Ann Covell is a British citizen and had a long career in the U.K. health service research sector and has served as a Justice of the Peace. Her interests include history, writing, and politics. She is the author of *Remembering the Ladies* and *First Lady Jane Pierce*.

I dedicate this book to my beloved late husband, John E. Covell, who gave me the gifts of time and encouragement to write it. God chose to call him home before I could complete the work.

Ann Covell

THE OTHER ANGEL

AUSTIN MACAULEY PUBLISHERS™

LONDON • CAMBRIDGE • NEW YORK • SHARJAH

Ordering Information:
Quantity sales: special discounts are available on quantity purchases by corporations, associations, and others. For details, contact the publisher at the address below.

Publisher's Cataloging-in-Publication data
Covell, Ann
The Other Angel

ISBN 9781641829144 (Paperback)
ISBN 9781641829151 (Hardback)
ISBN 9781641829168 (E-Book)

The main category of the book — Fiction / Historical

www.austinmacauley.com/us

First Published (2019)
Austin Macauley Publishers LLC
40 Wall Street, 28th Floor
New York, NY 10005
USA

mail-usa@austinmacauley.com
+1 (646) 5125767

I would like to thank the staff at the Library of Congress for their ready assistance and patience as I researched the Civil War period, as well as the many Historical Societies for their assistance in helping me to ascertain appropriate information and facts relating to the 19th-century U.S. way of life.

Chapter 1
Rory Compton

The maid's light knock, together with the rattle of a tea-tray, awakened Marianne. She called out to Esther to enter, glancing as she did at the closed door of the dressing room, where her husband, Charles, had spent a restless night.

"Leave the tray. I'll see to it," she said, raising herself onto the pillows Esther had just shaken.

"Yes, Mrs. Compton," Esther murmured. She laid out Marianne's robe across the small couch at the foot of the bed, before closing the door quietly as she left. She was used to this morning ritual.

Marianne laid her head back onto the pillow and closed her eyes, thinking of the foul mood Charles had been in last night when he had at last come to bed, so restless that he resorted to sleeping on the chaise longue in the dressing room. She wondered if he would wake up in a similar mood this morning. A few minutes later, she hopped out of bed, donned her robe and poured tea from the delicate tea-pot into the matching cups. She grinned as she remembered how incongruous the cup would look in her husband's large, tanned, capable hands. She made sure she rattled the crockery and teaspoon loudly. Sure enough, Charles appeared, as she had intended, yawning widely.

She smiled fondly at her husband. His once fair hair was now almost grey, and there were fewer curls around his temple nowadays, though his eyes remained the bewitching blue they had been when she first met him. His face no longer held the look of youth though it remained as attractive to her as that first glimpse of him 20 years ago, when her friend, Beulah, now her sister-in-law, had first introduced him to her.

She passed a cup to him, stretching up as she did so to kiss his beloved face. He smiled at her, taking in her tousled, auburn hair, the figure that was not as trim as it once was, though still attractive, and her lovely petite face.

Marianne stared at the lines etched around his eyes and mouth, which had not been so visible six months ago. She knew the lines and his moods had hardened due to the longstanding worry about whether the naval contract for his Longfield Farm hemp crop would be renewed. The concern was not only within their household but in those of many Blue Grass hemp famers. When he had learned a couple of days earlier the navy had awarded Longfield a further three-year lucrative contract, his poor moods had not been alleviated. Marianne knew his personal relief was tempered with the knowledge that the majority of hemp farmers had not been so lucky.

"I've been thinking," she began now, in a voice filled with worry, "we should take a few days away now that the contract negotiations are done. We could go to Richmond for a few days. Beulah's sister would be delighted. Let's plan something, shall we? William can manage the farm quite well without you for just a few days."

Charles sipped his tea.

"I understand two or three farmers have already put up their land and buildings for sale," he said.

Marianne stared at him. He had ignored her comments altogether.

"I had letters from a couple of them yesterday," he said. "They were abusive. I can understand how they feel and I'd be the same if my contract hadn't been renewed. And I can understand why they don't want to change to growing wheat and vegetables, but I do resent their attitude towards me." He passed a hand over his face for a few seconds, his face a picture of despair when he lowered it.

"Maybe your brother will purchase some of their land," Marianne suggested.

"Well, he might consider it," Charles conceded, "though frankly I hope he doesn't. I'm not so sure I want John and his horses on my patch. Do you?"

"I'm not sure, either," Marianne said. "He probably wants your land though, simply because he feels it should have been his in the first place, as the elder son, though he says he needs it for his Horse Farm. He'll always believe it was his birth right, I suppose."

"Let's not go there again," Charles said. He gulped his tea, and looked down at her.

"We might think of a few days in Richmond, though not just yet. For one thing, I don't want our neighbors thinking we're skipping off on a jag while they're suffering. Right now, I want to see Rory before he goes back to school. I needed him yesterday, but I didn't see a sign of him all day."

"He'd taken the twins to the river again. He's so keen they can swim perfectly before he returns to school. In fact, he's taken them down there this morning, just to make certain, though he's already pleased with their progress."

"Well, I want to see him today, as soon as possible. Send him to me immediately when he gets back," he retorted.

Marianne looked up at the harsh tone of her husband's voice, one she had never heard before when speaking of their children.

"Is there something wrong, Charles?" she asked.

"Yes, there is," he answered, his face hardening. He glanced down at his wife's concerned face. "It's just a father/son chat before he goes back to school. Something about his future education, that's all."

"Tell me," Marianne said, "I want to know."

"It's nothing," Charles said. "I just want to exchange views on his future University courses. It's just financial planning, that's all."

She smiled up at her husband. She should have known. Of course he had to plan ahead, especially as Rory was now 16 years old.

"Oh, is that all, my darling. I don't know how long he and the girls will be. Mamma Baker has gone with them. She'll bring the twins back, so Rory can have a long swim on his own. As soon as he's back, I'll send him to you."

She did not notice her husband's face had clouded again as he picked her up in his arms and walked toward their bed. For the next half hour they forgot everything but themselves.

* * *

Rory Compton stopped to catch his breath at the gated entrance of Longfield, following his swim and sprint home. He stared at the beauty of the large mansion in the fading sunlight, admiring the curve of the long driveway that widened out into a circle to the front entrance, the well-stocked gardens, manicured hedges, and leafy imported trees. He understood why his father was obsessed with their home, built on the outskirts of Cynthiana, Kentucky. As Rory gazed at the house, he had no idea this was to be the worst evening of his life and a time when his father would shatter the close bond between them.

11

He knew the twins would have returned home by now with Mamma Baker, his former nursery nurse and now theirs, full of excitement as they ran to tell their mother that Rory had declared them excellent swimmers. He had spent most of his summer school holidays teaching his sisters to swim, cherishing every minute spent with them.

Rory swung his towel and jacket over his shoulder as he deviated to the right and ran the remaining few steps to the kitchen entrance at the back of the house.

Always running, never still, thought Bessie, the cook, as she watched him hurtle in.

It was one of the Big Bake Days, a day that signaled Rory would return to school the following morning laden with a large basket of food for the journey.

The kitchen staff looked up at his noisy entrance, most of them smiling. They had been expecting him. He noticed almost every surface was filled with fresh baked cakes and pies full of rabbit or poultry. He picked up a couple of still warm buns to assuage his hunger pangs and beamed at the little scullery maid who told him in a shocked voice that he was not supposed to steal the food. He tickled her under the chin and plonked a light kiss on her cheek.

She touched the spot where the lips of the handsome son of the house had skimmed her face, and instantly forgave him. Bessie, quick to notice the incident, pretended consternation, but her chuckles suggested this was no more than she had expected.

As he passed through the kitchen looking to pilfer more food, he bantered with Gertrude, a teenage mulatto, and with Aggie, a white girl of similar age, who was one of the so-called 'village trash' his mother liked to employ. He always paid special attention to Aggie whenever he saw her, hating as he did the focus of her being considered 'village trash', but today his eyes were on Gertrude. She was short in stature, her plain, dark features yet to blossom, though her buxom young figure was, he knew, a subject of earthy conversation among the male kitchen staff.

He went around the whole kitchen, praising the confectionery wonders as he stole the odd titbit and chortling as he wisecracked with the rest of the kitchen staff. His hunger assuaged, he prepared to leave, knowing he had yet to pack his school chest. He groaned at the thought, realizing Mamma Baker would not have had time to do it for him.

She bustled in just as he was about to leave.

"Master Rory, there yer is. Git to your papa right now. He's bin callin' fer yer since I gotten back with yer sisters. He sure is angry."

Rory frowned, more in surprise at the deterioration in her elocution than her message.

"Papa is angry. What for?" he asked with a laugh. "He's never been in a better mood since he heard he's got the new navy contract."

There had been fears for months within the Cynthiana farming community that the navy's contracts for Kentucky grown hemp might be terminated. They had all heard about the 'iron ships' that were being built, reducing the Navy's need for quality rope, and that Longfield had been among the limited number within the Blue Grass area where contracts had been renewed.

Rory walked with Mamma Baker along the passage leading to his father's study, which was situated adjacent to the staircase that led up to the main living quarters. He felt reluctant to see his father without tidying himself up and suggested he should go to his room first.

Before he could sprint off, Mamma took hold of his arm.

"You better get there right now," she said. "I've never seen 'im so angry for many a year. It seems to be about yer. What have yer done?"

Rory jumped as he heard his father shout.

"Baker, you get that boy o' mine here right now!"

The farm manager, William, appeared at the bottom of the stairs.

A grateful smile spread across Rory's face.

A handsome black man, a former slave emancipated and educated by Charles, William had been his father's farm manager for many years. He had always been a friend to Rory as the boy grew from a robust toddler into the scholarly youth he was now.

They glanced at each other, both puzzled at Mamma's attitude and his father's severe tone of voice.

"Massa Rory, go to yer pappy right now. He sure is tormented," Mamma said. There was an odd tenor to her voice, and her usual jocular, shiny black face was solemn. "He's been calling for yer to put yer face in his study-room ever since I got back to this house."

Rory continued to stare at her, wondering if this was one of her jokes. She was fond of playing tricks on him and the girls.

"You'd better get in there, Rory," William said. "He *is* in a bit of a temper."

"I'll go and freshen myself up before I go in," Rory said, "but I can think of nothing I've done to upset either him or my mother."

As Charles again shouted for Rory to be sent to him, William shook his head.

"Rory, you'd do well to go now. I don't think this is a laughing matter."

The seriousness of William's voice and the unusual behavior of Mamma Baker began to alarm Rory.

"Is Papa alright? Is my mother unwell? Has something happened to the twins?"

Both shook their head and William shrugged in bewilderment.

"You should get in there," Mamma warned again, her hands flapping around her face.

Rory glanced at William, who nodded his agreement.

Rory gave the damp towel he still carried to Mamma Baker, pushed his fingers through his hair, shook off a few pastry crumbs, straightened his shirt and put on his jacket. Despite his concern, he could not resist patting Mamma's large rear-end as he crossed into his father's room.

He grinned at his father as he entered with pretend nonchalance, his smiling face lit up with mischief.

"Has the sky fallen in, Papa?"

He was stopped in his tracks by his father's ashen face, the hostile eyes glaring at his only son as his fisted hands beat the chair arms in furious activity. "What is it, Papa? What's happened?" His voice was harsh with a sudden fear and he remained standing in front of his father's desk, though his legs were ready to give way. He was reminded of the time when his mother had taken ill a few years ago and he was sent to western Virginia to spend the summer school vacation with Aunt Delphia and his cousins.

Charles Compton threw a sheet of paper at Rory.

It fell onto the carpet and as Rory stooped down to retrieve it, he saw it was from his school.

"My school report, Papa?" Rory queried, puzzled.

"Read the letter, boy, read it," Charles bellowed. He stood up in his agitation and paced a few steps before sitting down with a heavy sigh on an adjacent sofa.

As he read the letter, Rory's heart sank.

Mr. Smales, the headmaster, had written concerning a future academic plan he and Rory had discussed prior to the summer recess. Rory had promised to confer with his parents at home, but had not done so for a couple of reasons. The main one was the probable reaction of his father. He spoke now of the second reason.

"Papa, you have been so worried this summer. You've not been here for much of the time because you were either with Uncle John in Lexington, or Louisville or with naval officers. I didn't want to burden you with my plans at this early stage when you were so worried."

As far as Rory was concerned, this was a true and reasonable explanation and he waited for an invitation to sit beside his father to discuss the matter, but it was not forthcoming.

Charles glowered at his son without comment. It had been obvious to him, as he read the headmaster's letter, that Smales had based his professional recommendations for Rory's future education on his current academic status and potential. He remembered how, three years ago, Rory had been defined as an academic genius in scientific and mathematical subjects, and Smales had taken the boy under his wing. The school board had utilized his gifts by appointing him, at the age of 14, to act as the school accountant while the post holder undertook a three-month sabbatical.

Charles Compton had been delighted to give permission for this exceptional honor.

Shortly afterward, Charles and William had agreed an easier accounting system for the farm would be advantageous and free up some of William's workload.

Rory was flattered when asked to work on the project, utilizing the expertise achieved during the significant school experience. He also agreed to undertake the regular auditing of the new system.

Reminding Charles Compton of these and other academic achievements, the headmaster had suggested that his protégé could achieve a university degree within two years, rather than the usual three, particularly as he was already studying Greek and Latin, essential subjects for acceptance to Michigan Medical School. Prior to entering that esteemed institution, Smales warned that Rory would be required to gain experience by working for a year alongside a physician in some capacity. The headmaster had worked out a program that would get Rory into the medical school by the age of 20, rather than the usual age of 21, though there was a need to apply for special dispensation now. Smales had also advocated that when Rory gained his doctorate, he could apply for optional medical work in Europe for a couple of years, where specialty training was more advanced. The headmaster suggested the European experience would serve Rory and his future patients well and his letter sought permission from Charles before taking the plan forward.

Charles was enraged, not only at being left out of the discussions, but at the fact that his son wished to work as a medical doctor and not in the business he would one day inherit.

The subsequent quarrel between father and son was aggressive.

A natural diplomat, Rory tried not to allow his passion for his chosen profession to rule his arguments, as he attempted to explain why he wanted to enter the medical profession.

"Do you remember when Dr. Wallace was trying to deal with the outbreak of typhoid in the po' white village, about four years ago? His nurse left him because she was afraid of getting the disease herself and Mrs. Wallace had to help," Rory said, as he tried to jolt his father's memory.

"What the hell's that got to do with this?" his father yelled, snatching the offending letter from Rory's hands.

Rory told his father of an ambition to help poor, but dignified people that had been developing since he was a 12-year-old boy. At that time, he had assisted Dr. Wallace and his wife with menial, though essential tasks, as they fought the epidemic. It was during this time Rory had first come across the folks often referred to as 'village trash'. In his opinion, these folks were not trash at all, but proud folks who worked hard to care for their families in difficult circumstances, with little help from the more affluent population of Cynthiana.

"For the first time in my life I realized the way that some folks have to live," Rory said. "Frankly, Papa, the social system sickened me then, and it still does."

He tried to explain how he had vowed to help those poor people somehow.

"I saw the personal sacrifices Dr. Wallace and his wife made throughout that whole episode and I was glad to be part of their team. I was so proud of their humanity. They both put themselves at risk, Papa. That's where my conviction that I must become a doctor came from, and I'll never change my mind."

His father would not listen or try to understand. He ranted about how he wanted his only son to take over the business in due course.

"It's your heritage!" Charles hollered. "Why do you think I'm doing all this?"

"The girls could take it on. You know Mary has shown signs of having a high intellect and she deserves a chance of an education and to go into the business as much as I do," he snapped, "and I for one wouldn't wish either of my sisters to be denied that opportunity." His lips curled in defiance of his father's anger.

"Mary and Betty will marry and their children will bear another name. I want Longfield to be inherited by grandsons who bear the Compton name and by their sons in due course." Charles put his head in his hands.

For an instance, Rory felt strong sympathy for his father.

"Papa," he said, "I may or may not marry and have sons, but if I do, my sons will be allowed to follow their own heart. That may well include the leadership of Longfield. In the meantime, I could, of course, accept an appointment on the company's board and be willing to…"

He stopped short as Marianne, having heard the commotion, rushed into the room.

Without a word, his father threw the offending letter at her. After reading it, she looked from one to the other, shocked and speechless. The row flared again. Rory became defensive following further abusive comments from his father. His white-faced traumatized mother, caught in the crossfire, begged them to stop. Rory attempted to remain controlled, but as he endured his father's aggression and emotional badgering, his discipline began to disintegrate. Against his nature, Rory allowed his own passion to rule his thoughts.

Charles took hold of his son's collar, his angry face only half an inch from Rory's.

"You're my only son. This is not about me or you, but about this family. I want a Compton dynasty to be part of local history and culture into the next century and beyond. That's what I'm working for."

He stopped, fishing out a kerchief to wipe away the spittle that had gathered around his lips.

Rory turned his face away in disgust at his father's display of fanaticism.

Charles continued the onslaught.

"You have a duty to me and the generations that follow us. I will not allow you to exploit the family's future to fulfill your childish aspirations. Understand?"

He bellowed the last word into Rory's left ear.

Rory saw the muscles clenching along his father's jaw line. He felt a hardening of his own stomach, his throat closed up and he could not speak. For a few moments, he felt disorientated. He wanted to storm out of the room, but instead he glanced at his mother, whose hands had rushed to cover her mouth, and her eyes wide. She stood there pale-faced, staring at her husband following his rant.

Rory closed his eyes briefly and on opening them, took a deep breath, passing a hand over his clammy face before he answered. His voice was icy with no sign of the jaunty teenager he had been a few minutes ago.

"I suggest you go and make yourself another son. You're both young enough to do so. Because you're sure as hellfire not using my life to fulfill your dreams…"

Rory heard his mother cry out as she rushed out of the room.

Charles let go of his son's collar as he aimed a fist at him.

As it connected, Rory flew across the room, blood spurting from his nose, top lip and forehead as he fell. He could taste the blood and as he felt it running down the side of his mouth onto his neck, his tongue snaked out in a useless attempt to stem the flow.

His father walked over and looked down at him, his face and eyes suffused with contempt.

"Never speak like that in front of your mother again."

His father spoke with an awful quietness, his face expressionless as he stalked out of the room without another word.

He saw William walking toward the kitchen entrance and called to him.

"Clear up that mess in my study," he said roughly. "No questions. Just clear it up."

William nodded his assent.

Mamma Baker was waiting in the kitchen, while the house staff enjoyed a light supper in the kitchen annex.

William beckoned her to follow him.

They had both heard the angry altercation between father and son, but had the wisdom to retreat to the kitchen when they had heard the approach of Marianne.

Within a minute or two, the curious William had sidled out again to listen.

Rory lay on the floor, eyes closed, blood obscuring his features. He appeared unconscious, but groaned as William and Mamma lifted him onto the sofa that Charles had so recently vacated. They made no attempt to prevent Rory's blood from spilling onto the sofa's fabric.

William snapped out an order for warm water and clean clothes.

As the reek of blood filled the room, Mamma rushed out to bring clean clothing for the suffering boy, taking the ruined ones away.

William opened the room's only window in an effort to dispel the stink.

"No comment to anyone," he warned Mamma as she left, knowing full well that she would not utter a word.

Dinner was cancelled.

Marianne later spent an hour with Rory, devastated as she murmured soft endearments before returning to her distraught husband. She was not present as William and Mamma half-carried her son to his room once the house was quiet.

The boy sat on his bed, and looked at the neatly piled clothes and books ready to be packed into his school chest. Stifling the prick of painful and angry tears that threatened, Rory was appalled at the suddenness and violence by which his father had attacked him.

Neither Mamma nor William had commented as Rory explained what had happened, though both stayed with him for most of the night. They remained impassive except for the anger that shone out of Mamma's dark eyes from time to time.

She held Rory to her as she had done so many times before when he was a toddler, as large tears flowed once more from his swollen eyes.

William sat still for a long time, for once not knowing how to approach his employer, blaming him as he did for Rory's predicament.

They spoke only in short whispers when his mother crept in around midnight, so that they would not awaken him.

A telegraph message was sent to the school stating that Rory would not arrive for a few days due to an injury during earlier strenuous exercise. The same story was given to the house staff.

Three days later, Dr. Wallace declared his patient well enough to travel, and the following day Rory left Longfield for the railroad station, accompanied by William.

He had seen his father only once during that time, in the presence of the doctor, though there had been no discussion other than his recovery progress. As he left, his mother and sisters waved him off. His mother said little, but she kissed him and asked him to write to them soon.

Rory promised he would. He laughed with the girls at something funny; one of them commented on his damaged face and promised he would draw a picture for them on his way back to school, something interesting he might see on his way. They always liked that. He had looked round, hoping to see his father. He did not appear and Rory had muttered that he must say "goodbye to Papa", but his mother held him back.

"Let him be," she said. "He'll come round, I know it. Write to him in a day or two, and I'll write to Mr. Smales and ask him to release you for a long weekend in a few weeks."

Rory smiled at her, satisfied with the promise. He kissed his mother, hugged his sisters once more and made an uneasy departure from Cynthiana.

* * *

Rory did write to his father, apologizing for his rudeness, making no comment on his ambition to become a doctor. He did not receive a response, though Rory knew from his mother's letters that Charles had been away again. His mother described the weather that had prevented everyone from going far for over a week and delayed his father's return home. The rain had been almost constant, and much heavier than she had ever seen.

"There have been floods in some parts of the area, and mud inundation has spoiled some of the crops. With the cancelling of hemp contracts and the loss of vegetables, this is going to be a lean winter for many," she had written.

William had also written to him about things in general, as he often did. *"We can't even allow the horses and carriage out because of the heavy mud,"* he told Rory. *"That's one of the reasons your father's return has been delayed."*

Rory received a later account of the weather conditions within another letter from his mother.

"We're having a family day out next Sunday," she wrote, *"visiting the Turnbulls. As you know, their navy contract wasn't renewed, and Bill Turnbull is wondering whether he should increase his cattle herd, rather than turn to vegetable growing. He's asked for your father's advice. The weather has brightened and rain hasn't fallen for over six days, so we think a family outing would be good for the twins and the Turnbull children. William and the coachman have gone along the route and feel satisfied that it's safe. We are going to use our best horses. Mamma Baker will come with us. We're all looking forward to this trip as apart from Papa, we haven't been out of the house for weeks now."*

Rory could sense how relieved they must be at this opportunity for an outing after so long.

* * *

There had been much excitement and jollity as the family set off on their trip on that Sunday morning, William had later told John Compton. The only fuss there had been was when Betty jumped out of the carriage to retrieve her new doll she had left on the hallway table, which she wanted to show to the Turnbull children. A further, though softer, rainfall during the afternoon had delayed their return home, according to Bill Turnbull. When they had not arrived home within half an hour of darkness falling, William and two male members of staff set out to escort them back, but were unable to complete their journey due to a heavy landslide about two miles from the Turnbull farm.

It was not until first light on the following morning that the full extent of the devastating landslide could be ascertained.

Rescuers found the family and Mamma Baker buried beneath heavy mud within the upturned carriage.

The coachman was discovered several yards away, buried in deep sludge.

Betty's doll was found in a nearby bush, unscathed except for the mud, as if it had catapulted from the coach.

The horses, still hitched to the vehicle, were also dead.

William informed John that an inquest into the gruesome accident was requested prior to the organization of the funerals.

* * *

John Compton, now Rory's legal guardian, journeyed to Louisville to bring his traumatized nephew to his Lexington Horse Farm.

Rory hardly spoke during the journey and ate very little.

John's wife, Beulah, and his sister, Delphia, who had journeyed from western Virginia the day before, were horrified at their nephew's appearance. His previous well-toned body appeared emaciated, and his bright, intelligent eyes were mere specks in his pale, pinched face.

The local doctor declared Rory's body unable to withstand further days without nourishment and Delphia immediately took over the care of her nephew.

Dr. Wallace, Rory's former mentor, was asked to visit his patient with a view to providing a second opinion, which the younger, less experienced local doctor appreciated.

At the request of John and Delphia, the executors of Charles' will, the ever faithful William remained at Cynthiana to manage the business pending further arrangements.

William was glad to do so, determined as he was to look after Rory's inheritance until the youth came of age, assuming he could survive the present crisis. William dared not think of the consequences if the boy succumbed to his deep grief.

Chapter 2
Recovering

"I've been dreaming again," Rory said.

His eyes were closed. He felt Aunt Delphia's presence, heard the hiss of curtains being drawn back, felt a shot of cool air on his face as a window opened.

He lay quietly.

His aunt squeezed his hand, noting the pallor of his cheeks, and the dark circles under the eyes.

He opened his eyes and tried to smile at her, even though both knew her presence was unwelcome. He was aware she had nursed him over the past weeks, but had often expressed ingratitude.

* * *

"Rory never mentions his father," Delphia had told Dr. Wallace during one of his fortnightly visits from Cynthiana. "When I try to speak about him, Rory begins talking to himself under his breath. I can never make out what he's saying and it's as if he's putting up a barrier that I'm not allowed to get through. Sometimes he bounces a knuckle against his teeth for no apparent reason. I know the signs now, so when I see that sort of thing, I know he's distressed. I'm not getting anywhere with his state of mind."

"Well, there *were* two traumas in a short time involving his father," the doctor had emphasized. "It's as if he's repudiating his father's memory because he can't accept what's happened. He's only 16, and the awful incident in his father's office was a severe enough crisis in his life. To lose him and the rest of his family shortly afterward is an intolerable additional burden for someone so young. When he's able to overcome these crises, he'll stand a chance of getting his life back."

"I would say 'if' rather than 'when'," Delphia had retorted.

"Always think positively," the doctor shot back with a sad smile.

"How are you feeling this morning, Rory?" she now asked, taking his wrist to check his pulse.

He pulled his arm away. She had asked the same question yesterday morning, and the one before that. Yesterday, he had mocked her question out loud in a silly, affected voice and his answer had been the usual one.

"I just want to die. I want to be with Mama and my sisters. You'd all be better off if you'd let me die."

Delphia had never replied to the daily comment until yesterday, when she had retorted with just one word.

"Perhaps."

He had opened his eyes wide in amazement at that bolt out of the blue.

"You know, I've been thinking about that," Delphia had gone on to say. "Have you considered that God may have plans for you here on Earth? What's happened to your intention to become a doctor? Who knows, you may be destined for great things in the medical sphere with that God-given intellect of yours."

"How did you know about my ambitions?" Rory had asked, astounded.

The answer should have been obvious.

"Your mama wrote to me after you'd returned to school. She told me there had been an almighty donnybrook over your ambitions."

So, when Delphia asked today how he felt, he did not answer the question immediately, but waited for a few seconds as if thinking about it.

"I'll have my bath first and then my breakfast at the table instead of in bed, please," he muttered.

Tom, the elderly black male servant assigned to Rory's personal care had been waiting at the back of the adjacent anteroom door that housed a tin bath and water closet, waiting his cue to enter the bedroom. "I'll go and bring the hot water, ma'am," he said, a large white towel already draped over his right shoulder.

"The doctor told me yesterday that the exercise program is working well and he's pleased you're eating more, because that's important for your physical recovery," Delphia said to Rory.

She didn't tell him both she and the doctor remained worried about his continued dark moods, though she noticed he appeared brighter today. Now, taking advantage of her nephew's apparent improved mood this morning, she spoke to him.

"Rory, isn't it time you told someone about your dream? You know Dr. Wallace thinks talking about it would help you to overcome this daily ordeal. Go along with his advice on this. Talk to him. He's told us of his experience in Europe with this kind of illness, and the Europeans do seem to have learned a lot about melancholia and associated problems."

Rory didn't stare her out as he had done in the past when the subject was broached. He wouldn't look at his aunt and shook his head, his face lowered toward his chest.

"I daren't talk about it. I daren't even think about it all, I can't *bear* it," he whispered, turning his face to stare out of his bedroom window.

His answer jolted Delphia. He had never said anything like that before. Her response was immediate as she took him in her arms. This time, he allowed her to do so.

"Oh, Rory, my dearest, I do understand. It's how I felt for months after my husband died. When I eventually spoke with your dear Mama about how I felt, she helped me find my way back. So, just remember that when you feel you can talk, I'll be here. And if you don't want me to repeat anything to Dr. Wallace, or anyone else, then I won't. I know the same goes for Dr. Wallace. You can tell either of us anything, you know you can. So, trust one of us, please, for your own sake."

He had no chance to respond, as Tom and one of the footmen had returned with the hot water. As the footman poured it into the tin bath, Tom gathered up the boy's day clothes and turned to help him out of bed, an unnecessary action, as, for the first time since he arrived in Lexington, Rory got out of bed without help.

Yes, thought Delphia, *there's a definite change in him this morning.*

It was then that she made an impulsive decision. Today Rory would have his breakfast in the dining room. She knew it was a big change considering he had only just decided not to have his breakfast in bed. Big change or not, she became certain it would be therapeutic for him to eat downstairs, just this once. She informed Tom of the change, avoiding Rory's reproachful glare.

While he was bathing, Delphia arranged for a light breakfast for the two of them to be set up in the smaller dining room, overlooking the main garden.

Rory returned from his bath, fully dressed and ready to do battle, judging from the look on his face.

"There'll only be the two of us." Delphia said, before he could open his mouth. "If we go down now we might just catch the glints of sun on the river. It's the right time of day."

His scowl reverted to a look of astonishment.

"The river! Are we near a river?"

"Yes, the Kentucky River, It's a tributary of the Ohio River. I thought you knew it was just half a mile away."

"I may have done once. I've f-forgotten a lot of things s-since…" He stammered a little and didn't finish his sentence.

Delphia took advantage of the pause to walk to the door.

Rory tried to hurry after her, but had to slow down, his weak legs still unsteady.

Tom took his arm, and with the help of the polished wooden banister, they descended the short stairway together.

"I asked for a table to be set at the patio, end of the dining room," Delphia said to Rory on their way downstairs. "We may be able to see the river from there if the sunlight is just right."

Airy and light, with a whiff of cleaning wax mingling with the inoffensive odor of a breakfast recently served, the room radiated the affluent middle-class Kentuckian tradition.

He watched the swaying of the imported willow trees that allowed the sun to glint on beds of carefully tended flowers, only to overshadow them again with an elegant swish of a branch.

"Where's the river? How far away is it? Where does it leave the Ohio River? Can we go to it today?" His questions rattled across to her like bullets.

Delphia pointed toward the spot where he should look, but though he squinted hard, he was unable to see any ribbon of flowing water.

"It takes about half an hour to walk from here, but we often get a glimpse of it when the sun's in the right place," she told him. "I think I'm right in saying that the Ohio River divides twice at a confluence nearby, forming two rivers, one of which is the Kentucky River. You may want to check that to make sure I'm right. I'm sure your geography is better than mine."

He looked at her and, to her astonishment, grinned. She knew he'd seen through her tactic when he said, "Give a boy a task and it'll help his mood and ego."

They both laughed.

Another first, thought Delphia.

"The strip of river which we sometimes see does look lovely when it sparkles in the sunlight," she said. "I'm sorry we can't see it today, but the sun doesn't seem to be touching it this morning."

"It depends on the time of day, and the clouds," Rory told his aunt. He stared into the distance, straining to catch a glint of sun shine on water.

"I'll have to measure up the distance from a terrain chart and calculate the best times," he mused to himself, expression now lively as he reasoned out the mechanics of achieving this.

"I taught my sisters to swim in the river near Longfield, you know. They were brilliant, both of them."

As he said this, Delphia noticed the anguish in his eyes that usually appeared whenever he spoke of the twins was not there, as he described his joy of teaching them last summer.

"I'd like to swim again," he said, nodding his head in anticipation at the thought. "Can we walk down to the river today?"

Delphia shook her head.

"Frankly, Rory, your legs wouldn't be able to stand a long walk. The doctor did explain to you, didn't he, that your thigh muscles have atrophied over the last few weeks, though they have improved because of those starter exercises."

He nodded.

"While they're not strong enough yet," Delphia went on, "we can get them healthy so you can attempt an hour's walk later."

Disappointed, Rory retaliated. "You said it was only a half-hour walk."

"A full hour because you'll need to walk back," Delphia replied with a grin.

He groaned, but returned the grin.

"If you keep up with the newest exercise plan you should be able to do it soon," she promised. "Spring isn't all that far off, and then it should be warm enough to swim."

Rory beamed at her, and she realized she had discovered a weak spot that would, perhaps, motivate him during the difficult weeks of intensive exercising.

The sight and smell of the breakfast when it came galvanized both aunt and nephew. Delphia was pleased to see Rory enjoy the well-cooked food, though he could not manage it all, pushing the plate away after only a few forkfuls. She was disappointed, as she realized that the healing process may have started but was likely to be slow.

"Tell you what," Delphia said. "Let's begin your new exercises today. We can check with the local doctor about your progress next week, and that should give us an idea of when you could be ready for a longer walk. You'll get a better idea of progress when you are able to walk round the gardens and explore the farm. Would you like to do that? You've hardly seen any of it, have you?"

"Well, yes I would like to," Rory said. "I was only about eight when I last came and my cousins didn't have much time for me, really, so I didn't get to see much. That's when the twins were born, and Aunt Beulah had gone over to Longfield to help my mother."

He smiled at his aunt and yawned. "At this precise moment, though, I'm not ready for much yet, because I feel exhausted. It must have been that walk downstairs. Maybe I'll rest here for a while and read."

Delphia agreed, and when Tom returned to take his charge back to his room, she asked him to bring down Rory's books that were on his bedside table.

"And the paper and pencils," Rory called out, "and if you can, try and get me a ground chart that covers at least five square miles around the farm. The butler or my uncle may have one."

Within 15 minutes, Delphia had settled Rory into a high-backed chair with a few soft cushions, together with books, pencils, writing paper and, wonder of wonders, a terrain chart of the farm area that included the river boundary.

"It'll be quiet here for a while and you never know, you just might catch a glimpse of the sunlight on the river. We can begin your exercises in a couple of hours."

* * *

Over the following days, Rory's health improved and he began to take breakfast in the dining room. His mood lightened as he worked on a projected time chart of sunlight over the river, hoping the low clouds would not obstruct his calculations too much when he 'unveiled' his creation.

The day arrived when he was ready to present his document to Aunt Delphia and Aunt Beulah. Even Uncle John found time to be present. It was, as far as they could see, a complicated document, full of figures and arrows and drawings, though his uncle appeared to make some sense of it.

"It's a timetable," Rory told them. "See these times marked here? Well, these are my projections of when the sun will fall on this point tomorrow and for the next seven days."

He gestured to the points on his paper and indicated points on the horizon.

"Let's see over the next few days if my calculations work out," Rory said, with some apprehension.

John ruffled his nephew's blond curls, impressed at his achievement.

"A good try, boy. Good work. Your father would've been proud of you." He did not notice the frown that came over his nephew's face, or see Delphia flinch.

The schedule proved to be reasonably correct on most days.

"Some low clouds hampered sight of the river on two days," Rory explained, "but that doesn't matter because you could see the sun making a gold ring around the clouds, which I thought was a marvelous sight in itself."

Everyone, including old Tom, was verbose in their praise of him, and Rory's face glowed with pleasure. He set about preparing a new chart for the following week.

"Just to make sure I've got it right," he said, with quiet humility.

Following his morning exercises, it was now custom for Rory to explore the estate with either Aunt Beulah or Jacob, the head gardener. Tom was sometimes allowed to walk with them, if Rory felt weaker than usual. This new companionship had improved his ambivalence to exercise and walking, and his general appetite and moods had also perked up. Even so, there were a few dark days when the nightmare returned to plague him.

Dr. Wallace continued to visit him every two weeks and noticed one of the dark moods. He spoke with Delphia about it.

"His dream does return sometimes," Delphia told him, "but not to the same degree as before and perhaps only every seven or eight days."

"That's a whopping improvement, especially when it was a daily event not so long ago. Will you keep a detailed note of the days and times when the dream returns, and the extent and depth of Rory's mood following an episode? That'll help me to make a better assessment when 1 come back. It's obvious that he's still vulnerable," he said.

Rory was now at ease with Aunt Beulah, as she was with him.

Up until recently their relationship had been uneasy, as neither had been able to overcome the strained acceptance of the current situation. Despite her kindly nature, Beulah had tended to resent the atmosphere that prevailed as her sick nephew took up so much time and space within her well-run household.

Rory had sensed her unease and responded in kind.

But even though it was customary for Jacob to accompany them on most of their daily walks around the gardens and farm, occasionally Beulah and Rory would go alone and spend the morning together.

Beulah began to enjoy the hours of easy chat and light exercise.

On one of those days they stopped to rest awhile, sitting down to reflect quietly on the neatness and beauty of the large gardens. As they sat, Beulah stared at her nephew's face in repose. He was a handsome boy and already towered over her tiny frame. His shoulders showed signs of future broadness and muscle, and his blond curls were brushed back from his forehead and sat alongside thick brows that showed off his intelligent, kind blue eyes. He reminded her of his father at that age.

He lifted his head and locked eyes with her.

For a moment, they stared at each other.

"What's that look for, Aunt Beulah?" he had asked with the impish grin that crossed his face more and more these days.

"I was just thinking how well you look nowadays," she said.

He gave her a smile, one which touched her heart without warning, startling her.

The incident was over in a flash, but both seemed to know that something significant had occurred.

Rory didn't understand exactly what, except that his aunt seemed to have become his friend, rather than a relative he hardly knew.

Beulah realized that a special bond between the two generations had been created, and knew Rory's future was as important now as that of her own two sons.

"He's such a delight to be with, nowadays," Beulah said to Delphia, a few days later. "I can't forget those first weeks when he was so ill, and the weeks when he was so frightening in his melancholy, but I feel that I know him now. He has a real feel for gardening and farming, a natural to follow in his father's footsteps. He'll make a success of Longfield when he inherits it. And, isn't he like Charles?"

While he enjoyed his aunt's company, Rory preferred to spend time with Jacob when she went about her duties as mistress of the house.

A gentle mulatto who soaked up Rory's comments and compliments, Jacob had bonded early in their relationship as they chatted about the garden layout, the plants, and the difficulties of caring for the imported trees and how the master was so keen in keeping the garden area well apart from the farm.

"Yo' sure is like yo' uncle," Jacob said to him one day.

Rory liked the way the mulatto spoke, though on occasions found it difficult to understand.

"What do you mean?" he had asked.

"Well, yo' feel the plants are folks who need to be courted and well-fed, protected just like I protect my own chillen."

Rory enjoyed hearing about Jacob's many problems about the garden or his family.

"I got two daughters," Jacob told him one day. "One is like her mother, hardworking, keen to do things proper. We call her Bethesda, Beth for short. But my other, Maya, she's reckless, lazy, but so sweet to know. You can't help but love her somehow. They are both beautiful, but Maya is so vain. She stares into her Mama's looking glass all the time and wonders about her future beau."

"How old are they?" asked Rory, intrigued.

"Maya's 13, Beth's almost your age, 16 next month."

Rory knew Polly, their mother, who was Beulah's main cook. He also learned the couple was among the slaves his grandfather had emancipated years ago.

Rory discussed with Jacob how he had calculated the timing of sunlight on the river, and one day Jacob took Rory to view the river from a closer vantage point. He promised he would take him closer one day, when the doctors agreed.

"Do people swim in the river?" Rory asked. "I thought I saw a silhouette down there once."

"What's a silhouette?" Jacob had asked, puzzled.

"It's a sort of dark shadow outline of a person's body. I suppose you could call it a trick of nature, when the person can't be seen properly in full sunlight."

"Oh," said a still puzzled Jacob. "Well, your two cousins and your uncle never swim, and nobody else would come round these parts," he replied, though his eyes had shifted away.

"I suppose you dredge it from time to time?"

"Your uncle gets someone else to do that," Jacob agreed, "and it's needed to keep the banks clean and prevent it from silting up and flooding."

"So, you don't know whether it's safe to swim in or not?"

31

"I do allow Beth and Maya to visit the shallow part down there," he said, gesturing in such a way Rory was unable to discern where exactly he meant. "The girls can't swim so we won't allow them to go anywhere near the deeper parts, so I can't really say if it's safe or not."

"When I get down there, I'll soon find out," Rory said with confidence.

Jacob felt sure he would.

* * *

Almost every day during the following weeks, Rory explored various parts of the extensive estate. The improvement in his general health was most obvious in the extra weight he had gained. His face showed little sign of the pale, gaunt, wretched look of a few weeks earlier. He tended to laugh more, even when he fell one day, trying to catch one of the estate's playful dogs.

As his walking improved, Rory enjoyed strolling along the long drive away from the main house to the gate, usually in the company of Jacob, but sometimes with Beulah or Delphia. Rory delighted in the way the expansive iron gates, inscribed with the name 'Compton Horse Park' swung open in an imperious manner, suggesting it was beneath its dignity to allow the visitor in, or even out.

The walk began with the long flight of steps from the house, through the flowered gardens and lawns toward what appeared to be arenas to the left and to the right, like those he had seen when a European circus had visited Cynthiana years ago.

On one occasion, looking to the right, he noticed activity in the arena. Jacob told him it was the Compton Horse Training School patronized by sons and daughters of the 'rich folks' in the area.

Rory noticed two little girls practicing dressage. He stared at them for a few seconds and then turned away.

"Those little things are only six or seven years old," Jacob told him, pointing to the little girls. "They're the daughters of Mr. Kennedy from the Blue Water Farm."

The girls reminded him of Mary and Betty, and it hurt him to hear their happy shouts and laughter. He could hardly bear it, and tears coursed down his cheeks, which he tried to hide by cupping his whole face in his hands.

Alarmed, Jacob led the sobbing youth back to the house, and called for Tom, who in turn called for his mistress. Even Beulah was unable to console him, as Rory cried out for his mother and sisters.

"Mama, Mama, Mary, Betty," he wailed over and over again.

In his head, he could hear his mother's soft voice, the giggles of his sisters, even the laugh of his father.

"Papa, Papa," he cried out once and then wept again as if his heart was being squeezed.

He fell onto his bed, which shook as pain racked his whole body with tormented sobs.

Delphia and Beulah listened to Jacob's account of Rory's behavior and realized grief had once more overtaken him.

Delphia sat with him the whole afternoon, unable to stem the suffering and distress, until fatigue from the emotional upheaval overcame him, and he slept.

* * *

When Rory awoke at last, Beulah was there. She helped him to get up and bathe his face, before taking him down to her sitting room where she had already organized refreshments. She allowed Rory time to eat and drink as they made tentative small-talk, and watched him relax in the quiet atmosphere of her lovely, ladylike room.

After a while she went to a cupboard.

"Can you lift this box out for me?" she asked.

He took it to the large table under the window and they opened it together. Rory saw that it was filled with old papers, charts and drawings, which had belonged to his grandfather.

She allowed him to explore it, taking time to explain the various documents that he found of particular interest.

There he studied the initial plans for the house in which they now lived. As they studied the old plans, Beulah explained that when Rory's grandfather had inherited the farm, most of the farm work had been carried out by slaves. She reminded Rory of how the political parties, churches and even families throughout the country were split on the status of slavery, and was delighted with Rory's knowledge of the current divisions within Congress on the matter.

His grandfather, she said, had chosen to free his slaves, giving them an opportunity to work for him for wages. Those choosing to do so could pay a nominal rent for a shack with a promise that the estate would help them to renovate the premises. When the renovations were completed, the deal was that the workers would pay a reasonable market rent.

Rory marveled at the benevolence of Grandfather Compton, regretting he had not known him. He had heard similar anecdotes of his grandfather's kind-heartedness during the past few weeks.

He decided to talk with Uncle John about him, even though he had not noticed any affinity between John and what he now knew of his grandfather. Uncle John was, he knew, a hard-headed business man through and through.

Rory felt he and his grandfather would have been as close as friends as they were as relatives. He wondered aloud what his grandfather would have made of him and the tearful episode displayed today.

"He would have understood," Beulah said. "One of my most vivid memories of your grandfather was the day your grandmother died. She had fallen a few days earlier and never recovered, and he blamed himself for not being there to prevent the fall. It became an obsession with him. He never got over it. The sad thing was that no one could have prevented her fall, because she was stubborn and had declined any help when she went for a walk through a newly planted wood area. Apparently, her skirt had become caught in some brambles and she fell over, and broke an ankle. She was unable to get up and wasn't found for hours, by which time she had become unconscious."

Beulah picked up a drawing of the couple from the box.

"A neighbor drew that for him from memory," she said, and as she looked, her eyes filled with tears. "She was the last person on your grandfather's mind when he died nine months later. This drawing was in his hand when he died. You see, he knew that the grief inside him would never go away, that it would always be there, for the rest of his life, and he felt too old and lonely to want to suffer any longer. He wanted to go to her, so he allowed himself to drift away."

Rory stared at her.

"That's exactly how I feel," he said, "I feel so hopeless. There's nothing I can do to bring them back and to tell them how much I loved them all, even Papa. What's the point of going on? It's all so pointless." His tears began to fall.

Beulah held him close. "The point is your grandfather had a successful life, but without his wife at his side he had no hope left for the future. But it's different for you, Rory. You're young and have so much to offer the world, and your grandfather would want you to fight for it and achieve your potential. You were very young when he died, and I know you can't remember him, but he always knew, always said, that you were going to be special. What he felt and why I don't know, but that's why he had left the Cynthiana land to your father rather than allowing his whole estate to go to John. You see, he wanted you, his special grandson, to have an inheritance and he knew your father would do a good job of building it up."

Rory looked at her in bewilderment and shook his head at the revelation.

"I'm not special," he said.

"Yes, Rory, you are," responded Beulah, "and do you know, he would have been so proud of your ambition to become a medical doctor. He recognized that there was something unique in you and you must not let him down. You have to achieve that ambition, if not for you, then for him."

* * *

Despite her words, Rory suffered the nightmare that night for the first time in weeks, though thoughts of his grandfather helped him overcome most of the melancholy the following day.

A couple of days later, he took the same walk to the gate with Beulah, although this time he diverted his eyes when they passed the training arena. Looking to the left he watched, instead, a number of young boys jumping their horses under strict instruction. As he and his aunt walked through the tunnel of trees that concealed the house, they came into an open area. To the right, he noted the well-nurtured paddocks in which grazed a number of mares and their foals. To the left he could see the fences of what appeared to be a racing track. Jacob had already told him that this was a cross-country course for more serious horsemanship instruction. There were stables, rooms for the estate clerks, and a few small cottages where he was told the groomsmen lived. Further down the drive, into the distance, he stared at the two terraces of small, clean, well-kept homes. He guessed they were the shacks his grandfather had renovated.

During the next few days, Rory met a number of the farm hands, and chatted with them as if he'd known them all his life. It was good to banter with lads of his own age, and sometimes he would stand and cheer a game of 'kick the ball', wishing he was strong enough to join in.

Rory shared his uncle's enthusiasm for the Horse Farm and when John was absent, Beulah gave permission for him to assist the stable hands.

"I've seen how he reacts when he's with the horses," she told Delphia and Dr. Wallace. "I do think that the activity with the stable boys, who are of his own age, as well as learning about the horses, will help his emotional health as much as his physical health."

Everybody agreed, even John when he was told.

Rory began by skipping out the dung in the stables and 'rugging up' the prize horses in the stables and in the paddocks. He learned to use lighter rugs during the daytime and heavier ones at night. As his strength and general mood improved further as a result of this activity, he was able to take the feed buckets to the stable horses. Each horse had an individual colored bucket bearing its name, but he was not allowed to fill those. That was the job of Larry, the head groomsman.

"Why can't all the horses graze in the fields?" he asked Larry one day.

"Your uncle's horses are specially bred for racing or for sale to other enthusiasts. In time we can identify the best racers and put them into the stables for special care and training. Those horses require planned meals, as well as hay, particularly when they are competing. The breeders are often the offspring of some of our best racers, and the sale of those and their progeny is when Mr. Compton makes good money," Larry explained in the Lexington brogue that was so unlike that of Cynthiana folks.

"Does my uncle make money by racing them?" Rory asked.

"Yep, he sure does," Larry said with a robust chortle, ruffling the boy's golden curls. "The trouble is, he's running out of space and can't expand. He wants to take over your Longfield as soon as he can, as you might well know."

He glanced at the boy and his face dropped, realizing he had spoken out of turn as he watched Rory's laughing face turn to one of frowning concern.

"Tell you what, let's get down to the river today. I want you to see the little boat I'm making," he said, hoping this would take the boy's mind off his last comments.

They rode on horseback to the river, Rory holding onto Larry's pants belt. He had no time to worry about Larry's indiscretion for a time, though he did worry about the comment later that evening. He thought he would ask Uncle John what Larry had meant when he next saw him, but on further reflection decided not to, just in case he landed Larry in trouble for gossiping.

As Rory explored the farm's geography, he was astounded that for weeks he had remained unaware of its size, cocooned as he had been within his own wretchedness. His father had rarely mentioned his brother's farm and the majestic horses on which much of his wealth was based. He listened carefully to the workers, and the enormous pride each had in his work. The majority were from the 'po' white' village a couple of miles east, though Beulah surprised Rory when she pointed out the hired black people who worked alongside them.

"We don't buy slaves," she had explained to him, "but your uncle does need to hire some from neighbors at busy times."

Rory did notice, however, that the slaves were well-fed and cared for.

He was delighted with everything; not only the horses, but the different breeds of cattle and the acres put out to orchards and vegetables, so different from the Longfield hemp farm. He welcomed the peace of the picturesque gardens and the chance to use his own gardening skills. He even pondered on how he could improve the Longfield gardens, but most of all he wanted to get to the river and swim.

Day-by-day, as the shadowy mists in his mind lightened, Rory appeared to be more optimistic. The nightmares did not happen so often now, and thinking of his grandfather, he began to consider returning to full-time study, though loathed to leave his aunts and his new way of life.

There came a day when he joined Delphia for breakfast in the old morose mood and excusing himself, his food half-eaten, he sauntered onto the patio, where he sat on the top step, arms slung between his knees, staring out at nothing. He was brought back to Earth by a sudden piercing yowl. He jumped with alarm, and looked into the haughty face of a huge, beautiful animal.

"Who are you?" Rory asked the cat, annoyed at the interruption.

The cat simply yawned and looked away.

Expecting the dignified animal to stalk off, Rory was surprised when she suddenly jumped onto his lap, her wide green eyes staring into his. He realized this was Delphia's cat, a blue Persian she had brought with her from western Virginia.

"Go away, get off," Rory growled, putting out his tongue at the staring animal.

The cat continued to look bored, but stayed put.

Rory shuffled his knees, hoping the movement would shift the animal.

She did not budge.

"What do you want?" yelled Rory. "Get off me, you awful thing."

He heard a chair scrape the carpet behind him, but thought little of it, as he tried to stare out the cat's unmoving gaze.

"Well, Cat, or whatever your name is," Rory said.

The cat continued to stare at him.

"Do you ever dream?" Rory asked it.

The only response was a lazy blink.

"Well, I do," Rory said.

The cat blinked again.

There was silence for a few seconds and then suddenly, to Rory's own astonishment, he found himself providing a vivid abridgement of this morning's nightmare to the cat.

He told her of how, in the dream, he found himself running to catch his family as their coach and horses rattled past him. He was annoyed because it was raining hard. His father had ignored him completely, as had his mother as he shouted to them to stop. His sisters leant out of the window, telling him to run faster. For once they were not smiling. He heard their voices and couldn't understand their derision or the white, taut face of his parents, as they looked straight ahead.

At last he caught up with them. His mother turned her head, and looked at him, expressionless, except for one short moment when Rory saw a brief look of regret as their eyes met.

Then Mary came to the window. She laughed at Rory. She told him she was sorry they were late, but it had been Betty's fault, because she'd forgotten her doll and they had to go back for it. Mary stretched out her arms to Rory, who tried to get hold of her hand.

His father turned around then and turned the whip on Rory who let go of his sister as he felt the pain of the whip across his face. His father's face changed from the taut expression to a savage grimace, as he laughed at his son.

"Off you go, boy!" he had shouted. "We don't want you with us. Go away."

With an awful suddenness, the carriage crashed into a wall of mud and disappeared. He heard the screams of his sisters.

He stopped at this point, looking again at the cat.

"That's when the dream usually finishes," he said, seeking solace by thrusting his hand gently through the animal's white, soft fur.

The cat purred with pleasure.

"But this time the dream didn't finish then, because suddenly I was through the wall of mud myself. I had to push the mud away, but I could hear my sisters chattering away. They were laughing by now, probably enjoying watching me trying to push my way through to them. I heard Mama tell them not to tease me. 'He can't get through to us,' she had said, 'we'll have to leave him, girls. I've just seen my parents and your Compton grandparents. They're waiting for us, so we'd better go.' Her voice was clear and I fought harder to get to them. Then, I woke up and found myself back in my own bed. I heard myself shout that I hadn't been able to save them after all, despite the chance to do so."

Rory shivered as he ended his story by telling the cat how Tom had mopped his wet face and damp body down when they woke him from the nightmare, and of how Beulah, who had heard the commotion, had taken him in her arms, soothing him with her gentle voice.

"So, what do you think of that?" he asked the cat, who appeared to have listened with fascination.

The cat stood up, her claws padding around Rory's knees, before she jumped down. She twined her body around his legs before leaving for her next venue of interest.

Rory felt strangely bereft now she had departed.

"Well, you certainly made a friend of my cat," said a voice behind him.

He jumped, startled. Rory and Delphia stared at each other for a long moment.

"What's your cat's name?" Rory asked.

"Strange as it seems, you actually got it right," she said, "it's Kat."

She laughed at Rory's astonished face, explaining that her daughter, Laura, had named her.

"It's a shortened version of Kathleen," she laughed.

"I'd like to meet Laura again," he said.

Then, with a suddenness that shook Delphia, the boy's face crumpled as he broke into heartrending sobs. Delphia drew her nephew to her, arms encircled around his shaking body as if to shelter him from his torment.

Minutes went by before he pulled himself away from her. She now knew what the dream was and realized how he must feel; he had failed to save his family. She wondered how to help him.

He pulled out a handkerchief and blew his nose so hard she thought it might burst.

"You said I had got it right. Well, maybe I got the cat's name right, but if only…"

He stopped, sniffed again, searched for a clean kerchief.

She gave him hers.

After another good blow, he told her about the last time he had seen his father.

"I know that my dream is really about what happened on that day," he said, "and I've tried to keep the thoughts of it out of my mind, but each time I dream it seems more vivid. The memory just consumes me, every single day, even though I try not to let it. Today, it was even worse, because the face of my father was terrible in that last dream – full of hate. I can't forget that he died hating me. I wish I could, but I know it's going to be with me forever. It's a terrible thing to bear. It's terrible, terrible…"

He sobbed and Delphia was afraid for him. She knew she must send for Dr. Wallace today. She held him close to her.

Rory's mother had written to her about the row between Rory and his father, so Delphia was not surprised the persistent nightmare encompassed both that and the accident. She realized that Rory had not had time to make peace with his parents and felt the hopelessness of never being able to do so.

She decided to be blunt.

"Did you know that your mother had suffered two miscarriages?" Delphia asked.

Rory looked shocked, and shook his head.

She told him the devastation his parents suffered on each occasion.

"I'm telling you this, so you may understand why your father became so unbalanced that day," she said. "What you said about making another son would, without a doubt, have hurt your parents, though I am aware from your mother's letter, that your father's reaction was one he very much regretted. They realized, too late, that they should have let you know much earlier about those miscarriages."

Rory nodded, unable to speak as he took in this sudden revelation.

"Now, listen to me, Rory. I would like to give you some advice. Do you want it?"

He nodded again.

"You want to make peace with your father. You may not agree with what he said or did, but you want to make peace. Am I right?"

He nodded yet again.

Then she said something strange.

"Write to him, Rory. Write anything you want him to know. If you're not sorry, tell him so. If you regret anything, tell him. You should also tell him how you feel about becoming a doctor, and why."

She saw the cynicism in his face, but continued.

"You may want to write just one letter, or many more. Only you can know that. Just write. Then give it, or them, to me. I won't read them. I promise that. But I will keep them safe until you tell me to destroy them. You will know when that time comes." When she had finished, she studied his face.

His incredulous expression had transformed to one of understanding.

* * *

Rory did write a letter to his father and told him many things he wished he had told him before, of his hopes, expectations and of how he could not give up his dream of becoming a doctor. He spoke of his renewed vigor to ensure the future success of Longfield and promised that his father's dreams would not die either and he would ensure the Charles Compton dynasty. He wrote much more, from the heart, and felt tranquil and soothed as a result. For the first time in weeks, he could sleep untroubled. The next day Rory gave the sealed letter to Delphia for safekeeping.

Eventually the nightmare vaporized and Rory began to discuss his future education with Uncle John and Mr. Smales.

Chapter 3
Laura Parker

Laura sighed.

"That's the tenth time you've sighed in just two minutes," whispered Agatha, who sat behind Laura's desk.

Laura giggled, loudly.

Two girls seated near to them tut-tutted their annoyance at the small disturbance.

The teacher glared at Laura, who hung her head to hide a cheeky grin.

"Why do you think Abigail Adams is so funny, Laura Parker?" asked Miss Greening.

"I don't think she was funny, Miss Greening, in fact I admire her a lot. She was the woman who asked an incumbent president to 'remember the ladies' after all. I would have done the same thing and I was smiling only because I don't think we can make comparisons between her and Dolley Madison. That's all."

Heavy tapping on their desks by her fellow students told their frosty teacher they agreed with Laura.

Miss Greening tapped her own desk for quiet.

"You obviously were listening," she conceded, glowering at Laura, "but do try and be less disruptive in future."

The bell clanged for the end of the school day. Aware that the popular Laura had prevailed over the spiteful Miss Greening, the students clustered around her. Most had noticed Laura's unusual lack of enthusiasm and restlessness during the day and expressed their concern. She told them nothing of her anxieties, though she continually touched the letters hidden inside her pocket.

The students had two spare hours prior to their evening meal, during which time they could write letters home, or prepare clothes and books for the next day. Many in her class year were allowed to walk into the village, a half-mile from the school, as long as they were accompanied by at least three others. Today, Laura chose not to walk, surprising her closest friend, Agatha, who loved the daily journeys along the peaceful lane, for it was there that she might catch a glimpse of the most wonderful looking boy she had ever seen.

Laura, who had three brothers, was not particularly interested in boys, or the chat about them that seemed to occupy the leisure time of her companions.

Just four years earlier, Laura had been a rowdy, raggedy farm hand of a girl, often dressed in her brothers' castoff clothing they had outgrown. She loved the land and the hurly-burly of farm work, but most of all she loved her three brothers and tried to emulate them in all they did. She took exception though, to the noisy games of football and wrestling, preferring the swing seat her father had made, just for her. When she was small, she would allow her mother to put her in a dress and tie a ribbon in her long hair only on Sundays, in honor of their church service visit.

Since her father's death when she was seven years old, following an accident with a borrowed horse and a new unfamiliar horse-drawn cultivator, her mother, Delphia Parker, had run the large agricultural farm that combined a successful piggery.

Laura had been heartbroken and inconsolable at the sudden death of her beloved Papa for a long while, which was why her mother allowed her to help the boys with the farm work instead of teaching her household skills. It had also helped Delphia that Laura had taken her brother, Vinnie, younger by two years, under her wing as they shared their grief at losing Papa.

Together, the two of them learned about the land and farm chores and were inseparable, until Delphia noticed, as Laura entered her teenage years, that her daughter had reached the life-changing era of adolescence, with its inevitable mood swings, apathy and listlessness.

At a loss of what to do at that time, Delphia had written to her brothers' wives, Marianne in Cynthiana and Beulah in Lexington, seeking their advice.

"It took Laura a long time to get over her father's death," she wrote, *"and with the running of the farm and the household, I'm afraid I've neglected her needs and allowed her to become a tomboy. To be honest, she's devoid of all lady-like attributes. She's seen in the neighborhood as an extension of her brothers, and I can't see any future marriage prospects for her, although of course she's not quite 14. She could read by the time she was four years old, as you know, and is now as good as her father was at*

accounting. She has a flair for teaching, and is now busy teaching Vinnie the skills of bookkeeping. But, her deportment is so sloppy and her language is not what her father would have liked. Her one redeeming feature is that she's inherited the Compton good looks."

Delphia's passionate plea for help was a welcome project for her sisters-in-law. Each aunt took a turn at hosting Laura in their homes for three months. Laura was delighted with the environment of both homes, though she did not see much of her cousins, except for the dear little twin infants at Longfield.

"Both of my aunts have been so kind to me," Laura wrote to her mother, *"and I love the relaxed atmosphere here in Kentucky. My uncles appear to have more money than you have, so they can afford to buy labor. I wish you could afford that, Mother, as it would give you and my brothers a bit more time to relax. I do miss you all. How are you, and how is my darling Vinnie? Tell him I think of him often."*

"All's well here," her mother replied. *"All the boys send you their love. Lawrence has a girlfriend. She's got such a lovely nature and he's infatuated. They met after I employed her to help with the vegetable lifting, a few weeks ago. He really is besotted. She's Frances Langridge from Birch Farm. You'll have seen her about. Vinnie sends his special love to you. He misses you also, as we all do."*

On another occasion, Laura informed her mother of how tidy she had now become.

"You won't recognize me, Mother, because I can't abide anywhere to be untidy now, and that includes my own dress and hair."

Lawrence answered that letter.

"I don't believe for one minute you are tidy. Your definition of tidy is probably pushing your shoes and stockings under the bed instead of putting them neatly at the side, and trailing your clothes all over the floor. Am I right? When you come home, you'll have to be tidy, because my bride-to-be is staying in your room, and honestly, there's much more room now, she's sorted it out. Hope you can make the wedding."

When Delphia's sisters-in-law recommended at the end of the six months that Laura could benefit from attending Gosling's School for Young Ladies in Keene, she wrote to her mother.

"My dear Mother, I would so love to go to that school. Both aunts went there when it was first opened, and that's how they met apparently and have been friends ever since. I never knew that, did you? Please, please Mother, do say I can go. You did tell me long ago when Papa died, that he left something for my wedding dowry – well, I'd rather go to school with that than have a wedding. I'd like to become a teacher instead of getting married. Please let me go."

Delphia discussed this with her sons, who each said such pleading could not be ignored.

Laura started at the school at the beginning of the September term in 1856. So thrilled was she, she made no fuss when she was allocated the tidied up attic room at the top of the stairs to sleep in during the school breaks.

Frances was now well and truly established in Laura's former room and in view of the pending wedding nuptials all agreed Frances could stay where she was. The wedding was brought forward and took place before Laura left for the next school term.

"I wondered why the wedding was brought forward," she wrote to her mother, when she heard her first nephew had been born just six months after the wedding. *"I couldn't really believe it was just so I could be her bridesmaid before going back to school."*

Laura was pleased to hear the couple, who had begun to build their own house within the farm grounds during the summer, was ready to move into it before Christmas, as she realized she would have her room back when she returned home.

"But what does it matter where I sleep?" she had asked herself. "Especially, when there's a beautiful little baby Parker in the world." She couldn't wait to meet him.

Laura had felt isolated at the start of her school life, but had kept her unhappiness to herself. Some of her rough edges had been smoothed by her aunts, but she did not fit in with the elegance of her new surroundings and the gentility of her fellow pupils. She had decided not to tell her mother about this, but did write to Aunt Beulah.

"I know full well that there is contempt from the girls in my class when my manners slip, and they often do," Laura wrote.

Beulah did not worry too much as Mrs. Gosling, whom she had known since girlhood, had told her Laura's sense of humor had prevailed.

"The older girls appear to be quite taken with your niece," Agnes Gosling had written, *"She's an unusual girl, whose strength of character they've noticed though don't realize that's what it is. Laura has become popular throughout the school against all the odds."*

Mrs. Gosling knew of Laura's background and had noted her pupil's aptitude for learning, leadership and burgeoning popularity. She assured Beulah she would keep a watchful eye on her progress.

Laura's sense of isolation had receded by the start of her second year. To her surprise, it was at home where she now felt excluded. To her brothers, she appeared different and they didn't know how to treat her, not even Vinnie. The uncomfortable feeling of not appearing to fit in at her home would have been difficult to deal with, had it not been for Lawrence's wife and the baby. The two girls became firm friends and Delphia saw it was good for Frances to have younger female company. Laura doted on her nephew, allowing her sister-in-law time to get on with her chores.

Delphia wrote to her sisters-in-law in reams about her grandson and almost as much about the conversion of her unsophisticated daughter into a polite, almost cultured young woman in just one year.

"What a change there is with Laura. She's quite the lady now, though there's plenty of room for improvement. Mrs. Gosling takes a special interest in her, and I think in another two or three years, we'll be seeing a cultivated, refined young teacher in the family. I can't thank you enough for recommending the school. Nowadays, she even refuses to help Vinnie with the farm chores, which has surprised all of us, as the two of them were never apart in the old days. And she does keep herself well-groomed. The two elder boys tease her about it, but she doesn't mind. Her father would have loved this change in her, as much as I do."

Laura loved going home, knowing she would return to Keene, and occasionally when out for an evening stroll with her brothers. Her old exuberance returned on those occasions, but ceased after an embarrassing encounter with two of the sons from a neighboring farm.

"You should have seen it, Mother," Vinnie said to his mother on their return, one evening, laughing as he told the story. The other boys tried to stop him, but he persisted.

"What?" Delphia had asked, her own laughter stimulated by Vinnie's uncontrollable giggles.

"Well," he said, "she was doing cart wheels. I dared her to do three in a row and on the third one, in mid-wheel, with her skirt falling over her face, Jack Fenning and his two sons happened to be passing. And there she was, my so-called dignified sister with her bloomers in full view for all to see. We were all so embarrassed, except for the Fennings. They loved it."

His mother was angry, more with him than with the culprit.

"You should never tell tales of ladies," she scolded.

"Oh, Mama, she certainly was no lady," Vinnie giggled.

He was shocked when a great clout from his elder brother landed on his head, followed by another from Brett, his other brother.

Laura flew up to her room, sobbing her eyes out.

"Now look what you've gone and done," shouted his mother, slapping Vinnie hard across his legs.

Laura forgave Vinnie his indiscretion, but was sorry her mother did not forgive *her* for 'shaming the family' in the way she had.

"You still see yourself as a farm-hand," Delphia had complained. "This lack of feminine finesse was one of the main reasons that I sent you off to the school in the first place."

The incident had proved to be a good lesson well-learned, and Laura became once again the quieter, nice-looking teenager her aunts and the school had made her, and of whom her mother approved. Laura realized she did not, after all, relish the slatternly farm-hand image that she had once had.

On this quiet day at the school in her fourth school year, at the end of which she would graduate, Laura found a quiet corner in the library, after she had finished her chores. She took from her pocket the letter, received from her mother who was still in Lexington, together with that received three days ago from Frances. She knew the contents of both by heart.

The substance of both letters was similar, and while her mother's included an additional worry about cousin Rory, Laura's main concern was the possibility of a potential problem between her mother and her brother, Lawrence.

The gist of the problem facing the family was that Frances was expecting the birth of twins, which would swell her growing family to seven. She had already given birth to three children in as many years. Frances had stated their current house would be too small for the larger family, so had requested permission to move into the family home inherited by Delphia. The proposal was that Mother could live in their current home, with the idea of Vinnie taking it when he married. Brett, who had married a year earlier, would remain in the house he had built for his own bride. A new house would be built on Dibbins Plot, a single-acre unused corner of the farm, for Delphia and Laura when Vinnie eventually married. The boys felt that the new house would enable their mother to live a peaceful retirement away from the everyday problems of farm life.

"Don't they know how that will make her feel?" she had shouted at the walls on re-reading Frances' letter. "My mother kept that farm going when we were children, and now they are discussing throwing her out of her own home. I won't allow this while I'm around."

She was angry. The letter implied that the boys expected their mother to retire and hand over the business to them, as did the proposal to build a house at Dibbins Corner, a few miles from the axis of the farm. Laura knew her mother would come to the same conclusion and would be desolate at the thought.

"Mama's mind is as sharp as it's ever been," she had yelled into the room.

It was true Delphia had devolved aspects of the farm management to her sons bit by bit, to ensure stability following her own demise, but she had always made it clear that until that time, she wished to retain overall responsibility.

"And why not?" Laura yelled again, banging her fists on the table in front of her, "the farm is *hers.*"

She realized she was shouting, and glanced round the library to make sure it was empty, and then walked to the open door to see if there was anyone around in the outside corridor. To her relief, there was no one, and she closed the door, feeling foolish.

"Well, they would never hand the baton to me to take over this place if they overheard that rant would they?" she sniggered to herself, and though remaining aggrieved, managed to calm herself.

Frances had written to Laura out of friendship suggesting it was a logical step to ensure future family continuity and development. From the gist of Frances' letter, it appeared she expected Laura to agree with her. Her mother's letter had provided the same facts, but Laura knew that even though her mother would take a reasoned view, she would feel like a feeble old horse put out to pasture for the rest of its life. Laura herself could understand the rationality behind the proposal, but remained sensitive to mother's feelings. She wondered if an extension could be built to Lawrence's present house, but then realized there was insufficient land available to do that without compromising the main agricultural area. She was worried, however, that the lack of solution other than that put forward, could lead to family friction. The urgency was that a decision needed to be made prior to the birth of Frances and Lawrence's twins.

As it happened, Delphia had arranged to attend the school the following week for the annual Three-Day Exceptional Holiday, an innovation inspired by Mrs. Gosling to which parents were invited. Many did attend, taking accommodation at the nearby village, which was in turn a boost in income for the local residents.

That will be a suitable time to discuss the family quandary, Laura thought to herself. She knew that tossing ideas around had always been a part of her mother's business plans. Relieved at this thought, she turned to the rest of her mother's letter and her comments about Rory, with whom her mother appeared to be besotted.

Laura could remember travelling to Cynthiana with her mother when she was about five years old to stay with Uncle Charles and family. Rory was just a quiet four-year-old boy, redeemed only by a mass of blond curly hair. He appeared to prefer his own company to that of others. She had found him rather odd in comparison to her noisy brothers, not realizing her own behavior was unlike that of other little girls Rory had known. It never occurred to her he found her odd. Even now, Laura had the impression he was still that weird boy. She was curious enough to want to find out.

After telling her about the improvement of Rory's overall health, Delphia's letter confided with her the difficulties of being a joint executor in the administration of Rory's affairs.

"As you know, Uncle John's also an executor, and because he's Rory's legal guardian, he seems to have taken on all decision making. He hardly refers to me."

She described her misgivings about decisions he had made without referring to her.

"The main problem revolves around the house and some of the land at Longfield. It seems that maintaining the house and staff is expensive, especially with no one but staff living there," she wrote. "The house and the farm business are well-run by Uncle Charles' farm manager, William. He's a very decent person and a good manager. As you know, he's black, a former slave whom Charles freed when he inherited Longfield."

"Therein lies the problem," Delphia's letter continued. "When Charles was there, it didn't matter to business colleagues and local farmers that they had to deal with a black man from time to time. They always knew that the main man was Charles, you see, and that William was working under his direction. Now, though, any decisions made by William are being frowned upon by business colleagues, and even some of the farmers. It seems that there is jealousy about because Longfield achieved a new navy contract while other farmers did not, and William is bearing the full force of that jealousy. If William was a white man, or if there was a Compton living there, John's elder son, Timothy for instance, I do feel there would be a different atmosphere. But John seems intent on undermining the whole of Longfield's future business."

Laura was shocked at that last remark which gave her a lot to think about.

With a growing sense of excitement, an idea began to form in Laura's alert mind. The idea soon became a conviction.

"How would it be," she asked herself, "if Charles Compton's sister was to live at Longfield?"

If what she was being told was true, having Delphia, a blood relative and an experienced farm manager, living there, assisting in the management, might well alleviate the situation. It might also give the Parker family more time to resolve the current difficulty, and Mother would not be made to feel dispensable.

"The thing is," Laura said to the air around her, "someone has to persuade both Mama and Uncle John about this."

Another thought struck her. *What if John disagreed with this possible solution?*

She smiled as she realized that even if John did disagree, Rory himself might be willing for Delphia to look after his home and oversee his inheritance. She threw the letters into the air and laughed out loud, scarcely able to breathe in her excitement.

Chapter 4
Rory and Cousin Oliver

John Compton broached the subject of Rory's further education with his headmaster, Mr. Smales, on the lines of the original plan. Smales accepted he would make all arrangements, on the understanding Rory would undertake tutorials in Latin, Greek and French in Lexington, rather than return to the school. He had already located a tutor, Jeff Alderson, who taught those subjects to a group of three or four youths, under the patronage of a local banker, who agreed Rory could join the group. The pupils met Monday to Thursday during a normal school term period. Smales also arranged that he would supervise the extra tuition required for the university entrance examination one weekend per month.

John was reluctant to accept the arrangement at first.

"School will be good for him. He'll be among youths of his own age," he said, "We can't keep him locked away from real life forever, you know. He needs to be stimulated in his education but also be amongst his peers."

"I agree with you up to a point," Mr. Smales said, "but let me tell you about a boy of similar intellect who came across my path a few years ago. He was a quiet, shy type, with his head in the clouds, until he got into the higher classes. He reached adolescence and boys being boys, he was led astray by the carnal inclinations and drinking habits of a few fellow pupils. Older pupils have more free time away from the school on one evening a week, and on Sundays. These rules led to the boy's academic ruination and he now works as a lowly administrator in his father's business, married at the age of 19 to the girl he made pregnant. He is miserable and his intellect has atrophied under the barrage of married life, three children, and the tedium of his job. I believe, Rory has a stronger character than that particular pupil, but I've told you this true story to illustrate the importance of your decision right now."

Delphia and Beulah were present at that initial interview. Delphia was the first to join in the conversation

"I agree with Mr. Smales' plan. We've all been worried about Rory's mental state, but I think we can say now he is well enough to proceed down a more normal path. However, I think it would be detrimental to return him to Louisville right now. He really would feel isolated without his family around and be in danger of relapse in my opinion."

"He wouldn't be alone," John responded. "He'll have the companionship of youths of the same age."

Beulah glared at her husband.

"He's happier nowadays *because* he's here," Beulah said, her face pale in her concern for their nephew. "Rory's not a person who would welcome the isolation of a school that is so far away at this time. He's got used to us and feels secure in our love. I agree with Delphia, that he could regress without our support even for a short time. We've all done so much to get him back to reasonable health and he requires stability, not another upheaval. That's evident to me."

Delphia spoke up again.

"John," she said, "Rory is a sensitive boy. He's been seriously ill, but has had the courage to overcome it. He's so much better now because of our farm and all of us. He shouldn't be ripped away from his new life and sent back to an environment where he had to overcome black thoughts of the fight with his father, and where he learned of the death of his whole family. Sending him back there would be cruel. If you insist he goes there, I for one will never forgive you. And neither will he, of that I am sure."

"I agree with you," Beulah said. "He's now come to terms with his grief to a large extent, though he'll never forget what's happened. To send him back to Louisville, where the old wounds would surely open up again, would be unwise and put him right back to where he was a few months ago. I'm all for Mr. Smales' plan."

"It isn't that I don't want him around here," John said, "I would miss him if he went back to Louisville and so would many of my workers. He's popular with them. All I want for him is to be as happy as he appears now," John said, never a defeatist.

Mr. Smales had been listening, dismayed at the lack of accord within the family. He decided to intervene with something that might lead them to a solution.

"Why not get the opinion of Dr. Lawrence?" he asked.

Everybody agreed with this obvious solution.

The outcome of Dr. Lawrence's advice was that Rory met Mr. Alderson on four days a week, together with three other youths.

Each student took turns to host the others once a week in their own home. Monday was the Compton's day. Rory enjoyed striding out on the other mornings, his books tied with a leather strap slung across a shoulder. The others arrived on horseback, but Rory did not feel confident enough as yet to ride, to the light-hearted derision of his fellow students. He settled into study straight off and excelled.

Thanks to their common interests, the lively youths soon became friends and often met at the local hostelry on Fridays. The intention was to discuss the week's work, though the conversation usually turned to the ubiquitous question of how to attract this girl, or that one, where to take her and, to Rory's embarrassment, what to do with her. Rory was the youngest by three years, and two of them, Patrick Bellowes and Francis Bellingham, hinted that he should listen and learn from them. Fred Hetherington, a quiet, much shyer boy, said little on the subject, but as he could speak with authority on horsemanship, his credibility and popularity survived.

Late one Sunday afternoon Rory found himself alone. Uncle John, Beulah and Delphia had started their journey to Longfield earlier that day, with a plan to call on a couple of acquaintances en route. Rory would have liked to travel with them in order to see William, from whom he had not heard for weeks. He had spoken of his wish earlier the preceding week but his preoccupied uncle had mumbled something about not wanting to inconvenience the folks he had arranged to call upon.

"In any case, this is the weekend Mr. Smales is here for your tutorials," his uncle explained, in a tone that brooked no argument, "and I don't feel it's a good idea to cancel those."

Rory wandered into the library where he usually studied and sat down in one of the comfortable chairs near the window. He opened a book and studied for a half-hour before he realized the sky had darkened. He wondered where the maid would leave his dinner. He thought for a while about the maid. She was pretty in a way, though messy in hair-dressing and deportment. He wondered what the soft curved shape, accentuated by her tight dress looked like uncovered. He blushed at his thoughts, deciding that he was allowing the bawdiness of Patrick and Francis to fill his mind a little too much. He did not realize his own burgeoning instincts were responsible for his vulgar, though enjoyable thoughts, as he attempted to concentrate on the exercises he had been set.

He was suddenly startled by a voice behind him.

"Do you think you should be trespassing in another person's library?" asked a tall youth, glowering down at him. He was thin

53

and looked tired, his unshaven face accentuating the blackness of his hair. His dark brown eyes flashed angrily as he strolled into the room as if he owned it.

Rory sprang up. The man looked familiar, though he could not place him. He watched as the stranger let himself down gently into the opposite armchair.

"I've been riding all day," the man said, explaining his obvious pain.

"I'm Rory Compton, and the owner of this library and the house is my Uncle John," Rory told the unwelcome visitor, who looked even more familiar as he grinned at the nervous boy in front of him.

"Well, in that case, you must be my cousin Rory, and I must be your cousin Oliver," he said.

He laughed at Rory's obvious surprise. "I should have remembered you were still here. Sorry, completely forgot. How are you? I am so sorry about your family. It was a terrible thing to happen."

They shook hands, and Oliver grinned again. Rory's heart twisted for a moment as he noticed the grin was exactly like his father's. No wonder he had looked so familiar. They chatted away easily for half an hour, and during that time decided they liked each other. Rory felt they could be friends.

"I'm hungry," said Oliver, "Let's see if we can find our supper, shall we?"

They found the shapely little maid fluttering about the small dining room used for incidental meals. She had obviously been prepared for Oliver, as the table was set for two. She stayed to serve them. Her eyes followed Oliver's every movement and her blushes deepened each time he spoke to her. At his request she trotted off to the cellar to fetch the particular wine he had requested.

Rory grinned as she left.

"She's yours for the asking, it seems," he said, laughing.

He surprised himself as this speech was so unlike him. It was almost, he thought, as if Patrick, or even Francis, had been behind the chair prompting him.

Oliver looked long and hard at his cousin.

Rory expected a string of expletives following his undignified rudeness, and he felt ashamed of his coarse remark.

"You've heard about me, haven't you?" asked Oliver, a sadness in his voice and facial expression.

"Of course I've heard about you," Rory said, "you're my uncle's second son; my cousin; a little older than me; you don't like your school very much; a bit artistic; supposed to be quiet, though you haven't shown me that side of you this evening. Yes, I know about you."

"Yes, yes," Oliver said, "I mean the other part of me. You mentioned the girl, the little maid…"

His voice trailed off.

"I just meant that she likes you, she's attracted to you…Christopher Columbus, don't tell me you've got a bad reputation with women at your tender age?" Rory laughed, realizing Oliver would get on like a house on fire with Patrick and Francis, though he calculated that Fred would be too quiet for him.

"Actually," said Oliver, his voice subdued, "I'm not keen on girls, as a matter of fact."

Rory was astonished.

"I didn't know that," Rory now said, somewhat abashed, "but who cares? I certainly don't. You are who you are, and that can't change. You're a splendid fellow as far as I know."

Oliver smiled, and shook his head.

"I don't mean…" he blurted out, "I'm not…well, what I mean to say is the reason I don't like girls is because they caused me and a friend a lot of…well, we both vowed to leave 'em alone…not that we did anything …what happened wasn't our fault…" Oliver realized he was gabbling and stopped.

Rory stared at him, not really understanding all this baloney. "What the heck are you trying to tell me?" he said.

Oliver told him. "I used to go to another college in Louisville – it's closed down now. Well, one weekend, there was a special course for senior students. All other students went home for the weekend except me, and another student, Frederick, whose family lived in New Hampshire, too far away for him to go home for just two days. My own family were away, so I couldn't go home either. We were given a lot of freedom that weekend and allowed to go out with the senior students on the Sunday evening. One of the seniors, Russ, was put in charge of us. He'd volunteered to do so though he hadn't really wanted to go out. He'd arranged to meet a girlfriend, who'd cancelled at the last minute and he was unhappy about that to say the least. The other lads met a group of girls, who were soon the worse for drinking, and allowed themselves to be used badly. I was disgusted, not only with the feral behavior of those seniors toward them, but of the girls themselves, as was Frederick. We did enjoy wandering around the town with Russ, though, and stopped a couple of times to get beer from quieter taverns. Russ regaled us with the virtues of his beloved Sophie. I remember thinking how wonderful it would be to have a girl like her to think about. On our way back, we saw a group of guys in a large group, looking down on what we thought was a fight on the ground. When we got there, we saw one of them taking advantage of a young woman lying there, almost unconscious with drink. Then another one, one of our students as it happened, said 'my turn' and started to abuse the woman spread-eagled on the roadside. Russ suddenly shouted out and pulled up the guy and socked him. The group of youths ganged up against Russ, but he didn't move as he stared down at the woman, who was in a shocking state by now, rumpled, soiled, and giggling.

I remember Russ shouting 'It's Sophie. What've you done to my Sophie?' He shook off the guys holding him and fell to her side, and tried to keep her awake."

"By then a posse of older men had arrived and shouted to the gathered youths, who took to their heels. They carried the girl off. I don't know where or how they'd been alerted. All I remember is Russ leaning against the wall, sobbing. Somehow we all got back to the college, and the headmaster was informed the following morning by the staff member in charge of the building that night.

"After breakfast, everyone was called to the assembly room. It was there we heard Russ had hanged himself in his room. Frederick and I were appalled, devastated. We were interrogated for a long time because we had spent the evening with him. We both vowed we'd never allow ourselves to be in that sort of situation, and we made a pact to be celibate for the rest of our lives."

"When did all this happen?" Rory asked

"Two years ago. The college closed due to the scandal that followed. I've not changed my mind about celibacy and women since that time."

"Who did you tell about this?" asked Rory.

"The headmaster and those investigating why Russ hanged himself, as well as my father," Oliver said, "but nobody, except Frederick, understood what the episode had done to me. I don't know why I'm telling you, really. It's because I trust you, I think."

"Well," said Rory, "I can understand how it's affected you so badly, and it must have been an awful experience. It's an affliction that may disappear with time, especially if you get some help. I have a good friend, a doctor, who might help you. He helped me a lot."

Oliver looked at him.

"You've got a wise head on your shoulders," he said, "and I must admit that the horror of it all has begun to recede, but I still shudder at what I witnessed…and the outcome of it all."

"Now that you've told someone else, it might start to dissipate further and one day you'll be famous with your pictures. Everyone will realize your extraordinary artistry and be proud of you," Rory said, referring to Oliver's enthusiasm to work with the renowned photographer, Mathew Brady. During their earlier conversation, Oliver had spoken with enthusiasm about Brady, whom he had met in Washington.

Oliver nodded. "There's just one more thing," he said. "You actually know my companion of that night. He's Frederick Hetherington, and such a shy chap who needs a bright companion, just as I do. We both find it difficult making friends, especially since the incident, so we've linked up and are great buddies. Maybe we'll get over the horror together, who knows. I feel better already, knowing that you know why I'm a bit of an oddball. My father and brother have no time for me. So, it's a good thought you've given me, Rory. Thanks."

Rory grinned at his cousin.

"Look, old chap," he said, banging Oliver smartly on the back, "if you've got any more confessions, you'd better come out with them right now. I'm not one for thunderbolts out of the blue, you know."

Laughing, the cousins shook hands again and drank the wine that the blushing, tousle-haired maid had just rushed in.

The following day, the students and tutor duly turned up for their first session of the week, which happened to be at the Compton's place. Oliver was not to be seen, but Fred was his usual, quiet, self-effacing self.

Following a busy schedule, Rory remained in the library to finish off his notes after the students had left for the day. A half hour later, Oliver popped his head round the door.

"I've asked Fred to stay for dinner. Do you mind?" he asked.

Rory did not mind, and said so.

"There's a letter for you," Oliver said, handing it to Rory. "It came this morning. Should have been delivered on Saturday, apparently, but the mail guy was held up. It's come from Cynthiana by the look of it."

Rory recognized William's writing, and ripped open the envelope. As he read, the eager smile on his face slipped bit by bit, and by the time he had finished his face was rosy with anger. He took a few minutes to calm himself, and then went out, seeking his cousin.

He found him in the kitchen, where he and Fred were enjoying an odd-looking concoction of food that consisted of two pieces of bread with a chunk of sliced chicken placed between them, which they were eating with their fingers. Oliver caught his cousin's astonished expression.

"Don't look like that," Oliver laughed, "Fred made 'em. They're not much to look at but are very good."

"It's called a sandwich," said Fred, "named after a man called the Earl of Sandwich in England in the last century. He sort of invented them because he didn't like leaving his gaming table to eat his dinner with everyone else at the dining table. Do you want one?"

Eager to fulfil his errand, Rory declined.

"Can you do something for me?" he asked Oliver. "This letter's from my father's farm manager, and he refers to some points he made in previous letters he sent me. Your father's got them in a desk drawer, and I need to refer to them again. Do you think you can get them for me, please? I don't like to pry in his things."

He showed Oliver the envelope delivered that day, suggesting that the envelopes and handwriting would be similar. He told him where he guessed they would be, and crossed his fingers in the hope he was right as Oliver dashed off to look. Within a few minutes, Rory had possession of three opened letters from William, each addressed to him, but which he had never seen. He had taken them from Oliver with a nonchalance he had not felt, making reference again to the foreign dish with a shudder, as the laughing Fred and Oliver returned to it with relish. Back in the library, he read the letters with measured deliberation, at the end of which his face had darkened with fury.

The next morning Oliver was surprised to find a note, asking Fred to give Rory's apologies for the rest of the week's study sessions, and to say he would catch up with everything the following week. He wrote that that he was going to Cynthiana but gave no further explanation.

The housekeeper informed Oliver that Rory had left that morning for Cynthiana, and had told her he would probably return with his aunt and uncle.

Chapter 5
Longfield's Future

Rory arrived at the railroad inn in Cynthiana by mid-afternoon and reserved a room for three nights. His small leather travelling bag, packed by the housekeeper, was large enough to hold his new suit, with a change of clothing and nightwear.

"I don't know where he's going, or why," the housekeeper had said to her husband, an under butler at Lexington earlier that morning. "He's very courtly nowadays, fully in charge of himself. You can't help but compare him with the ailing boy he was, when he arrived here last September."

"He ordered the small carriage last night to take him to the railroad for the early train to Covington, and then he'll get the train from there to Cynthiana," her husband had responded, as he gulped down a hasty breakfast.

Getting Rory ready for his sudden trip had held up his wife's morning routine so things were running late.

"I can't fathom why he didn't leave with his uncle yesterday," she'd replied. "He would've saved the cost of the train, and I've heard it don't save no time, what with having to change at Covington."

* * *

Rory had found the journey arduous, and was glad of the warm broth offered by the innkeeper's wife, Janet Atherton on arrival. He was aware William no longer resided at Longfield, but the innkeeper knew where to find him. A few hours later Rory and William were enjoying a delicious hot meal together, cooked specially for them by Janet. They said little as they ate in the small dining corner of the large, noisy room where patrons rolled cylinders of cheap tobacco leaves lolled against a counter with their even cheaper drinks. For the first time in his life, Rory drank a strange-tasting brew from a tankard. He liked it and asked for another. William shook his head and winked at the innkeeper as he requested two mugs of strong black coffee to follow the succulent apple pudding. This was all served by a chirpy girl called Bessie, who showed much interest in Rory, though he did not appear to notice her.

The current situation at Longfield was the main topic for discussion that included the downgrading of William's role during the past months. William spoke of the somewhat hurried departure of Ronald Selby, Longfield's auditor, whom Rory had come to know when he and William had established their new accounts system. Mr. Selby, the respected sole owner of a professional accountancy company, had continued to advise Longfield on taxation liabilities. He was also to be their fall back for auditing services should Rory's future university commitments limit his time.

"I remember how Mr. Selby used to talk about his retirement," Rory said. "His wife was so anxious to return to their roots in Carolina. He said to me once, he didn't think he'd make it, but hoped his savings and the sale of his business would enable his wife and family to do so in due course."

William nodded. "Yes, I remember that, and I often felt sorry for him. I can understand why he accepted the offer from Norman Sampson, the new owner. The story goes that Sampson is keen on horse racing and breeding, and wanted to come to Kentucky because he thinks this is going to be the horse county of our country. He wants to be a part of its growth."

"Did Sampson tell you that himself, William?" Rory asked.

William shook his head. "When he realized your uncle was a horse breeder, he was quick to make his acquaintance, but ignored me most of the time. He and your uncle became close, which surprised me, as I think Sampson's an uncouth lug. Your uncle did tell me that Sampson's keen to become established in the area, and that's why he made Selby such a generous offer he just couldn't refuse. To old Selby the offer would have seemed like a miracle that gave his family the chance to fulfil their dream. No wonder he accepted it."

"Where have the Selby's gone? Do you have a contact?" Rory queried.

"No, that's just it. No one appears to know where his wife's relatives actually lived in Carolina. To my knowledge, the Selby's never made close friends while they were here."

Rory was thoughtful for a while. "I do remember Mr. Selby once saying that he couldn't be friends with his clients as he knew too much about them, though he did say this with a wink of the eye," he said.

William nodded in agreement.

"So, who is this Norman Sampson? What's his background?"

"Nobody knows much about him, except he's keen on horse racing. Most of Selby's clients remained with Sampson when he took over, probably to maintain continuity in these days of uncertainty. That goddamn naval contract business has left a lot of worried folks around here," William said, shaking his head.

"Did he know you and I maintained our own ledgers, and that Selby only advised on the annual taxation position since our changes?"

"Your uncle wasn't aware you had been so involved in the business and was taken aback when I told him. Frankly, he was scathing about the arrangement. As you were still under your doctor's care, he said he had no option but to appoint Sampson to look the books over. He was within his rights to do so, of course, as an executor of your father's will. I did try to tell him how you came to be involved," William continued, "but he just couldn't believe it. He said that if it was true, your father had been unethical. I told him that Mr. Jefferson at the bank could verify our professionalism, but he didn't want to know. He just wouldn't listen."

"What did you think about all this at the time?" Rory asked, tenacious in his efforts to ascertain as much information as possible.

"I felt your uncle's attitude was odd, given you're his nephew and it was, after all, your father's idea. Your Aunt Delphia said she'd told him about your school record. He didn't return the ledgers to me, and when I asked for them at the end of the week, he told me he'd passed them to Sampson. He bawled me out when I protested."

"You're saying that Sampson had access to the education and the household expenses ledgers, as well as the business accounts?"

William nodded. "I told your uncle that the education and household ledgers were nothing to do with the business and that they were my responsibility until you inherited. He told me to mind my own business. I said that was what I was doing on behalf of the executors and reminded him your Aunt Delphia was also an executor. After that he ordered me out of his sight. This was said in front of one of the house maids who had just arrived with his morning coffee. I think that's when the rumors started about my so-called book-keeping incompetence and my position came into question."

William winced at the thought and cupped his face in his hands, in obvious distress.

"Did Uncle John check with Mr. Jefferson at the bank?" Rory asked. His own face was tense as he witnessed William's pain.

William shook his head.

"Your uncle said it wasn't necessary. It was just my rotten luck that Jefferson had been transferred to their Manchester branch in New Hampshire for a couple of months, otherwise I would have gone down to see him myself, to ask him, and to have a word with your uncle. I haven't seen the ledgers since they were handed over to Sampson, though I've made careful notes for entry when they do re-surface."

"And by this time, Selby had left the area and was unable to either substantiate or disprove the insinuations?"

William nodded again.

"Did Sampson spend a lot of time at Longfield?"

"Yes he did, and your uncle seemed to welcome this. They were very buddy-buddy, and it was around this time I noticed staff and customers were disrespecting my own role even more. Rumors began about my supposed incompetence, and how I had been so lazy I had allowed you, a school-boy, to do the book-keeping for me. The biggest blow was when your uncle told me Longfield was losing money. I knew it couldn't be true."

Rory's mind was whirling. The situation seemed far worse than William's letters had implied. His breath became labored in an effort to gain control of his reeling thoughts and panic. He felt a strong need to be alone for a while.

"I need a bit of fresh air, William," he said, "I'm just going for a short walk to calm down. I won't be long."

William nodded, feigning a sudden interest in three little boys, visible from the small window of their meeting room, playing 'kick-a-stone' on the cobbled street.

A cobbled street's a damned silly place to play 'kick-a-stone', he thought, trying to clear his own mind of the anguish within him. His shoulders sagged as he watched their carefree play and to his dismay, unbidden tears began to run down his strong, though woebegone, face.

When Rory returned half an hour later carrying a tray of coffee and cookies, William handed Rory a series of balance sheets prepared by Sampson, commenting they had been carefully scrutinized by Uncle John. They appeared to indicate discrepancies between income and expenditure, resulting in serious losses.

"You can see that the presentation differs from ours, but it's clear there are discrepancies. I asked again to see the business ledger so I could make a professional judgment of their accuracy. It was then I was told one of Selby's staff had mislaid the ledgers temporarily because they're in the middle of re-decorating and hadn't yet set up a regular file system."

Rory hooted with derision. "Heavens to Betsy, did my uncle believe that?"

"He seemed to," was William's only comment, as he gulped down his coffee, reaching for a cookie with a shaking hand. He saw Rory noticed the shake, and once more he cupped his face in his hands, his shoulders heaving slightly.

Rory left his seat and crossed over to William. He put his arms around his friend's shoulders and cradled his head against his own chest until the silent weeping stopped.

As William recovered, he spoke of how Sampson had laughed in his face, as he confronted him over a minor problem.

"He called me a black amateur, and told me to go away. I felt like punching the man up to the moon," he said, smiling now at the thought of doing so, "but I didn't because I saw your uncle's expression had changed. He was glaring at Sampson and I waited for him to reprimand Sampson, which he had a right to do, but he didn't. He just looked down at his hands, fiddling about with his wedding band. Later that day, I told your uncle I was due time off and as I had not had any since the accident, I would start the following day." He looked at Rory, who nodded for him to go on.

"So here I am," William said, "I've not been dismissed, but I'm not fulfilling my management role either."

Janet Atherton popped her head round the door. "Do you want something substantial to eat? It's well past noon, and I've got steak pie and hot gravy if you want some."

They did want some, and for an hour they were able to forget the plight of Longfield's management problems, especially when William ordered tankards of the cold brown brew Rory had enjoyed the evening before.

"Just a small tankard for each of us," William said. "We don't want to sleep through the afternoon, do we?"

"I take it neither my aunt nor my uncle is aware of the copy ledgers in the bank," Rory said once they had eaten.

William shook his head.

Rory could see the tension in William's face; the accentuated frown lines across the brow and the shifting of his feet indicated he was uneasy. He could not believe this worried man was the suave confident one whom he had looked up to since childhood. If his uncle and Sampson were out to destroy his dear friend and mentor, he realized their tactics were working.

During that afternoon, they discussed William's last letter to Rory.

"This letter told me that you had an odd meeting with one of the naval administrators," Rory reminded William. "What was that all about?"

"Ah, yes," said William. "Look, I'll start from the beginning of my involvement with the naval department. When I became the agricultural manager at Longfield, I worked within the different aspects of the farm, the corn, vegetables and fruit growing and hemp, though by degrees I found myself in charge of the naval contracts for hemp. This was one of my main jobs for years and I built up camaraderie with the naval contacts by letter, and later by telegraph. The main person I dealt with throughout those years was Dennis Linford, though we had never met. So, when a request arrived for Linford to visit our farm, I was thrilled. I was to meet him face to face at last. This request came out of the blue, with very little notice, and we assumed it was a courtesy visit, perhaps for their future reference. We considered it an important honor. Because of my connections, and in spite of the troubles I was up against, your uncle asked me to arrange a soiree to welcome the naval officer. I worked in close contact with Linford on the arrangements."

William then spoke of John's concern about the possibility of a final decline of the Kentucky hemp market, and had asked about potential plans to cover the eventuality. He said, John suggested consideration should be given to the early use of the existing hemp land for horse-breeding.

Rory made no comment, but asked William to continue his account of the naval officer's visitation.

"As arranged," William said, "Linford was greeted by your uncle and aunt as executors, but I was astonished when Sampson was included in the welcoming party. I hadn't expected him to be, as my role during the event was to ensure smooth running during the evening, but I did feel Sampson's inclusion was unwarranted."

"I was intrigued at Linford's appearance," William continued. "I had expected to see a tall, well-spoken man with impeccable manners and dress. I first noted the untidiness of Linford's dress, with scuffed shoes and no neck-wear from the back of the room, as your uncle didn't introduce me to him until much later. I don't know why I should, but I felt personally embarrassed at the girth of the small-statured man and the sound of his grating laugh."

"I saw ladies wince as he leaned over them, spitting out crumbs into his raggedy beard as he spoke with a mouth full of food. He wouldn't have the white wine, and I heard him say it was flapdoodle fit only for children, though he snarfed down glass after glass of red wine. He gave a short speech that didn't mention our farm or its product. Instead, he told naval jokes that were unseemly in that mixed company, and his speech was slurred. I thought he was objectionable, as did most of the guests."

He stopped to take a gulp of water.

"When did you get to meet him?" asked a fascinated Rory.

"Well, your uncle took his time but eventually introduced me to Linford toward the end of the visit. Up close to him, I could see he was ugly and he smelled unwashed. His beard was still full of food crumbs, and his breath smelt of wine. I put out my hand to shake his, and made a comment about the length of time we had worked together, but he didn't say a word. He just stared at me. All of a sudden, I noticed that the folks around had gone quiet. Like me they'd seen Linford raise an eyebrow and an expression of disbelief on his face. He looked at my hand but refused to shake it. I can remember thinking what an objectionable creature he was."

William stopped again, took another swig of water and rang the bell.

"Can we have some more coffee?" he asked the maid, his voice wavering a little.

William and Rory did not speak again until the coffee arrived, but after a couple of swallows, William continued his story.

"Do you know what happened next?" he asked Rory, who shook his head

"Well, he actually said 'man alive', and then he laughed in my face, calling me a blackie. He said 'I've been working with a blackie and never knew'. He had a look of disgust on his face and he looked round at the guests in surprise, as if seeking their support, though he didn't get it."

Rory poured out more coffee, and noticed that William's hand shook as he drank. Rory turned to his own coffee, unwilling to watch his friend as he clutched the cup tightly, as if seeking support in his suffering from the inanimate object.

"Linford then turned his back on me, and he took your uncle and aunt by the arms and walked out with them toward the garden.

I did see your aunt pull her arm away, and walk off in another direction, but Linford didn't seem to notice in his arrogance."

He stopped again, eyes moist, as he gulped down the rest of his coffee.

"I recognized the consternation among the guests. It was intense. A number came up to me and apologized for the behavior of the naval representative, and the party came to a sudden end. It was one of the worst evenings of my life, though I was pleased to see I had everybody's support. I saw your aunt turn to look at me, but I left before she reached me, as I didn't want her involved in the chat that was going on."

"Did my uncle apologize to you?" Rory asked.

"He showed little concern over the incident, but I did hear more than a few of the departing guests saying that the affront to me had been contrived by him. It is difficult for me to comment on that, but I must say I have wondered."

"Did the incident have any effect on your authority after that?" Rory asked.

"Yes, it did. Any scuttlebutt, however untrue, does have an adverse effect on the victim. I carried on, mainly because of the support I had from your aunt, but I was depressed, and perhaps not at my best."

"After that event, the popularity of our other products waned, and there was a lot of gossip about the way our farm was managed. Following Linford's outburst, there were many people who began to wonder who was in charge as malicious tittle-tattle against me continued."

As Rory listened, enthralled, he began to wonder if the whole incident between William and Linford had indeed been contrived. Surely, though, his uncle would not stoop to such tactics, but if so, why?

"What I never discovered from Papa was why Longfield was the only farm around here that achieved a new contract. Why was that?" he asked William.

"It's because we grow the more elite hemp preferred by the navy. Our well-cleaned fiber ensures their required consistency and superiority, and we achieve this by our 'water rotting' system. Our neighbors denounce this because it's so labor intensive," William informed him.

"It occurs to me," Rory said, "that this trouble could have been created as a result of sheer jealousy among the farming community following Longfield's success in achieving a new contract. There could have been, though I think unlikely, some prejudice against black people given the current politics. I can't believe, though, that my uncle would have contrived against you, so who, I wonder, is responsible?"

He stopped, wondering how to proceed following a sudden instinctive disquiet that now overwhelmed him. It was obvious to William that Rory had an idea in his head. Knowing him to be a youth of considerable intellect, William smiled and nodded toward Rory, to encourage him to proceed.

"Do you think Sampson could have been involved in that incident against you?" Rory asked. "From what you've told me today, I'm beginning to think he knew Linford well, and that somehow there is collusion to get rid of you. There's no evidence, I know, but I have a sneaking suspicion about Linford's unexpected interest after all these years. I'm also suspicious about Sampson's sudden arrival. What do you think?"

"There *is* an element of jealousy about the contract, but that sort of jealousy would not be used by the good folks around here to undermine an innocent man's honor. It's unjust and farmers would not tolerate it," William said. "Like you, though, I do have doubts about Sampson. However, Linford has been with the naval authority for years now, and I don't think they'd employ a man of poor character for so long, even though he presents as a bit of a roughneck," he said in his measured way.

He stopped for a moment and looked at Rory, with a dejected look of regret.

"That incident with Linford has been unsettling but I'm a free black man with my papers, and with all my experience I can find another job."

Rory's misgivings were enhanced when he realized William appeared to have made a decision to leave Longfield.

"Would you be willing to stay at Longfield if there was a Compton living there?" Rory asked. He sensed this was the right time to ask the question, following his long chat with Aunt Delphia and Laura a few weeks ago.

"I'll stay to clear my name," William responded, "but after that I may well move on."

Rory already knew from William's last letter that following the Linford brouhaha, the matter had been referred to his father's attorney, who had recommended a formal meeting to discuss the future. His aunt and uncle had agreed to the proposal.

William spoke of how the legal team remained cautious about offering further solutions at that stage, as they were bound in law to ensure the wishes of Charles Compton and the protection of his heir above anything else.

Those invited included the heir, executors, auditor and an assistant, and the legal team.

William was aware that John, as Rory's guardian, had already pronounced his nephew not yet well enough to attend. He himself had not been invited, even though he had neither resigned his post as general manager, nor been dismissed.

"Well, I'm even more adamant now that I'll attend the board meeting," Rory said. "If I hadn't received your last letter, I would have been ignorant of all this mess. My first question will be to ask why you have not been invited."

Once agreement was reached that deceitful or dishonest behavior may have been perpetrated over the past months, William and Rory worked through the rest of the afternoon and evening formulating a plan. The whole of the next day was spent researching salient points that each had identified. Numerous telegraphed messages were exchanged between Cynthiana and the naval establishment where Linford was employed, as well as visits to their local bank, Mr. Jefferson having now returned from New Hampshire.

Rory placed all the telegraphed statements, bank statements and his notes into a small official-looking leather purse loaned by William, and organized a carriage to take him to Longfield the following morning.

William saw Rory off. Although Rory had suggested he should accompany him, he declined. Rory wore the well-fitting new outfit that suited his tall, lean frame. His stark white shirt provided a nice contrast to the slight tan he had achieved through his outdoor life in Lexington. In all he looked every inch a young, personable diplomat. His face declared the Compton good looks and the breeding of an educated young man; his former listlessness had been replaced by a determination that belied his youth.

He did not know that he struck a stark resemblance to his resolute grandfather, James Compton.

He reached the servant's entrance of his home, having timed his journey to arrive in advance of the start of the meeting. He walked unnoticed toward the small ballroom where the meeting would take place. As he approached the door, he heard an angry voice and the sound of a hard slap.

A young voice yelped as a bad-tempered voice asked why 'those dang ledgers' had been brought along. Rory sneaked a stealthy peek round the door. A youth, probably no older than himself, was rubbing his right cheek.

Disconcerted, Rory drew back.

"You told me to bring *all* the Longfield documents so we could be prepared for anything," the youth whimpered, shrinking away from his attacker.

"Not those, dumb head. Put them somewhere out of sight."

He walloped the boy across the other cheek with his cane, this time bringing tears to the boy's scared eyes.

Rory heard a gentle creak, then a thud, a familiar sound but one he could not place. After waiting a couple of minutes, he sauntered into the room.

He was aware that the boy and the bully were staring at him. The seats around the table had been allocated to individuals, and Rory, showing none of the nervousness he felt, carefully examined the name cards. Noting that the auditor's name appeared next to his uncle, he removed the card, crossed out the name, and carefully wrote his own name on the reverse, before replacing it. He grinned inwardly at his own daring and at the man whom he took to be Sampson, remembering William's description of him.

"Do not interfere with this table plan. This is to be a private meeting, so I need to know who you are," snapped Sampson.

Rory's response was haughty and he enjoyed putting the man down.

"Mr. Sampson," he said, "you are not heading this meeting, so do not speak to me in that tone. My name is Rory Compton and this property will be mine when I come of age in the not too distant future."

When he realized who Rory was, the auditor, with petulant reluctance, obtained an unused card and placed himself and his assistant in another spot next to the attorney's assistant.

Meanwhile, Rory moved his placement card so he would be sitting across from the auditor and ordered Sampson to re-organize the place names accordingly. He had not expected to have this opportunity to wrong-foot Sampson at such an early stage and struggled to suppress his triumph as he took his seat.

Delphia and John entered the room 10 minutes later, followed by the attorney and his assistant. All stared in disbelief at the boy, but managed not to verbalize their surprise.

Sampson looked apprehensive as he shifted uneasily in his chair.

Rory noted his agitation and how Uncle John avoided Sampson's glances.

As everybody settled, Rory kept an eye on Sampson's assistant; a shy creature, tall, dark, scrawny, with sharply chiseled cheeks that spoke more of lack of nourishment than good looks. The left cheek bore a red, swollen blemish. His huge eyes gave an impression of a startled young deer ready to run at the slightest movement. Sampson introduced him as Ronald Bishop, his assistant.

As Rory studied Bishop, he noticed that he looked fixedly at him, before shifting his eyes side-ways to the left. He did this a number of times, and William wondered whether this was an affliction or affectation, and felt sorry for the youth.

"Where is William?" Rory asked, when the introductions were completed, pretending surprise at his absence.

John answered.

"There have been some changes within the organization lately," he mumbled, "all to do with William's appointment as the general manager at Longfield. It seems some customers don't like black people taking over."

John went on to say that on top of that, accounting discrepancies had been suspected.

Rory did not respond, but asked why the previous auditor had resigned

"Surely I should have been told about that, especially as I've been my father's official auditor for the past two years."

Sampson looked up in shocked surprise, as did the attorney.

"You looked surprised, sir," Rory said to Sampson. "Surely you will have noticed my initials at the end of each page of my ledger. I always initial them on completion of an audit."

"I may have noticed them, I can't remember," Sampson responded with such politeness that he almost fawned over the boy. "If I did, I wouldn't have realized they were your initials." He smirked at Rory.

"If indeed they were yours," he added.

Rory was grateful when John spoke up about his nephew's educational background and his achievements to date, and was backed up by Delphia. Those present were impressed with the exception of Sampson, who was taken aback by the revelation. He glanced at John from time to time, a worried frown on his face.

Rory had meant at this stage to have complained about his own exclusion from the meeting and that he had not received official notification, but changed his mind. He decided not to incur the displeasure of his uncle, having concluded the pleasure would be outweighed by any antipathy he created toward himself as a result.

John's opening remarks covered the reasons for the meeting; the main ones being the existing management problems at Longfield and the alleged pecuniary difficulties.

"Did you bring the ledger?" John asked Sampson, who tapped Bishop's shoulder.

Bishop fished it out of his case.

Sampson did not notice Rory's immediate look of surprise as he proceeded to discuss some of the anomalies he had discovered, which he felt could be the reasons for the discrepancies.

Rory realized at once that this red leather ledger was not the original green leather one he had worked with. Emboldened by his absolute certainty, he asked to see the ledger and reached across the table to receive it. Sampson demurred, but John and the attorney insisted that the auditor should hand it over. During that brief exchange, Rory glanced at Bishop, who continued with his peculiar gaze followed by the side-ways shift of his eyes.

Rory studied the document carefully, running a forefinger swiftly down the columns page by page, making notes at the bottom of each. It did not take him long. He felt Bishop's gaze, and looking up saw a beseeching look followed again by the strange eye-dance. Rory glanced away, puzzled, though a growing suspicion began to form that unless the boy was a coot, he was trying to tell him something. Ignoring Bishop's appeal for the moment, Rory began his attack. He picked up the ledger, and glanced briefly at the back of it, before returning to his notes.

"I see the ledger dates from just over three years ago, at the time our new accounting system was instigated," he said.

"That is correct," Sampson answered.

Rory felt like slapping the man's face to wipe away the smug expression, but instead smiled at him.

"There are discrepancies on those pages pertaining to the past 12 months," he stated, indicating the ones he had marked. "The totals are incorrect and the discrepancies are compounded page by page throughout. There are also further errors of addition on some pages," he said.

Sampson's surprise was genuine. Everyone could see that.

"What do you mean? No accountant would accept a summation of a child who has simply run a finger down a column in the way you just did. Of course the totals are correct. I would have seen any errors. I resent the implications of this child's comments, Mr. Compton."

He turned to a worried looking John.

Before his uncle could answer, Rory interceded.

"Mr. Sampson, I may be young in years, but I am not a child as far as my mathematical abilities are concerned, as you've already heard. From an early age, I've had an ability to calculate instantly and with accuracy. I've written down my calculations with my pencil underneath your own figures. They can be tested right now."

He passed the ledger to the attorney.

"Sir, would you like to do a test on any two pages you choose and compare your results with Mr. Sampson's and my totals."

Rory noticed that Uncle John was about to interject, and dared to scowl at him. He was gratified when his uncle changed his mind.

The attorney glanced at John and again at Sampson before doing the calculations, at a much slower pace than Rory. He concluded that Rory's figures were correct. He chose another two pages, just to make certain with the same result, and then another two. Sampson's face paled as he and the attorney stared at each other until Sampson turned to glare at Rory.

"Now look, you sassy young snip…" began Sampson.

When Aunt Delphia exclaimed at his words, Sampson had the sense to change tactics. In a more good-natured voice, his mouth twisted into a grimace that was meant to be a smile, he informed Rory the entries must have been completed by a new employee who was, by the look of things, somewhat incompetent.

"I'll rectify that when I return to my office," he said.

Rory snapped back quickly.

"You intimated a moment ago that you had found them to be correct and gave an impression you had checked them yourself."

There was complete silence in the room, as the attorney and Rory stared directly into the shifting eyes of Sampson.

Rory broke the long silence.

"For the last two years I've completed the entries in the official ledger. This ledger shows no sign of my handwriting whatsoever. Neither mine nor the farm manager's initials are visible."

Sampson did not respond.

Rory closed the ledger and looked at the trademark engraving on the back cover.

"This is a brand new ledger," he said to the meeting, holding it up. He showed it to the attorney, pointing his finger at the engraving.

The attorney studied it, and turned to John.

"The engraving shows the date of production of this ledger to be this year," he said.

John held out his hand to receive the book, and stared at the trademark and the date. He flicked the ledger open to the first page, and saw the date of the first entry to be just three years earlier than the date on the back. He glared at Sampson over his spectacles.

Again, Rory broke the silence that ensued.

"There are other discrepancies," he said. "First of all, the original ledger is green, the same color as the duplicate in the bank vault, not red, as this one is. Secondly, I noticed two important accounts are missing in this record. Where are the figures for Beaumonts of Manchester, England and for Hornimans of Boston, Mr. Sampson? The high income from these sources is significant and not included at all, which probably accounts for the alleged revenue shortfall you are about to announce. Where is the record for these companies, Mr. Sampson? And where is the original green ledger?"

There was absolute stillness in the room. No one spoke. Rory glanced across at Bishop. The eye-dance had become even more pronounced and he suddenly understood it. He thanked the boy with an imperceptible nod and a slight smile.

Sampson tried to yank back the ledger but Rory held onto it.

"I venture to suggest, Mr. Sampson, you assumed this ledger would be readily accepted, knowing that without William present, there would be no one to challenge it. You did not bargain for my attendance here today either, or my input into the accountancy management of Longfield, did you?" Rory asked.

He watched as Sampson attempted, unsuccessfully, to recover his composure. Rory was now standing, bent slightly forward, his hands spread out on the table. He glowered down at Sampson, his face strengthened by his belief in Sampson's delinquency. He heard a small gasp from Delphia, not realizing he presented an uncanny resemblance to his grandfather. Delphia, John and the attorney glanced at each other in speechless awe, as Rory continued his relentless verbal attack on the hapless auditor.

"Will you tell me what happened to the original business ledger?" Rory asked. "Indeed, where are the other ledgers, the ones for the education expenses and household expenditure? Have you brought them with you today?"

His icy voice chilled all those in the room.

Rory was shrewd enough to realize that Sampson would be aware of the need for absolute proof of any wrong-doing. If the original business ledger could not be located, Rory knew from Mr. Jefferson, the bank manager, that the signed copy ledgers in the bank would be proof enough. They had calculated there was no way Sampson would have had previous knowledge of any copies as William had not mentioned them to either Sampson or to John. Mr. Jefferson had confirmed there was no record of Sampson having been given such information by any bank employee.

"Well, they either got lost during my office alterations or failing that they may have been destroyed by some transgressor, who wanted to hide something. There has been so much trouble already and I didn't want the Compton name to be further dishonored. That's why I decided to start a new ledger," Sampson managed to splutter.

As he spoke, he glanced at John, who nodded at the sentiment expressed toward the Comptons. Rory pushed back his chair, glancing at Bishop as he did so. Following a brief eye deflection and a half-nod from Bishop, Rory strode confidently toward the grand piano, and pulled out its stool and lifted the creaking lid. Three green ledgers were revealed. He pulled them out, and allowed the lid of the stool to fall. He heard the familiar thud as it came to rest, a memory from his childhood and the same sound he had heard earlier that morning. He handed them to the attorney who scrutinized the copy of the original company account ledger, seeking the names of the two missing lucrative accounts. He found them. In the meantime, John glanced through the education and household accounts ledgers.

While this inspection was going on, Rory used the opportunity to pass a note to Delphia. A couple of minutes later she excused herself, muttering she wished to organize refreshments. Meanwhile, Rory got to his feet again and stared at Sampson, who had so far made no attempt to move. He spoke to his uncle who now had the three green ledgers and the red one in front of him.

"Uncle John, will you give me the final balance in the education ledger, please," Rory asked.

John gave it, explaining to the meeting that the larger sum represented legacies from Rory's maternal grandparents for his education. The smaller one was a legacy from Grandfather Compton, meant for the education of his sisters. The total amount was large.

At this point Sampson rose, but sat down again as the attorney and his assistant stood dramatically and moved to his side. He looked defeated.

"I found out yesterday all those funds were transferred early last week from the account we hold in the Bank of Virginia into an account in Ohio, in the name of Delaney and Sampson," said Rory, his voice as casual as if he was reporting on the outcome of a local tennis tournament, "as were other monies, which we can now see were amounts paid to us by those customers deleted from the fraudulent ledger."

He turned to the attorney. "The Ohio bank has been requested by the Marshal's office to freeze that account, and it will be possible to recover the money in due course," he said.

The attorney, now gripping the left arm of the putative transgressor as his assistant held the other, could do nothing else but nod in surprise.

Rory grinned. "It gets worse," he chortled, his teenage humor overcoming the seriousness of the situation as he looked around the shocked faces of his audience.

He glanced at Delphia's serious, pale face as she re-entered the room. She nodded twice, and Rory's knew this was no time for levity, however light-headed he was beginning to feel.

He explained how William had contacted naval authorities yesterday, via the telegraph system, concerning the recent visit of Dennis Linford, and was informed the man had passed away a few months earlier. Pending the appointment of a replacement, Linford's assistant, Jack Delaney, had been carrying out his duties. Photographs of Linford and Delaney had been telegraphed through to Cynthiana and it was apparent that Delaney had impersonated Linford.

Rory, now sure of himself, had once more taken up the stance of his late grandfather, his erudite face stern.

"Delaney was arrested last evening for the serious crime of impersonating an administrative officer of the government's navy and on suspicion of misappropriating bank funds," he said.

Sampson leapt to his feet. "I had nothing to do with the misappropriation of funds. And it was not me who impersonated Linford," he screeched.

"Nevertheless," said Rory, "the appropriate authorities have been informed and you will be arrested for conspiring to assist an impersonator of a government department officer, as well as on suspicion of being the instigator or accessory to a bank crime."

Sampson sat down heavily. He glared at Rory. "You have no proof of any wrongdoing on my behalf. I did not transfer the money to Ohio. I did not impersonate Linford. You have to prove any wrongdoing before you can arrest me."

The attorney answered Sampson, jerking his arm as the man tried to shake loose from the strong hold on him.

"You can be arrested on suspicion of wrongdoing, Sampson. I am sure we can prove your links with Delaney, but apart from that, it's evident the supposed company ledger you tried to present this morning provides erroneous information and blatant inaccuracies. We might not be able to prove you hid the original ledgers, as they were found on Longfield property, but I do not underestimate the value of witnesses. In the meantime, there is sufficient cause to detain you. We shall sort out the truth in a court of law."

The threat strengthened Sampson's resolve. He managed to jerk away from the hold of his guards and made a dash for the door. He did not get far. As he wrenched open the door, he found his exit blocked by two large uniformed guards.

Delphia would later explain that Rory's note had encouraged her to alert the already assembled Marshall's contingent, who had been advised by William of an imminent denouement, prompting them to guard exit routes.

There was chat about the naivety of Sampson and Delaney in putting their name on the Ohio Bank account.

The auditor assumed they would have had to supply identification prior to opening such a large account, and had not had time to obtain false identification. Although they were obviously part of a gang of fraudsters, it was apparent they were in the throes of cheating on their 'syndicate partners' and had to move quickly to ensure capture of such a large haul for themselves.

"They took a risk in using their own names, but probably thought they would be withdrawing it in the near future and felt the risk was worth it," he said. "They almost got away with the fraud and had it not been for young Rory and William, they would be well away now."

During the evening following Sampson's arrest, John asked Rory to take a walk around the estate with him. Rory was pleased to hear his uncle praise his astuteness and to hear how proud he was of him.

"It puzzles me why Longfield was targeted and why William was so maligned," said John.

"Well, it's now been confirmed that the two of them are part of a large gang of swindlers that looks out for vulnerable companies they can hoodwink," said Rory. "Delaney would have known, through working alongside Linford, about the vulnerability of Longfield in the immediate uncertainty following my father's death. We'll hear more about how and why their plan was hatched at their trial, I suppose."

John nodded.

"I'm sorry William became a target for slander just because he's black," he said, "but getting rid of him was probably crucial to completing the fraud within their short time frame. I reckon that when Linford died, they came up with the idea of impersonating him to demean William. The fact William stuck it out as long as he did will have surprised them."

He patted his nephew's shoulder. "What a lucky fella your father was, breeding someone like you," he said.

"Aunt Beulah said I take after your father," Rory said, "my grandfather Compton."

"Yes, you certainly do," John agreed. They were quiet for a while as they walked.

After a few minutes, John spoke of his brother.

"I spoke with your father a couple of weeks prior to the accident," he said. "He was heartbroken over the estrangement between the two of you. He told me how wrong it was of him to deny you your right to become a doctor, and admired your tenacity in sticking to your guns. He was looking forward to seeing you again, so that he could tell you this in person and how he was going to help you achieve your ambitions. He told me he lashed out at you because of the hurt to your mother."

"I do so wish," said Rory, "that he had written to tell me that. I did write to him, but I'm afraid it was all about my grief rather than his. I'm ashamed; I didn't even think about his own feelings and let my pride come first. I was bereft when I heard from Aunt Delphia about the miscarriages."

"Maybe your father wanted to say it to your face," John said, "rather than write a formal letter. Think of it that way, for I'm sure that's what he felt."

They did not speak for a while, until Rory spoke of Longfield again.

"Uncle John," Rory said, as they returned to the house. "I suppose you know Aunt Delphia is having a bit of a hard time with her family right now. She's agreed to change the housing arrangements over there, but she's convinced they want to run the farm themselves, without her input. It's been her long-term plan to hand it over to them eventually, but I don't think the boys understand how hard it is for her being pushed out so soon. After all, the farm has been her life's work and she feels dispensable and wretched."

John agreed and was about to say something, then changed his mind.

"I intend to qualify as a doctor but as that will take me a few years," Rory said, "I can't be what you could regard as a visible owner here at Longfield. But Delphia is my father's sister, and a true Compton at heart. Do you think she would consider coming here until I qualify, so that she's seen as the 'Compton' family presence everybody seems to be hankering after?"

"Let's ask her," John said, having spied Delphia walking down the driveway to meet them.

"Where have you two been?" Delphia cried when she saw them walking toward her. "Laura's due back here in half an hour or so, and I did want us all to be here when she arrives."

"Well, I'm having a bit of trouble with this boy. He had the nerve to ask if you would stay on at Longfield until he's finished his studies and returned home as a doctor. What a cheek, eh?"

Delphia's look of delight and relief told Rory everything he needed to know, as did her rapturous hug.

"Yes, Rory I'd love to, so long as William will stay. I couldn't do it without him," she said and they all agreed that she could not do without William.

The three Comptons went together to search him out.

Chapter 6
Rory, Laura and Beth

Rory squelched along the soft, black mud of the pathway that would take him down to the river. He relished the silence of the new day as he watched the thinning, grey mist spiral out into a soft shade of rose, revealing the tender blue of the sky. He caught his breath at the spectacle. As he walked, he realized that it was not so silent after all. Here and there was the rustle of a little creature, eager to get out of the way of his boots, the whispering of the tree boughs as they swayed and dipped to the gentle breeze, and the dawn chorus as birds raised their voices in praise of this new day.

At least Rory hoped that is why they sang, and even considered raising his own pleasant alto voice to sing along with them, then thought better of it. As he walked, he savored the idea of the few weeks respite from study, prior to going to the Ann Arbor University in September. Today was the second Friday of June, and he looked forward to meeting up with his fellow students at the hostelry at noon.

He had decided on a slight deviation that morning, when he came across a path of the river he had not ventured down before. As he caught sight of a shining ripple of water captured in the emerging sunlight, he thought it would be a wonderful place for this morning's swim, and moved quickly toward it, shaking off his casual clothing as he went along.

He spied a dry bush where he bent to store his clothes and drying cloth, and prepared to run down to the riverbank. Just as he was about to head to the water's edge, a sound interrupted him. He watched the water ripple as the naked body of a girl rose from a shallow pool, her pale skin glistening in the soft gleam of the sun. Another girl appeared, a little older and equally naked. She shivered and said they must hurry back.

Hurry back to where? Who are they? Rory thought. He knew there were no girls of their description living at or near the

Compton's farm, and it was a good mile away from the po'-white village.

He dared not move, as he watched the girls wade onto the bank. They were young and both very lovely. The full-breasted older girl had long, light-brown fine hair and Rory watched her towel it dry, and commence combing it. He admired the way her right arm arched in an attractive curve as she combed. He heard her urge her companion to hurry. The younger girl, showing early signs of feminine beauty, had allowed her darker hair to stream about her face and was not bothering to dry it. Suddenly, she stopped dressing and stared straight into the bush where the almost naked Rory stood. Hardly daring to breathe, Rory was sure she could see him now the sun was bathing the bush with its bright light. What was he going to say to these glorious creatures? Would they realize he was not spying on them? Would they believe it was pure chance he was there at all?

"Hurry," said her sister, for it was obvious from those lovely faces they were of the same stock.

"Look!" the younger one cried out. "There be an angel. Be'ind dat bush. Look! Look!" By this time, the sun had disappeared behind a cloud, and Rory realized that the bush had darkened and he was once more obscured.

"You're sure a fanciful one, Maya. Git on, we's gotta git back before we missed. Ye'd better jest hurry now."

Rory was mystified. Their accent was definitely not of the local farming community. He decided they must be from the village though he thought they sounded similar to the black cook, Polly, back at the house. For a fearful moment, he trembled in the agony of which way they would return, but they took the opposite way, along a short track and over the brow, before dropping out of sight.

As he swam, he knew that the sight of such feminine beauty would stay with him for a long time. The images of the girls played havoc in his mind for much of the morning, dissipating only as he and his fellow students planned their leisure time.

For the next two weeks, the boys swam, strolled, hiked, explored, played ball games, built a somewhat unstable flat-boat, ate, drank (a little) and were to all intents and purposes self-sufficient young men, eager for university life and their new-found sense of freedom. They were often accompanied by Oliver, whose relationship with their fellow student, Fred Hetherington, was now well accepted.

Following those care-free weeks, Rory's companions were snatched back into their family folds for participation in trips to and from far-away relatives. Oliver was invited to the home of Fred's relatives in Nashua, New Hampshire, leaving Rory to fend for himself.

He took himself off to Cynthiana for a two-week visit, where he found Delphia happy in her new role, and anticipating the arrival of Laura, who was leaving school at the end of the week. Laura had elected to stay with her mother in Cynthiana until she found a teaching post near her family home, and had informed Rory of her plans in a letter.

"I wonder if Laura will revert back to her old tom-boy image she had in Virginia," Rory had said to his aunt the day before she arrived.

"Somehow I don't think so," said Delphia, her voice full of pride. Her daughter had turned out well so far.

"She learned a lot by living with your mother and Aunt Beulah before she went off to school, and those years at the Keene school cemented what she had learned. She loved her experience there and that's why she's so keen to become a teacher."

"She's a determined girl and wants to teach under-privileged children in a po'white district, or even open a school for the black children who don't receive schooling," Rory had said, proud of his cousin's ambition.

"I can't see any possibility of such an opportunity hereabouts, unless she finds it for herself," said her mother, a frown furrowing her wide brow.

"Well," said Rory, "she'll find her own niche, either here or somewhere else. I get the impression that she'll get there, wherever that is, come what may."

He was glad of Laura's company, and found her effervescent personality and easy chatter welcome and charming. They could talk about anything and it was as though they had been together their whole lives. Rory found relief in being able to talk about his sisters, whom he missed as much as ever.

Delphia had made no changes within the house prior to Rory's visit, but together with his aunt and cousin, gradual changes were made. One of the first was the allocation of his own room to Laura as she would be spending more time than him at Longfield. Laura loved the room and the wonderful views and it was this gesture that put the seal on her increasing affection for her cousin.

Rory spent much of his time with Dr. Wallace and his wife, and together they planned the intervening year between university and medical school, even though it was two years away. When he was not with the Wallaces, Rory divided his time between William and Laura, though often the three shared walks together. Laura's sparkling personality was always a welcome interlude, and the three were soon close friends, with a bond of mutual trust. The two weeks passed at high speed, and Rory regretted the arrangement with Mr. Smales to spend two weekends with him in Lexington during August, in final preparation for university.

"I'll write and cancel the arrangement," he had said to Delphia.

Much as she loved Rory, his selfishness irked Delphia and she made her feelings known.

"Mr. Smales has given you a lot of his time at some inconvenience over the years," she had said, "and he may have cancelled much of his own family time to spend those weekends with you. Your cancellation is unjustified, especially as he's done so much for you."

It was Jacob who came down to Cynthiana to take Rory back to Lexington.

"You look good, Mas'a Rory," he said as they set off on their journey.

Long as it was, Rory preferred this mode of travel to the tedious, bone-shaking rail journey. They chatted about the goings on at the farm since Rory had been away, though most of the chat was about Jacob's daughters.

"My girls won't keep away from the riverside," Jacob said in the attractive mulatto cadence Rory loved listening to, "and my old wife is afraid that one fine day, one or the other will be drowned, especially the young 'un, Maya."

Although Rory was aware Mr. Smales would provide study exercises following his visits, he had wondered what he would do with the rest of his time in Lexington. He now saw the opportunity to engage in a worthwhile project during the few weeks prior to going to Ann Arbor.

"I taught my sisters to swim," he said. "Will you allow me to teach your daughters? It won't take long and I can have them swimming as well as me before I leave." Jacob agreed and it was arranged Rory would meet the girls and their mother in the near future to talk it over with them.

"They've grown up a bit now," Jacob said, "especially Beth. She's a respectable girl who sews for your aunt on occasions. Your aunt tells me Beth'll make a good lady's maid one day. But Beth wants to be able to read books like you and Oliver. I can't show her how because I can't read. They both like it when Oliver's here and he reads to them, and your friend Fred does sometimes, but they long to be able to do it for themselves."

He looked hopefully at Rory, who recognized the plea.

"I didn't know that Oliver and Fred read to them," he said, surprised.

"Oh, yes, though Oliver's not here much now, but Fred is still working with your old tutor, and he gets plenty of free time. Lonely without his pal, he is."

"Good for Fred," Rory said, "maybe you can ask him to teach the girls to read."

"Have done, but he's too shy, I think. He says he'd rather make pictures with that new-fangled box Oliver gave him last time he was home. Oliver used it for his work, but he's got a newer one now, so Fred gets his cast-off," he chuckled.

"Well, I can teach the girls to swim in the few weeks before I leave for university," Rory told Jacob, "but it'll take much longer than that to teach them to read and write. I don't mind starting them off with some writing exercises before I go, then we'll see. It may be possible to teach them to read and write during the long holiday from university next summer, once they've learned the basics."

Jacob seemed satisfied with that.

Rory spoke to Aunt Beulah during dinner about the proposed swimming lessons and was surprised by her comments.

"You've never met the girls, Rory, so try not to show surprise, as it would humiliate them and their mother."

Rory gave her a perplexed glance

"You see," she continued, "those girls look white, but they are daughters of mulattos, as you know. Their particular heritage is complicated. Some could say they are quadroons, as their maternal and paternal grandfathers, as well as their great-grandfathers were white, though their grandmothers and great-grandmothers were black slaves. With all that white ancestry, it's not unusual for children of later generations of black people to be born with pale skin and fine hair."

Rory realized the mystery of the girls he had seen down at the river recently was solved. Overnight he tossed and turned, unsure now that he wanted to undertake the swimming lessons, but knew that it would be difficult to reverse his offer. But when he saw the girls a few days later, he realized he did not, after all, want to renege.

They had been well groomed by their mother prior to the meeting and looked even more beautiful. He decided he would spend more time than he had intended teaching them their letters.

Aunt Beulah accompanied them for the first swimming lesson. She had already explained the swimsuit design they should wear, as recommended by her nephew, and there had been a rush to make them in time for the first lesson.

"The suit should be in two pieces with long pants to the ankles and a tunic that reaches just above the knees." Rory had suggested. "It's no use wearing those voluminous swimsuits with frills and flounces that are shown in the lady's magazines. They're too restrictive for committed swimmers. They should be made from good cotton to prevent them from sagging when wet, and the legs of the pants should not be wide, otherwise they'll get water logged. I'll be teaching them to use their feet as well as legs and arms, so it's important not to have any restrictions."

Beulah had smiled at his enthusiasm.

She and the girls' mother liaised in the planning of the summer's swimming and reading lessons. Rory recruited Fred Hetherington to participate with the reading and writing exercises, and as Beth was eager to learn how to speak French, Fred agreed to help out with that also, with the promise of a financial donation from Rory.

Beth had captured Rory's heart, of that he was in no doubt. She was so beautiful that when she was near him, he could hardly breathe. He was afraid she would hear his heart racing. He daren't look at her swim-suited body he had so recently seen in a more graceful state of nature, nor could he look into her innocent, sometimes quizzical, eyes. Instead, he found himself gazing at her naked feet as she walked toward the water, every step exquisite as far as he was concerned, each footmark a work of art. He would ensure, as he gave instructions, that he was at her sister's side, in an effort to tune out all distractions. When it came to individual physical contact with the movement exercises, he found as he helped Beth, the very air around him appeared to compress around his body and his chest tightened. He did not realize then that these painful physical symptoms were the beginning of his adult life. Through sheer tenacity, he managed to overcome the anguish of this first love, realizing that unless he was ruthless with himself, he could not complete the task.

By the end of the summer, Beth and Maya could swim with ease, and Beth was well on her way in her efforts to learn how to read and write. Maya was slower in academic accomplishments, but had learned how to adapt to the social requirements of mixed company as Fred Hetherington and others included her in informal recreational events. She had discovered a capacity for teasing and flirting.

Beth reached the age of 16 just prior to Rory leaving for university. There was a small celebration in honor of the birthday. She was now of an age where she could be employed within the Compton household. Beulah, who had been present at Beth's birth and was very fond of her, wished to train the girl as her personal seamstress and maid. First of all, however, the girl must be educated to the standard that she set, which included an improvement in her elocution. As Beth would be 'living in', Beulah felt she would be in a good position to improve her pronunciation and articulation. She was also aware Beth was a quick learner and something of a mimic, so felt the task may not prove too arduous.

Rory and Fred, together with the two girls, had become close, thanks to their shared summer experiences. Beth, who had noticed Rory's apparent antipathy toward her, was detached for a while, but her own intelligence, natural friendliness and positive thinking helped her to accept the situation.

"I find that when I'm with Rory and Fred, I copy their inflections and vocabulary," she said to Beulah one day, during one of her elocution lessons. As she learned from them, she also began to adopt Beulah's mannerisms. She told herself that the apparent lack of rapport between her and Rory could be due to her unrefined demeanor and manners, and she was determined to secure his approval.

"After all," she said to herself one day, as she took a lonely walk down by the river, after Rory had left for Ann Arbor, "I shall never love another boy as much as I love Rory Compton." Beth spoke to the air and for all she knew, to the birds and the bees, and she laughed out loud at the thought.

When Rory returned to Lexington a few months later, he was delighted with Beth's speech improvement and general appearance. Gone were the untidy skirts and beads; she was now clothed in a well-cut skirt and blouse that she had made herself, with dainty ear and neck jewelry she could now afford to buy on market days. She proudly informed Rory that she had made three sets of clothing, each in a different color, with fabric donated by Beulah.

"Her reading ability is outstanding," Fred Hetherington had reported, "though she needs a lot more practice in writing. That's bad, though not as bad as Maya's which is three times worse. Maya's not as keen to learn as Beth, but she's a good reader, though she does like me to read to her."

"Are you reading something to them right now?" asked Rory.

"Yes, Hawthorne's *The Scarlet Letter* which they really like. I didn't think they would, as it can be a bit stark in some parts. Maya in particular loves the characters."

"Well, thank you for what you've done, Fred. I thought you might have given them up by now."

Fred laughed. He did not say that he welcomed the extra cash in his pocket donated by Rory.

"One thing that has surprised me," Fred said, "is that they both have exceptional artistic skills. Maya's facial portraits are outstanding and so professional, and while Beth can draw portraits quite well, her particular skills are with buildings and maps. She can look at a scene, or a picture, turn away from it, and in 10 minutes or so produce an almost exact replica of the scene. It's a rather curious flair for girls from their background."

If Rory heard a slight hint of racialism in those last words, he ignored it, and they spoke of other things.

"How's Oliver nowadays?" Rory asked. "Is he still with Mathew Brady in his New York Gallery?"

Rory had been pleased when Oliver had been employed as an assistant to Brady, who was probably the most gifted of American photographers at that time, winning prizes in various international exhibitions. As well as working at the New York, Oliver also spent time at Brady's galleries in Washington.

"Yes he is. He's lucky to be there. Did you know Brady is quite famous nowadays, and he's a semi-official photographer to the presidency?" said Fred, full of pride at his friend's relationship with such a famous man.

"I hardly ever see or hear from Oliver since he began working with Brady, who's a workaholic and expects his staff to be the same," he went on. "Oliver and I don't have much in common now and I'm aware how enthralling his present way of life is. I enjoy his friendship, but I'm beginning to think it's not worth staying in Kentucky to complete my classics course. I may as well return to New Hampshire, but my father is adamant I complete my study here."

"When you've finished the course perhaps you can find a job in New York to be nearer to Oliver," he suggested. He was surprised when Fred responded with a casual shrug.

86

"I'm not sure we want the same things anymore," he said, "and my father wants me to go into his business when I've completed my education, but yes, you're right. I could get a city job quite easily, I would think."

He went away happily, while Rory thought over his own plight, for he too needed someone with whom he could discuss his own problem, that of his ardor for Beth. He was aware that he and Beth could never have a long-term relationship, but his infatuation had now become so intense that concentration on his studies had been affected.

He did find a listener when his cousin Timothy paid one of his infrequent visits home a couple of days prior to Rory's return to Michigan. His advice was simple.

"My dear cousin," Timothy said, "believe me, in a year this girl you can't live without now will be a distant memory. You're suffering from sheer animal lust, nothing else. Girls come and go, just as lust does. You know, you're almost a man, with a man's desires and her beauty just happens to tease your masculinity. Look, I can take you to a place tonight where you can relieve your passion for a bit. It's an easy way out of what you're going through right now, believe me."

Timothy took him to a large house in a discreet area within the outskirts of Lexington, where he appeared to be well known. He whispered to a well-dressed woman who wore heavy jewelry and too much perfume, who introduced Rory to a buxom girl dressed in a flimsy loose gown covering visible scanty underwear. She led him by the hand to a room where he spent a few memorable hours. He had learned more than he had bargained for and left Kentucky a day later feeling like a king.

Rory spent little time in Kentucky during the next two years. When he did return, with high honors, to fulfil his year with Dr. Wallace, Beth and Maya had become skilled in reading and handwriting. Beth, who had achieved above average accountancy skills and could write and read in both English and French, had become Beulah's personal companion.

He learned Fred was still in Kentucky where he had undertaken a teaching post in a recently opened school, having failed his university entrance examination for the second time. He kept in touch with Beth and Maya. Maya was now in the employ of the Huntington family, a long-standing and affluent Lexington family. Beth told him of how 'little Maya' had prospered.

"Aunt Beulah recommended her to the Huntington's, based on the fact that she was literate and well spoken. She's a housemaid, hoping to become the personal maid to the eldest daughter," she said.

What Beth did not know was that Maya flitted around the Huntington Mansion in the well-cut formal uniform of the household, glorying in the sumptuous surroundings. She had made up her mind; she herself would become the mistress of such a property. She just had to find the right person and get him to propose to her. She was aware she had the natural skills and beauty to do that and assumed it would be an easy task. She so loved her new home; she was reluctant to return to her parents on her alternate weekends off, though once there, she wallowed in the comfort of being doted on by her parents, particularly Jacob who adored his favorite daughter.

Rory's home was once more at Longfield, though he spent much of his time at the Lawrence medical surgery. When at Longfield, mainly at the weekends, he spent most of his leisure time with Laura and Delphia, either in the fields or just trekking around the estate, which was now thriving, though the constant threat of losing the naval hemp contract hovered over them. William and Delphia kept a careful eye on the future of other agricultural aspects, and Rory could see that the adverse effects of what they called the 'Sampson era' were long gone.

From time to time, he travelled over to Lexington for a few days. During those visits, he noticed Beth had blossomed into a lovely, rather stately young woman of immense intelligence, who was an asset to Beulah's household. She did not impose her status on the staff, and was popular wherever she went.

So efficient was the Beulah/Beth team they both had ample free time, and Beth was able to enjoy the days Rory spent with them. Rory, who had indulged in a number of love affairs at university, had never forgotten his former lust for Beth but their current friendship was now based on the relationship of two young people who had grown up together. There were still occasions, however, when her more mature beauty took his breath away. Occasionally, Laura would take time from her work as William's assistant to travel with him to Lexington, and the three would glory in long walks together.

They liked to punt down the river in the old boat built years ago, enjoying intellectual conversations that would often turn to the political situation within the country. On one of their walks, Rory spoke of his general contentment and hoped Laura and Beth were as happy as he.

"Everything seems to be running so well for the Compton family," he had said, "both here in Lexington and in Cynthiana."

Laura thought he should always keep in mind the danger of losing the hemp contract.

"If that happens," Rory said, "there's the option of growing more corn for distilling, especially as Kentucky whisky is so popular. That's something I have in mind for Longfield, and I've already asked William to examine the option; what land and labor we would require, as well as the sales outlook for the product, should we ever be in that position."

Beth was impressed. "A possible good solution," she conceded, "and it could ensure continuance of employment for your existing labor force, and even provide jobs for those who can't make a living from their own small farms."

"We might even be able to contract some of those farms to grow corn for us," Rory said. "That would be a boost for the poorer farmers, wouldn't it? What do you think, Beth?"

"Well, yes, it is a good idea to be thinking ahead and not be surprised at the need for change if it happens," she said, "but I do believe there is an even more worrying factor that could upset the overall way of life here in Kentucky, indeed within the whole country."

Laura and Rory stopped in their tracks, surprised at Beth's somewhat tragic and worried face.

"Ah," said Laura, as she remembered an overheard similar conversation between Beth and Beulah on Wednesday. "Do you mean the tensions created by the alleged fraudulent election in Kansas last March? The one that ensured a pro-slavery majority?" she asked.

Laura was herself sympathetic toward the escalating anti-slavery crusade.

"Yes," Beth agreed, "as well as last year's Kansas-Nebraska Act that appears to have divided the Kansas territory into two. The president should never have signed that in my opinion. He would have known that Kansas was meant to be a free state as it lies north of the Mason-Dixon line. After all, it *was* established back in 1820 within the Missouri Compromise. Now, of course, there's uncertainty about its status. The whole incident has created unrest and I am worried it might escalate. I get the impression there might be more of this sort of thing to come."

"Do you think Kentucky is vulnerable as an uncommitted border state? And perhaps alongside Tennessee and Virginia there might be an escalation of problems surrounding the slavery issue?" Rory asked.

Beth shrugged her shoulders. "Our politicians are even finding it difficult to answer those sorts of questions," she said, "but I do think about them, and wonder how it is all going to end."

They also discussed the general economy of Kentucky, and agreed there was reason to believe that general unrest, country wide, was looming.

"I think it could be worse than that," said a moody, somewhat morose Beth.

Rory promised to discuss the issue with his fellow students as they were from varying parts of the country and their views might feed their next conversation on the subject. Then he laughed, and took hold of a hand of each of his companions. He began to run and they had no option but to run with him, and soon they were their laughing, cheerful selves again, as they reached the river to eat their rations.

The year rolled on and the friendship between Laura and Beth blossomed. Delphia and Beulah were eager to meet nowadays and visits between their homes became more frequent. The early rapport between Laura and Beth improved. Delphia and Beulah could see the friendship of the girls was good for both and saw to it that they had plenty of free time during the visits.

When Laura left school, she had spent much of her time helping with the administration of the farm, though did not attempt any of the heavy farm work as she had done in Virginia. She also helped with the local church work, and when she heard a new school for girls was to be opened shortly in Cynthiana, under the patronage of a local philanthropist, Laura sought out the benefactor, Walter Twigge.

Mr. Twigge, inspired by a Lexington philanthropist and friend, David Sayre, the creator of the successful Transylvania Female Institute in Lexington, had donated a small, two-story building and funds to set up a school for the education of girls between six and 12 years of age. His four granddaughters, who did not like their formidable governess one bit, were destined to attend the school and Walter had offered the job of head teacher to John Macmillan, a tutor with a high reputation. However, Twigge's enthusiasm soon turned to gloom when he realized the laxity of the State courts responsible for the division of counties into educational districts.

They moved at such a leisurely pace and he felt the school opening was so far away, it would not happen within his lifetime. Without the support of the influential David Sayre's office, it may not have been possible, but together with that influence and the daily persistence of Mr. Twigge and his attorney, the school was inaugurated within the year.

The concept of a girl's school was well received and supported by the well-to-do Cynthiana community and even the less wealthy made efforts to claim places for their girls. When Laura first approached Walter Twigge, he and McMillan were delighted to offer full-time employment to this bright and articulate young woman, especially when they learned of her own educational background. They had the funds to pay her, in the knowledge that an anonymous benefactor had, through an attorney, promised further capital within a couple of years.

Delphia and Laura had settled down in Longfield, and though each loved their own home and family, Longfield had somehow become so much part of their identity they felt reluctant to leave. Laura, in particular, had vowed she would stay in Cynthiana to work at the new school, knowing deep in her heart that it was the hope of seeing Rory from time to time that held her firm.

During one of Rory's rare weekend visits to his home, Delphia and William discussed the need to replace Laura, whose administrative input had become invaluable as William's work increased.

"We need a good accountant," William had said, "and though I've looked around, I haven't come across a decent candidate yet. Laura is hard to replace."

Rory solved that problem within two minutes.

"Is young Ronald Bishop still working at the Terry Light Transmission Company?" He remembered the boy with affection and it was he who had orchestrated the existing job for the innocent young lad after he had been caught up in the Delaney/Sampson debacle.

"Yes, he is," answered Delphia, "and I believe he's done very well and got a promotion recently. And, what's more, he plans to marry. He's saving hard to buy a small home."

"I suggest you offer him the job of Senior Clerk at Longfield, and pay him accordingly. We do owe him, after all, and William will welcome him, I'm sure," Rory said.

They grinned at each other, pleased they could show their gratitude to young Bishop.

Following their most recent visit to Lexington, Laura had arranged to stay on after her mother returned to Longfield. Her teaching role at the new school was marvelous but tiring and everybody had suggested a short holiday. Beulah ensured that Beth had plenty of time to spend with Laura, and their friendship became even closer during those happy, restful days.

Laura was always fascinated by Beth's high intellect and depth of conversation when they walked along the river banks and stony pathways of the estate. She was surprised when Beth occasionally lapsed into her colloquial diction when speaking with her parents, and could hardly believe the swift return to her educated accent when she left them. They saw little of the tall, slim, fashion conscious and lovely Maya during that time, as she had developed a retinue of young friends who seemed to follow her everywhere during her weekends at home.

A couple of days before Laura was due back in Cynthiana, Beth asked Laura if she would like to visit one of her friends, Clarissa Alexander, who lived on the edge of the po'-white district.

"I met her about six months ago," Beth said. "She was out for a walk by the river, and I'd seen her before but she was rather aloof, so we never spoke. One day, though, she fell and I heard her cry out, so I knew she was hurt."

Beth began to laugh.

"You should have seen her, doing her best to look dignified as she tried to get up with a sprained ankle. Somehow, my parents and I, together with an old door and a garden barrow, got her home. All her dignity had gone by the time we got there. We had a good old laugh about it once she was settled and comfortable, and we've been friends ever since. She works hard to keep their household going, so I have to go out and see her. It's my day to visit her so she'll be expecting me, and I know she'd love to see you as well.

Chapter 7
Laura and Beth Meet Clarrie

Beth and Laura took the short route alongside the river to the Alexander's farm. The cool air was zephyr-like under the blue sky and mild sunlight, and it seemed no distance as Beth related Clarissa Alexander's troubled life since moving from Boston to Kentucky five years earlier. Within half an hour they diverted to a well-worn woodland path that opened onto the small 10 acre Alexander plot, in the middle of which stood the neat farm buildings and house.

Beth explained how Clarissa's father, Stuart Alexander, had been an apothecary with a qualified medical doctor, Gerald Green, in Boston. Stuart and Gerald had met as students at Philadelphia University, where Stuart's talent for chemistry drew him to the advanced apothecary course. In due course, he and Gerald established a medical practice, where each performed their individual skills. 15 years slipped by almost unnoticed. As Stuart gained experience in his craft, he earned the respect of the Boston medical world and was a reassuring stalwart within the Boston community.

Medical training improved significantly over those years, and the new generation of physicians became more conversant with the chemical intricacies and art of compounding ingredients into medical cures. These 'new' doctors became the forerunners in the craft, eventually leading to the reduction in an apothecary's status. When Doctor Green decided to retire to Maine, his share of the practice was purchased by one of these newly qualified physicians, George Houseman, an arrogant man who was unwilling for Stuart to retain equal status with him, partner or not. Neither Stuart nor his wife Martha, could accept this demotion, even though they had retained their social position and decided to bring their retirement dream forward by a few years.

They purchased the run-down, small farm on the outskirts of Lexington, but two years later, Stuart suffered a fatal heart attack while out in the field with the old plough they had inherited with the farm. The plough was made to be pulled by two men, or a donkey, neither of which were available to Stuart. He pulled it without any support though it was hard work as it clanked away. It had, along with the other farm equipment, proved to be in need of small but constant repairs, which depleted their budget. Stuart had decided to replace it when the farm became profitable, and he and Martha had been confident that this would happen if hard work and enthusiasm had any influence on the matter. Martha blamed three days of hard work with this plough for her husband's sudden fatal heart attack, but his death made it financially impossible to consider its immediate replacement.

"It was so sad," Beth said, "and even more so when Martha's younger son was killed in an accident with the same plough a year later. He had left it for a moment and somehow it overturned when he returned to it, and he was crushed. He was killed instantly according to the doctor. Nobody ever discovered exactly what had happened, though it was suspected he had unharnessed himself to chase away a stray dog that was getting in his way. She also explained that Martha's elder son, Tom, wasn't interested in the farm, and was a bit of a dreamer.

"He does try, alongside his sister," she said, "but although Clarrie's strong and sturdy, I do wonder how on earth she manages to do everything she does."

Beth told Laura of how shocked Martha and Tom were when they saw how little remained in their bank account following Stuart's death. The bank manager, Mr. Bennett, confirmed that their savings had been eroded over those first two years due to labor costs, farm appliance repairs, and a decrease in the sales of their crops.

"Mr. Bennett also told them the dwindling sale of Kentucky hemp was the main blame factor," she said, "and he's right. The gradual withdrawal of lucrative orders for Kentucky hemp has had an indirect effect in creating the Alexander's economic crises."

"That's because, I suppose, the hemp farmers are able to utilize more land to grow vegetables, fruit, and tobacco instead of hemp, and the farmers can afford to sell their crops at the markets at a lower rate than the small farms." Laura suggested.

Beth nodded. "No doubt at all," she said.

Laura wondered whether the improvements in ship building negating the need for quality hemp rope, was worth upsetting the overall economy of the hardworking farming community, with its impact on businesses and consequent hardships on family life.

"It depends on what you think is more important, I suppose," said Beth, "Is it better to have poorer farmers across Kentucky or the improved security of our country in building iron ships?"

"I was told corn has become an important product in the distilling of Kentucky whisky, and the better off former hemp farmers now have more acres to spare so they're able to grow more corn, in order to increase their revenue," Laura said.

"Well, yes," Beth agreed. "Not only that, they have more room to increase their cow herds to produce quality milk and cheese that's sold at a price lower than the poorer farmers can. So, the richer farmers can pull themselves out of a financial mire, but not the po'-white folks, who are already so poor they're half starved."

"It's no wonder the Alexander farm is failing," Laura said, "because they can't sell their produce unless they offer it at a fraction of what it's worth. They want to grow more wheat, but it's both labor and appliance expensive. They simply can't afford to do it."

The two girls looked at each other, worry crossing their concerned faces. It seemed to them that further deterioration of the lives of country folks was inevitable. As women, they could do very little about it. They were not allowed into the local political arena. They sighed at what appeared to be an unsolvable problem.

They were silent for a while, until Beth changed the subject with a wide smile.

"Wait until you meet the two children Martha and Clarrie rescued from a terrible situation," she said.

Laura was all ears. She was interested in anything to do with children.

Beth told her how the children had become part of the Alexander household a few months earlier. The boy, Jack, about 12 years old, helped Tom with light farm chores, while the girl, Frances, who was probably a couple of years younger, insisted on helping Clarissa and her mother with small, though time consuming chores. This released Clarissa for bread making, a new aspect of their business that brought in much needed income each market day, and one of the reasons they wanted to grow more wheat for milling.

"I was with Clarissa when she first came across them," Beth said. "They came from an itinerant family who made a living from selling bits and bobs that were probably stolen. They sold next to nothing in this area, but folks round here are neighborly and donated food to help feed the large family of all boys, except for one little gal. It was probably this generosity that persuaded the itinerants to set up camp not far from the Alexander's farm."

"Folks around here often heard screaming from the camp, though most of it was the boys' rough games. But, one day when a farmhand was out for a walk, he heard such appalling screams that he ran over to the camp. He saw a huge man he thought to be their father, beating two little children with a line rope and a cane.

"The unconscious gal was bleeding while her brother was so badly beaten, he didn't have the strength to get up from the ground," she said in a subdued voice.

"The farmhand carried the little gal to the Alexander's farm, with the lad limping at his side. When you meet Clarrie and her mother, you'll see why they took them in without hesitation," continued Beth, who had noticed Laura's appalled expression.

Beth described how Martha had taken off the dress of the girl, noting that the back of the funky skirt was red with damp blood. She also realized the girl wore no underwear, and when she saw her blood-stained upper legs, knew there had been an unspeakable assault. At first, the boy denied having seen the actual attack, but knew that 'Big Bill' had "dun sump'n" to the child. The frightened girl held out her arms to her brother and wept loudly as he comforted her. Martha was so patient with the girl, and extracted the account of what had taken place. Her suspicions had been correct.

"It had been easy to believe the girl's story. She told of how her brother had tried to rescue her from the attacker." Beth continued. "It turned out that the man wasn't their father, but a nomadic who had joined their group sometime after their natural father had died. Her brother's interruption of the vile offence against his sister had inspired the cruel beatings. When the boy described what he had witnessed, the angry farmer returned to the itinerant's camp and beat the perpetrator unconscious. We later learned of how the remaining family group of six boys and their mother stood around watching and cheered whenever the farmer landed a punch."

"Apparently, the farmer knocked the brute out and shouted that he was going for the sheriff. Sure enough, the sheriff arrived with a posse of three deputies an hour or two later but the family had cleared off, leaving behind a dreadful mess, as well as the two children still with the Alexanders. Later, we all heard of how the body of a man, his arms and ankles tied with rope, with signs of a heavy beating, was found in a nearby rocky crevice a couple of weeks later, obviously thrown there by his assailants. It was never proved this was 'Big Bill' though many suspected it was. Some also suspected his attackers could have been the itinerant family itself, though nothing had been heard or seen of them since the family skedaddled."

"Do the children miss their family?" Laura asked, horrified at the story and at how their mother and siblings could discard them so easily.

"No way," Beth told her. "The little souls didn't even have proper names. The girl had been referred to as 'Little Bug' and the boy had been given an obscene name – I can't repeat it. Clarrie's mother gave them new names and the children are so proud of them. It almost makes you weep when you call out to Frances by her new name. Her sweet little face lights up and you just want to pick her up and hug her. Frances can't remember her father, but Jack does and both wanted to keep his last name – Bellwood. So, Clarrie's mother had them registered as Frances and Jack Bellwood. Having their own name and identity seems to have given them confidence, somehow."

Laura was amazed that such cruelty to young children could exist, but as they were almost at the Alexander's place, decided not to pursue this new worry. She would instead discuss the situation with her social-minded Aunt Beulah as well as with Rory, who was due home shortly. She vowed to herself she must 'do something' one day about such treatment to children, but could not, as yet, conceive how she could go about this.

It was within this background the well-spoken, gracious Clarissa greeted them at the farmhouse gate, acknowledging the presence of Laura with a touch of shyness as she enveloped Beth in a warm embrace. Laura, whose imagination had been caught as Beth told her story, was surprised there was nothing in the girl's face and discreet glance that indicated any personality. Her voice as she greeted Beth was soft, almost dove-like. Laura had visualized a tall girl, beautiful, full of fervor and a 'get-on-with-it' conviction.

She was of average height, with brown hair and eyes, and a tanned, weathered look to her skin. Her hair was styled into two neat coils that hung above her ears. She was dressed in a clean calico dress, though her well-polished boots looked shabby and down at heel. The girl's deportment was probably her best feature.

She's quite homely, Laura thought, somewhat disappointed.

"So, this is Laura, is it? I was beginning to wonder if you were a character in one of Beth's books. She's always reading, you know," Clarissa said, shaking Laura's hand.

As she spoke, a half-smile spread over her face, transforming it quite suddenly, as though she had just walked out of the shadows of a copse into sunlight. Her smile broadened and her voice was now clear and firm. She no longer appeared plain or lacking personality. Clarrie looked at her in surprise as she realized Laura was gaping at her.

"What's up?" she asked, laughing.

Beth giggled

"I'm sorry. I didn't mean to stare, Clarissa. I have heard about your family's struggles over the past few years, and do admire you so much. It's wonderful to meet you," Laura said.

Clarissa laughed.

"Call me Clarrie, please. Come on, let's get some tea and you can meet Mother and Tom."

The three girls linked arms, not realizing then that this small gesture signaled the beginning of a unique friendship.

Clarrie's brother, Tom, was a tall, raw-boned lad, and bashful as he eyed Laura for the first time. Browned by the heat and wind, with a straight back and tough-looking muscles, he stood awkwardly, unsure of how to address this young woman, with hair that shone like a halo around a face so lovely that it took his breath away.

Prodded by his sister, he and little Frances began the process of laying out the tea service, as Clarrie brought in the ready-prepared Boston afternoon tea. Mrs. Alexander, a gentle, articulate lady, who insisted on being called Martha, was a charming, thoughtful hostess. Clean and neat in her shabby dress, she made Laura and Beth welcome as she helped to serve the home-made brew, and freshly baked bread and home-churned butter. She had pulled out a jar from her cherished stock of home-made apple jelly, and there were delicious-looking tiny cakes and a large fruit cake that looked so delectable that Laura could hardly take her eyes away.

Laura felt that nowhere could she have enjoyed such a simple but delicious meal more than in this clean, shiny, well-brushed home. Frances hovered shyly in the background, until Laura gently coaxed the child to sit next to her and asked where Jack was.

"He's too shy to meet a proper lady," Frances answered.

Laura blushed and asked permission to seek out Jack and bring him into the group.

It was not long before she allowed herself to be led back to her seat by a beaming Jack, who clutched Laura's hand as if he would never let it go. He told her of how Martha had shaved his and his sister's heads to get rid of the long, filthy hair that had never been washed, and had tended the sores and scabs on their scalps. He was proud of the fact that the hair was growing now, so they would be able to go to the public school quite soon. He also read her part of a page he had copied from one of Clarrie's old books. He had been an excellent learner under Martha's tuition, as indeed had Frances, though she was not as interested. Martha had made arrangements with Mr. Bennett, the bank manager, who helped her out in many ways nowadays, to talk to his brother-in-law, an attorney in Lexington, about the legal aspects of keeping the children with her.

"Martha likes to meet people like you," Beth said to Laura as they walked home. "She rarely meets an educated person. I think it would be nice for her to meet with your Aunt Beulah, but when I mentioned this to her some time ago, she hinted she couldn't afford to buy a new gown for the visit."

"My aunt wouldn't mind what her gown was like, she would just welcome her as a new friend," said Laura, who knew how much Beulah missed her own mother's company.

After a second visit to the Alexander's farm, Laura, always outspoken, took it upon herself to invite Martha and Clarissa to tea the following week, anticipating the excuse of the gown.

"I was in the same position when I went to stay with Aunt Beulah for a few weeks years ago," Laura responded. "It was worse for me because I couldn't sew, but my aunt's seamstress came to my rescue. She re-fashioned two of my dated dresses. Mother insisted I took them with me on my visit to Uncle John's, and made them into something wonderful. Let's look at your old gowns, and see what miracle Beth can suggest."

The four women spent an hour together in Martha's bedroom before Laura and Beth began their walk home, carrying between them two gowns for alteration; one for Martha, the other for Clarrie. They had promised to visit Beulah when they received her official invitation. The girls barely noticed the weight of the garments in their elation at having achieved this promise.

Their joy was short-lived. They were almost home when they were met by Beth's distressed father, Jacob, in the small pony-trap.

Maya had not returned home. She had said she was going swimming, but that had been hours ago. They feared she may have drowned. Beth, knowing her dreamy sister often had her head in the clouds, sighed in exasperation.

"She prob'ly dun a wrong turnin' and gotten de Lord knows where – she dun dat afore," she said to her father, lapsing into her natural diction for his benefit.

She turned to Laura.

"My sister has done this before but she always turns up. I suspect she has an admirer," she whispered.

Laura heard the peevishness in her friend's comment and was surprised.

Carefully placing the gowns in the trap, Laura sat down beside them, allowing Beth to sit alongside her father. As they sped back, as fast as the little pony's trot would allow, she thought of the pleasure with which dear lonely Aunt Beulah would receive the news of Martha's potential visit.

When they arrived, Beth found her mother had already checked the places where she knew Beth and Maya visited. Her one remaining hope was that Maya had gone to the Alexander farm with her sister.

Beth knew of another place – one Maya had found accidentally a few weeks ago, during a lone walk. It was a small sheltered copse, dark and apparently forgotten. A place for a quiet picnic, Maya had said, or a secret rendezvous with a lover. Beth said that she should stop reading those dumb-ass magazines with half-witted stories that she found for a penny in the local market, and concentrate on the quality literature Fred and Oliver had introduced her to.

"Fred's given me a book called *The Scarlet Letter* but it's too hard for me to read. He reads it to me sometimes, which I like. When I don't understand some of it, he explains the words to me. He's good is Fred. I shall bring him here," she had sighed.

She tended to speak in the 'white-person's' vernacular in the presence of Beth nowadays, rather than in their colloquial tongue.

It was Beth who found Maya. She was fully clothed except for her bloomers which had been thrown onto a nearby bush. When her mother spied the garment, she ran toward the bush and tripped, falling heavily to the ground. Those who heard the thud as her head hit a large rock knew it was the sound of death.

Jacob ran to his wife and his howl of anguish shattered the usual quiet of the peaceful copse, sending small animals scurrying away. The birds even stopped singing.

Someone would tell, much later, of how he watched in horror as one lone leaf slowly fell from a tree, finally landing on the shattered head of Jacob's wife.

"I can't get that darn fallin' leaf outta my 'ed, nor that sound when 'er 'ed 'it the rock," he was heard to say many times a day for weeks.

Beth noticed horse hooves in the soft earth and followed them. Her cry of horror told the stricken searchers. She had found her sister. Maya's head was hurt, bleeding, but she was still breathing.

"Who's done this to you, Maya? Who's done it, Maya?" cried Beth, bending her head toward her sister.

"The other angel," Maya whispered.

Beth stared at her in exasperation.

"Maya," Beth shouted. "Tell me. *WHO DID THIS?*"

*"*Not the first one, the other angel." Maya gasped as her eyes fell back.

Those words were the last that Beth would hear her sister speak. She felt the small shudder of Maya's body in her arms and heard the last breath of life escaping, as she held her sister tightly to her. She was stunned, not knowing who or what Maya had alluded to.

Maya's body was carried gently to the pony trap. Her beautiful face had been carefully cleaned, and her head was now covered in a large bandana through which blood still seeped. They left behind a pool of dark blood in the hollow in which Maya had rested. Another trap carrying her mother, now held in her father's arms, followed.

When Martha met Beulah at last, it was not the cozy afternoon tea that Beth and Laura had envisaged. The reception following the joint funeral of the Compton's cook and her daughter was destined to be the first occasion that the two mothers met, but was not to be the last. Neither wore fashionable funeral gowns and neither cared about that one little bit.

Official investigations were carried out, theories investigated, rumors acted upon.

Except for the horse hooves that had led Beth to her sister – evidence which had been almost demolished due to the heavy footprints of rescuers, stretcher bearers and onlookers – no indication of what had happened to Maya was discovered.

Beth made a silent vow that one day she would solve the mystery. In the meantime, she had to deal with her stricken father.

Everyone was alarmed by Jacob's daily suffering. He attributed Maya's vicious death, as well as his wife's, to his own neglect by allowing his favorite daughter too much freedom to wander. He hardly noticed Beth, which was hard for her, but she tried to understand, the burden of self-blame made his grief even harder to bear. She encouraged him to take care of the gardens which showed signs of abandonment, but his grief stricken mind blamed his previous addiction to work for the supposed neglect of his child.

Jacob had shown great anger at his imagined ineptitude as a father so most were surprised when he added to his elder daughter's grief by hanging himself under the large oak tree near Benson's paddock. The main question asked within the community was why he did not take into account the effect his suicide would have on Beth, the only surviving member of his family.

Beth survived the disaster, with the help of the Compton family, Clarrie and Martha. She kept to herself the vow that one day she would discover who Maya's killer was, the same person who was responsible in her mind for the deaths of her parents. She was convinced she would.

Somehow Beth retained her own tenacious and well-balanced character, as she expanded her experience and education. She became a beautiful, serious-minded intelligent woman, who did not smile so much, unless in the company of her dearest friends, Rory, Clarrie and Laura.

Chapter 8
Changes for the Alexander Family

Clarrie looked across at the recently built house where the old fermentation vats had stood for many years. It was medium sized, with four upstairs rooms, including a bathing area, three downstairs reception rooms, a kitchen and a bright dining room adjacent to a covered patio. Douglas Bennett himself had commissioned and supervised its building. The house was surrounded by a medium high perimeter wall, with a gated entrance that offered privacy when required. A newly laid lawn, fresh shrubs and sculpted hedges were visible from the refurbished farmhouse where Clarrie lived together with her mother and the Bellwoods. Young imported pine trees were planted against the outer line of the wall, which Clarrie knew would in due course offer more privacy to the occupiers.

"Who would have believed this three years ago?" she asked herself, staring out at the Alexander farm's changed outlook.

Her eyes turned to the old stable, now painted white, which housed the Victoria carriage, purchased six months ago from a struggling farmer east of Lexington. She looked across at the immaculate orchard, where newly planted apple trees harmonized with the old. To her left, she could see the renovated farm buildings that had once housed farm machinery now donated to farming neighbors, and was now their pristine depository for the flour purchased from Malone's Mill. She saw again the long lines of agricultural crops almost ready for harvesting, and the new shack built especially for their modern plough. A smart new stable to the far left was home for their four horses while adjacent stood a wooden shack for their delivery carts.

From her bedroom window, Clarrie could also see the farmhouse garden where Frances was wandering, posing in her first 'grown-up' long gown ready for today's big party. Gone was the white coverall and white clogs that Clarrie had stipulated to be worn by all the bakery workers together with a white head bandeau, conscious as she was of the need for high standards of hygiene. Beth had made the first six coveralls and bandeaux, though her role as Beulah's personal maid and companion kept her well occupied. This task had now been allotted to an efficient little seamstress, Chloe, a daughter of the housekeeper. Chloe worked on the project each day after school ended; she had already produced half a dozen spare garments, and was busy on the next batch.

Frances' whistle rendering of Martha's favorite lute music to be played at today's family party drifted upward. Clarrie giggled at the somewhat unmusical sound, though felt this was more acceptable than the raucous din her own singing voice sent forth. Frances had remained a small scrap of a girl, and while she would never be a beauty with her scraggy legs and long, thin face, Clarrie knew her personality and good humor held everyone in thrall. She did notice, however, that her chief baker had made the best of herself today as she looked forward to the day's celebrations, just as she herself had tried to do.

Clarrie checked her reflection in the long cheval mirror, once the property of her maternal grandmother and the thought that she looked as good as she was ever going to get, before crossing the passage toward her mother's room. She couldn't really believe *The Day* had come at last – her mother's wedding day. Carrie smiled at the thought of how Douglas Bennett, their former bank manager, had courted Martha over the past three years, and how she had finally capitulated to his courtship. When Martha had agreed to marry him, he asked permission to build a house for them on the land laid spare when the vats were removed.

Clarissa heard her brother Tom's voice downstairs and the excited twittering of young Frances, and thought of the other major changes in their lives. Tom was now the head gardener at the Compton's mansion. He and his wife, Florence, lived in Jacob's old cottage with their small son, and another baby was on the way.

* * *

She thought of how Douglas Bennett had become involved with the Alexander family and of how, prior to his retirement, he had been prone to taking what he felt were 'special' accounts under his wing. One such account was the Alexander farm following the death of her father. Tom had been named on the account alongside his mother's, following his father's death, even though he had been an under-age youth without administrative authority. Douglas approved of Stuart Alexander's foresight in ensuring his wife retained legal rights to the destiny of the farm. He had always felt the strong beliefs of Abigail Adams, who had, in the early days of the Union, advocated equal fiscal rights for wives and spinster relatives, should have been listened to. 'Remember the ladies' Mrs. Adams had urged her disinclined husband, President John Adams.

Douglas had noted the gradual decline of the Alexander farm funds, as the variable economic situation played havoc with Kentucky's economy, as well as that of the nation. He took it upon himself to visit Martha Alexander. His main message was that the business must diversify if it was to continue, or that Martha should sell the farm and settle down in a small home with '*vest-pocket*' capital. He was aware her friendship with Beulah Compton had raised her social profile, a useful asset if she had to re-establish herself elsewhere. Following a lengthy interview, he left a doubtful Martha with ideas spinning around in her brain.

His comments had been inspired by the sumptuous afternoon tea Martha and Clarrie had served him. Home-made bread and butter, little cakes with colorful chopped fruit adorning the tops, a fruit cake served with cheese, which he thought eccentric but nevertheless munched with relish.

"Serving cheese with fruit cake is a custom from the north of England where my grandmother lived before she came to America. The cake is made from her original recipe," Martha told the fascinated Douglas.

A widower of more than 10 years, Douglas was rarely served food as delicate and flavorsome. Neither had he experienced such warmth and comfort as he found within this delightful household.

"Have you ever considered setting up a bakery?" he'd asked.

The idea had overwhelmed Martha. She was astonished when Tom and Clarrie accepted it with enthusiasm, especially as she knew that her daughter's earnest ambition was to become a nurse.

Tom, whose heart was not in the routine daily grind of farm life, left all decisions to his mother and Clarrie. He longed to accept the offer made by John Compton to take on the job as his full-time gardener, with the added incentive of Jacob's former home. If the family farm was sold, a solution that he had hitherto preferred, he could accept John's offer without fear of disloyalty to his mother and sister. Perhaps he could then consider marrying, for he was a youth going about his business with his head in the clouds with love for Florence from the nearby Whitehead's farm.

Once the bakery option was accepted after much talking and planning, Martha conceded that her son could consider settling down as he wished. She reminded him, however, of his duty to her and the farm over the following months.

"I'll need your help full-time at the farm for the harvesting and grinding of the apples, as well as organizing the seasoning process. The vats will need to be thoroughly cleaned before we use them for this year's processing, and then you'll have to help with transporting the fermented pulp to the cider maker's tanks."

These tanks were situated a few miles away, where the cider making process would be completed, and required careful planning with a team of experienced workers. Tom groaned at the thought but knew Clarrie would help him with the planning.

"There's also the wheat harvesting and getting it over to Malone's Mill for grinding and sacking," his mother reminded him. This final batch was designated for their new enterprise, and Martha thrilled at the thought. She smiled a lot nowadays.

Clarrie had always supported her brother wherever she could and realizing his genuine antipathy toward farm work, was glad when the planned changes enabled him to accept Compton's offer. Jack and Frances were adamant they would assist with the farm poultry and small cattle herd that produced the household's eggs, milk, butter and cheese, and proved more than eager to support the bakery project.

"I love baking bread," Frances had said, "and I've read some of those household magazines that Mrs. Compton sends us sometimes. Will you let me try to make some of those tiny little cake things with sugary toppings, and big fruit cakes?" she asked, her face pink with excitement. Martha agreed it would be something different for their customers, and that they could at least give it a try.

Clarrie and Martha often reflected on the enormous task of planning, not realizing in their early enthusiasm just how much there would be to do. One of their first tasks had been to negotiate a deal with the Lexington Apple Cider Company about the future apple transport and processing of their fruit, the costs of which had been a major factor in the decreasing viability of their farm. With Douglas Bennett's full support, the Cider Company agreed to remove the Alexander farm's fermentation vats to their own land in time for the next season, thus taking on the grinding and fermentation processes. They also agreed to purchase the annual apple harvest direct from the Alexander farm, who would undertake the annual harvesting and delivery of the unprocessed fruit.

Douglas had been concerned the current costs of producing and milling their own corn were unfeasible.

"I believe it would be expedient to purchase the bakery's needs direct from Joe Malone's Mill, rather than growing your own corn. This would save the cost of planting, harvesting and labor," he said.

Martha considered the suggestion with some reluctance. "What about the poor folks who rely on us for work on our farm?" she had asked, anxious about the families of the seasonal workers. However, Clarrie and Tom both welcomed the idea.

"We shall need the labor in the bakery if it takes off," said the practical Clarrie, "and it would be year-round rather than seasonal, so the folks we hire would have full-time employment with us. Maybe not at the beginning, but from the public interest we've had in the bakery, I think we're certain of some success."

Martha was thus persuaded and their business plan was accepted. Martha and Tom were able to arrange a short-term bank loan to assist with the immediate costs of establishing the project.

There were early signs of success for the embryo bakery, as new orders for both bread and fancy goods arrived on a daily basis. The energetic Frances introduced a series of sweet-cakes and puddings which sold so quickly that she often worked overnight to fulfill orders for the next morning. Further help was hired and it was here that the blossoming Frances proved her diplomacy skills, adept as she was in ensuring a happy working spirit.

The family began to realize their unique products were a welcome source of diversion during these dark days of economic turmoil and talk of unrest twixt the North and the South. The Alexander Bakery soon became a household name within the larger houses of Lexington.

"I want a large basket of bread and your fancy cakes sent over to Longfield every Friday," Delphia had said, and it was not long before orders began to arrive from other Cynthiana residents.

* * *

There had been great excitement when Martha's wedding plans were announced. Preparations for the wedding feast did not take precedence over the daily orders, but with the help of extra staff, funded by Douglas, the wedding day went without a hitch. The bakery closed down for the day, as family, neighbors and employees congregated to witness the union of two beloved members of their community, followed by a sumptuous banquet and dancing. Rory had skipped a few days from university to be at the event, to the delight of his family and his three friends, Laura, Beth and Clarrie.

The four of them spent the following day together, wallowing in reminiscences of how life had changed for all of them. The girls accompanied Rory to the railroad the following day, and returned arm in arm, still in holiday mood. It was a wrench to return to normal duties.

Clarrie and her mother were well aware that Frances and Jack Bellwood were the mainstays of the project, each as enthralled with the preparation of products as with the selling of them. They were 'natural' bakers. Jack was also blessed with a financial acumen that, under the guidance of Douglas, added to his effectiveness. Like his sister, he had a sense of humor, and it was hard for anyone to imagine life without the two former waifs. They were family now and had never given cause for anxiety. Martha suggested they should take a few days off in lieu of all the extra work involved in preparing for the wedding, but they did not take advantage of the offer, stating they would save the days for a special occasion.

"I can't imagine what special occasion will arise," said Martha, "but hopefully something will persuade them to take a break."

* * *

Three weeks later Clarrie had been startled by a young soldier, dressed in the Confederate grey uniform, who looked familiar. He had knocked loudly on her office door and at first she could not understand his accent, though detected a slight Southern twang.

"Are you the boss lady I've heard of?" he asked with such abruptness that Clarrie was taken aback.

She nodded.

"Ah'm searchin' for mah brother and sister. They were brung to this farm back along by a farmer who stopped their beatin'. Ah knows that 'cos I followed him. Ah wish ah'd stayed with the two mites but 'ad to get back to see our ma safe from that blackjack what beat up the little 'uns."

Clarrie stared, for she now recognized the soldier as an older, slimmer, taller version of Jack.

"That would be Jack and Frances Bellwood, my bake-house managers," she told him, her tone indicating she would stand no nonsense from the stranger.

"They've got new dubs. An' kept our da's name! That's good. The old dubs were disgusting. The blackjack give 'em to us. I changed my name as well, when I enlisted for this army."

He looked down at his uniform with pride.

"The dub I 'ad was even worse'n theirs," he added with a grin, so like Jack's that Clarrie smiled back at him.

"Me and two of mi brothers made sure the blackjack did'na beat up any of our family agin," he said. "We stuck together for more'n a year after that, then our old ma found another fella to be with, so I up and went."

He told her that he was a registered soldier in the 1st Cavalry Regiment of Virginia, and was now known as David Plowman.

"I met a guy on the way when I left my family an' we buddied up for a while," he explained. "When he was sick he tol' me I could have all his things if he died, which he did. Ah took his name, but sold up his things to get him a decent burial. He'd 'ave bin kinda pleased to know that."

He grinned again and Clarrie's fears melted, realizing that he was here just because he needed to know how 'the little 'uns' had squared up in life. Clarrie offered refreshments, and explained how Jack and Frances had prospered. She sent a message, inviting them to her office and witnessed the hysteria of recognition, the exclamations and tears of surprise and disbelief. She hastened away, tears in her own eyes, leaving them to get to know each other.

David was able to stay for a few days before he returned to his regiment, and his siblings spent most of their time with him. Clarrie shivered as she overheard his final remarks to Jack, as they shook hands before parting.

"There's a war a'comin'," David warned. "Make sure you fight for the right side." He patted his uniform with dignity. "The southerners will get our country to where it should be."

Clarrie arranged for David to be taken to the railroad that would carry him back to his regiment. Jack and Frances had purchased a first class ticket for him in gratitude for having sought them out and he left with a hamper full of good things for his journey – enough to share with his fellow passengers or save for the lads back at his camp. David had become popular during those few days and everyone was sorry to see him go, particularly the young girls who smiled, dimpled and batted eye lashes whenever they caught sight of the handsome stranger. It was whispered that he had got to know two or three of them rather well during his short stay.

For a few days after David's departure, Jack was subdued. Everyone thought he was missing his brother, but Frances knew, as did Clarrie, he was worried about the possibility of war. He did not want a part in any aggressive consequences of the country's current political instability.

Chapter 9
Further Changes for Clarrie

The work of the bakery continued. As their business advisor prior to his marriage to Martha, Douglas had advocated the sale of the cattle herd, thus saving on cattle feed and veterinary costs, as well as freeing Clarrie from time-consuming dairy chores.

"Your milk, butter and cheese needs can be purchased from the local market at much less cost, and that'll help your neighbors indirectly, as they have little else to sell," he had argued. "You also need suitable transport to deliver your products to the large number of customers you've now got. The sale of the cattle would help with the cost of purchasing delivery wagons."

It had been a difficult decision for Clarrie as she loved her cow herd, but she had to accept the rationality behind the proposal.

Her own management abilities soon led to increased free time and she used this to study books loaned to her by Rory, now an earnest medical student. Clarrie spent many hours poring over them; scribbling lists of questions for Rory to answer when she saw him again. Now the Alexander Bakery had taken off, and her mother and Tom were settled, she sensed this was now the time to strive toward her own ambitions.

So, when Clarrie was asked to help out at the local doctor's surgery during a measles outbreak, she was ready to accede to Doctor Lawrence plea for help. He knew full well that Clarrie's real ambition was to become a nurse. Laura happened to be visiting Lexington during a break from school-teaching when the request was made and Clarrie asked whether she could also assist. Aware of Laura's teaching background, as well as her love of children, Doctor Lawrence agreed.

"She'll be an asset. A team with you and Laura is just what is needed," he said.

In their attempts to avoid the spread of the virulent disease, the two friends planned a rota for locating the stricken in their homes.

"We'll have to identify which houses are in quarantine and which aren't," said Clarrie, "otherwise the doctor will waste a lot of time if he has to visit every house."

In order to identify the 'measles' houses requiring a visit from the doctor, one of Clarrie's tasks was to take the doctor's pony and trap out each early morning, calling on homes where her home-made signs, bearing a large red 'M', were displayed in a window or garden. She and Laura had distributed these within the community on the first day, asking occupants to hang the signs in their windows or gardens, if they suspected an outbreak of measles in their home.

When visiting any home with suspected measles, the doctor and all members of his team donned spare bakery coveralls as some protection against contamination.

For the isolated cases in a household, and where it was necessary to provide special care, Mrs. Wallace had sorted out a quarantine room with water and washroom facilities in the city's communal hall that she, Clarrie, and Laura set about cleaning and sterilizing.

The two girls made straw mattresses and covered them with old bed sheets begged from wealthy Lexington houses; forgotten nightwear was retrieved from storage boxes in many a nursery; children's outgrown clothing was donated following an urgent appeal to her friends by Beulah Compton, as was purified water, canisters of hot nourishing soup and pans of cooked vegetables. The whole community was eager to assist as Clarrie and Laura labored to help the doctor and his wife. At one time there were 20 very sick children and three adults in the make-shift hospital, all of whom required attention day and night, though many affected children and sick parents were able to remain at home.

When checking on the 'signed' houses each day, Clarrie's official-looking white garb and her efficiency led to confidence. She was able to provide preliminary advice and a potion made up by the doctor's wife to help with early symptoms. Clarrie found insufficient water availability and the lack of plumbed closets were the hardest problems to overcome in their efforts to stop the spread of infection. They added water canisters and wash-bowls onto their trap load, together with digging tools so that they, or the householders, could dig an earth closet where required. Somehow Laura and Clarrie managed this extra chore, leaving the doctor and nurse time to administer their own skills when visiting 'home' or 'hospital' patients.

The two friends worked most days and sometimes at night in their efforts to maintain clean straw beds and linen as well as the quarantine room sterilization. Martha and Beulah made daily visits to collect donations from those householders who continued to give. The outbreak was contained within three weeks, the fear of an epidemic much reduced when the make-shift 'measles hospital' had only three patients.

Only one death was recorded; that of an elderly man, Jonathan Blowers, whose farm-house had somehow been overlooked, situated as it was in a heavily wooded, dark copse. He was the grandfather of a five-year-old boy who had been brought into the hospital at the same time. The boy's father, a school teacher now settled on the Kentucky/Ohio border, had made a surprise visit to his parents with his son. He had been shocked to realize the dire circumstances under which they were living, generated by infirmity and old age. He realized he must return to his old home here in Kentucky to care for them and decided to return to Ohio to bring his wife to help. He left his son with his doting grandparents confident they would look after each other for a few days. There was now an adequate rail service between Lexington and his Ohio home, and he had promised a return within four days with his wife.

They did not return.

When Clarrie met the pale, skinny little boy wandering down a track near the Blowers' farm, old tears having streaked his filthy face, she discovered an appalling state of affairs when the child led her to his temporary home. He had told her that 'grandma' had gone to sleep and 'wouldn't wake up' and that 'gramper' was too sick to sit up in bed. The stench in the room was terrible, the old man feeble and delirious, his dead wife at his side. Noting the absence of drinking water, she ran to her waiting horse and trap taking the boy with her. Allowing the boy a few sips of water, she dashed back to the old man to give him a few sips, and put a damp cloth across his hot forehead. She also left a soaked cloth over his lips so that water would, hopefully, drip into his mouth, to provide some measure of hydration, though she knew it was not enough. She noted the red blotches on his abdomen and neck, similar to those on the little boy's body that were not consistent with a measles rash.

She returned to the boy, gave him a few more sips of water, realizing that he would drink the whole amount if she allowed it. Knowing the dangers of this, she rationed his intake as she hurried back to the hospital. She had already stripped the unwilling boy of his filthy clothes, putting them in a large sack she had left at the farmhouse. His scraggy little body and head were now swaddled in a large sheet, leaving just one arm free. Clarrie suspected typhus, having read about the disease in one of Rory's books. She knew that typhus could result from lice and human feces, both clearly apparent in the house. The doctor would know for sure what it was.

Little Rupert Blowers, as Clarrie now knew him to be, appeared to be sleeping as the trap clattered into the yard. Within a minute she would see the doctor and rush him to the boy. Then she would identify an isolated room – just in case it was needed. She could hardly believe that they had almost contained one potential epidemic, only to discover another more virulent one in their midst. She prayed she was wrong.

As the doctor rushed to Rupert, he gave a swift instruction to locate a small empty room with easy access to water. The bemused curator, excited by the unexpected change of procedure, knew just the right room and he and Clarrie set about clearing it of furnishing, replacing it with a sterilized table and bedding. Laura rushed around the room, carefully cleaning every nook and corner to her friend's standards. Clarrie excited the eager curator even more as she barked orders at him to bring additional bedding, a tin bath, warm water and soap to the room 'as quick as you can'. He knew he would not be given any details of the panic, as he was sent to locate a further table, sterilize it and then bring it to the new treatment room.

What all the fuss was about he could not honestly say, but what a time he would have telling his tavern friends tonight of this unforeseen adventure. He had been disappointed when the doctor, who knew him as a gossipmonger, insisted he must not discuss anything of what he had seen or heard about this crisis. The loyal curator never ever breathed a word. He felt important for once in his life to have been trusted by such an eminent man as the local physician.

Rupert responded well to the soothing warmth of the water tub as he was immersed. Without comment, he allowed Clarissa to hack away his lice-ridden hair, which was placed in a bag that Laura sealed and threw into the nearby furnace used throughout the measles outbreak for burning contaminated sheets and clothing. The girls lifted the cleansed Rupert onto the mattress and left him to the care of the doctor.

Typhus was confirmed.

Clarissa could hardly believe it.

"TYPHUS," her mind shouted at her. "Pray God we can prevent further infection."

Her reading had informed her that the disease was not passed between humans in a clean environment, but nevertheless she insisted she and Laura should bathe and change their coveralls in order to soap and rub away any possible contamination. Prior to this, they had completed the thorough cleaning and sterilization of the small room and their used coveralls and cleaning rags were burned. Laura, who had planned to return to Cynthiana and her school in a few days, was informed that she could not return there for two weeks during the recognized Typhus incubation period.

A horse and trap was sent to the Blowers' home, with a specially prepared casket as well as a stretcher and clean sheets. The driver and assistants were provided with coveralls and head covering. A similarly clad priest accompanied them. Clarrie insisted that as much of the sick man's hair and beard as possible should be removed at the house. He should also be stripped of all clothing and swaddled in a sheet. Everyone had been impressed by her efficiency and attention to detail, especially when she ordered that the horse, as well as the cart, underwent the same cleansing and sterilization process.

Rupert and his grandfather lay in the solitary unit for two days before the old man died. The boy was unaware of his grandfather's death as his own frail life ebbed and flowed. A small burial service was held for Mr. Blowers and his wife in a far corner of the Presbyterian churchyard, where they were buried together, three-feet deeper into the earth than was usual. Their grave was covered with a large flat stone and Laura buried a cherished chain and cross close by; she wanted to leave something that showed the couple were not forgotten.

The farmhouse was burned to the ground, as well as a few adjacent trees and bushes, on the orders of the governor, who had accepted guidance from his health advisor. He had heard that the dead man's son, who would have inherited the property, had been listed as 'presumed dead' following a rail accident. Later the governor would officially thank the doctor and his team for preventing a potentially dangerous measles epidemic, but no mention was ever made of the prevention of a typhus disaster.

However, the incident ensured sufficient pressure within the governor's office to ascertain just what fate the Blowers' son and his wife had met, especially when Laura contacted the office about re-locating their child to Cynthiana, in her care.

To everyone's relief, Rupert gradually recovered, though it would be a long time before he would regain full strength. He was depressed as he realized his grandparents, whom he hardly knew, had died and that he was now an orphan. Laura remained in Lexington for the required two weeks, and spent much of her time with Rupert. She knew in the way his little face lit up whenever he saw her she was important to him, and was becoming anxious about the day she would need to leave. During the last week she learned much more of his happy life in Ohio and how he grieved for his parents and their life together. She was astounded when he asked her one day about the Orphan Train.

"Now I'm an orphan, will they put me on the Orphan Train to the West?" he asked nervously. He said he had heard about orphans who were put on the train from New York to the west, and became white slaves to the farmers.

"Well, you won't be going on it," she said. "For one thing, you don't live in New York. I can say though what you have heard are just silly rumors."

She told him what she knew about the Orphan train.

"It began in 1853, by a man called Charles Loring Brace, who founded the Children's Aid Society in New York. He'd been devastated at the plight of thousands of homeless New York orphans who roamed the city's slums with no hope of a better life. His idea was to transport some of the orphans to the West, where they could be adopted by farming families, and have a chance of proper family life."

Laura told him she was a member of a local group raising money for the organization, and reassured him the orphans were never treated as slaves by the farmers.

"I would be the first person to complain to the top, to the President himself, if such were true," she said.

"Don't worry about it, Rupert," she said. "I'll see you'll not be alone, because I shall take you with me to Cynthiana when you're better, if it's at all possible. I'll need to look into the legal aspects, of course. But you'll definitely not be going on the Orphan Train, as good as it is."

She watched his face change from worry to relief and was pleased with her sudden dramatic decision, though felt scared all of a sudden.

Christopher Columbus, she thought to herself later, *what am I going to do with a little boy in my busy life.* She knew, however, she could not, indeed would not, reverse her decision.

Two days later they received good news. Following the governor's orders further efforts had been made to ascertain exactly what happened to Rupert's parents. It was reported that they had been found and had survived the train crash. His father had suffered broken limbs, head wounds, cuts and amnesia.

His mother, who had suffered a miscarriage brought on by the trauma, had been taken to a hospital for women and had not been listed as a victim of the accident. She was in pain and confused, distressed that she had lost her baby, and did not know where her husband was, so the nurses decided she could stay until she recovered.

"The hospital caring for Roland Bowers didn't know the name of the one amnesiac in their care for some unknown reason, possibly due to the administrative chaos when so many injured patients arrived, and had not connected him with the train accident," a representative from the governor's office told them later. "By the time we trawled through all hospitals records in the accident area for a second time, Roland had recovered and remembered who he was and where he was supposed to be. It was the quick-thinking hospital clerk who had spoken with him following his recovery who telegraphed our office," he said.

Laura returned to Cynthiana with some regrets, particularly at leaving Rupert. His parents had not yet arrived in Lexington by the time she had to leave, but were due at any hour. She wished she could have met them and wondered if she would ever see dear little Rupert again.

Chapter 10
Thanksgiving – November 1860

When Laura returned to Cynthiana, she noticed a change in her mother, an alteration so delicate she could not define it at first. As her mother dashed out to greet her, Laura studied her unusual dress. She was wearing a white, low-cut linen gown with roll-backed sleeves that struck a flattering contrast to her tanned face and arms. She also wore jewels in her ears.

Laura could not help but stare as she realized there was a slight touch of rouge on her mother's cheeks, enough to enhance her lined, though still lovely face. Used to her matter-of-fact enthusiasm for most things, Delphia's skittish behavior over-rode Laura's immediate pleasure at being back at Longfield.

She had known from Delphia's last letter her mother had been helping out at the school and had expected to see a tired-looking woman who was glad to see her daughter, if only for her to take up the teaching burden once again.

"The headmaster is concerned your students are missing out on the curriculum," Delphia had written, *"so I've offered to take on the first year infants to ease the restructure of the teachers' schedules. He wants, above all, to ensure continuity within your class and to maintain your standards. It's all worked out very well so far, and I for one am enjoying the change."*

Laura continued to stare at her mother during the evening. Quite out of context of their current conversation, Delphia would begin to hum or sing at odd moments as her eyes danced. Even her voice had changed to a bubbly lightness Laura had never heard before. At one point during evening, Delphia rose to prepare a light supper. Laura could not believe her eyes when she noticed her mother's sedate walk had also changed as she positively skipped into the kitchen. She had heard of older folks suffering from softening of the brain, but surely her mother was too young. Worriedly, Laura followed her mother into the kitchen and watched as Delphia stood in the middle of the room, stretching her whole body in long, fluid movements, her face radiating the glow of a much younger woman.

That's the way Martha Alexander looked on her wedding day, Laura thought.

Then she froze, her mind in a whirl.

That's it. Mother's fallen in love, she thought, *but with whom? Oh dear, not with William. Like him as I do, I can't do with him as a stepfather. The folks around here would be appalled, and what would happen to Rory's estate?*

She was aghast at the realization that even if mother and William did not marry, everybody would soon become aware of their affair if mother persisted in this adolescent behavior.

The impropriety of it all, Laura thought.

She could hardly breathe in her distress

"Who's the lucky man, Mother?" she asked in a voice as natural as she could make it, though she knew it shook.

"Does it show that much, Laura?" Delphia replied, clasping her hands to her chest.

Laura simply nodded her answer.

"Who is he?" she repeated.

Delphia touched her arm and held on to it for a moment.

"You won't believe it," she said, "I don't suppose you'll even approve."

"Mother…" Laura said, her annoyance now apparent.

"While you were away I had to liaise with him quite often. Or rather, he liaised with me. The school means so much to him, and whenever he had a problem he would come to me because I was always about at the school, you see. Quite often the things he enquired about could so easily have been dealt with by the headmaster. But the more I saw of him, the more we both realized how much we had in common, and here we are now, in love with each other."

Delphia's gabbled speech and silly grin irked her daughter.

"Mother," Laura yelled. "Who are you talking about?"

"Walter Twigge," Delphia said. She laughed at Laura's surprise as she took her by the waist and jigged her round the kitchen. "Laura, don't look like that, be happy for me. We're going to be married."

That night over supper, they both admired the large solitaire that Delphia now wore, as did the staff when they noticed it. Walter had joined them for dinner, and Laura was encouraged to speak of her own adventures during the past weeks. Delphia was proud of her daughter's input during the health scares, but stunned when Laura told her how near she had been to having an adopted grandson. She admonished her daughter for what she considered sheer stupidity.

"How could you have cared for a young boy grieving for his parents? How could you support him when your whole life is taken up with supporting your students? Had you thought it through, Laura?"

"Yes, mother, I agree with you, it was a stupid, impulsive promise to him. I've realized that already and learned my lesson. Rupert's happy with his parents now, and for that I thank God, but I really do miss the little fella."

Before Delphia and Walter set the date for their wedding, they travelled to Virginia to discuss handing over the farm to the boys. Walter wanted Delphia to be a full-time wife in Lexington and not have the worries of the farm to consider. Both felt that handing the farm over at this point would save problems in future years.

"Don't worry," Walter had told them, "I shall provide for your mother and sister when I am gone to my Maker. All I want now is for you to have the farm and for my future wife to be worry free from now on."

Once that business had been settled to everyone's satisfaction, Delphia and Walter considered the date for their wedding.

"You know, Walter," Delphia had said, "Beulah and I discussed having a Thanksgiving social in November. Why don't we have the two events around that date and perhaps share the event while our family and friends are all together anyway. I don't really want a big fussy party just for us, do you?"

The idea was welcomed by Walter and the whole family.

Delphia and Beulah had considered this date realizing the joint celebrations would be a good family tonic following the turbulence of the presidential election. It had been Sarah Hale, the editor of Godey's monthly magazine for women, who had inspired them. As far back as 1846 Hale had begun a magazine campaign for the establishment of an annual national observance of Thanksgiving. Hale's preferred date was the last Thursday of November. She had even written to President Zachary Taylor in 1952, who had shrugged off her plea, as had his successors, Franklin Pierce and James Buchanan.

Beulah and Delphia were strong followers of Hale's notion, and decided to hold their event on Thursday November 22, 1860, 16 days following the presidential election. The wedding would be a couple of days earlier. They figured that the menfolk would have chewed over and dissected the election results and the character of the president-elect to a point where nothing more could be said. This would ensure, they hoped, a family reunion unsullied by too much politicking.

Beulah longed to see her widowed sister, Sarah Willoughby, who lived in Richmond, Virginia, an almost inaccessible journey, given how far away it was and how unkind the terrain was to travelers. They had had no physical contact since the death of Sarah's husband four years earlier. Although rail roads were being constructed, a viable route from Richmond to Lexington was not likely in the near future so Beulah sent an invitation to her sister in plenty of time to plan her journey to Kentucky. She did the same with Delphia's sons, who would also need time to plan in between growing tobacco, maintaining the piggery and vegetable growing.

Preparations began in September; Sarah and her maid/companion, Anne Featherstone, arrived at the beginning of October for a lengthy stay. The original list of 27 adults plus Delphia's seven grandchildren was reduced when the Parker family decided they could spare only one of their large brood, Delphia's widowed younger son, Vinnie. There had been overall disappointment when it was decided the grandchildren should not be deprived of their school time.

* * *

By this time the presidential election campaign had reached fever-pitch. There had been much discussion within the Kentucky newspapers, households and street corners on the division of the Democratic Party into northern and southern factions and the consequent formation of the Republican Party. The long speeches throughout the state by worthy men such as Stephen Douglas, John Breckinridge, Tennessee's John Bell and a scarcely known candidate from Illinois, Abraham Lincoln had been dissected word by word. Lincoln stood as the Republican candidate, but the fact that he and his wife had once lived in Kentucky engendered as much interest as there was for the Southern Democratic candidate, Breckinridge, whose family was 'old' Kentucky.

Surprise swept through many States when Abraham Lincoln won the popular vote with a 39.8 percent share, even though there had been little support for him from the South.

In the days that followed Lincoln's triumph, the Compton household was in a state of jitters, although no one was completely sure why. Kentucky, a slave 'border state' appeared in general to be neither for, nor against, current political disputes.

"You know my views," John Compton had said to his business friends down at the old clubhouse near his racing course. "I tend toward the preservation of the Union."

His unease grew as he listened to speculation that old Tom Barnby had sparked.

"I'm not sure about Lincoln. I think he's a man of integrity, but he's also a man of unestablished political acumen, and that could well undermine any thoughts of unity between the North and South. You have to have a president who can bring folks together, not push them apart out of sheer ignorance," Barnby had said.

While Barnby's remark had aroused doubts in the immediate aftermath of Lincoln's success, no Kentuckian really thought that the president-elect's victory would spark off further friction. Newspaper theorists discerned that while the slavery controversy was tangible, it was the southern disputes over state sovereignty that dominated many a rowdy public meeting. It was when news began to seep through of pending secessions in the south that a sense of imminent disaster emerged. People everywhere became restless, with tempers and tantrums flaring within hostelries, on the streets and within households.

The Compton kitchen was no exception. A row with the capacity to blight the Thanksgiving event boiled over. Everyone knew who had been invited. Mrs. Wilson, the Compton's black housekeeper, resented the fact that Jack and Frances Bellwood, had been invited as guests, as had Sarah Willoughby's companion, a rescued Richmond 'po'-white' orphan and, even worse, in Mrs. Wilson's opinion, so had Beth, "that blackie born with the chalk-white hide that brings shame on our own community."

There had always been an element of pretension among the servants of high-placed families such as the Comptons, and the talk downstairs was that the inclusion of those four guests was an affront.

"If they think I'm going to serve that mulato and the southern trash, or those bakers, they don't know nothing," was Mrs. Wilson's general appraisal.

John Compton was surprised at this attitude. "It's a scary time for slaves and servants, indeed for all of us, nowadays, and I understand that, but I treat all my servants with respect and will not allow prejudice in my house. These four people are proven family friends, and they shall remain as our guests. But what's the solution to all this fuss and feathers downstairs? It's a Thanksgiving family party not a rabble-rousing opportunity!"

It was Martha Bennett who solved the difficulty, during one of her visits to see Beulah.

"You could invite Mrs. Wilson to take tea with you and Beulah and accuse her of spoiling your surprise."

John and Beulah just stared at her.

She laughed at their startled expressions.

"You could suggest to her you would like staff to eat their Thanksgiving supper at the same hour we will be sitting down for ours. So long as they cook the food, set the tables and the dishes in the dining room, you can suggest we will serve ourselves, just as they will be serving themselves downstairs. Tell them in this way the staff will see that you are giving thanks to *them*, not only for the good food but for the folks who look after the household every day."

John spluttered and stuttered at the effrontery of the suggestion, but Beulah and Delphia were in full agreement. He soon realized that he had no alternative but to accept the enthusiasm of his wife and sister, as well as that of their good friend, Martha.

"I have a further suggestion," said Martha, delighted to have an opportunity to offer subtle thanks for everything her friends had bestowed upon her over the past years. "Let it be known that you will not require a cooked breakfast the following morning, as plans have been made for the bakery to supply your guests with baked goods mid-morning at my home. That way, everyone, including the staff, can have a few more hours in bed. Baskets of our best baked goods will be sent over for their own breakfast, so no cooking is required. You could suggest that you had already planned this additional 'morning' holiday but were leaving it as a surprise for them all."

John and Beulah Compton discussed their 'surprise' with a surly Mrs. Wilson, who had bustled into their drawing room later that afternoon with an air of trouble about her. She left with an air of importance, glowing with the knowledge she alone knew about the small holiday in store.

The incident did, however, unsettle John and Beulah, who wondered if this act of disrespect in their own household was a sign of things to come should Lincoln's presidency fail to improve the apparent undercurrent of ill will in the nation.

* * *

Delphia and Walter's wedding took place quietly at Longfield two days prior to the Thanksgiving event. It was an informal ceremony, attended only by the family and those who had travelled for the Thanksgiving celebration. Delphia and Walter stood together, his right hand resting gently on her shoulder, his face strong, firm and smiling. Delphia, an attractive blush spreading from her coiffured head to her neck, looked lovely as her jeweled dress winked and shone. Following the short ceremony, family photographs were taken by Oliver, who had become a celebrity for his portrait work. Everybody was moved by the couple's obvious happiness, both wearing grins that couldn't be contained. There was much embracing and plenty of 'ooh's, aah's,' and 'how you've grown, I wouldn't have recognized you' floating around as the wine flowed. Laura and Vinnie, their faces shining with happy tears, couldn't have been happier at their mother's choice of a step-father.

"More important than that," said Laura, "is her choice of a husband. Just look at her. She's ecstatic."

Rory, now a qualified physician, who had returned from his studies in France and would not have missed the event for anything, also shed discreet tears as he remembered how Delphia had supported him all those years ago.

The happy bursts of laughter and the many signs of affection within the group contributed to one of the best weddings John Compton had ever been to. He was pleased his sister had found such happiness and blubbed into the last of his many drinks before Rory escorted him to his own room to 'sleep it all off'.

The dawn of the Thanksgiving party flowered into a perfect morning. The staff jostled and bustled about, cleaning, cooking and setting tables with shining silver and crockery. Everything had to look wonderful for Mr. Compton, the only master they knew who had ever organized a servant's party. Mrs. Wilson elbowed her way around with a huge grin on her face for once, thanking God for the way of life they were honoring today. The younger house maids rushed to finish chores so they would have time to titivate their hair and best dress for their own evening event.

The 'serve-yourself' meal upstairs was a success and everyone enjoyed the informal novelty of the occasion as they walked around with loaded plates.

At first, the young men stuck together in a group; Timothy and Oliver Compton had been asked to 'look after' Vinnie, who had lost his wife in childbirth a year ago. Vinnie had been in Lexington for a week and it had been agreed with Delphia's other sons that he would stay for another two or three weeks. He had remained the diffident young man he'd been on arrival, with a tendency to spend much of his time with Aunt Sarah's maid, the shy Annie, a kindred spirit if ever there was one. While Timothy and Oliver found their cousin Vinnie agreeable, they were grateful for the company of the livelier Jack Bellwood in their group. The four young men were soon joined by Rory. He had told his listeners he would travel to Vienna for a further year of European medical experience in that city and also take his new wife, Marie-Louise Alazet.

Laura was watching the group and wondered at the sudden whoops and back slapping that had followed one of Rory's comments. She was too far away to hear what he'd said and wished she could join them but her sense of propriety, driven into her during her school years, prevented this. She would wait for an invitation to join them, or wait for Rory to come to her.

She sighed as she turned away to join Clarrie, who had been chatting with her brother Tom and his wife Florence, who were full of baby talk and domestic bliss. She remarked on this to Clarrie, who beamed across at them.

"Tom's happy doing what he's always wanted to do," Clarrie remarked.

They both smiled as Jack and Frances ambled over to them.

"You didn't tell us Rory was married," Jack blurted out.

"He says his wife's father made him leave her in Paris because he's heard about our political problems," Frances said, eager to get in her own words of the sudden news.

Their silence and shocked expressions made Jack realize he had made a blunder. He passed on to a story of how Beulah's sister had fed her dog, Basker, with too many sweet-meats, resulting in him vomiting over Dr. Wallace's shoes.

Laura heard little of how wicked Basker had been, as she tried to take in the other information that had been so casually given. Rory married! She caught sight of little Annie Featherstone in deep conversation with Vinnie and wandered over to them, setting up an over-bright, inane conversation about the behavior of dogs.

However all she really could take in was the happy face of her beloved Rory to her right. He glanced at her once, and catching her gaze had winked at her.

She had not returned his smile. She was bereft. Rory, the only man she thought she could ever love, of whom she dreamed day in and day out, could not be married, could he? Surely he would have told her. She had thought he had loved her too and that one day they would marry, as cousins often did. She had waited for him. Clarrie stared at her friend, taking stock of how hard this sudden slice of gossip had hit her. She understood Laura's misery.

Beth, Clarrie and Laura spent the rest of the evening together, each surprised that Rory had not told them his news but keen to catch up on other gossip. Laura and Beth were thrilled to hear that Doctor Wallace had appointed Clarrie as the head nurse in the new building he and his wife had built on the site where the Blowers' cottage had once stood.

"An unexpected inheritance made it possible for the doctor to purchase the land and build a clinic. It had long been their dream to provide medical assistance to the po'-whites for an affordable fee," Clarrie said.

She hugged Laura. "It was our work during the measles epidemic, and the initial control of a potential typhus outbreak that inspired them to think of me for the post," Clarrie had said, "plus all the general medical knowledge dear old Rory managed to get through to me."

At the mention of Rory, the trio became quiet for a while, until Clarrie spoke of how she had never dared dream of being in such a good job.

"When Dr. Wallace offered me the job, I jumped at the chance. Jack's administrative expertise has increased under the guidance of my step-father, and he was more than willing to accept my share of the bakery's work. Mother's pleased also, as she knows my heart is really with nursing," she told them.

Laura told them about a further development in the measles and typhus episode.

"You remember Roland Blowers, whose father had typhus?"

Clarrie nodded. "Shall I ever forget?" she exclaimed.

"Well, would you believe it, he applied for my teaching post when I was appointed as headmistress. There'd been quite a few applicants, one of them being a local girl whom I know well, and I'd already decided she would be ideal for the post, so I'd just skimmed through the other applications. I hadn't really noticed the name of Blowers or the Ohio address, but Walter pulled out his application and invited him to the interview, along with three others. To cut a long story short, he proved to be an excellent candidate.

"I'd never met him, so didn't recognize him at all at the interview and his name didn't ring any bells. It wasn't until he mentioned his son, Rupert, I realized who he was. What a quandary I was in, as I knew both of them were ideal. It just so happened Rory was at Longfield, settling some of his estate business before returning to Europe. I discussed the dilemma with him and Walter, and they both agreed the school could afford to employ both candidates, each having individual skills that would enhance the curriculum and future income."

Beth and Clarrie were not surprised when Laura also revealed it was Rory who had turned out to be the school's benefactor. He had invested the funds his father had set aside for the education of his two sisters and promised them to Walter Twigge should the need arise.

Laura explained that Roland Bowers had purchased a small home a couple of miles from Longfield from the proceeds of his father's land sale.

"So my original dream of young Rupert being near me came true. How's that for sheer coincidence," she said. "Roland's wife, Bonnie, has never really recovered from the train accident, and is quite frail. We've become friends and she told me of how Rupert had always talked of coming to Cynthiana to see me so that when they came across our advertisement, Roland decided to apply. Rupert attends the school, of course, and he's a bright boy. We are all looking forward to a good future for the little fella who survived typhus."

Clarrie and Beth were overwhelmed with Laura's story. For a while the disquiet created by Rory's marriage was forgotten.

Laura also told them that of her two proposals of marriage.

"The first one was from a local trader. I'm afraid I was rather cruel to the poor chap, but honestly, if you'd seen him…" She laughed at the memory.

"The second one was harder to turn down. I couldn't be cruel with him because it was from Oliver."

Taken aback at this incredible news, Beth and Clarrie listened to Laura's story about her cousin. He was now a well-known photographer in Washington, having been apprenticed to his idol, Andrew Gardner, for a while now. Oliver had made a name for himself with the artistry of his compositions and had concentrated on portraiture.

"He became tired of this," Laura said, "and began to take action pictures wherever he saw an unusual incident; a drunken man beating his wife in the street, a filthy woman and child weeping with hunger outside a store that refused them entry, cattle running amok and creating severe damage along the main street of a small community in Maine, and a man who had been hung in a tree to die."

"He showed me pictures of happy scenes as well as those of misery, most of which he sold to newspapers along with the story behind the picture. He said that editors snapped up his work and I'm not at all surprised. Some of the pictures are magnificent. My aunt and uncle are now, at last, proud of their talented son."

She stopped, giggling at the shocked faces of her friends.

"Oliver's a sensitive guy and as I'd not shown any desire to marry, I suppose he'd assumed I was the pious, sexless, school mistress type. He said it was legal for cousins to marry and if I married him, he would not expect anything from me once I had produced a child. An important part of his offer was his promised support of the school at all times. I couldn't, of course, accept the proposal, but he is my dear cousin and I do love him as such. I did remind him that he was one of the country's most eligible bachelors. All he would say was he was shy with most women and didn't get on with them. I didn't know what else to say, really, but he said he would probably stay a bachelor for the rest of his life, and would be happy to do so. He said he'll leave the procreation of his father's future heirs to his brother. He's another who seems to have an aversion to marriage. That's odd when you realize how happy his parents are together."

All Beth and Clarrie could do was stare at her in open surprise. Laura laughed again at their open mouths and furrowed brows.

"What happened to his old friend, Fred Hetherington?" ask Beth, who had fond memories of both Oliver and Fred helping her and Maya to read and write.

"Well, he did stay on at Lexington for a while when Oliver went to New York, but he left when he failed a second attempt to get a university place. Beulah thinks he went into his father's law practice on the outskirts of Nashua in New Hampshire. As far as I know, he's not now in touch with Oliver."

They went on to discuss Oliver's older brother, Timothy, who had successfully passed-out at West Point, and had seen service as a second lieutenant out west, under the famous Colonel William Harney. When she had sent her invitation to Timothy, Beulah had insisted that he should apply for leave to attend this important family event, though none of them expected him to turn up. When he arrived a few days earlier, his parents were overwhelmed and Oliver found himself busy taking family photographs to symbolize his brother's rare presence.

Timothy had been the star of the Thanksgiving evening as he regaled eager listeners with news of the 'other U.S. skirmish' and of how he had helped to scatter a large force of war-painted Cheyenne warriors.

His tale-telling ceased only because the large room had, on the stroke of midnight, filled with shy-looking maids, cleaners and washers-up, as well as the loftier servants, grooms, gardeners and assorted manuals. Among them were a small number of unknown young colored people, hired for the day and invited to the 'do' downstairs. All now stood around the room, bewildered, bashful, quiet, as the 'upstairs' crowd gazed at them dumbfounded.

A somewhat pompous John Compton, always a bit of a dramatist, took a step onto a low bench that had already been placed for him. He allowed his gaze to sweep around the room, finally settling on Beulah. He cleared his throat and began.

"This is an important day," he began, "and I am grateful to my wife and my sister for organizing this Thanksgiving evening." He stopped, astonished that he, the Master, was being interrupted by his listeners, albeit with loud cheers, whistles and clapping. He allowed the applause for half a minute, grinning down at his wife and sister as they blushed and smiled.

"Tonight is a celebration of the bounty provided by the good Lord, who gave us all health and the capacity to make things grow so that we can live and eat well. This bounty does not just arrive; it is the fruit of the labor of everyone who works on this plantation, whether it's the planting of the corn and vegetables, the harvesting, or the preparation for market. It's from the men who care for our horses – yes, *our* horses, yours and mine – for they provide the means by which we receive most of our revenue. I want everybody here in this room to know how I appreciate *all* the work done. For instance, I admire the two little girls I see scrubbing our front steps each morning, Fanny and Jennie."

He looked round the room and spying the blushing girls presented them with his most gracious smile. They blushed, and he knew that the servants would remember the incident, and imagine that if he knew the names of the lowest of the household hierarchy, he would also know who everybody else was.

Beulah, taken by surprise at her husband's words, looked around the group of eager listeners, and could swear she saw them all stand more upright, squaring their shoulders as if it were they who had earned the compliment. Henceforth, they would probably do anything for him, she thought, just as she did, really!

"Friends, let me tell you I notice more than you think, and every day I see nothing to complain about – I see your enthusiasm, your loyalty, your neatness, and your personal manners. In fact, I see YOU. I know each and every one of you and I hope that we will continue to be together for a long time to come."

He stopped for a few seconds. His tone and expression became more serious as he continued.

"Some of you are bonded, but you are as valued as much as anyone else in this house tonight. There is a system of bondage within our state, just as there is in many states throughout our Union, but I hope you will agree that everyone here, bonded or not, is treated with fairness and consideration. You always will be. My father endorsed the bondage system many years ago for economic reasons and I reckon that most of us have become used to the idea, but I am aware that a few plantation owners have abused the system. Fortunately, they are in a minority and to my knowledge, none are within our state. What I will say tonight is that none of you will ever be abused. If there is ever a man or woman among you who has cause for suffering because of your tasks here, I need to know, and if there is unfairness, it will be dealt with. I promise you that."

John stopped for a moment, aware from the facial expressions of his audience that he had made an impact.

"However," he said with a twinkle in his eye, "I should add a qualifier to my last comment that discipline over any misdeeds will continue, as I know you will all realize." The last sentence was said with a wide grin, which brought the same response from his listeners. He knew he had got the right message across.

"Ladies and gentlemen," he said, looking carefully around the servants, "my family wishes me to thank all of you for your hard work throughout the year. Special thanks to the housekeeper, cook and kitchen staff for providing such a wonderful feast for us, and I trust yours was as good as ours. We do not take you for granted, and thank you all for sharing this special occasion with us. There is a small gift for each of you as you leave – please accept this with mine and my wife's warmest regards and enjoy your extra free hours in the morning."

At a signal from Beulah, the family and guests stood and applauded the servants as they left the room, some faces flushed with pleasure, others awash with tears. Fanny and Jenny, staring in awe at the master as they passed him, were rewarded with another special grin. Knowing he had achieved his staff's future loyalty, something he felt he may need in the days ahead, John felt that if tonight's proceedings had created a precedent for future years, it was well worth it.

Delphia was by now aware that her son, Vinnie, a tall, hollow-eyed boy, with a pinched, pale face that could be handsome when he smiled, had not fitted well into the family. Everyone had known beforehand that his wife had died last year following the birth of their still-born son, and made allowances for that. He himself had never met his cousins before, though had heard of them, and had seen his Aunt Beulah and Uncle John only twice in his life. Indeed, he had met his step-father only twice. He was shy with everybody except his mother and sister and his diffidence was a barrier that no one had been able to jump over.

Under the care of his mother and sister however, he made some progress. He enjoyed days out with Laura, and her friends, Beth and Clarrie, who took him around the Compton Plantation, the bakery, down the river on a skiff, long walks through the wood when the winter weather allowed, and trips on the now well-used passenger rail lines. These new experiences, so different from his active, busy life on the Parker Farm back home were never-ending wonders. Gradually, Vinnie's appearance changed; gone was the hangdog expression, the good Compton looks were almost restored and his natural exuberance flickered. Delphia was exasperated with herself; they had all assumed that hard work and familiar surroundings would help the boy to overcome his tragedy and she now realized that an earlier holiday with her in Kentucky would have been more expedient.

The arrival of Beulah's sister, Sarah, and her companion, Annie, had also made a difference and Delphia would say later that fate had intervened. From Vinnie's first meeting with Annie, he appeared smitten with the quiet, pretty little thing. She also appeared to be equally infatuated with him. During the week that followed the party, this grew into deeper affection, then love.

Vinnie had been due to return to his home a week after Thanksgiving, but Delphia telegraphed her elder sons to say she wished him to stay longer, as their brother's health was improving, She thought this was partly due to the change of surroundings and his growing affection for his Kentucky relations. Oliver produced an amazing family photograph that showed Vinnie's improvement. She telegraphed it to the Parkers, with a note to say she and Walter would fund the cost of a hiring someone to take on Vinnie's share of the farm work for a few more weeks.

When Vinnie approached Sarah seeking permission to marry Annie, there was a general stir of disquiet. She and Beulah had not anticipated this. Who would look after Sarah when she returned to Richmond?

To everyone's surprise Beth offered to travel back with Sarah as her permanent companion. She had explained to Beulah that ever since the pre-Thanksgiving confrontation with Mrs. Wilson and the comments about her skin color, she had felt uncomfortable being there. The possibility of staying within the Compton family, through Beulah's sister, but moving away from her current discomfort, had given Beth the courage to make the offer. She and Sarah liked each other, and though she undoubtedly loved her current mistress, as well as her closest friends, her need for a change was apparent and understandable.

During her interview with John and Beulah, she was tearful but adamant, she wanted to leave Lexington. John felt it necessary to tell her how different life would be in Richmond, of the possibility the city may secede and become part of a Confederacy rather than the Union.

John and Beulah had discussed the proposal with Sarah, who was more than happy for Beth to take over from Annie. Sarah did not want to stand in the way of Annie's future happiness and was glad that the girl would be stepping into a fuller life with a partner she adored. She thought it would be wonderful to have Beth with her.

John felt it appropriate to remind Sarah of Beth's background to which Sarah responded that she was already aware of Beth's heritage, and would be the last person to unnecessarily disclose Beth's birth circumstances. Thanks to Beulah's and Rory's past intervention, as well as her friendship with Laura and Clarrie, Beth had matured into a well-spoken, educated and gracious woman. Sarah reassured them she would be introduced as a companion recommended by her very own dear sister.

She knew Beulah had already discussed the problems of a marriage with Beth, and that even her marriage to a white man could produce a colored child. Beth had informed both John and Beulah she was aware of this and it was the reason she had never considered marriage to anyone, irrespective of bloodline. She was, she told them, interested only in being a good companion to Sarah within a new environment, meeting new challenges and in due course finding a way of helping others. When John questioned her about what she might want to do, she was unable to say. She said if she was meant to do something, the Lord would ensure she knew about it.

When Beth's parents had been emancipated years ago, John had ensured their daughters were also freed from legal bondage. Her parents had been registered under the name of 'Compton' according to the tradition for slaves at that time, and had retained the name when John freed them. Beth now asked Sarah if her last name could be changed to Willoughby and both John and Sarah were happy to organize the legal change prior to the journey to Richmond.

Annie and Vinnie's quiet wedding took place in the plantation's chapel the week before Christmas; the Parker brothers and their wives had journeyed over for the event and to take the bride and groom back home with them. Oliver organized pictures of the occasion, some of which would travel back to Richmond for Sarah's friends to coo over.

Two days later Rory was due to return to Paris to meet up with his wife prior to travelling to Vienna in January. He had stayed longer than planned due to Vinnie's wedding and Beth's move to Richmond. On the final evening, he found Beth in the small garden laid down years ago in memory of her parents and sister, as he knew he would.

"It will be strange knowing you're not here in Lexington," he said to her, "but you're moving forward now. I would urge you not to look back, not to picture your life here as the only one there is. You're educated, intelligent and articulate, and have made of yourself a very able woman. I'm proud to be your friend."

Rory took her slim frame into his arms and hugged her as if he could never let her go. He looked down and stared at her face as if capturing every line and expression within his memory. Finally he suggested she should not waste any chances in life.

"Don't *take* any chances, though, if you have any doubts. You're a wonderful woman, Beth, and I couldn't feel more proud of you than I already do, but I have a hunch you'll further surpass your many achievements," he said, as he released her from his arms.

132

They looked into each other's eyes. Beth was never sure of what exactly happened next, as she found herself held against his chest, his arms wound around her, holding her with a ferocious intensity. She managed to twist free of his arms and lifted her own to fend him off, though somehow they came to rest on his shoulders and slid around his neck until her hands met at the back of his head.

He appeared to shudder slightly and she heard him groan before whispering her name.

As she opened her mouth to speak, his lips closed upon hers in a hungry, long, selfish kiss. He would not, could not release her from it. She felt his fingers trail along her spine. Her head began to spin as the sensation of sinking into him shook her, and she struggled to release herself from his grasp. He pulled her toward him. Her body seemed to melt as the indescribable sensation overtook her again. She experienced a wave of desire to belong to his body, be one with it. When at last he took his lips from hers, she whispered his name.

"Rory. You're my life."

She trembled within his arms as they clung together, each listening to the two heartbeats, oblivious to anything else. The world stood still as Rory filled Beth's heart, her mind, her whole being. She had never known such strong emotion before. Then the real world returned. What had seemed like an eternity of being locked together was less than a minute. Beth had realized she would have to go; if she stayed she would be unable to resist her longing for him.

"We cannot do this, Rory. I have to go."

He was taken aback, his passion unprepared for her reaction.

"No, don't leave me now, Beth. I need you."

"Let me go, Rory. I want to go. You're married now. You know we can never be together."

He knew he had no choice but to release her, though his longing was equal to hers.

"Dear Beth, you will be in my heart always. I have loved you for a long time," he moaned.

They were both in tears as they returned to the house, not knowing when or if they would ever see each other again. She realized if it were not for her ancestry, she would have been the one he would have chosen to travel to Europe with. She knew also, he did not realize she was so much in love with him that she could not bear the thought of ever meeting his French wife, which would be inevitable if she stayed in Kentucky.

Beth was excited as she and Sarah began their two-day journey, though sorry to leave her friends who came to wave them off. Laura and Clarrie had promised to accompany Beulah on future visits to Richmond and John promised that extra efforts would be made to see more of them in the future.

Life was going to be very different, thought Beth.

Chapter 11
Beth Moves to Richmond

Richmond was exciting, though Beth missed the open spaces of Kentucky. She was surprised at the limited space around Sarah's home. The long plot of land at the back of the tall three-storied house, with its paraded rows of various vegetables, was a replica of those on either side, as was the small square at the front, sprouting flower shoots that would soon bring color to the garden.

She enjoyed her new life and soon came to love the neat house and its cheerful chintzes and carpets, polished walnut furniture, the comfortable luxury of soft chairs set around the fire-side and the gentle swish of drapes as they moved in the breezes drifting through the long open windows. Her own room, adjacent to Sarah's on the mid-floor, was cozy and private and where she spent her spare time reading. Letters to Kentucky chronicled the daily events of Beth's new life, kept alive by her daily entries into the diary presented to her by Rory.

Beth was introduced to Richmond society as Sarah's companion who had once served her sister in a similar capacity. She soon proved to be indispensable. Sarah's friends were enchanted by the sudden romance of Annie, but welcomed this impressive, striking new companion with open friendliness tinged with curiosity.

Beth dressed herself in immaculate though plain clothes and maintained Sarah's more colorful outfits in pristine condition. She sewed new undergarments, learned new ways with hair-dressing and even dared to fashion her own hair into the current southern city styles. Her cultured Kentuckian accent, honed by her years in the Compton household, was pleasant to their ears, and visitors soon learned that this intelligent girl could hold her own in any conversation.

Sarah's friends, many even stouter than she, admired Beth's trim figure, and wondered how she could stay so slender in spite of the enormous dinners eaten within that household.

"What were your parents like? Do you have siblings? Do they mind your move to the South?"

Sarah tended to answer those early questions.

"Beth's younger sister died early, as did her parents. They died soon after her sister did, probably because of a broken heart. My sister Beulah was fond of the whole family and took Beth into her own when she was orphaned," she explained.

Noting her poise and obvious education, it was easy to accept the story, and gradually their curiosity dissipated.

Beth was accepted, for the first time ever, as a beautiful white girl, but she found it difficult to embrace this charade, and it afflicted her conscience from time to time. She was proud of the heritage she could not own, and had not bargained for the feeling of deprivation that overwhelmed her from time to time. However, Beth knew she must go along with it for Sarah's sake, as she attended dinner parties, afternoon teas, art galleries and theater visits. Her interest in the city's culture surprised her; she enjoyed the museums and art galleries, attended church services and undertook simple walks around the city with Sarah, who wallowed in the company of her talented, attractive companion.

That this peaceful pace of Richmond life would not last was clear even to the newcomer, as winter turned into a sunny though rainy springtime. Hostilities broke out among the 'yes' and 'no' factions of the city whenever secession was discussed. Tension abounded. Longstanding friendships were shattered by rowdy arguments about the future of their beloved Virginia.

Richmond had by now become the headquarters of the Confederation and the home of the newly appointed Confederate President, Jefferson Davis.

It was a time when innocent people were suspected or held responsible for political misconduct. Sarah's acquaintants, the quiet Van Lews who lived near the Saint John's Episcopal Church, were under suspicion for something or other, though Beth could not fathom why.

"It all adds to the excitement of my new world," Beth wrote to Laura and Clarrie.

Laura showed Beth's letters to her mother as well as to Beulah and John, who would shake their heads in a kind of sorrow at the news of the warlike belligerence within the southern states. Like most Virginians, many Kentuckians hoped that the state would not secede.

As the talk of possible war cantered on in Kentucky and other states, Beth's letters became less garrulous about the political restiveness of Richmond, at Sarah's request. The little she did write gave an impression of general unease throughout the city, though not enough to worry Beulah about the welfare of her sister. Beulah had already written to her sister and suggested she came to live with them in Lexington until the current situation resolved, but Sarah preferred to be in the home that she and her dear husband had built together and where her life's main memories were.

It had not taken Beth long to become aware that Sarah had a secret place where no one else was allowed. It was the tiny attic that had been her husband's hide-away. When she missed her husband most, Sarah would ask faithful old Tom, a former black slave who had been with her for many years, to pull down a hidden robust ladder that she would climb with expert steps to the tiny room. When she realized Beth had learned of this special place, she told her how she could almost smell her husband's presence there, and would sometimes light up and smoke his old pipe. In one of her letters to Kentucky, Beth described the habit of pipe-smoking among some of the gentlewomen in that community, which was supposed to be a secret though in reality it was a well-known habit. Laura's letter saying she must at all costs refrain from the practice, had caused Beth to chuckle, but also made her feel homesick for days. She missed those great friends of hers so much.

Beth longed to hear how their lives had changed, if at all. She wondered if she would ever see Rory again and how their friendship might change once he was back in Kentucky with his wife and child.

He had written to her from Vienna, and she read and re-read the letter two or three times a day the first week she had received it.

"Life is hectic for me, nowadays," he had written, *"because although I'm under training here, as I'm qualified in medicine I'm expected to carry out the same work as the regular doctors. I can cope easily with the general ailments, but I've been amazed at the problems many of the former soldiers have had following their time in wars over here in Europe. I pray to God our own country will not turn into war. Whoever claims to be the winner, the losers are the men on either side who are maimed, both bodily and mentally."*

"I've coped with my stint in the surgical wards, and am amazed at the strength of mind those men have in coping with their disabilities. Some have lost limbs, some their sight. I saw one man today who has lost both arms and one leg, though he was as cheerful

as ever, and has learned how to shuffle his rump from his bed to a chair. He loves the idea of being looked after by the cheerful nurses and he's one of the lucky ones, as both his wife and mother have accepted their new role in life as his carers. He just thanks God he still has his sight. How brave is that? Many with lesser physical disabilities have been rejected, their families unable to cope with what is, to them, a very different person. It's heart-breaking.

"I feel powerless when I see an undamaged body that's shaking without control, and know the damage is in the poor man's mind, resulting from the horrors he's seen and undergone. To me these men are worse off than those who have lost limbs and are the most likely to be rejected. There are a number of great fellow medics who are beginning to study this phenomenon and we all hope that treatment and medication develops within the near future to help these patients. I can't bear the thought that these men may spend the rest of their lives in the darkness of sheer horror and despair."

It was at this point that Beth broke down. She knew without doubt if her sister Maya had lived and had been disabled either physically or mentally following the attack on her, she would have devoted her life to caring for her.

Rory finished the letter with an apology which helped to uplift her morose mood.

"I am sorry for my behavior when I last saw you, dear Beth. I am aware of my blunder and I should not have inflicted it upon you, especially as you have your new life in front of you. I did not realize myself the full strength of my love for you until I held you that evening. Somehow, though, I remain selfish, as I can't fully regret my action. I feel glad that you know my true feelings for you, but If I have caused you pain as a result of my selfishness, I hope you will forgive me."

Beth had been relieved to receive the letter and hugged it to her, as the healing of her own confused mind began.

A second letter received a few weeks later contained news about the forthcoming birth of his first child.

"I am anxious that our child is born in Kentucky, as I want all our children to have U.S. citizenship," he had written to Beth. *"My father-in-law is proving difficult as he wants his first grandchild to be a citizen of France. He's a strong character and I don't want to*

be the cause of family friction, but he agreed to Marie-Louise marrying a foreigner, so he will have to take the consequences of that. She will be sailing to New York with some of my colleagues when she'll be just under seven months. She's due at the end of June. The journey is not as long nowadays as it used to be and she'll have the medics to keep an eye on her. I've arranged for William and Dr. Wallace to meet Marie-Louise and take her to Longfield. I've also suggested that her parents travel with them and even offered to pay their passage. I will not compromise and Monsieur Alazet will have to settle for that."

He told her the risk of a civil war was another factor in Monsieur Alazet's argument that his daughter should give birth in France. Beth wondered how Rory would overcome the problem, for she could see both sides of the predicament. She told him so in her reply, suggesting the child would in all likelihood be born long before there was any talk of war in America, if indeed it ever came to that.

"There may well be a skirmish or two down here," she had written, *"but it should soon be over."*

Beth spent the rest of that evening writing to her friends, taking care not to say anything about the rumors that were rampant in Richmond about an imminent attack from the North. She believed they were spread by the 'yes' faction in order to frighten folks into voting for their cause. She mused on this thought as she began writing her daily diary notes. When she finished, she sat for a while, hugging her diary to her, as she remembered the old days of four care-free friends sitting and laughing together on the river bank on a sunny Sunday afternoon in Kentucky. She also thought of her sister, Maya, and her tragic death all those years ago, and of her parents. While she could accept her mother's sudden death as a pure accident, she could never forget the mysterious circumstances in which Maya had died. One day, she would get to the bottom of that mystery, she promised herself for the thousandth time, as she pushed her neat writing box and pencils into a drawer.

It was quite late, and Beth realized how tired she was as she sank onto her bed, fully clothed, thankful she could now rest. She laid her head on the soft pillow and, not meaning to, fell asleep. She slept until a heavy knock on her door startled her. She did not know what the time was, but realized there may be a problem with Sarah. She hurried to the door to find a disheveled, shaken Sarah, her cheeks and neck flushed. She was wringing her hands, eyes large, round and afraid. Beth caught her as she almost collapsed into the room.

"Beth," Sarah cried, having gained her balance. She stood holding the wall, unable to say another word, her breathing distorted, the facial flush increased.

Beth wondered if Sarah was in the throes of a heart attack. She helped her to the one soft chair in her room, and began to massage the back of neck, a sure way of calming Sarah down. Within a minute Sarah was composed, her breathing back to normal. She turned to look at Beth, eyes tragic, tears rolling down her face.

"Beth, we are at war. The Confederates have shot at our flag. Fort Sumter has been attacked. One of Mrs. Van Lew's servants has just been to tell me the news. It happened a few hours ago. Oh, Sarah, what will happen to our lovely Richmond now?"

"What will happen to our wonderful country now?" Beth muttered.

She was distraught. She had not realized how hard this news would affect her. How could it be that people of one nation were prepared for deadly combat against each other, and for the destruction of a government 'of the people, by the people and for the people?' So many had fought and died for the creation of the Union decades earlier.

She remembered Rory's letter and the horrors created by the European wars. Her immediate thought was that she must help to stop this useless conflict. She fell to her knees, laid her head on Sarah's lap and wept. This time it was Sarah's turn to bring solace to her beloved companion. The thought of Rory's distress at this news was uppermost in Beth's mind, adding to her own grief, as she wondered what would happen to his family and his way of life now. She dreaded he would remain in Europe, but also realized it was the most sensible solution.

Chapter 12
The Civil War Begins

Kentucky remained neutral when secession of the Southern States began in December 1860, though citizens were aware of the 'yes' and 'no' agitators. The Compton family, along with many others, was not surprised that South Carolina had been the first to secede though were jolted when another five states within the southern 'cotton kingdom' followed a month later. The family was concerned as signs of military aggression became evident, knowing they could affect every state to the north and south. John feared for his sons, nephews, and business projects.

A few days prior to the Sumter attack, John had been with professional associates discussing how the government could avert a conflict. One conversation led to a discussion of how safe the Union's Fort Sumter was, situated as it was just off the Charleston Harbor in South Carolina.

"The Confederates will realize Sumter's a complication," John Compton had said to his colleagues. "The Fort is bound to be attacked and destroyed."

"Seems to me a fort attack is certain," the youngest, most cynical member of the group, Marvin Everet, retorted, "though it could take place at Pickens down in Florida, if not at Sumter. It could even be the fort based in Texas or on the banks of the Mississippi. Davis knows that just one shot fired at our flag, wherever it is, will create a serious confrontation."

The gloomiest member of the group, George Clarke, spoke up. "I've heard from my cousin, who's a senator," he drawled, sucking on his pipe, "that when Lincoln took office, one of the first things he heard was the shortage of arms and food supplies at Sumter. I can't understand the reason for Lincoln's delay in dispatching an expedition down south to support the fort."

"I'd gamble that William Seward played a part in the delay. Never did trust that fella," said another pipe-smoking codger, as he swigged back a mouthful of Kentucky whisky.

141

Ron Jennings, a new member of the club who leaned toward the 'no to secession' faction, stood up, red-faced and angry. "Well, whatever you might think, Seward is a fine secretary of state, a great guy to back up the president. I'm one of many who are uncertain about Abe Lincoln. I can't understand how a man who has served only one term in Congress, and is a lawyer in a minor law company, has become president. Thank heavens we have Seward around," he said.

A listless looking man, Robert Small, who tended not to join in political discussions, looked up as Jennings reclaimed his chair following the outburst.

"Seward's a selfish man who wants to be president. I don't trust him. Thinks he can run rings around Lincoln. The talk is he gave Lincoln flawed advice. I do know, any information Lincoln receives will be considered with careful thought and acted upon one way or another. Lincoln has a lot to learn, but he has a steely strength of will and he's clear in his role to hold the Union together. He believes it's his duty to do so."

Someone asked Small why he was so sure of Lincoln's personal integrity and Seward's lack of it.

"My son-in-law's a congressman, my nephew's a senator. They hear things others don't," Small responded, before swilling down his drink and walking away with hunched shoulders, as though he might have said too much.

* * *

When Lincoln at last agreed to send much needed supplies to Sumter, the South Carolina governor was alerted, who informed General Beauregard. A swarthy Creole, Beauregard was the commander of the Confederate military forces, and he had laughed out loud at this news.

"Fort Sumter is in Confederate territory and should be in Confederate hands," he commented to the Confederate secretary of war, L.P. Walker.

It was Walker who instructed two of Beauregard's staff to row across Charleston Harbor to the fort, carrying a white flag and a written demand to surrender arms. Major Robert Anderson received the document, but refused to acquiesce. Walker, who wished to avoid bloodshed, responded to the negative response by stating he would prefer an amicable surrender, but intimated there was no immediate rush to bombard Sumter. With no sign of an approaching supplies ship from the north, he felt sure Anderson would capitulate when the fort's dwindling rations ran out.

By now the Confederate President Davis had stepped in making it clear there would be no further delay. On April 12, a second communication was rowed over to Major Anderson who replied he may surrender in three days unless he had contradictory instructions from his government. The polite patience of the two Confederate aides ran out. One of them, Captain Stephen Lee, wrote out a second ultimatum based on verbal instructions he had already received in the event surrender was denied. Forty-eight courteous though decisive written words proclaimed the Confederates would open fire if Anderson did not surrender within an hour. The document was dated 12 April, 1861 with the time of handing it over to Anderson stated as 3.20 A.M. The Confederate aides were escorted from the Fort with notable courtesy and rowed back to shore. At 4.30 A.M., the first shot of the Civil War was fired.

Clarrie was one of the first in Lexington to hear how the war had begun thanks to a letter Jack Bellwood received from his brother, David Plowman, and had shown to her. Plowman, it appeared, was one of the nearest to witness the firing of that first 10-inch mortar. His letter implied that the noise emitted from the blast was akin to the 'sound of madness'.

"It brought every soldier in the harbor to his feet and every man, woman and child within the vicinity from their beds to their rooftop," he wrote, *"and none of us fully understood during those first few minutes that this was the beginning of war."*

Plowman's account suggested it had been a spectacular sight; one old man had said there had been 'nothing like it since Bunker Hill'. The bombardment lasted for many hours. Fires appeared almost everywhere within the fort, but though there were injuries, no one was killed. Plowman also wrote he had witnessed the refusal of Congressman Roger Atkinson Pryor to fire that first shot, after which Edmund Ruffin, a 67-year-old with long white hair was chosen to do so.

"I would have given anything, I had to have been in Ruffin's boots right then," he wrote to his brother.

Plowman's letter mocked Anderson's inability to put up a fight.

"Anderson was forced to surrender when he ran out of material to make powder bags to keep his guns working. He hadn't even realized that The Star of the West had attempted to enter Charleston harbor with full supplies and had been sent packing by warning shots from Confederate gunners. Why the coward didn't realize this, or retaliate against those shots toward an obvious federal ship, we'll never know."

He ended his letter with the hope his brother would accept his previous advice to enlist with a Confederate company to fight against the Unionists. Jack hated the mocking derision slung at the brave Anderson and made a decision. He knew then it would be with the Union forces if he was conscripted.

The shocked Washington White House half expected an assault, either from an internal coup or an assault from without. Within 24 hours of the Sumter defeat, Lincoln had summoned 75,000 militia volunteers and almost 93,000 men were provided to serve the traditional three-month militia term, a stopgap sufficient to hold Washington, Maryland and Fort Monroe. In spite of that, Harpers Ferry fell on 18 April, and much of the Union's most advanced arms-making machinery was dismantled and moved to Richmond.

Meanwhile, Lincoln declared a blockade of the Southern coasts and ports, having perceived the importance of the sea. He also called for a further 42,000 volunteers; 230,000 volunteered, all of whom were placed on the registers. The president had no qualms in disregarding the constitution as, without congressional authority, he spent millions of dollars on acquiring the Union's biggest army ever.

Throughout that spring and early summer, there were small skirmishes, though the public anticipated fighting would end with an almighty battle between the two factions. The first skirmish was on 10 May, when Union troops took arms from the Missouri state militia near St. Louis and Union troops occupied Alexandria in Virginia on 24 May.

Both sides were eager to destroy the other, intent on taking over the other's capital city. However, the Union army lacked a skilled fighting general. Irvin McDowell, who had served in Mexico, appeared to be their most experienced, though he had never commanded over 35,000 men. McDowell's lack of experience was apparent on 21 July, when the first big battle of the war took place at Bull Run, Manassas, not far from Washington. This ended with the disordered Union army in retreat. The Confederate General

Beauregard refused an order from President Davis to follow them, on the basis of food, transportation, arms and ammunition shortages as well as the acute tiredness of his troops. The first important battle of the war, which many had anticipated being the final one, ended in a stale-mate, with the loss of 2,400 men, but did prove that neither army was an easy target. It was now obvious this war would end later rather than sooner.

Sarah and Beth, along with many Richmond residents, were distressed when Virginia seceded to the Confederation in July, and were terrified to hear the Confederates were massing at the important Manassas Rail Junction.

The talk in Richmond and the surrounding area had stressed the Union would scuttle the enemy with ease at Manassas and march down into Richmond, taking control of the town and President Davis. Pillage and rape was expected. Beth had never believed the rumors of defilement of women or of the vandalism that would follow the Union army's entry into Richmond. Instead, long lines of Union prisoners were marched into the city, and placed into the Libby prison.

"The state has voted to secede, and though we can't agree with that decision, we have to be seen to accept it if we are to live here. We can only help the Union cause by being discreet about our loyalties and wait for an opportunity to do something about it," friends had whispered to Sarah.

* * *

Within two weeks of the Manassas outcome, Miss Elizabeth Van Lew visited Sarah with her friend Eliza, to request Beth's company at a small party of younger women. All of these women were intent on providing parcels of food and small comforts for delivery to the Libby prisoners. Elizabeth had sought permission to do this from the prison's governor, utilizing her persuasive powers of speech as well as a basket of home-made bread, ginger cake and buttermilk for his own use. She also suggested the parcels for the northern prisoners could assist him to make better use of his scarce financial resources. He had taken time to agree, but in due course parcels of home-knitted socks, caps, clean patched shirts and trousers, pairs of old boots and a few tattered old books were delivered to the Libby. Once a week cans of home-made soups and bread rolls were conveyed to the prison.

The governor established a policy of close scrutiny in the presence of Elizabeth or Eliza, when anything was delivered. A sense of trust prevailed, and Elizabeth was allowed to visit some of the imprisoned officers. Over time a hazy model of military information was developed, utilizing intelligence from existing prisoners and the continual daily flow of new prisoners. Elizabeth was responsible for monitoring the information and for masterminding its progress to the northern authorities. To enable this, she established a significant secret network of agents that included clerks working in the Confederate War and navy departments, as well as a personal friend who worked as a maid in the home of President Jefferson Davis. Beth, who had heard a little about this group, though not enough to realize who organized it, wondered how she could participate in this world of espionage.

Chapter 13
Laura's War Begins

Rupert Blowers, now a healthy looking youngster, raced to the seat under the larger of the oak trees in the school garden, where he knew Laura would be. He was clutching two letters. It was a warm, early April day as Laura rested, recovering from her morning with class Three. When Rupert reached the tree he handed the letters to her.

"There's one from your mother and the other's from Richmond," he said, full of his own importance.

"How do you know that?" Laura asked, with a grin.

"I recognized the handwriting," Rupert said, hoping she would open Delphia's letter so she could tell him the latest news.

"I miss seeing your ma."

"So do I, Rupert," Laura answered, "but with two of my brothers dashing off to join Lincoln's volunteers last year, what else could she do? My sisters-in-law have to do the men's work in the fields now, so Mother had no option but to go there to help out. At least she has Mr. Twigge with her."

She put the letters into her pocket so that she could savor them after the long school day.

"Do you think my father will allow me to volunteer?" asked Rupert.

"No, he will not," she replied a little too quickly for his liking.

Rupert shot her a look of surprise. It was not often she snapped at him.

She saw his hurt and ruffled his hair.

"For one thing, you're not old enough," she said, "and you've got your education to finish. That's going to be another four years at least. This skirmish will be over in another few months anyway."

She watched Rupert as he loped off, remembering the first time she had seen him all those years ago. He was taller now, his body taut and tanned. She smiled after him.

I really do love that boy, she thought, *and there's no way he's going away to fight.*

A few hours later she ripped open her mother's letter. She was standing near the long window in Longfield's quiet library. A minute later she collapsed onto the nearest chair, ashen-faced. The letter contained news of the death of her second brother, Brett, killed during the Fort Donelson battle. Lawrence, her elder brother had also been wounded in the battle for Fort Henry, and was now on his way home, minus his left leg. Brett had been one of the first to respond to President Lincoln's pleas for army volunteers, and Lawrence followed shortly afterward. Vinnie had remained with the farm at his mother's request, as she required at least one man to support the farm. Laura thought back to those battles in the early days of February, just over two months ago. She'd had no idea her brothers had been fighting there.

A maid, Polly, entered the library carrying Laura's tea and a small slice of her favorite cake.

"Miss Laura, are you ill? Oh, what is it?" she gasped, as she saw Laura's huddled figure on the chair. Her grey face appeared to have aged 20 years.

Laura sat up straight, her face expressionless, before dropping the letter she'd clutched in her right hand. She rushed out of the library and made for her own room. As Polly knocked on Laura's door a few minutes later, she listened to her heart-rending sobs. They were similar to those she had heard only last week at her aunt's home when news of her cousin's death in battle had arrived. Polly could not read but guessed the dropped letter had contained bad news. She returned to the library where Laura had dropped it, picked it up and dashed to William to tell him what she had just seen and heard. She handed the letter to him. After reading it, William instructed her to check again on Miss Laura in five minutes. Laura refused to let her in and told her to go away. Polly made a further two attempts, at five minute intervals, before returning to William.

When William knocked on Laura's door, accompanied by Polly, and called out her name, she opened it. Her face was so woebegone and ashen as she swayed at the door, both he and Polly thought she was about to faint. William caught her in his arms and between them he and Polly settled her down on her rumpled bed. Polly fetched a blanket to cover her, as William dried her tears with a wash-cloth found in a drawer. For a while he held his dear friend in his arms as he tried to hush her weeping. At last she stopped, and William pushed her back onto the pillows with such gentleness that reminded Polly of her own husband's loving manner.

"Just stay here with Miss Laura," he instructed Polly. "I'm just going to order warm soup and tea for her. I'll be back soon."

Despite her distress, Laura could see William's dilemma. He'd had to ask the maid to stay, while he did the fetching and carrying as it was impossible for him to remain alone in the bedroom with her. She decided to intervene.

"I'm alright now, William. I'll come down to the library and will tell you what has happened. I would like the soup, though. I'll be there in a few minutes," she said.

William nodded and as he left he heard Laura ask Polly to fetch her some hot water so she could wash her face.

Alone in the library, she found the letter from her mother which William had returned. She gave it to him to read. He did not tell her he had already seen it.

"I'm just unable to bear the thought that dear Brett, my precious brother, so full of joy and fun, with such love for his family, is now dead. I can't imagine the injuries he must have suffered. And now his dear body is buried in a mass grave alongside unknown men."

Large tears spilled again from her eyes.

He offered the small hand-towel he had brought with him, as she spoke of her torment and her fear that their burial may not have been blessed. She also spoke of her own intolerable misery at the thought of her mother's anguish and that of Brett's wife and children.

He took her in his arms and she laid her head against his shoulder, as she spoke of her distress for her elder brother's terrible injury and loss of a limb.

"It's just doubled the agony I'm feeling for darling Brett," she said, "and I just wonder how Lawrence is going to cope with such a disability."

"Even he can't anticipate what his reaction is going to be when he's back at the farm," said William. "I don't know Lawrence well, but he appeared to be a strong man of spirit and dedication on the one occasion I met him. He's your mother's son, and he'll overcome the disability, glad that he's alive to be with his family. It'll take time, but he'll be alright, just wait and see."

Polly, who was standing in the background waiting to serve Laura with her soup, thought that William's response hit just the right note, knowing how empty, trite words were unwelcome. She had learned that from her own aunt's heartbreak only last week.

Both she and William stayed with Laura as she tasted the soup, disappointed that she pushed it away after only a few sips. Laura began to talk of the stories her cousin Rory had told about some of his patients in Europe, former European soldiers who had suffered in their wars.

"I remember how Clarrie and I just listened awestruck as Rory described how he had treated those men. Their physical injuries had healed, but their minds were destroyed forever from what they had seen and suffered in battle."

She was silent for a while, her thoughts far from cohesive as she tried hard to think how she could help those soldiers who would return from the war with similar mental conditions. She could reach no conclusions, and she felt crazed with her own grief.

Her sobbing had now ceased, and she felt able to release poor Polly, who had remained standing for over an hour, ready to help her if required.

"I shall be alright now, Polly. Please don't worry about me. It was the sudden shock of it all. You may leave me now, and thank you for staying. I am grateful."

"Thank you, Miss Laura. I won't wish you 'good night' for I know you may not sleep well, but if you should need anything, you know there'll be someone downstairs who'll hear your bell."

She gave a quick curtsey and left, closing the door behind her.

She asked William to stay for a few more minutes and invited him to take a seat nearer to her. Before doing so he opened the library door wide. Laura knew it was his sense of etiquette and did not need to comment. She began to talk with him about the comparative peace of this Blue Grass locality of Kentucky following earlier attempts to draw the neutral state into the north/south conflict.

"You know, many folks I've spoken with have barely felt the physical impact of this war apart from the Confederate's capture of Columbus in the south west last September," she said, "but I'm beginning to hear more and more that neighbors are losing family and friends in battles. Only last week, Polly told me about her cousin's recent death, which has left the family in a dreadful state. She is so scared her husband may get killed."

They spoke of the Confederate's victory in the battle of Columbus on the Mississippi, undertaken despite the state's proclaimed neutrality and of how this had prompted the state's congress to call for war against the southern invaders.

"I really couldn't believe it when that happened," said Laura, "and how it's led to the formation of the Kentucky Confederate Government a couple of months later."

"I'm not sure how long that government will exist," said William, "but so far it's made little if any impact. Kentucky might well become a Confederate state in the future, though I don't think the majority of Kentuckians will want that. Our own elected state congress has not stood down, so we're not yet bound under the southern regime despite their victory in Columbia, as it hasn't been legally elected."

"I'd also come to that conclusion," Laura said, "but does Jefferson Davis and his generals understand that convention?"

William cracked his knuckles as he sought a response, while Laura tilted her head from side to side, as if weighing choices. They stared at each other, seeking mutual reassurance, and seeing none shrugged their shoulders in unison.

"Oh, if only the Union hadn't lost Columbus, we wouldn't have had the battles at Henry and Donelson and my brothers would still be safe," she said, as she attempted to stop further tears welling up.

"Yes," said William, "if only. It's inevitable, though, that the Confederates will make other attempts to gain full control of Kentucky, even though our own state government proclaimed neutrality. We live in an important strategic area, and the fact that our population is split between Confederate and Union sympathizers doesn't help. I fear that Kentucky may be in for further fighting."

"Yes, I've realized that myself," Laura said. "Did you know, William, there's been another serious impact on Kentucky traditions. My Uncle John has already sent all of his horses to safe places further east. I'm not sure just where, as he's keeping that to himself, and I don't blame him. He says they would otherwise be commandeered for army use, whichever side wins or claims them. I believe other horse farms have done the same."

"Yes, I've heard that, though it's supposed to be a secret. It's hard to disguise a large movement of well bred horses, and I'm glad your uncle and his neighbors had the foresight to move them while it was still safe to do so. If they aren't here, they can't be taken. That's been good planning."

"I do hope that my Brett hasn't died in vain," Laura said, as heavy sobbing again overtook her.

William was annoyed with himself that their talk of possible further conflict in Kentucky had caused her further distress. He wept with her, both at the futility of this war and the sight of Laura's distress and rang the hand-bell for a maid to help Laura to her room.

The following day, her grief still raw following a sleepless night, Laura wondered how she, a solitary schoolmistress, could help to alleviate all misery and suffering brought on by the conflict. She knew she owed it to the children to try, but a feeling of inadequacy overwhelmed her. She thought of how Rory would advise her, and longed to see him.

Laura knew her intense, emotional response to her personal loss would never leave her, though her natural tendencies allowed her to reach out tenderly to those families who had suffered similar trauma. She also realized some of the children who had been withdrawn from her school due to lack of family funds, were as much victims of the war as their fathers.

Laura did not read Beth's letter until a few days later. When she did, she realized the unrest gripping the Richmond populace. She noted Beth, who loved the social activities she shared with Sarah Willoughby, had shown no regret they had ceased, but had enthused over a 'special job' she was about to undertake, though gave no hint as to what it was.

That's just like Beth, Laura thought, *to keep me in suspense like this. She's saving it all up for when we meet.*

"There's a lot to be said for living in Richmond," Beth had written, *"though I have to say that the shortage of food is serious. Jefferson Davis calls for 'fast days' every so often. We're not bowing to his orders, so we do tend to fling that instruction aside and use the day as an excuse to gorge on what we have left in the pantry."*

Laura suspected that Beth had mentioned the food shortage to her in the hope that she would send a food parcel from Kentucky. She discussed the possibility with William who alerted Beulah in Lexington. No one knew if such parcels would reach their destination, but Laura was aware that efforts would be made. Aware that travel was difficult nowadays, she did not anticipate seeing her friend for months, but longed to see her and Clarrie again, almost as much as she yearned to speak with Rory. She needed the advice of her three friends most especially at this time, now she was experiencing the greatest pain she had ever borne. Knowing this was impossible, Laura set her mind on how she could help the war effort.

Within two weeks, she had established a branch of the Soldiers' Aid Society and reorganized the school curriculum to ensure sufficient time for making woolen scarves, ear muffs and head-covers for the soldiers. The sewing of buttons onto donated jackets and trousers was also a feature of their work. Some of the more articulate, older children were given the task of writing letters in their own words to serving soldiers, emphasizing the gratitude of all students for their services to the Union cause. Within that short time, she also became a representative of the local U.S. Sanitary Commission. She was aware, however, that these additions to her workload would not go far enough.

As the days passed, she yearned even more for Rory's wisdom as to how she could cope with her own perceived ineffectiveness as well as his thoughts on her evolving plans. She had not dared to discuss these with Aunt Beulah or Clarrie during a recent visit to Lexington, and was grateful in one sense that her mother was so far away. She knew for certain that Delphia would have attempted to dissuade her from her plans. In the absence of such support she turned to William, who listened with understanding as well as alarm.

However, Laura was obliged to write to her mother and step-father about the school. She wondered if and when they would receive her letter, as postal services had declined as had the possibility of transmitting telegraph messages.

"There's been an increase in the number of children being taken away from the school, as fees can't be paid while their fathers are away," she wrote. *"As a consequence our income has been affected. On top of that, the junior class teachers, Robson and Swires, have volunteered to serve Lincoln and will be leaving at the end of this term. Tillotson is thinking of doing the same, though he's in his early forties. It's hopeless trying to fill the vacancies. Roland Blowers also tried to register as a volunteer, but he's been declined due to the injuries he got in the rail accident years ago, which leaves just Roland, Audrey Singleton and me, unless Tillotson is turned down due to age. Audrey has recommended two of her friends who might help out"*

Laura's letter asked for advice about the possibility of closing the school. Her step-father's response was swift and delivered in person.

After completion of classes on Friday afternoons, it was Laura's general rule to discuss the next weeks' work and administrative issues with her staff, the head boy, head girl and two parent members of the board. The chairman of the school board and other officials did not attend these meetings, so it was something of a surprise when, two weeks prior to the end of term, Mr. Twigge arrived, together with two other board members. Their unexpected entrance created substantial unease, made obvious by the amount of shifting in chairs, heel-tapping by some, throat clearing or rigid posture. Everyone except Laura and Walter Twigge were frowning.

Mr. Tillotson spoke out of the corner of his mouth to Audrey Singleton without moving his head.

"Don't look so worried. Nothing's ever what it seems."

She looked at him with sudden hope.

"Do you think it's going to be alright?" she whispered.

"Not sure," he said, with a grin, "it could be even worse than we think."

He smiled as she glared at him.

Laura introduced Mr. Twigge and the official board members, and apologized for the absence of Dr. Rory Compton. Mr. Twigge rose and the listening audience tensed.

"We have a dilemma with the number of students leaving our school, but an even greater one is that created by staff leaving to join the army," he began. "However, my main quandary is that our headmistress, Miss Parker, has handed me her resignation in order to support the work of the Union. My personal hope is that this war will soon be over and that she will return to Cynthiana. However, Miss Parker has already indicated that she will not return to the school as headmistress."

He ignored the stunned faces of his listeners as he commented on the school's academic achievements during the year, as well as their work for the Soldiers Aid Society. He congratulated Mr. Robson and Mr. Swires, and commiserated with Mr. Blowers and Mr. Tillotson that they had not been accepted by the army.

"You may be disappointed," he said to the two men, "but your skills are needed here in Cynthiana. Without teachers of your caliber, the fate of our young people may well be in jeopardy."

His speech was interrupted by general applause and the grins of relieved staff. He waited, smiling, until it stopped.

"I have liaised with my fellow benefactor, Dr. Compton, who is unable to return from Europe until his hospital contract expires later this year. He agrees with me that the school can remain financially viable, and he has donated a substantial sum to the school that will match my own contribution."

There were more whoops of relief.

"As Miss Parker's resignation will come into effect at the end of this term, we have had to move quickly to ensure the continuity and stability of our school," Walter said.

Complete silence followed as reality set in and the urgency of the situation registered. Shocked faces spoke volumes as they glanced at Laura. Audrey Singleton did her best to hold back her tears, without success.

Walter waited for a moment. With a lowered head he tightened his lips and swallowed hard, unable for a moment to hide his own disappointment that his step-daughter had decided to leave the school. In a quieter voice, though smiling, he spoke again.

"I am sorry Miss Parker is leaving us, but I'm very happy to announce that earlier today, Roland Blowers accepted the board's offer to become our headmaster from the next term. Mr. Tillotson has accepted the post of deputy head. These offers have been made after careful consideration and the board is confident that our decision will be in the best interest of this school."

It took a few seconds for the unexpected news to be absorbed before the startled meeting agreed with enthusiasm. Roland Blowers rose to thank the board for their confidence in him.

"I never dreamed that I could ever be a headmaster," he said, "and I know I have a hard task ahead of me to maintain Miss Parker's standards of care. I have known her for quite a while now, and all I can say is that she is a wonderful woman. I don't know what path she'll be following after she leaves us, but whatever it is, she will bring competence, joy and love to her new project. She will be taking with her all our love and respect. The pleasure and privilege of knowing and working alongside her will be forever in our hearts here in Cynthiana."

During the long applause no one appeared to notice Audrey Singleton swipe at Mr. Tillotson with her rolled-up meeting papers. At least, no one seemed to except Laura. She couldn't hear what Audrey had said to him, though she watched him laugh and pull her to him. She didn't seem to mind.

Mmm, thought Laura, *at last he's had the courage to let her know how he feels. It'll work out for them, so at least some good has come out of all this.*

She sighed again and thought of Rory though this time it was not with longing but with exultation he had, once again, secured the future of the school.

Now that her beloved school was safe, Laura commenced the finalization of her own plans, which she kept to herself, confiding only in William. But for the first time since the death of her brother, Laura now looked forward to the future.

Chapter 14
Beth's Secret

Sarah's household was aware of the current unease in Richmond, where talk of war was paramount, as was the low food supplies available within the city. Some blamed this on Lincoln's naval blockade tactics, while others thought it was due to the poor rail links in the South. The declaration of 'fasting days' by Jefferson Davis had proved unpopular, and public opinion was that the fresh supplies were being hived off to his soldiers. There was a significant rise of anxiety, gloom and lack of trust among the city residents who resented the presence of the grey-uniformed soldiers within their society.

As Sarah Willoughby pondered on this, she was startled though not altogether surprised, when Beth announced Miss Elizabeth Van Lew had called without the usual courtesy of advance notice. Sarah assumed this might be in connection with the current food situation within the city.

"I wish to discuss a private matter with you," Elizabeth said without any preliminary discussion, on entering Sarah's neat, warm drawing room. She dismissed Beth with a curt nod toward the door.

"Beth is my companion. You can say anything in front of her," Sarah retorted, her right hand signaling to Beth that she should stay.

"I do understand that, Mrs. Willoughby, but I must insist that only you hear what I have to say."

As irritated as she was with her visitor's attitude, Sarah's curiosity was aroused. She nodded to Beth in silent agreement, though her mouth twisted in annoyance. To show her displeasure, she shrugged her shoulders and sat down without inviting her visitor to do so. She stared out at the summer colors of her garden in an attempt to recover her poise. As Beth left the room, Sarah turned and glowered at her still upright guest, before inviting her to sit. Elizabeth did so, not in the least unnerved at the obvious snub, though she was surprised. Although she did not know Sarah very well, she was aware of her reputation as a polite and charming hostess.

"I did not appreciate your discourtesy to my companion, Miss Van Lew," Sarah said with quiet emphasis, though her voice trembled as she strove to control her pique

"Do call me Elizabeth, please. I didn't intend to be so rude, but you see, I have come to speak to you about Beth," Elizabeth said. "I believe she's one of us, a Union supporter."

Her words were simple, but Sarah could not have been more stunned. She stared at Elizabeth for a few seconds.

"What are the views of my companion to do with you or anyone else, Elizabeth?" Sarah asked, repelled by the political implication

"I need some support in an important matter," said Elizabeth, "and your companion is the most likely person I know who could help. However, we must be assured of her loyalty to the Union cause and her personal integrity."

"We? Who are 'we'?" Sarah asked, her belligerence emphasizing her continued annoyance.

"One of the main reasons why I think your companion may be able to help the Union cause in Richmond is her relationship with you," Elizabeth said, ignoring the question. "I'm aware of your loyalty to the cause. I wish to confide in you, though I trust you not to divulge anything that I am going to say. Can I rely on you?"

Sarah was intrigued. "I am loyal to the Union, of course, and I assure you that anything you say to me will not go any further."

Elizabeth informed a surprised Sarah of a Union spy network within Richmond, led by her and her mother. Sarah was aware that the Van Lews were allowed by the governor of Libby Prison to carry supplies of home-made food and old clothing to the imprisoned Union soldiers but was amazed to learn of Elizabeth's espionage activities. As she listened, Sarah's senses were excited and she even felt jealous. She wished she could be part of the spy team. Neither names nor actual activities were mentioned, but Elizabeth emphasized the success of their operations during the past few months. Not all of her supporters lived within the city boundaries, she said, and she spoke of one in particular.

"I'll call him Peter though that's not his real name. He lives a quiet life outside the city, deep in the countryside. I can't say where, for your sake as well as his. The less you know, the easier it will be for you to continue your usual way of life."

Sarah nodded eager to hear about Peter.

"It's crucial that any military or political information I send to Washington or to the military generals is accurate and timely. Any miscalculation could be devastating and there's always the danger of infiltration. We need to remain vigilant at all times. For some time now two of our agents have delivered valuable and vital details to the Union army using a unique scheme established by Peter," Elizabeth said.

Sarah gaped as the incredible story unfolded of how Peter's dog, Tramp, became the hero of the fantastic episode Elizabeth now related to her.

"Earlier this year, Peter's terrier dog vanished. The family and house staff searched high and low, inside and outside, for most of the afternoon. They couldn't find him. The next morning, some of his staff, whose rooms were situated above the cellar, reported barking and distressed howls during the night which ceased just before day break. Although the cellar had been searched the day before, a new search began in that vicinity. Either the din of the search or the sound of Peter's voice aroused the dog because the howling began again. Within a few minutes, they realized that Tramp was behind the wall of the cellar, though no one could locate an exit or ingress. They had no option but to break down that part of the wall in the vicinity of the barking before the filthy little dog leapt out, straight into Peter's arms.

"You can imagine everybody's relief, and all understood when Peter ushered them out of the cellar saying that he wanted to calm Tramp down. He said this was best done alone, though the truth was that he'd realized there was a man-made cave or a tunnel behind the wall and he wanted to investigate it."

Elizabeth smiled at Sarah's gasp of surprise. "He calmed Tramp down and returned him upstairs, forbidding anyone to venture into the cellar until repairs had been carried out."

Elizabeth explained that Peter and his handyman, Amos, returned to the cellar later that morning. Their candles created bizarre shadows on the walls as they accessed the open space which was about six feet high and square.

"To use Peter's words it was eerie and the cavity stank of damp earth, wet stone and vermin. He said the walls were rough and clammy, littered with spiders and their webs. There was no detritus on the irregular ground except rodent bones and a few rotting vermin corpses, as well as the scratchings made by dear old Tramp."

"Peter also told me how he was knocked almost unconscious by a sudden blow to his forehead as they moved forward, resulting in blood pouring down his face. Poor Peter had dropped his candle, but Amos used his as he returned his steps on hearing the thud and Peter's shout of pain. It wasn't until then that they realized they were now at the entrance to a tunnel, about five feet high, though Peter had not realized this until his head crashed into the top of the tunnel's entryway. Due to his height of around six feet, Peter was unable to proceed unless he crawled, which at that stage he wasn't prepared to do. Amos, being short in stature with a thin body frame, decided he could go on while Peter remained in the cellar waiting for his return."

"Amos followed the tunnel, using his left hand to hold his candle, and the other to touch the rough wall as a navigation guide. He often stumbled as his candle shook, but after five or six minutes he noticed fresher air, and felt rocks and tree roots underfoot. Outdoor light penetrated the end of the tunnel and you can imagine how relieved he was. When he climbed outside he saw that dust, dirt and broken spider webs had settled on his clothes, arms, hands and boots. He told me much later that when a rat jumped onto his shoulder just as he emerged from the tunnel, he was terrified for a second or two, and let out a great squawk. Who could blame him? Amos said the rat scampered off, more frightened than he was."

"He managed to clamber through an enormous barrier of brambles and thick bushes. From the outside, he realized the tunnel exit was about a quarter-mile to the right of Peter's garden, and invisible to any by-passer thanks to the thickness of the vegetation and a large oak tree standing by it. It was now obvious how Tramp, always fond of burrowing, had gained entrance to the tunnel in the first place. We've concluded that once inside the tunnel, poor Tramp became disoriented in the darkness and when he found himself in the larger chamber he stayed there, howling to be rescued."

"It's a wonder that no other animal had discovered the tunnel earlier," Sarah commented, "but then, I suppose there could have been some that did, but managed to get out of it."

"Well, that's as maybe," Elizabeth said, "but it was a lucky chance for our cause we were alerted to it by dear old Tramp."

Elizabeth picked up her now lukewarm cup of chamomile tea, and sipped it as she watched Sarah mop her brow.

Sarah took up her own cup and drank in nervous noisy gulps before ringing for a further supply. She emphasized to the maid that it should be piping hot and accompanied by a few sweetmeats.

"Could you ask that Beth brings it in 15 minutes and be ready to stay with us?" Elizabeth asked. Sarah nodded her agreement to the maid, eager for Elizabeth to continue her story.

"Well, when Amos got back to the large chamber where Peter was waiting, he was quite out of breath," Elizabeth said. "It was then they had a further slice of luck. I believe Amos leaned on what they had thought was part of the wall so that he could recover. As he did so, it moved. They realized it was a rock and behind it they found men's clothing in an old sack. It was old and filthy, but dry. Peter found a fragile drawing in the pants pocket requiring delicate handling, though it's in reasonable condition given its age. The drawing appeared to be of a tunnel at the end of which was a large tree. Another document included a number of extraordinary drawings, with written descriptions of what each one represented."

Elizabeth coughed and blew her nose. She stared out of the window for a while as Sarah sat in suspense, waiting for her to continue and trying not to show her impatience.

Eventually Elizabeth continued her narrative.

"Peter and Amos undertook another voyage of discovery the next day. Poor Peter had to crawl through the tunnel which turned out to be an ordeal for him because the confined space was hardly wide enough for his body. He realized he wouldn't be able to undertake the journey very often. It didn't take long to confirm the oak tree Amos had noticed was the one referred to in the document.

"With the help of those flimsy diagrams, it took just over a week to locate a small cavity that had been hewn out at the side of the trunk, probably during the Revolution period," Elizabeth said. "The carpenter had also made a small door for access. According to the diagram, this hideaway had been sculpted by a clever carpenter who had somehow made it invisible within the rough contours of the tree. His artistry was so good that it was impossible for others to detect the well-concealed opening."

Sarah frowned, unable to envisage the whole contraption.

"How did they discover how to open the door?" she asked.

"They had checked the drawings and discovered an inconspicuous pressure point that unlatched the door," Elizabeth said. "I know it sounds incredible, but it really does work, though I believe they had to use beeswax to free the workings. When they managed to open up the cavity, they found a wooden, tin-lined box. Further scrutiny of the drawings showed a similar cavity at the back of the tree trunk facing toward the tunnel entrance, which gives access to the same box."

Sarah was staggered at the revelations and unable to comment. Tilting her head to one side, she pursed her lips and stared into her garden. She blew out her cheeks as she ran a hand through her hair. She wondered if she was dreaming. She turned to Elizabeth with a frown, gathering her thoughts.

"It's almost too incredulous to accept," she said in a tremulous voice. "That carpenter must have been a genius. I wonder how long it took him to do it. She shook her head, squashing her eyebrows together, "Are you sure of all this?" she asked.

Elizabeth nodded.

"What I can't understand is how Peter managed to locate the cavities in the tree trunk? Surely the surface, even the color of the bark, would have changed over all those years, what with weather, climbing rodents, even other creatures."

"Remember, they did have the benefit of the drawings," Elizabeth said, "and it might not have taken so long if they'd been careless of being seen at the oak tree too often. It's not a regular walking or horse-riding route, you see, but discretion was essential, as you can imagine. So they agreed to spend only about an hour a day there, even though there was little chance of being noticed."

She smiled at Sarah's astonished expression.

"Spying is a dangerous activity, and we must be so careful at all times," Elizabeth said. "During the Revolutionary War, our army officers were able to utilize some of the skills gleaned from the Europeans, who were competent plotters. Also, our own George Washington was a competent spymaster during that war. Both Washington and his generals left scripts about their experiences, from which we have learned, though apart from that, we had to more or less start over again. You see, when the United States settled down, the art of spying declined as there was no further need for it. Not until now."

"Yes, I can see that, though I thought that part of the role of our overseas ambassadors is to keep their eyes and ears open for news of value," said Sarah.

She knew that from her late husband's cousin, who had served somewhere in Europe. "That's spying, isn't it?"

"Yes, to a certain point," Elizabeth said, "but war-time espionage and spying is a different thing, especially now. We're fighting to retain the Union our ancestors gave their lives for. As citizens, we can only do so much to help the military achieve their objectives by presenting them with up-to-date intelligence about the enemy. However, we first have to obtain it and that's where the true art of spying is important.

"Our Richmond team is small but essential, living as we are in the Confederate's capital, and working well, but there have been past problems created through careless planning and talk. We have to prevent recurrence. That's one of my team's main priorities, and always uppermost in our minds.

"I can't divulge too much, of course, but there is evidence that Jefferson Davis has used intelligence gained through espionage to achieve some of their success. We suspect some of this information was gained through careless indiscretions of Union agents. President Davis has a clever team, and we must be clever enough to overcome them."

Elizabeth stopped to blow her nose and once more stared out into the peaceful garden.

"I can tell you now that Peter has established a new plan, utilizing the tunnel. The previous plan worked well, but we were always anxious Peter could be followed when he set off to issue a courier with instructions, even though we had no evidence of that happening. It was for that reason, we decided to change the couriers anyway, for their sake as well as Peter's, a tactic we learned from a European agent."

"How sure are you of choosing the right people? Are they always men?" Sarah asked.

"Sarah, that's a good question," grinned Elizabeth, pleased at her insight. "And yes, we do have female spies. I'm not a man, am I? We also have to be so careful in our selection. For one thing, we need to ensure the safety of our agents isn't jeopardized, either by their own careless talk or that of family and friends. For Peter's new plan, we needed to appoint two couriers who live alone, with no wife or family to worry and wonder why they needed to leave at short notice every so often.

"It was a difficult task but eventually Peter discovered two such men; one is a childless widower who jumped at the chance of being useful. He presented as a man of means, and doesn't have a job. The other is a reticent younger man, who ran away from home a couple of years earlier. He rents a small cabin and carries out odd jobs for smallholders around his district. Apparently, he earns sufficient to sustain his health and cleanliness. He doesn't appear to want much from life, except the end of this skirmish between the North and the South, and a need for recognition of sorts. I've been assured they are discreet, articulate men, able to read and write and passionate supporters of our cause. What's more, they passed the rigorous testing of our interviewers," she said, ending with a laugh.

Sarah had noticed that Elizabeth laughed a lot.

"We reassigned the original couriers and appointed the chosen two. Neither is aware that the other exists. It's not likely they will come across each other because of their differing social backgrounds and also because they live in opposite directions from Peter's vicinity."

"How do you alert Peter that you have information and how do you get it to him?" asked the wide-eyed Sarah.

"I send a basket to Peter's wife with a home-baked cake, together with the latest copy of Godey's Lady's Book. Within the book I pencil in a code giving Peter the date and time when we require a courier to be available. My mother sometimes sends a chatty letter to Peter's mother, the sort of thing elderly ladies say to each other, just in case a curious busybody looks inside. Sometimes, for the same reason, I send the mixing instructions for the cake if it's a new flavor.

"Hidden underneath the lining of the basket is another thicker lining, a sort of pocket that covers the full base of the basket. I sew the sealed document intended for the military into that pocket, and the whole thing is lifted out, ready for delivery to the military. It's undetectable in the basket, because the top lining is sewn in on top of it, and looks permanent. When the basket is returned to me, I sometimes need to replace the linings, but I have a large roll of the fabric for that purpose."

Elizabeth told Sarah of how prior to the new system, Peter would leave a coded note at the house of the chosen courier, arranging to meet for the hand-over of the package.

"I can understand how that system would be impracticable if Peter was ever followed," Sarah said, though she remained amazed at the care and thought that had gone into the planning. Her attitude toward the imperious Elizabeth thawed. No wonder she had insisted on confidentiality, she mused. She smiled at Elizabeth, full of admiration for the remarkable woman.

"How has your new plan improved the system?" Sarah asked.

"I can't say more about our new scheme right now. I wish to request your permission to approach Beth to help us to identify what could be a flaw in the new plan."

Sarah was taken aback. "How can my Beth help?"

"I've already intimated that we have to be very careful about newcomers to Richmond, and I hope you will forgive me when I say that your companion has been observed over the past few months," Elizabeth said, once again ignoring the question.

She put up a hand to stem the anxiety she knew Sarah was about to release.

"I have to say that your choice of companion is excellent, not just because Beth is a Union supporter, but because her demeanor, discretion and intelligence are beyond reproach. She's an ideal companion for someone like you, and I commend you on your choice."

The diplomat in Elizabeth knew well enough that her comments would please Sarah who was gratified at the praise.

"You have my permission to discuss any proposal with Beth, so long as there's no danger to her, but if she has any objection, I will not try to change her mind. It will be Beth's decision. I also reserve the right not to release her if I think she could come to any harm," Sarah said.

Elizabeth inclined her head in agreement.

When Beth returned, bringing with her a tray of chamomile tea and a few broken sweetmeats salvaged from the cook's depleted larder, she was apprised of Sarah and Elizabeth's discussion. As she listened, she sat straight as a rod, shoulders pressed hard against the chair back. From time to time, she smoothed down her dress, nodding sometimes, though hardly daring to breathe in case she distracted Elizabeth. She forgot to pour out the tea and as her excitement intensified, she felt her chest tighten and heard her own fast-beating heart.

When Elizabeth completed her oration, she asked Beth if she had understood what she had been told.

Beth nodded. "It's obvious," she said, "that your new plan involves the courier picking up through the cavity in the tree. I see, this would remove the need for Peter to deliver the package to the courier, which could have put both of them in some danger. The other advantage is that no one other than Peter is aware of how the document is delivered for eventual collection by the courier."

She frowned a little as a thought struck her. *The couriers would have required instruction on how to access the side cavity though, wouldn't they? Who instructed them?*

She noticed Elizabeth's face had become stern and introvert.

"It was Peter who showed them how the door is opened. He used a facial disguise and a western accent to prevent future recognition."

Elizabeth's deepening frown suggested she was troubled. When she spoke again her voice was slow and deliberate.

"Two other people know who delivers the package besides me – Peter and Amos." Elizabeth looked at her two listeners for a few seconds. "It's Amos who delivers the package into the back cavity."

Beth was astonished at the revelation. "Why?" she asked. "That's a potential risk to him as well as our cause, isn't it?"

"Peter is the obvious choice for delivery, but his stature and large body frame makes it difficult to crawl through the tunnel, "Elizabeth said. "There's also his fear of confinement in a small space to contend with."

She shuddered.

"I can understand that fear. Amos knows the tunnel well by now, and understands how to access the back cavity, so he's the logical choice to take Peter's place. He doesn't know what the package contains. According to Peter, he just does what he's told to do. He's not educated and can't read or write. The main thing is that he isn't inclined to go against Peter, who is confident he can trust Amos."

"What about the danger to Amos? Is he aware of this?" asked Sarah

"No one else knows how the package is delivered to the collection point, so he's not in personal danger," responded Elizabeth.

"The plan appears perfect," Beth said, though her disappointment that Amos was involved had been evident. She summed up what she had understood from Elizabeth. "We can assume that the couriers are unknown to anyone except Peter and those who interviewed them for the job. As you said, Peter doesn't even know where they live, but that doesn't matter as he won't need to deliver the package to them anymore. Amos will never be seen delivering the package so he'll remain anonymous. There's just one more thing, though. The courier would need a horse to make a quick getaway with the package. Where does he conceal his horse? He can't leave it in the vicinity of the tree as it would attract attention."

Elizabeth looked hard at Beth, more impressed than ever with her quick, logical thinking.

"You're a very perceptive young woman," she said, smiling. "Yes, you're right. If he approached the tree on horse-back and dismounted to retrieve the document, it would look odd to any by-passer, never mind an undercover agent. And if he hid his horse while he walked to the oak, the horse could whinny in disapproval, as they do, and that could also alert a possible enemy agent. It's for that reason we have instructed the couriers to leave their horse at Johnson's Point a quarter of a mile away and walk up to the oak."

"Who chooses the courier for a particular job? Do they do it in turns?" Beth asked, encouraged by the compliment.

"I choose which courier to use," said Elizabeth. "Nowadays, either I or a close friend of mine informs the couriers. Both of us are adept at dressing up as poor women selling matches and potatoes, and we often glean information through this. The sight of one or the other of us in one of our guises is commonplace nowadays, and causes no particular comment if we approach homes to sell our wares. We can easily plan a route that makes it easy to drop a coded note through a particular door."

Beth was ready to ask a further question but Elizabeth put up a restraining hand.

"Just so you know," she said with a playful wink, "the main reason why my very trusted friend participates is that she's a different stature and girth to me. It's useful to put more than one character out there, because if the same one was noticed to do this on a regular basis at the same door, it may well create unwelcome attention. We both have three different disguises we can use."

"You've thought of everything," said Sarah, beguiled by the conversation.

"You certainly have," agreed Beth, "but how certain are you that your own home is not observed? If an old seller woman is seen leaving your house, won't that create suspicion?"

Elizabeth grinned, "My dear Beth, you really are into our way of thinking. We tend to use a dilapidated old barn at the back of my home which isn't visible except from one small side window of my room. It has a back door and we enter and leave by that means through one of the fields round the back of the house. One of us will dress in the appropriate garb in the barn and leave while the staff are having their morning break."

Beth nodded her satisfaction at the answers.

Elizabeth poured herself a cup of tea, not wanting it to become cold. She had noticed how Beth's disposition had changed from one of mocking incredibility to curiosity, as lips parted, her upright, taut body tilted toward her, eyes glowing with an unexpected brightness.

Sarah poured tea for herself and Beth, and offered the sweetmeats. The three women finished their tea before Elizabeth spoke again.

"By the way, we arrange a specific pick-up time from the tree cavity, because we know the approximate time it takes for the courier to walk back to Johnson's Point to pick up the horse and ride from there to the army venue. Both couriers are aware that if their arrival at a military base is outside the anticipated time, we would soon become aware and start asking questions. The implementation of this strict timetable enables us to be certain the courier has neither time nor opportunity for decoding the message or passing it on to the enemy for copying."

Elizabeth noticed the swift rise of Beth's eyebrows and the edging of the girl's chair as it crept closer to her own, as if she didn't want to miss a single word. It was at this point Elizabeth delivered a dramatic announcement.

"We discovered the last two documents have been tampered with and changes were made to our coded message. They were sent within 18 hours of each other and we didn't receive the message from the army's scrutineer until after the second one had left. Apparently, the changes are subtle, though not enough to get past their expert. Courier A delivered the first document and Courier B delivered the second one," Elizabeth said.

The statement was received with amazement and chilly silence.

"So, it looks as if the couriers are in in collusion," said Sarah at last, breaking the quiet hush.

"It's not easy to accept that conclusion," said Elizabeth. "There's no evidence to suggest they are. Both Peter and I are convinced there is no collusion between these two men and they are as true to our cause as we are."

As she said this, Beth was surprised to see Elizabeth's demeanor change. Her shoulders slumped and she stared at Sarah for an overlong moment while she clasped and unclasped her hands. Beth realized Elizabeth was making an effort to calm herself and it made her uneasy. She broke the silence.

"There's a traitor in our midst then. We could blame the couriers, or Amos. We could even blame Peter," Beth said, "but from what I've heard, it's unlikely to be any of them. Of course, the only solution to this problem is to cancel the plan altogether and find some other way of sending messages to the military, or revert to the original one,"

"Not yet," said Elizabeth, now recovered. "If we do that the traitor will realize we know about them and take steps to ensure we don't find out who they are. We must try and catch whoever it is. Otherwise there could be massive consequences for the whole of our organization. We need to use our own undercover skills to ascertain what has happened and who is responsible.

"Peter and I have already drawn up a plan, and this is where you, Beth, could be of great service to our cause. Are you willing to consider becoming a temporary agent?"

Beth, intoxicated with a need to assist this impassioned ideologist, agreed to help. She accepted the invitation without even glancing at Sarah.

It was to Sarah's credit that she smiled at her.

"Good for you, Beth dear," she exclaimed, her face displaying her love and admiration for her dear companion.

Beth stood up, wide-eyed and delighted, hardly able to contain herself. In her euphoria she walked around the room in short self-contained steps, hands clasped to her chest as if overwhelmed as Elizabeth thanked her.

Sarah hugged her and dismissed Beth's worries about how she would manage while she was absent from her post for two or three weeks. Beth did not realize Sarah's thoughts were fixed on how she could use this story to regale her neighbors in the future, when it was safe to discuss such matters.

"I do believe the two new couriers are the culprits," Sarah grumbled, as Elizabeth prepared to leave.

Elizabeth smiled. "Perhaps you'll be proved right, Sarah," she said, "but I also believe Peter and I are justified in our doubts. I'm also convinced that Beth will be a great asset to our cause within the next weeks."

* * *

Three days later, Beth was ensconced within Peter's household as an assistant to Peter's accountant and scribe, James Trotter. James had often asked Peter if he could have support in the office, but he sniffed at the sight of Beth.

"She's the best I could get," Peter had told him, "most of the younger educated men have volunteered for the army, and it's difficult getting an older man to be subservient under a younger one. I do understand your need to have help, James, and I've done my best, but you'll just have to make do."

When she first met James, Beth was dressed in a shapeless long black skirt and a white, high collared blouse. A baggy purple tunic worn over the top of this emphasized the slimness of her body. Her hair was tied up in a rough, untidy mass on her head and her eyes were hidden under ugly, plain eyewear borrowed from Elizabeth's hoard of disguises. She was quiet and eager to help James. By the end of the first day, he felt that despite her awful appearance, her soft smile and gentle educated voice were acceptable, as was her ability to carry out his instructions.

"I'd have preferred a male assistant," James said to her within minutes of her arrival, "but when this silly little conflict with the North is over, Mr. Jolliffe will hire one. So, you're only temporary. Don't forget that."

That was the first time Beth had heard Peter's surname, and she realized she would have to be careful not to use the false name of Peter. Beth found James easy to get on with and they worked well together, so much so that the backlog of paperwork was soon demolished.

She had been allocated a bedroom near Peter's mother. Everyone knew this was the only spare room within the house so the arrangement was not a surprise, though one of the older maids felt she should have been offered the room, while 'James' girl' could have had hers. When James told Beth of this, she could do no more than shrug, and say she went where she was put and had no say in it. James told the maid of her reaction, and that was the end of that potential problem. However, Beth realized from the incident that James was fond of a bit of scuttlebutt, and remained as reticent as she could without being ungracious.

Beth had already been informed that she would see little of Peter, as it had been decided he would feign a mild illness for a few days.

"However," Elizabeth had said, "if we discontinue for too long, the traitor may conclude we are aware of enemy infiltration and go to ground. It's urgent we ascertain who is responsible, for the sake of our whole Richmond espionage operation."

At the end of that week, James, realizing his work load had depleted, asked for a few hours off each day during the following week. He told Peter's wife he had not had a break for five months, except for Sundays, and needed time to catch up on rest and sleep. Mrs. Jolliffe had already noticed his pale face and listlessness as well as the tired lines around his eyes, and spoke with Peter, the upshot of which was that James should work in the mornings only, just for one week.

James' absence made it easier for Beth to spend time traversing the tunnel and the ground around the entrance. She learned the mechanics of the cavities, found a comfortable spot where she could safely view anyone approaching the oak tree, spent hours walking, all the time looking for nooks that could hide a person, or a house that could well be temporary enemy territory. She clocked up the time taken to walk between these houses and Peter's, and within three days pronounced herself ready to go ahead with Peter's plan.

A basket from Elizabeth arrived on Thursday afternoon and the pickup time was arranged for Friday afternoon at 4.15 p.m. It was delivered to James' office so was received by Beth. She took it to Mrs. Jolliffe who, knowing Beth's true role, showed her Elizabeth's coded message within the Lady's Book, hand written in pencil on the second last page – F415PM. She realized 'F' meant Friday and 415PM was the time.

Beth was in position by 2.15 P.M. on Friday. Dressed in black from top to toe in thick trousers and a long coat, her head covered in a helmet and a mask over her face, she left the tunnel and delivered the package into the back cavity. She inched her tiny frame behind the heavy vegetation toward a spot hidden by foliage she had identified earlier in the week, where she had a good view of the oak tree. Twice, she made a noise as a foot struck a twig. She stood still for 60 seconds on each occasion, before moving on, just as Peter had taught her. She had already discovered an old tree stump which she could use as a seat. The bracken covered wall provided a back support, necessary if there was to be a long wait. She knew that the dark interior of her leafy nest, together with her dark clothes and mask excluded the possibility of being seen if and when anyone appeared near the oak tree. Nothing whatsoever occurred until 4.15 P.M. except for the gentle movement of a rodent or a bird hopping onto the surrounding hedge, hoping to find sustenance.

The document was collected by the courier. A check of the time from Peter's pocket watch loaned to her for the exercise revealed that he had left at 4.19 P.M. She returned to the house, cold and disappointed at the negative outcome. Once she had thawed out with hot soup and thick home-made bread, she was able to draw the features of the courier. Peter later verified he was the younger of the two new recruits.

The following morning, Elizabeth learned the courier had arrived at his destination well within the time allocated and the document was intact without changes.

"This is not such a bad outcome," Peter said. "It proves that this courier is in the clear."

Beth had to make do with that, though she remained disconsolate that the exercise had failed to highlight a possible infiltrator. It was decided they would carry out the same operation the following Wednesday.

The basket arrived on Tuesday afternoon. Beth had expected it, but James, now more alert and less listless, took the basket on arrival. Beth had already noticed that he was in a much better frame of mind than hitherto and that the short break the previous week had done him a lot of good.

"What's that?" she asked.

"It's another cake for the old lady. I hope she doesn't like it, cos she'll send it down to us if she doesn't. According to these baking instructions it's something quite different in flavor," he said, waving a handwritten page in the air. He picked up the Lady's Book, flicking the pages without interest until he stopped at an advertisement, commenting on a new shirt available at one of the larger stores in New York.

"Don't get any of these clothes in Richmond nowadays," he commented, "and I'd really like that one." He showed Beth a picture of the latest design in men's wear and she agreed he would look good in it. He flicked through to the end, stopping briefly at one or two more advertisements, before returning the book to the basket. "By the way," he said, "did we get one of these baskets last week? I should have warned you that they come from a friend of Mr. Jolliffe's old ma from time to time, though usually in the mornings. At least they used to be friends afore they got too old to visit."

"I expect they still are friends," said Beth with a laugh, "especially if she's sending her some home-baking. But I don't recall something like this arriving last week," she said, glad of the false eye-wear that hid her eyes as she spoke the lie. The less he knows, thought Beth, the better, as he left with the basket over his arm, to deliver it to the younger Mrs. Jolliffe.

At 2.45 P.M., the next day Beth made her way to the hiding place. She had been given the package for posting into the cavity and knew the courier was due to pick up the package at 4.45 p.m. Twenty minutes earlier, Peter had called James to his office, and Beth knew they would be ensconced together for at least three hours. She had dressed in the cave, taking care to add an extra layer of underwear to combat the chill of waiting.

This time she had to wait for 30 minutes before she heard the cracking of twigs and ruffled dead leaves as boots crashed down upon them, as well as the scurry of disturbed rodents and the stir of birds flying off in alarm. Swallowing hard, her heart beating so fast she was scared he would hear, she stared at a male of medium stature. He wore black, probably for the same reasons that she did. His head was covered with a woolen cap pulled down over his ears, his face blackened with soil or soot. She was unable to make out his features, though studied the shape of his face. She watched him fiddle with the unlocking mechanism and heard him curse as he pulled his right hand away with a sudden movement. He stared at the hand, and she could see a thin trickle of blood as he lifted it to his mouth to flick away the blood with his tongue. She almost gasped aloud as a sudden gleam of sun highlighted a glint on a finger. She stared hard. It was a ring, one with a shape she had seen before. The blood continued to spurt, and again he flicked his tongue across his hand, so that once more she caught a glimpse of the ring.

Yes, definitely," she thought, *I've seen one like that somewhere.*

All of a sudden she felt afraid. What would she do if she made a sound to startle him? What if he saw her? She felt as if she could collapse, but dared not lean against the foliage in case it rustled with her movement. She remembered Peter's instruction in case of such panic and breathed in slowly, then exhaled with equal slowness. She achieved the rhythm taught by Peter and made no sound.

The blood now stemmed, the man began to whistle under his breath. It was an unusual sound, as though he was whistling through his teeth.

She recognized the tune. It was an old French nursery rhyme tune.

Where had she heard that sound before?

The man tried again to open the cavity, and the whistling stopped. He retrieved the package, pushed it into a small bag that lay across his body, and closed up the cavity. His low whistling began again, that strange between-the-teeth sound that was so familiar to her. She noted the time when he left. The whole incident had taken just over six minutes.

She was now able to stretch a little, before settling down again to await the next part of the adventure. She had time to pursue her thoughts as to where she might have heard that unique whistling before, and where she had seen a similar signet ring with a distinctive coat-of-arms shape. She realized she had not seen a ring of that design in Richmond, though it could have been worn by a visitor to the Compton's farm in Lexington. She pushed her memory back to her Lexington days, and tried to remember.

The man returned some time later and pushed the neatly bound package into the cavity, still whistling. This time she had heard the distant clatter of hooves and noted it had taken him five minutes to arrive at the tree after this.

He was whistling the same tune, a tune she had learned so well during her lessons a few years ago in Lexington, the lessons she had undertaken with Oliver's friend, Fred Hetherington. She had suddenly remembered it was he who had worn such a ring. She also remembered his peculiar way of whistling through his teeth.

The last she had heard of Fred was that he had moved back to New Hampshire to work in his father's law business. She could hardly believe that the shy, affable Fred Hetherington of those days was a spy. At least the whistling style and the ring seemed to tell her so. She wondered why he was in Richmond in the first place and pondered this turn of events while she waited for the courier to collect the package.

Beth was able to catch the features of the courier, who was older than the one she had seen previously. Early the next morning, the army telegraphed a confirmation that the document had been received within the time limit but it had been tampered with. She had drawn a picture of the courier and Peter confirmed his identity. Out of interest she had attempted to draw the face of Fred as she had known him. She was satisfied her memory served her well and that if she saw him undisguised, she may well recognize him again.

Beth's report and suspicions raised a number of questions that were hard to answer. The more immediate question in the minds of Elizabeth and Peter was how Fred, if indeed he was the miscreant, knew of the courier's collection time. The consensus was that it must have been a courier who had talked. They knew for sure that it could not have been Amos, because he had been working at Peter's sister's home for the past few days, helping with long standing repair work and could not have known about the delivery.

Peter, however, was unsure about Beth's theory.

"It's too much of a coincidence," he said, "and after all, you didn't see his face."

Beth knew her job was not yet over, and insisted her plan for tracking down the suspected infiltrator be considered.

"The only clues we have right now as to who the infiltrator might be is the ring and the whistling. I do think we have no other choice but to follow up on my suspicion. Surely you can't ignore it. We have nothing else to go on."

"Continue," Elizabeth said.

"Fred wasn't all that bright and failed to get placed in a university," Beth told them. "I know he returned to New Hampshire to work in his father's law practice. He would have needed to get a job when he moved here, as his family isn't wealthy. It would seem to make sense that he'd look for a similar position with a lawyer here in Richmond."

She looked at them. Elizabeth nodded, though Peter continued to frown.

"You said he was your tutor for a while. If it was Hetherington, perhaps he's got a teaching post." Peter said.

Beth nodded at the possibility, though kept her eyes fixed on Elizabeth as she spoke.

"We have no other choice but to follow the clues available to us, and I want to try to locate him. To do this, I need to spend some time checking out the vicinity where the law offices are."

Peter pursed his lips and crossed and uncrossed his long legs in irritation. He seemed tense and unsure, opening his mouth to say something then changing his mind.

"How would you go about seeking Hetherington?" asked Elizabeth, who had also noticed Peter's exasperation.

"I'd like an opportunity to stay in that area for a few days. I know what he looks like, his walk, his voice, his laugh, and yes, how he whistles. Although he'll look older, I'm sure I'll recognize him. If he does work in one of those offices, I'll find him. Early morning, mid-day break, or his return home, I'll be there, watching and waiting. Indeed, I might even be able to locate his residence."

She outlined her simple plan.

"I would need to stay in a suitable boarding house near the law offices. From there, I would be in a place where I could pretend to be visiting friends, which would be a good excuse to be out and about. My clothes should be discreet enough not to attract attention, but of a suitable style for the wife of a professional man. Do you have such clothes in your store room of disguises, Elizabeth?"

Peter stood up without warning and shouted out an expletive, clearly affected by Beth's plan.

"Look, Elizabeth," he said, "I do not condone putting this young woman into any kind of peril. She's already undertaken a hazardous task for us, and should be sent home right now. We have promised Mrs. Willoughby her companion would come to no harm and we owe it to her, as well as Beth, to ensure she doesn't."

Beth took a deep breath as she tapped the table top with one hand while she jerked her tunic down with unnecessary force with the other. The tightness in her neck and shoulders was plain to see, and her clenched jaw and angry eyes contorted with contempt.

"There's no other way of finding out if my theory about Hetherington is right or wrong," she said, her voice cold as the fingers of both hands drummed hard against the table. She stared at Peter and held up a dismissive hand as he attempted to speak.

"I was already in danger when I waited those cold hours for sight of a possible traitor. I put up with that, overcame it, and now we have some clue, however obscure you may think it is, I am going to do something about it, with or without your permission. Understand? I will use my own small savings to do it, but do it I will." She leaned toward Peter, looking confidently into his eyes.

Peter was shocked. He shook his head, and tried, without success, to maintain eye contact. He slumped into his chair, holding his head in his hands. Beth saw that his cheeks had reddened and felt sorry for her outburst.

"You're only a year older than my daughter," he muttered in a thick voice. "I can't bear the thought of her doing something so dangerous and I won't let you do it, Beth."

He looked up at Elizabeth. "We can't let her do this. It's too dangerous."

"Yes, Peter, we can, if Beth is willing. I will help her with the plan," said Elizabeth.

Elizabeth funded a new, though simple wardrobe and clean, modest lodgings within Richmond's business center. When Beth stepped out, she presented as a young woman of limited means, perhaps a school teacher or a governess on a holiday that did not merit a second glance. Neither her beauty nor her intelligence managed to shine through. With spending money donated by Sarah, Beth enjoyed her first two days alone in Richmond, visiting the shops and sight-seeing. In one shop, she purchased a baby garment and a soft toy which she planned to send to Rory for his son, who was nearing his first birthday. She hoped that the garment would be big enough for the child by the time he received it and decided she would return it the next day in exchange for a larger size.

She sighed when she thought of her three friends from Kentucky, wondering how each was. Letters were few and far between now. She hadn't received one from Laura for months, and the last one from Clarrie spoke only of how the conflict was affecting life in Lexington. She pondered on the cruelty of this conflict and yearned for their days of happy, carefree friendship of years past. She wondered what they would think if and when she told them of her current role seeking out Fred Hetherington.

By the fourth day, she had located the office where Fred had worked. She had seen him a day earlier as he hastened through a stream of pedestrians in a fashionable part of the city. He was taller now, thicker around the middle, his shoulders wide in a well-fitted suit. He would have made an attractive sight had it not been for the frown lines between his eye-brows. As he rushed past her, she stopped to look in a shop window, though she saw nothing of its contents as her eyes followed his progress through the reflections. She noticed him enter a large building. She glanced at the town clock and realized he was returning to work following the mid-day break. She sauntered around for a while, ending up in front of the offices. Across the road, she noticed a coffee shop which according to the sign in the window, closed in the afternoon and opened in the early evening,

Obviously to catch the office workers, she thought.

Beth returned to her lodgings and wrote a note to Sarah, asking her to arrange for Elizabeth to meet her the following day at 11 o'clock at her lodgings. She made her way to the coffee house in plenty of time to be sure of a window seat, where she pretended to read the newspaper she had purchased. She had found a newspaper to be a useful prop to hide behind as her hopeful eyes scoured the crowds for a glimpse of Fred. Right now she was ready to leap up at the first sight of him leaving the office, as she planned to follow him to his residence.

As it happened, she had no need to move. She saw Fred leave the office building and it was obvious he was making for the coffee house. She lowered her head to her paper, pretending to sip from her now empty mug. He glanced quickly around, looking for someone, and then sat down at the open counter. A waiter approached Beth and asked if she required another coffee. Relieved, Beth nodded her thanks, extending the correct coins in payment.

The coffee house began to fill as crowds emerged from the offices and it was difficult to keep Fred in sight, as she waited for his exit. The waiter brought her coffee, obscuring her view, and when he moved off, she was devastated to see Fred had left. In a panic she glanced out of the window, and saw him as he shouted out to a friend.

The two men walked off toward the vicinity of the theatre just around the corner. She knew then that she could not have followed him home that night, but that did not seem to matter anymore. She had recognized his friend and was so shocked, she could neither move nor think straight. She gulped down the hot coffee, needing it more than ever as she watched Fred and his companion, who was none other than James Trotter, Peter's assistant.

The next few days were a disappointment to Beth. There was no swift denouncement of the two. Elizabeth met Beth at her lodging house as arranged and was astonished to learn of the unexpected arrival of James Trotter. It was now obvious that he had been Fred's informer. Between them Peter, Elizabeth and Beth pieced together how James had fathomed it all out.

Interrogation of Amos revealed James had been in the cellar one day, a bottle of Mr. Jolliffe's best wine in hand, just as Amos had emerged from the tunnel. Somehow James had cajoled the simple Amos to drink with him, during which time he had extracted the story of the tunnel and its use. Although it was not intended Amos should be aware of the package contents, he had overheard a conversation in the days prior to being given his new task and began to wonder what was going on. Although a quiet, uneducated man, he had reached a quite thrilling conclusion in his own mind, but kept his own counsel. Amos, who was not accustomed to wine, soon became the worse for wear, and was distressed when his new best friend of the day, James, did not believe his version of his strange new task. Amos had admitted he showed James the evidence of the drawings as some proof of his story. He knew they were in a drawer of Peter's desk, to which James had a key.

"So that's how it was done," said Peter, relieved it was all over, though disappointed at his own carelessness, thereby accidentally alerting Amos.

Elizabeth shook her head at the idea of denouncing Fred and James.

"We don't have any explicit evidence of their involvement," she said. "Trotter had been clever in detecting the code written in the Godey's magazine, but he's obviously been well trained. We've now worked out for ourselves what has occurred, but if we denounce them we may have to account for how and why Beth was involved. This may put her in even greater jeopardy than you had envisaged a few days ago. We can't use Amos' statement, because it would mean denouncing him as an accomplice. We all know he was not a willing accomplice, or even aware he was divulging top secret information. Really, Peter, I would think we are as much to blame as Amos because we put him in that position in the first place."

Peter looked miserable.

"It's time he retired anyhow," he said. "My sister is so taken with him, she wondered if I could release him to her. He's turned out to be an excellent dog handler, and as she breeds and rears dogs, he would be ideal for her. I'll speak with him today and give him a month to get used to the idea and then he can move on. I shall miss him, of course."

"What will you do with James?" Beth asked.

"Oh, I think we can offer a job to him in Canada. As you know, Elizabeth, our organization has an outpost out there and would be grateful to receive him. I'll offer him a job and double the pay. I'll send Amos over to my sister for a few more days – she'll be glad of the help right now, and then get rid of Trotter. That way, we'll prevent any suspicions he's been identified as a traitor."

Peter knew his ambitious assistant would accept the Canadian job offer, but also discerned his journey to Canada may well be hazardous. He had heard of others in a similar position who had never reached their destination. He kept this information to himself.

"As for Hetherington," said Elizabeth, "Pinkerton's men will ensure he's made fully aware he's been discovered. He'll know he'll be under scrutiny from now on, wherever he is, and if he puts a foot wrong, this serious felony would be added to any new ones. Nothing would save him at that point. I have an idea that he'll be advised to return to New Hampshire, where I'm certain Pinkerton will arrange a continuous watch for some time to come."

Peter glanced at Beth.

"It's clear that your perception and tenacity has stopped a southern spy in his tracks," he said, realizing Beth's disappointment that there would be no immediate denouement. "Without your willingness and courage to undertake this task for our cause, we wouldn't be aware of the identity of two traitors. It's half the battle knowing who the enemy is. Thanks to you, these men will never be in a position to do further damage."

He looked down at the drawing Elizabeth had handed to him minutes earlier.

"By the way, did you draw this picture of Hetherington?" he asked Beth.

"Yes, she did," said Elizabeth, "and a very good one it is, having seen him in that coffee house. I shall ensure it's given to Pinkerton. What an achievement, Beth, not only did you identify a spy, but you damn well gave us a picture of the rogue. Now that is an unusual thing for a beautiful woman to do. We really will have to find you a position within our organization. What do you think, Peter?"

Peter nodded vehemently.

"Where did you learn to draw like that, Beth?" he asked. "You really are a very clever artist."

"My sister and I always had a flair for drawing," she said, "but my sister was better than me. As to where I learned some of my techniques, I don't think you'd believe me if I told you."

"Oh, come on. Who taught you?" Elizabeth said.

"It was Fred Hetherington," she said, "in the days when he taught me French."

Beth felt that of all the shocks of the last few weeks that statement may have been the biggest one of all, judging by their faces. Their joint laughter was uproarious and loud.

Beth returned to Sarah, though she was now received as a beloved relative rather than a paid companion. She was recognized by these auspicious people as a useful spy, and she knew she would never let them down. Her ability to memorize the written word as well as her propensity to draw scenes, faces and maps proved invaluable as she began her journey into wartime espionage.

She was happy for the first time in years, though this was moderated by the thought of her sister, Maya, who had also been taught by Hetherington. She could never forget how Maya had died so many years ago, and how that tragedy had led to the deaths of her parents. She renewed her vow to try to discover the mystery of how her sister had met her untimely death. She also thought of her three Kentuckian friends and decided to write to each of them again. She wondered what they would make of her new life if she was ever able to tell them about it.

Chapter 15
Laura's a Fighter

It was a fine early morning at the end of July 1862 when Laura left Cynthiana. She was confident she would not be recognized in the clothes she had purchased from Bert's Second Hand Store at Lexington market three weeks earlier. She laughed out loud at the thought of her incognito visit to the raggedy stall.

On that day she had dressed as a plump middle-aged woman, her head enclosed in a tight fitting grey scarf. William had secured two thin cushions around her, one emphasizing the buttocks and the other the bust line, over which she pulled an out-of-date, full-sleeved, long shift that showed only the fronts of dilapidated shoes. She'd rubbed her face with nettles to create a red rash, and hoped the unanticipated pain would subside soon.

She had enjoyed the charade, telling Bert that she was seeking clothes for her son who had registered as a volunteer for Lincoln's army. She said she wanted her boy to arrive well-dressed and wearing boots. She'd heard Bert was a strong patriot who was disappointed his own sons had not volunteered. She left with two pairs of patched black pants, an oversized jacket, a checked shirt and, wonder of wonders, two pairs of boots.

"They'll all fit him," Laura had said to Bert, "he's only little, just like his daddy."

She knew the boot size was fine for her, and the garments would be altered to fit when she returned to Longfield.

A week later, as she set off on her long journey, she looked like a young boy just off to serve his country, wearing a pair of men's pants, patched at the pockets, the jacket, now altered to fit her, an old shirt of William's and a pair of boots. Laura felt confident about her appearance. She adopted a male gait as she strode forward toward the railway. Her early farm upbringing alongside her brothers and male farmhands had taught her how to swagger like a man, what to say, how to say it and even express expletives so she could be considered masculine. She knew how to ride and shoot, how to skin a rabbit and cook it and how to shod a horse.

Excitement, confidence and a sense of relief grew with each step. Slung across her body was a sack filled with a spare set of clothes, socks and the other pair of boots. Coins had been sewn into various small pockets discreetly placed in the bag, as well as in the hems of both pairs of pants, that would not only add weight but be available when she required cash. She carried a small amount of loose coins in the jacket pocket for immediate use and a second smaller bag slung across her back contained food and water for six days.

"It seems that barbers are doing a roaring trade right now," William had said last night, as he hacked off her hair, leaving just sufficient for a barber to style into that favored by young army recruits. She planned to stop at the first out-of-town barber shop she came across, to obtain the neat, short cut of soldier boys she had seen in recent weeks.

She was glad for the first time in her life that her voice was deeper than most young women. William thought it might deepen further as she grew older though unlikely to change just yet. She retorted that her new choice of words would certainly take the edge of any suspected effeminacy, whereupon William urged her not to forget her manners and femininity when she returned home. They both laughed at the image of her arrayed in a beautiful ball gown and a jeweled hairstyle, while retaining her manly gait and bad language.

William had made sure no one saw her leave the house, though it was unlikely that anyone would have recognized the youth. As she strode along, she thought of her brother's cruel death and those of the men and boys whose blood had sunk deep into the earth as they called in vain for their mothers. Her soft heart went out to the parents, siblings, wives and children of the dead, in the knowledge of the deep grief they would endure.

She had planned a route to Herkimer County, New York, where Captain George McLaughlin was recruiting for the formation of the 153rd Regiment, New York State Volunteers. She had calculated it would take six or seven days to get there.

She was right in her assumption that it would be easy for a boy sporting a soldier-like haircut to hitch a lift here and there, or jump on an appropriate train. The journey turned out to be pleasant and she met only kindness by everyone who sought to help the quiet 'young boy' on his way to serve the country he loved. It didn't seem to matter whether the folks were Union or Confederate followers, as all sympathized with a young person who wished to serve his country. It took the anticipated six days before the weary Laura arrived at McLaughlin's Company G of the 153rd regiment, at Fonda, New York.

Laura's forged papers, organized by the faithful William, served her well. The physical examination she had dreaded was perfunctory. The coins and pebbles sewn into the hem of her pants enhanced her recorded weight and she passed an inspection of feet and hands as well as a cursory examination of the padded intimate area of her fully clothed body. She proved her competence in handing a rifle and was invited to sign a document that enrolled her as Laurence Compton Parker, 17 years old, whom no one suspected was a 20-something female school-teacher.

Company G was to be mustered into service in October and assigned to Washington City defense, but in the waiting time she learned that as well as providing guard and provost marshal duties, the privates would undertake daily drills in preparation for the time they would be required to face enemy in battle. This did not suit Laura's image of fighting for her country.

Laura suffered weeks of heavy drilling and shooting practice. She proved to be an exceptional, hardworking and intelligent trainee. She also learned the art of discreet washing and dressing in the well populated billets, although she was not alone in her wish for privacy as many of the new recruits found it difficult to expose their bodies publicly. The older recruits laughed at them.

"You'll learn not to be so fussy in a few weeks," they laughed, amid raucous comments. Laura learned to keep to herself, to avoid the rough, male day-to-day life. She began to realize her childhood days at the farm had been paradise in comparison.

She was billeted in a small hovel with three others with little privacy, though it proved easy to conceal her gender from the shy teenage boys. Laura tried hard not to behave in school-teacher mode toward them. She did, however, encourage them, in a paternal, protective way when they wept with fatigue at the end of each day of drilling and marching. After a few weeks, she had made so much progress she was designated as a tutor. Laura loved it all, though longed to get into the 'real war'.

She wrote to William about the scarcity of food rations, afraid her current loss of weight would be noticed and her gender discovered should she fall ill. Within a short period, she received food parcels from Cynthiana. The contents were soon demolished by her billet companions.

She did not have long to wait for her first real battle experience. By now, Laura was aware that following their defeat at the second Battle of Bull Run, Union morale was low, though this was restored to a degree when General McLellan was reported to have 75,000 men. Private Parker was one of them.

Laura wrote to Clarrie and Beth, to whom she had confessed her current life change in a previous letter.

"At dawn on 16 September our army confronted General Lee at Sharpsburg," she wrote, *"I was in Major General Hooker's corps and the next day he mounted an assault on General Lee's left flank. The battle was vicious, with repeated attacks by our troops; though the Confederate counter attacks were equal to ours. We got so close to each other, the Blue and the Grey jackets almost intermingling. We could see the faces of our opponents, young faces not much older than 16, looking as scared and perplexed as I am, sure we did. We had been taught to shoot on sight of grey coats.*

"None of us knew whose bullet it was that led to the whole face of one Grey disintegrate, though his body still moved forward, until at last he fell. I can't find the words to express my grief when the boy's body crashed down in front of us. I realized then my revenge for Brett's death was pointless. Why kill another young boy in such a dreadful way in order to feel better about one's own dead? I think we all felt the same. One of our boys covered the poor faceless Grey with leaves and made a cross from twigs which he placed on top of the pile as he prayed over him. We were ordered forward, and our religious soldier was shot dead within a minute of moving. I wanted to stop and provide the same rites he had recently performed, but wasn't able to. My own faith toppled that day. I do so hope it will return. Such fighting, such pain, so many wounded and dead, it is hard to describe the futility of it all when witnessed at such close quarters. My consolation now is Brett and Lawrence can't be hurt any more, but I've begun to worry about Vinnie, as well as the older students at my school."

By the time Laura's friends received her letter, the press had lauded the whole battle as hard-fought by both sides, proclaiming the resultant Union victory was gained only because the loss of so many of his troops had driven General Lee's forces from Maryland.

Clarrie in particular was shocked to realize her best friend Laura, her genteel, courteous friend, had taken part in the gruesome affair.

They received a further letter from Laura in early February 1863, and on this occasion Laura sent a similar letter to her mother and to Rory.

"Things change so quickly in the army," she wrote. *"One day McClellan is still our commander, the next we hear he's been fired by the president and Major General Burnside has taken over."*

She told them of how Burnside was eager to get into Richmond and rout the army and Jefferson Davis from their perches.

"Burnside set about devising a plan to capture Richmond by crossing the Rappahannock River using pontoons and outflanking General Lee. With a Union army of 120,000 against General Lee's 70,000 men, together with the speed Burnside had got his army to the Rappahannock, we all thought this was to be the final battle of the war. When the pontoons didn't arrive until 10 days later he'd lost the advantage. When they did arrive, he got the engineers to build them up as quickly as possible. The problem was that the builders were unable to work quickly due to heavy mud and Confederate snipers."

"To cut the story short, a small party of sharp shooters was sent in to gun down the snipers. I was part of that team. We managed to stem the firing, though when it began our sergeant in command was one of the first to get a bullet. The boys panicked, but I went into my schoolmistress routine and managed to calm them down. One of them took over the care of the injured man, and I delegated the remaining boys to various points where the snipers could be more clearly seen. I'd been in a position where I'd seen this more clearly than our sergeant had been able to, so there's no blame to him for not noticing. We did stop the snipers, but our efforts were too late. You'll know the story of Fredericksburg by now. The following day, those of us who had been sent to take down the snipers were awarded a full 24 hour rest period. It was a great boon, I can tell you."

Of those few soldiers left behind to rest that day, Laura was the only one unable to sleep. After an hour of listening to the snores of her comrades, she crept out of the tent and made toward a trench to relieve her gas-filled innards. Within minutes she was ready to return, when she heard a moan. The vicinity was quiet, with only the rustling of vermin. She moved onto her belly as quietly as she could. She heard nothing more and was about to return when the moan came again, louder this time. There followed a cry of pain. She heard a low voice asking for the child to be saved. She dared not stand, knowing Union snipers were on the alert for possible Confederate intruders. There was another moan, and then a scream that was quickly stifled.

Laura sent out a loud whisper. "Who is it? Where are you? Where is the child?"

"Here, I am here. My child is still within me. It's ready to come out…"

Laura ascertained the place from where the voice emanated, crawled out of the trench and turned to her right, away from the sniper's view. She almost fell into the next trench but saw nothing. She called out again.

"I'm here, hurry…hurry," a trembling voice answered.

This time Laura ascertained the direction of the voice and crawled toward a large tree. She knew the woman would be behind that tree. It was either a birthing mother or the enemy trying to trick a Union soldier over, but Laura knew she could not chance a child's life or indeed a mother's, and crawled across.

Within 10 minutes, she had delivered a scrawny baby boy safely, who bellowed as soon as he lay in her hands. She felt for her knife and swiftly made the cut to separate the child from the placenta, winding a piece of clean cotton, torn from her pocket, around his middle, before placing him into the weeping mother's arms.

"He is a beautiful boy," Laura said to his mother. "I'll come back with water and swaddling for him. I'll be a few minutes."

She made the mother comfortable. Slowly and painfully, she crawled back on her belly to the camp. The other troops slept on. She almost laughed as she contemplated how they would react when she was able to tell them of the adventure she had while they lay sleeping.

She wished them good dreams, as she gathered water, toweling and her own sheet. Her hand shuffled into her make-shift personal hold-all for other items, before hurrying out. This time, she ran under cover of the trees, and hoped that the sniper was asleep. She gave the woman some of the water, bathed and then swaddled the child in a towel, after which she attended to the needs of his mother.

She stayed with them, and helped the mother clamp the baby's mouth to her breast. Eventually all three slept. Laura had a rude awakening, with the howl of the baby. Startled, she shot up, knocking her head on a low lying branch. She cried out loud at the heavy blow, as blood gushed out of the cut on her forehead, loud enough to alert the sniper, who fired a warning shot. That shot set up a chain reaction. The sniper rushed from his lookout post toward the cries of the new-born and the shrieks of the mother, as did her fellow soldiers awakened by the din and the firing of a second shot, followed by a third.

Little did the now quiet child, gnawing at his mother's breast, realize he was the center of an almost biblical tableau on the banks of the Rappahannock River, a scene that would never be forgotten by the onlookers.

Mother and child were taken to the nearby Chatham Manor, an old, large house used by the Union as their H.Q. and field hospital. They were placed in the care of the two general nurses allocated to the force who were already busy with their first patients from the fracas taking place in town.

Later, Laura wrote to her mother about the baby and told of the trauma the innocent public suffered during these battles. She also explained why the first-time mother had been one of a large group of citizens fleeing the battle area, when the pains of labor overtook her. She'd strayed from the group to sit awhile until one of the pains passed, not realizing how near she was to giving birth.

Laura told her mother how she had been so concerned for the mother and baby; she had not thought to ask her name and now regretted the oversight.

"You'll know the outcome of that battle by now," Laura wrote, *"but the newspapers don't give the human stories we see. Fredericksburg citizens have really suffered. The town had been peacefully occupied by the Union once before, but when our forces arrived again, more than two-thirds of the population fled from their homes toward Spotsylvania County to seek safety with friends or relatives. I remember one incident in particular that occurred soon after the baby's birth.*

"During a marching exercise we turned into a sheltered path toward Willis Hill and saw crowds of distressed women and children hunched together. It was late afternoon. We realized they

were some of the Fredericksburg refugees. A few had thought to bring bed counterpanes, some had even brought bits of carpet, and they had stretched these for shelter over sticks stuck into the ground. I saw one woman walking along holding a baby to a breast, with a little girl of about three hanging onto her skirt, also crying, as she asked for something to eat. She repeated over and over that she wanted to go home to her papa. I ran over to give the mother a few broken cookies from my pocket and my water flask. Our sergeant yelled at me to get back in line, but I didn't. Most of the troops followed my example. Some gave their precious water. Our sergeant ended up doing the same, and even showed the women how to light a fire, so there would be some warmth as the cold of the night set in. No one spoke as we tramped our way back to camp as the sight of those fleeing civilians had outraged us all."

In another letter to Clarrie, to be forwarded onto Beth, she spoke of the mother and baby.

"When they were moved to Chatham Manor, I heard nothing further. I asked about them once or twice but was told to concentrate on whatever I'd been tasked with at the time. I realized the woman belonged to one of the groups fleeing the area and had somehow got lost but would love to know how and where they are now, indeed who they are, but probably never will. I do know, though, that the mother and baby will be well cared for at Chatham. I caught a glimpse of one of the nurses and she reminded me so much of you, Clarrie, and made me long to see you and Beth. I do hope it will not be too long before we can be together again. Have either of you heard from Rory? I haven't."

Laura did not know how long it would take for the letter to reach Clarrie, but hoped it would not be too long. She was missing Kentucky and her busy school life there, and letters from home were as important to her as ever.

Laura was recognized for leadership qualities as well as her valor on the battlefield and earned a recommendation for promotion to sergeant, which she did not accept. She realized it was a serious enough offence to have given false information to a recruiting board, and that inevitable imprisonment would follow if it became known she had not confessed her gender masquerade to a promotion board.

Burnside's Army camped in Stafford County behind Chatham in the winter following their defeat, while the Confederate army occupied Spotsylvania County across the river. Pickets from both sides kept up a careful patrol on their respective sides. Laura was often on picket duty and did not mind this as she was able to sleep in comparative comfort in a billet at Chatham House following a watch.

One morning, as she approached her billet following such a watch, she was accosted by two armed guards. Her companions were allowed to go forward to the billet, but she was frog-marched by the silent guards on either side of her. The guards left her at a closed door, which opened quickly as two further guards led her to a battered looking desk, behind which sat a senior officer, whom she knew to be Captain Wainwright. He was the one who had bawled at her in exasperation when she turned down the promotion recommendation. She glanced at a figure sitting in a chair in the corner of the half-lit room. He looked a bit like the picture of General Burnside she had seen, though he appeared more tired and disheveled. She wondered what she, a lowly private, was doing here in such presence, and her mouth fell agape as she stared at him.

"Eyes front, Private," Captain Wainwright snapped.

She turned her head and found herself staring into the impenetrable eyes of the tired-looking officer in front of her.

"You are Private Laurence Compton Parker?" His voice was clipped and aggressive.

"Yes, sir."

"When did you enlist in the Army of the Potomac?"

"In August 1862, sir."

"Why did you join up?"

"I wanted to serve the Union, sir. My brother had been killed at Fort Henry, another brother lost a leg at Fort Donelson. I felt useless and wanted to avenge them, I suppose."

"You suppose? Suppose? What does that mean?" retorted the stern officer.

"I wanted to be useful to the Union cause, sir. My brothers had fought and I felt it was my plain duty to them, and to fulfil my promise that I would do something to help, and be someone to carry on for them. They'd had the courage to leave their wives and children, and I was just keeping school in Kentucky. Why should I leave it to them to make the sacrifice?"

"Do you not think that educating children is a good war effort?"

"Yes, sir, I do. But there were men at my school who had volunteered but were not accepted," Laura said, "and they were good enough teachers to take over the headship from me and carry on with my work."

"Your work? You were the headmaster?" Wainwright leaned forward in his seat, his face belligerent as he searched her own.

Laura knew she had made an error in establishing her status at the school.

"My step-father is the founder and patron of the school, sir," she explained. "I received a good education and it was the head of my school who recommended me, sir. My step-father knew there would probably be a shortage of men, sir, if the war came about. He thought I would be too young for the army, and decided to give me early experience of managing the school, sir."

"But surely, Private your step-father would have realized that a young scholar like you would be ideal for our army, and that you would be one of the first to be brought in if we decided to conscript our men?"

Laura realized she was getting into deep water. She had to think quickly, though found it difficult to lie, especially in the august presence she felt herself in. She wondered at the inane questioning that seemed of little interest to a general. He surely would not be interested in a lowly private.

"You turned down the opportunity to become a sergeant. Why?"

The question was terse, but not unexpected.

"I did not wish to have the added responsibility, sir. I find it hard enough being a private nowadays."

She heard a smothered snigger in the background that turned into a cough, but dared not look over, keeping her eyes straight forward. She thought she saw a glint of humor in Wainwright's eyes.

"You did well when you took the lead after your sergeant was injured during the assault on the snipers." Wainwright said. "It was appreciated. I guess, also, that you were brave to bring that child into the world a few days ago. The mother has given me a full report of your bravery in getting to her in the first place, and I must admit that your presence of mind saved her life as well as the child's. You are to be commended on that action, Private."

"Thank you, sir."

"You consider yourself to be a man of honor, Private Parker, do you not?" Wainwright asked.

"Yes, sir."

"Yes, what?" the officer spat out.

Laura was perplexed, and then realized what she should have said.

"Yes, I am a soldier of honor, sir."

A voice from the back bellowed. "The question is, Private, are you a *man* of honor?"

Laura was stunned. She continued to look straight in front without looking in the direction of the voice.

She did not answer.

"Answer me, Private," came the menacing, authoritative voice

Laura now realized her deception had somehow been discovered.

"No sir," she answered.

"Then you must be a female," sneered the high-ranking officer, who had by now walked forward and stood next to Wainwright, who had risen to attention.

"Yes, sir, I am a woman," she said, looking straight into his eyes, hers not wavering.

"Well, it's not unknown for a woman to join the army. They do so for many reasons. They join to be near their husbands or sons, or for the adventures of war. Some join because they want to be near men, to offer themselves to men. This last is a common justification. Is it yours?" he hissed.

Laura was shocked.

"That is a gratuitous suggestion and I resent the implication, sir. I am untouched, sir, a fact that can be proved. I enrolled for the reasons I have already given you, sir."

She glared at the two men.

There was no mistaking her innocence or her fury. The older man laughed.

Laura expected Wainwright to be shocked but was surprised to see his relieved expression. He watched as the senior officer strode back to his chair, and brought it to Laura.

"Please sit, Miss Parker."

"Sir, I cannot. Not in the presence of officers, sir."

"Yes you bloody well can. And will. You're not in the Army now, you know. Besides, no officer can sit in the presence of a standing lady, madam."

A sense of pleasure washed over Laura. Now she could be herself again, even though she knew a prison sentence was likely. Without thinking, she discarded her usual male sitting stance as she sat down, knees closed, legs slightly to the left, ankles crossed. Her clasped, wrinkled hands lay on her lap.

The General, if that was who he was, offered a brief smile in her direction and patted Wainwright's shoulder twice.

"You know what you have to do now, Captain," he said and walked out of the door.

"That's Dr. John Letterman, medical director of our army, at least he is for the time being, though there are rumors Lincoln wants him for something else now. He's the man who is responsible for many of the better changes within our field hospitals and care of wounded men," Wainwright told her.

"Oh!" she exclaimed, somewhat disappointed. "I thought he was General Burnside."

"Well, Parker, you're nowhere important enough to think that a general would be interested in sorting out your gender," he said.

They both laughed, and the ice was broken,

It turned out that the mother and baby incident had led to her downfall. Wainwright explained how the mother, who had indeed become parted from her family as they trudged toward Spotsylvania, knew the tenderness and gentle manner by which the soldier had treated her was that of a mother or a nurse, as did Laura's competence during the baby's delivery. She had felt even more certain when Laura had cut the baby's cord with such professional skill and wrapped a firm bandage around the small wound. The after care of both baby and mother helped to define her suspicions that this soldier was a disguised woman.

It was when Laura returned from her brief absence with necessities for cleaning the two, as well as the 'home-made' cotton pads used for stemming the feminine discharge following the birth that she knew for certain. Why would a man carry those about with him in his battle-kit? And what man would think to leave another two for her use at the field hospital?

The nurses started the gossip, which filtered through the staff and it was not long before Dr. Mary Walker, a woman with the dual role of physician and nurse at Chatham, heard the story. She discussed the rumor with the visiting Dr. Letterman.

As it happened, Letterman was on a short courtesy visit to the Chatham H.Q. and hearing the story, he discussed the matter with the officers. A unanimous decision was made that the discovery could not be ignored, and that dismissal from the army and punishment was appropriate.

Letterman admired this woman who had deceived so many for so long, though could not make this apparent. Instead he wondered if there might be an opportunity for her to serve the Union in a different way, using her obvious mimicry skills. First, however, they had to ascertain who she really was and her credibility as a true Union supporter.

Events moved forward with speed. Wainwright ordered a bath for Laura, assisted by a female aide from Chatham. It took three baths before they both agreed she was thoroughly cleansed of weeks of grime, dust and non-washing. Feminine garments were brought to her. The word was put around the camp that Private Parker had been removed to duties elsewhere.

Laura was allocated a shelf in a small store-room for sleeping, the only available space left in the overcrowded hospital, and was allowed to recuperate for two days. Following a formal interrogation by Captain Wainwright and Dr. Walker about her background, she was allowed to consort with the female staff. She could not believe it when she saw her dear friend, Clarrie, who had been a nurse at Chatham Manor for three weeks.

Within a week, Laura was approached by a visiting officer, Colonel James Little, who gave her two choices. For two days he had studied the under-weight Laura, whom he thought must have been beautiful before she played her game of swapping gender. During the past weeks her hair had not been cut, and had grown quickly. She already felt the benefit of her improved diet, and her body shape had filled out as a result. She had a vivacious personality, and appeared to have retained her level of logic and intelligence throughout the trials and tribulations of the battlefield that no woman should have to go through. He knew that Laura had the capacity to become a desirable woman. Wainwright seemed to think so, as Colonel Little had noticed.

"You have sown your own fate, Miss Parker," the colonel said to her a few days later

"You must now prepare to reap the harvest. This could be a sad harvest that won't bear fruit in a cold cell of a female prison full of felons. Or it could be a fruitful one, with a high yield for the Union cause. You must make the choice: either enter the Secret Service or go to prison. I have to warn you that in some ways you could feel imprisoned by the conditions, but they offer more comfort than an airless room and a flea-ridden straw bed on a cold floor."

He explained to Laura what he wanted her to do, and without hesitation she accepted her new role, realizing that this is what she

192

had actually been seeking all along. She was to become a spy for the Union.

She was dumbstruck when she was invited to meet the person with whom she would be closely involved.

"Hello, Laura," said Beth, as she entered the room. "You look as if you've been pulled through a hedge backward with that haircut. Have you got your wig, yet?"

"It's better than it was three weeks ago," retorted Laura, staring with unmistakable envy at the light brown hair coiled high around Beth's head, framing a face that was lovelier than she had remembered.

As Laura listened to Beth's adventures as a runner for a spy ring in Richmond, she could not believe that this confident woman had been the shy mulatto of such a short time ago. Beth was, Laura decided, more open than before, not wrapped up in the shell of inferiority that she and Clarrie had tried so hard to crack. She hadn't mentioned the death of her sister Maya either that had once been the focal point of her existence. The two friends embraced and went out to locate their mutual friend, Clarrie

Chapter 16
Clarrie on the Front Line

The three of them spent time catching up. Clarrie spoke of her shock at the revelation Laura had joined the army posing as a male soldier. From the content of her letters it had been clear she was not acting out a part but was every inch a solid Union fighter.

She knew Laura had been brought up in a family of boys, and had enjoyed their rough, noisy activities as much as she liked to dance and play the piano. That had changed in later years when Laura assumed the role of a demure, well-respected school mistress. Clarrie had therefore found it impossible to see her as a soldier of war.

Although Laura had requested her friends not to divulge her secret, Clarrie had spoken to her mother of her worries. She wondered whether Laura had become unhinged with grief following the death of her brother. Martha had not agreed.

"More likely the tragedy spurred her on to be who she really is; a compassionate, adventurous woman who needs to spread her wings. It's significant to me she doesn't want to return to the school after the war. She's being true to herself, I think," Martha responded.

"Let's pray she'll return from the war," Clarrie had said, thinking about the long list of battlefield deaths produced almost daily in the journals.

Clarrie told her friends of how her days had been spent in her Lexington nursing station, though having trained three young women from the village to undertake much of that work, she also had time for the bakery. Her manager, Jack, had enlisted into a Union regiment, leaving Clarrie and her brother, Tom, to manage the bakery alongside Frances.

She told of how, over the past two years, Tom's health had deteriorated and Dr. Wallace had diagnosed a heart defect which he thought may be similar to that of his father. This resulted in Tom's application to become a Lincoln volunteer being rejected although he was able to continue some gardening work for John Compton. Tom and his family had by now taken up residence in his old home with Clarrie, to facilitate his eventual management role within the bakery. He had been surprised to find he enjoyed his new role as much as Clarrie enjoyed her nephew and niece and the constant chatter of his wife.

In spite of this, Clarrie felt dispirited, especially after receiving Laura's letters. She knew full well that the bakery could manage without her help nowadays, and was loath to undermine the confidence of her well-trained nursing assistants by overseeing their work too often. Occasionally she assisted Dr. Wallace. She confessed her restlessness to Mrs. Wallace, who suggested she should apply to become an army nurse. However, Clarrie worried about her brother and their mother and how they would carry on the bakery business alone, especially in view of her brother's precarious health. She still remembered the agony following her father's premature death.

Dr. Wallace agreed with his wife.

"They both love the work; it gives them something to work toward for the future of the children. You'll be more fulfilled caring for our injured soldiers, if you feel you could manage that sort of nursing," he had remarked with a stinging bite

It was just the challenge Clarrie needed. She applied to Dorothea Dix, the Union's superintendent of army nurses, to become a volunteer. With her experience and demeanor her application was accepted, and within weeks she found herself based on the battlefield of Corinth, Mississippi, immediately followed by Perryville, from where she wrote to her mother.

"I am appalled by what I've seen. I'm sure I'll never feel so horrified at anything that may happen in the future as I felt when I first arrived in Corinth," she said. *"It was bad enough dealing with those suffering hunger and fever, but the suffering and incapacitation resulting from their injuries was almost too much for my spirit to bear, but bear it I did for their sakes."*

Thereafter, she was sent to the Chatham Manor field hospital in Fredericksburg. She had no idea this was also Laura's present location.

She had heard of the Surgeon General, Dr. William Hammond and of Dr. Jonathan Letterman. Aware of Letterman's plans for improved medical resources and an organized ambulance corps for the removal of soldiers from the battlefield, Clarrie welcomed their successful implementation at Chatham. She had seen appalling injuries of soldiers at other field hospitals, aggravated by men being left untended on the battlefields, unable to help themselves.

In spite of the improved medical and surgical techniques and the prescribed number of surgeons and physicians, problems remained that affected the overall services, largely due to a constant shortage of medical supplies such as ether and morphine. But it was an improvement on her Corinth and Perryville experiences, and Clarrie remained enthusiastic about the effective triage system introduced at Chatham.

She soon discovered the system was effective in saving lives, though it added to the already long and difficult workload of the nurses. The space within Chatham Manor was overstretched as the need to accommodate more and more injured and recovering troops increased. Large store rooms had been converted into wards; soldiers were even placed on shelves to recuperate, due to the shortage of beds and space.

Although scrubbed daily, latrines soon became foul, and the problem of infection was ever present. As well as nursing fraught amputees in difficult circumstances, Clarrie's experience in preventing contagion was utilized to full effect, though she often felt it was a struggle they were losing. She longed to be able to discuss this with Rory, whose experience in Europe would have been invaluable.

Clarrie's work and that of her co-partner was exhausting, with only six hours respite in every 24, so she was not surprised when her colleague collapsed under the strain. Clarrie was left with just three orderlies to help her and there was one period of 48 hours when she did not sleep at all. One of the surgeons had made a case for additional staff and that very morning six nurses had arrived, with the promise of another contingency the following week.

Clarrie was ordered to take two days off. She used some of the time to write to her mother.

"On that first free morning, I was stunned to find Beth and Laura waiting for me to wake up. They were outside my little make-shift tent. At first, I thought I was hallucinating. You can imagine that we have been inseparable for the past two days. Somehow we all manage to sleep in my tent. When they've gone, which I understand will be in two or three days, I won't know what to do

with my free space, but while it's been uncomfortable, I wouldn't have missed their company for the world."

"They made certain I didn't get even a glimpse of the field hospital tents, and we walked in the safe area for hours, exchanging home news and I was able to tell them of my recent experiences. They were unable to talk of some of theirs. They're a bit of a mystery, and I don't know what's gone on with them over the last couple of years. They kept me away from the nursing scene, but we did help out with the camp's cooking in the evening. That was therapeutic for the three of us."

Clarrie told them of the dreadful day Jack Bellwood, her bakery manager, had been brought in. She had not recognized him at first. He had been left on the battleground for half a day before being picked up by an ambulance driver, who had investigated a movement in a hedge, followed by a long wail of despair. Jack was almost naked and what clothing he did have was scorched and tattered. His name tag had survived and Clarrie was devastated when she saw it: JACK BELLWOOD. He was in bad shape, and the surgeons decreed that he was too near death to attempt amputation of a leg so badly ripped that it hung on by a sliver of damaged bone and sinew. All they could do was to try to free him from agonizing pain during his last hours.

When Clarrie had noticed the name tag she looked more closely at his face. It really was Jack. He was crying out for his mother. This cry from injured soldiers always upset the nurses and orderlies; a soldier crying out for a mother who would never hear him, who would never know that she was the one on his mind as he lay dying. Clarrie spent as much time as possible with Jack, without neglecting her other duties. She talked to him about his sister Frances at the bakery, of the folks they both knew. She spoke of his brother, David Plowman, who had visited them out of the blue a while ago. At the mention of David's name, Jack appeared to rally for a while.

"Can I see him?" he tried to say.

Two days later, a few Confederate survivors arrived. When Clarrie began the necessary stripping of clothes and washing the blood and grime from one of them, she noted his name tag. DAVID PLOWMAN – Jack's brother! She ran the length of the long house, to find Jack. He had been moved and after a frantic search she found him again. He had somehow rallied that day and was calling for his brother.

197

"I know he's here, I know he's here," he repeated, over and over.

A couple of orderlies brought the injured, though ambulant, David to him. The brothers wept as they recognized each other.

"I knew you would come, I knew you were near," Jack said.

For the rest of that day David sat with his brother, sometimes holding him in his arms, other times helping to feed him. That night they lay down together, holding hands, talking, often laughing. Jack died with laughter on his lips at a light-hearted anecdote of a shared incident from years ago. His brother was comforted by the sound of that laugh at the end. He closed his brother's eyes and kissed him. "From Mama," he whispered, as he held his dead brother in his arms. Clarrie had been with them for that last half hour.

As she told Beth and Laura, she wept for her protégé Jack and for his sister Frances, but most of all wept for David, whose compassion had comforted his brother to the last.

"It seemed to me that the whole hospital grieved as the news got around. It hadn't mattered whether they were Unionists or Confederates. They were brothers who had, by some miracle, found each other again, young men who had been struck down in battle," she said to her friends, weeping and relieved she had been able to tell the story.

Laura and Beth also wept and the three held each other close, pondering the hand of fate.

"Just think, Clarrie," Laura said, "if it hadn't been for you, Jack and David would never have come together when it was most needed. Just think what you did for them."

Clarrie looked surprised, and then wept again, but somehow her friends knew the sharing of that story could have released their haggard, frail friend from at least one nightmare.

The mood changed when Clarrie told them of the happy day for the staff when a mother and new-born were brought in. Clarrie explained they had heard rumors the young mother, Maryanne, thought the soldier who had helped her was a woman. After listening to the intimate details of her care, one of the older nurses agreed that only a woman could have been so caring and gentle and the rumor spread. When Laura revealed she was the soldier who delivered the baby, Beth and Clarrie could hardly believe it and listened, overwhelmed as Laura told them of her serendipitous part in that incident.

"Do you know what the baby's name is?" asked Laura, "I've often wondered how they are."

"She called him Lawrence," Clarrie said, "after the soldier who helped her."

After a while both noticed that Beth had become silent. For a while they left her alone as she brooded. During their potato peeling session in the makeshift kitchen, Beth blurted out her concerns.

"I often think of how and why my sister Maya was killed. I wonder if I shall ever find out what happened to her," she said.

Clarrie picked up the knife she had dropped in surprise and rinsed it in a small bowl of water.

"I think it unlikely now, Beth. Remember how hard everyone tried to find clues following the accident. Apart from the horse tracks that you followed just before you found her, there was nothing. It was such a shame that the hoof marks were obliterated with everybody rushing to the scene when we heard you cry out. Why have you suddenly thought of it?"

"It wasn't an accident, I know it wasn't," Beth snapped. "Somebody killed her. I wish I could find out who it was, because they're responsible for the death of my parents as well as Maya's. I just need to settle it in my mind once and for all."

Her voice faltered as she looked at her hands, twisting them together.

Laura frowned. She had not heard any mention of Maya's death for a long time, but could understand how, within this atmosphere of illness, death and sheer misery, the deep grief had returned. She took the now weeping Beth in her arms.

"I can't let it go," Beth mumbled into Laura's now damp left shoulder pad. "I did for a while in Richmond, but it's back again. It's a dreadful weight. If I could just settle it, I might be able to leave it behind."

Clarrie watched the tableau as Laura soothed Beth. She was aware Beth might have become depressed by the sights and sounds of so many injured soldiers and the knowledge that many would probably not make it home again. She was sure Beth must be suffering from underlying grief that was ready to come to the fore in complex situations she found herself in. She had discovered this was a problem among the medical and nursing staff at army field hospitals. She would ask Rory about it when she saw him next.

By the time Beth left for Louisville, Kentucky, she appeared to have recovered, although she was less exuberant. Laura followed her a day later, and Clarrie returned to duty. She was astute enough to realize there was a reason for her friend's discreet exits and although she didn't comment, she remained curious. She returned to the wards wishing that she had been part of whatever the conspiracy was. What a joy it would be if they could spend the rest of this atrocious, senseless war together. However, she had returned to duty refreshed and determined to tackle the care of her patients, as well as working toward improved sanitation within the smaller field hospitals dotted about the terrain in tents.

Clarrie reflected on how, over the past years, her own experience and the knowledge gained through Rory Compton's letters from Europe, had made her aware that mental problems, such as depression, could be overcome. Research in medical and nursing care in Europe had progressed at a more rapid pace, he told her, and there had been progress in the prevention of pestilence infesting battlefields. He mentioned published articles which might assist her own studies and spoke of his own authorship of one printed in an eminent medical review in Vienna.

With this in mind, Clarrie had sought out Clara Barton, a nurse who served at Chatham. The two women were not in the same work group, though they shared similar views about hygiene on the operating tables and in the wards. During their many conversations, the two like-minded nurses reflected on Rory's experience in Vienna. Clarrie spoke of his work under the patronage of Dr. Ignaz Semmelweis, a leading European physician who required physicians and midwives to clean their hands rigorously before attending child birth. This had led to a dramatic reduction of maternal deaths due to child-bed fever. This result had not yet been officially accepted by the profession, though many European physicians, including Rory, took heed of the theory. Semmelweiss had also studied the prevention of contagion in other areas though again his conclusions had been discounted by the European medical hierarchy at that time. In spite of that, Rory believed his mentor was correct, and prevention of contagion on the battlefields was foremost in his mind.

Clarrie longed to seek his advice on the situation pertaining at Chatham. She knew that of the many scourges of a war hospital, the incidence of typhus, typhoid and dysentery, was paramount, made worse by poor ventilation and overcrowding. To alleviate the overcrowding at Chatham, a system of tents had been organized to house those who were on their way to recovery. The necessity for disinfecting operating areas as well as surgical equipment following each operation was foremost in both Clarrie's and Clara's minds. Together the two women organized volunteer groups of staff and recovering soldiers to help in the essential cleansing process.

When on duty as an assistant to the surgeons, Clarrie insisted there was sufficient water and carbolic soap available to wash hands thoroughly prior to and following each operation, as well as a fresh set of disinfected surgical appliances. She insisted the clothes of surgeons and operating staff were covered with aprons, each destined for either the laundry or the furnace at the end of each operation, Clarrie smiled as she remembered her own strict hygiene rules when the bakery was first opened, and how easy it had been to implement it in comparison to her current project.

Neither medical nor nursing staff got used to the grinding sound as the surgeon sawed off a badly injured limb. Once removed, it was skinned. The removed skin was sown over the wound to ensure a smooth stump. By now Clarrie had the courage to insist that this piece of skin should be washed, as well as the open stump, in an effort to prevent infection. At first the surgeons refused. They said that the ether sedation could wear off before completion if they added another few minutes to the process. They also spoke of the shortage of water and suggested that any water used to wash the skin and the stump could be better used to alleviate the thirst of patients.

One day Clarrie snapped back at the surgeon who refused her request. She pointed to a bowl of clean water she had already requested prior to the start of the operation, and glared at the surgeon.

"Do you remember the young boy who had his left leg and right hand amputated last Monday and how he screamed when he realized what you had done?" she asked. The disquieted young surgeon nodded.

"Well, he died this morning. His wounds were badly infected. Let's say this water here is his water ration for today, had he survived. The poor fellow won't have died in vain, will he, if we can save the next patient from a similar death by using his rations?"

The shocked surgeon acquiesced to Clarrie's request. He never refused again and in time Chatham's teams of surgeons ensured the procedure was part of their care plan. Within a month, Clara Barton's records revealed the number of soldiers dying from wound infections had been reduced.

"That is not to say that the problem of hygiene is over," Clarrie said to her own team. "It'll take ages before there's a general acceptance of increased cleaning in every corner of the hospital."

That project became her passion.

One day Clarrie was called to an inconsolable young soldier who had lost his right arm. When she tried to talk to him about ways of overcoming such a handicap, he yelled out in a series of expletives.

"It's not my f…ing arm, it's my bl…y ring. My f…ing wedding ring. I'd been married for just three weeks when I had to leave her to come to this hell hole. What will she say when she knows I've lost the ring?"

He was heartbroken.

Clarrie knew what she had to do. She hurried to the now stinking pile of the day's amputated limbs, praying they had not already been taken for interment. She recognized the soft, brown almost hairless arm of the young boy. During that particular operation she had worried about the future effect the amputation would have on the youth. She had also noticed the ring, but had not thought much about it as she dealt with the process of helping the surgeon patch the stump. She tried to ignore the stench as she pulled out the severed arm from the pile of rotting flesh and released the ring, a difficult task as the finger had swelled.

She took the ring back to the boy, who was overjoyed. The next day she gave him a chain she wore only occasionally.

"Let's put your ring on this chain, so you can wear it round your neck until your other hand becomes less swollen. It will in time, when your body gets over the shock of what's happened to it. You can touch the ring now, every time you think of your wife."

The boy's look of gratitude was worth the agony of searching the odorous pile of limbs and the smile she gave to him was radiant, her eyes glowing.

The men stared at her.

"Nurse, you are really beautiful when you smile like that. Do it more often," one of them called out.

She said she would try to remember, and left the ward, her stride longer and quicker than usual as the tears she did not want the men to see flooded her eyes.

Following the incident, she always checked the fingers of the patient and removed any rings before the operation began, carefully putting them into the tiny hand-made pockets she made in her limited spare time. She penned the patient's operation number to it. Patients were always thrilled at the safe return of their jewelry, and the system became part of the operation routine.

As time went on, Clarrie earned a reputation for her dragonesque attitude, but after working under her strict hygiene regime, one surgeon after another acknowledged the measurable improvement in the recovery of their patients. One likened this to the efforts of Florence Nightingale during the Crimean War. That comparison was, to Clara Barton and Clarrie, worth all the effort they put into their campaign.

When Dr. Rory Compton arrived for duty as a surgeon, their work still had a long way to go, but he realized the conditions at Chatham were superior to those he had seen at his first battlefield hospital, on returning from Europe.

Clarrie was not surprised to learn Rory had been allocated to Chatham Manor. There had been so many coincidences, not only in her own life, but the lives of other medical staff, who suddenly found a patient had been their next-door neighbor, a cousin, or even the brother-in-law of their best friend at school.

"What a pity you weren't here six weeks ago," she said, after greeting him. "Beth and Laura were here."

He did not believe her.

"Well, you'll have letters winging their way over to you," she answered, laughing, "because they both said they were going to write to you."

Clarrie was surprised to hear that Rory's wife and son were still in France.

"For once I listened to my father-in-law," he grinned. "It wasn't the right time to bring them over from Europe. They're safer there. Once this mess is finished, I'll go over for them."

His in-laws had suggested they would return with them and settle down in America. Both Rory and Clarrie grimaced at the thought and laughed.

Rory showed her a picture of his son, Louis Antoine.

"He's just like my sister Mary at that age," he told her.

It was a happy moment. Clarrie thought the picture of his wife, Marie-Louise, looked familiar. She wondered if he had shown her the same picture before. But it hit her suddenly that evening, as she was helping a soldier to wash his body with his remaining hand. The image resembled Beth as she had looked some years back.

The following day Clarrie spoke to Rory about Beth's near-breakdown.

"She was remembering her sister Maya's death all those years ago and I was so surprised, as I don't recall her mentioning it after she went to Richmond."

Rory was more concerned than Clarrie had expected.

"She's showing classic signs of depression. It probably resurfaced when she became involved in the war. What is she doing, exactly?" he asked

Clarrie grimaced and shook her head.

"She didn't even hint at it," Clarrie said. "Laura's also a bit of a mystery. She masqueraded as a male soldier for a while until she was discovered. It appears she's yet to be punished for that. I've heard of a similar incident, and the woman was slung into jail, though Laura seems to have been pardoned by the army."

"She stayed with me and Beth for those few days. Her hair had been cut very short in her days as a soldier. It's growing well, though still short. One day I heard Beth asking her if her wig had arrived, which was thought-provoking to say the least. They changed the subject when they saw me and frankly I had enough to think about other than Laura's hair and didn't follow it up."

"When she left, two soldiers accompanied her, though she wasn't under arrest as far as I could see. I don't know where she was going. Beth had left the day before, and I know she was going to Louisville. Her depression seemed to have lifted, though she wasn't quite as sparky as she had been. When she left, I heard her say to Laura that she'd see her soon, like they knew they'd be with each other in the near future. It's a mystery. Do you think they're into espionage?"

"Yes," was Rory's simple response, but he continued to look worried as he ran a hand through his hair.

Clarrie and Rory were happy to renew their old friendship, as they tackled the problems of sanitation and anti-infection together. It soon became clear to Rory, however, just how tired and ill Clarrie was. Her former colleague who had collapsed a while back had not returned, which did not matter too much as the hospital had almost emptied, as the wounded were returned to their families or city hospitals.

Some patients remained, but the staff was well able to cope with the decreased workload. Clarrie concentrated on her disinfecting and cleaning program, for it had been suggested that Chatham may be required as a hospital again in the future.

A former nurse, whom Clarrie had known well, returned to Chatham to open a soup kitchen there during the winter.

Everyone was aware the two armies were based on the opposite banks of the river for the winter. The Army of the Potomac occupied Stafford County, at the back of Chatham Manor, while the Confederates settled in Spotsylvania, across the river. They were waiting for the spring and whatever that season would bring.

Clarrie was ruthless as she went about her massive cleaning spree, carried out under the banner of the U.S. Sanitary

Commission. Chatham itself housed the Union pickets during this period. A few doctors remained for the benefit of the camp, one of whom was Rory, who kept a careful eye on Clarrie. In due course he attempted to persuade his friend to return to Lexington. She did not want to leave, feeling that she knew the house well enough now, and had cleaned almost every nook and cranny, in readiness for any further battle that some felt could occur in the spring.

"You're a brave woman," Rory said, "but it is not a brave thing to be foolish. There will be no battle during the winter months. If there is a skirmish at all it could be around Fredericksburg or even Chancellorsville, but we've learned so many lessons from the last battles, it'll probably be a smaller one. This really is no place for a woman. If you return to Lexington now, you can regain your strength, in the knowledge that you have made this house a suitable place to treat wounded troops, and if necessary you could apply to nurse here again."

"I can't leave, there's still much to be done. I want to be here in case there is another battle in the spring. I must know that this house really is capable of saving lives rather than destroying them."

She cast a beseeching glance at him.

"When I said this is no place for a woman, what I was trying to say is that the life you've lived and witnessed during the past months is not conducive to a young, tender woman like you, either physically or mentally. You've already suffered much adversity in your life. I know your character is strong, but you have to accept your flesh is weak. I can see signs of possible cardiac problems – your color, your breathlessness, your irritability. You may have inherited the heart weakness that's within your family, but more likely it's because you have overstretched yourself. You're at the end of your tether and don't realize it. You owe it to your family and to yourself to take a long leave now."

"I'm as fit as ever I was," Clarrie spluttered through clenched teeth, annoyed beyond belief at Rory's impudent and arrogant rant.

"Clarrie," Rory said, realizing her irritation, "you're one of my closest friends and very dear to me. I've been concerned enough to watch you over the past weeks, and I know full well that if you do not return home, even for a brief time, your health *will* deteriorate. Frankly, the risk of cardiac failure is painfully obvious to me and you may die. You could also be on the verge of a mental breakdown."

He saw her look of surprise and the angry confusion. He took her in his arms and held her for a few moments, before lowering her onto the long, battered sofa in the room. He continued to hold her close.

"Listen to me," he whispered, as she struggled to free herself. "Just listen for a minute. What I've said is not as surprising as it might at first seem to you. Let's consider everything in a rational way, as we've always done."

They talked, and Rory felt her relax, as her tears dropped onto his arms. He let her weep. When she calmed down at last, he spoke again, knowing that the tears had been the first tentative step toward her healing.

"You have seen so much suffering. You've heard screams of agony knowing you could not stop a young man's pain. You've watched the mutilation of bodies, knowing the rest of their lives were ruined. You've seen piles of putrefying severed limbs and seen death at its worst. Although you have worked miracles for those men, some died in the end. That could break any doctor, never mind a compassionate woman like you. You feel guilty because you couldn't prevent the deaths."

He stopped, allowing her time to take in what he had said.

"Yes," he went on, "you have given so much to those men; gentleness, compassion, love and care above your call of duty. You've fought the scourge of infection, and you've worked wonders here in that alone. You feel that all your efforts have been in vain, that you must carry on with this personal battle of yours. You probably realize Laura had similar feelings when her brother died and she tried to scourge herself of them by becoming him, a fighting soldier. You're neither mentally nor physically capable of doing what she did, but what you have done is equal to anything that Laura has achieved. Believe me."

Clarrie released herself from Rory's arms and looked at him, astonished.

Before she could say anything, he said, "What you don't realize is that all this has been a battle raging away in your psyche, destroying your peace of mind, your ability to sleep. Without those two essential aspects of life, your health has suffered. After witnessing so much suffering, your body is now telling you it's had enough. If you don't overcome this mutilation of your own mind and body, and break your obsession to keep Chatham going, you'll destroy yourself. Think, Clarrie. Think about it."

It was with some misgivings that Clarrie left a few days later for Kentucky. As she left, she heard the soft whisperings in the tree tops as they shook down moist droplets onto the few grass blades still standing. There were no bird songs and in the quiet of early morning, the only sound was her breathing, and the nervous stomping of the horse waiting for her.

All of a sudden a thought came, unbidden, that there would be no need to comb out a head of matted hair or a beard this morning, or ever again. The thought of the task sickened her, and she wondered why it had hit her right now. It never had when the hospital was full of scurvy bodies. A shudder racked her as she realized now really was the time to leave this house, this camp for soldiers whose trade had been unwilling slaughter.

As her journey home began, escorted by an orderly, she retained her composure. She was moving forward, she told herself, to a life where once more she could help to remove the burdens of everyday folks unable to help themselves. She would begin with the plight of those families now deprived of their men-folk, and the greater predicament, in her mind at least, of the men deprived of some of their limbs and means of livelihood.

She knew they would never forget what they had witnessed, or achieve complete peace of mind.

Rory hugged her as he handed her up into the dilapidated cart lined with old, clean blankets and a couple of cushions for comfort.

She had glanced round as she saw a movement at the door out of the corner of her eye. The small number of doctors, nurses and orderlies remaining at Chatham had gathered to wave her off, all smiling, wishing her luck. Clarrie waved back, her sense of loss hidden by her own smile.

She hoped it would not be too long before Rory could return to his home in Cynthiana. She had told him she would write a reassuring letter to Marie Louise in France as soon as she got home.

Clarrie sighed to herself as Chatham and the waving medics and nurses were lost to sight. She and Rory could have made a marvelous team as life partners, she thought, for what seemed to her the millionth time, though she had always known it had never been an option. Despite her long-held and unspoken longing for a future with him, she began to look forward.

She wondered how she could begin to assist those poor soldiers and families who had even more cause than she to remember the pain and loss of war. As she journeyed toward the rail connection to Kentucky, she began to draw up a plan for her new life.

Chapter 17
Laura, Beth and Espionage

"Spying and espionage go hand in hand," said Captain Welham, Laura's mentor. "Spying is the act of accessing confidential information for political or military use; the act of passing this information to appropriate factions is espionage. You will be involved in both."

Thus Laura was introduced to her new life, having been warned that her job was not all excitement and thrills as portrayed in Longfellow's Paul Revere poem.

Her first assignment was to uncover a plot against the Union forces involving the theft of raw materials from a small pharmaceutical company. She had assumed she would meet up with Beth once in Louisville, but apart from early contact with Captain Welham, she was left alone to learn the tricks of her new commitment.

Armed with a few tips and the name of a spy suspect, a well-to-do man known for his partiality to billiard playing, the daunted Laura soon learned the art of extracting information from alcohol-induced billiard players. Posing as a wealthy young man known as Larry, she became adept at the popular game. She had no difficulty in repudiating allegiance to either side of the current conflicts and was able to extract useful information when playing at fashionable billiard saloons or in the homes of wealthy folks. Within a month, she had infiltrated the social circle in which the thieves functioned and was able to identify three men and a woman as culprits. A couple of weeks following their arrest, the gang-leader was also apprehended.

Laura's next assignment required a new male disguise and she now presented as a chatty, shabby, rustic fellow, gleaning information here and there from unsuspecting individuals. Known as 'young Tommy' this untidy, lazy youth in their midst liked nothing better than sitting in drinking houses, enjoying a good old natter, returning the expletives learned during army days with gusto.

As 'Tommy', Laura soon became part of a band of youths whose sole *raison d'etre* was to harass and disrupt the ever-present Union forces. The gang was organized by a large bear of a man called Big Hal, who lived next door to a cranky old spinster, Mrs. Welland with whom 'Tommy' lodged. Laura did not relish being part of this team, but was obliged to do so if 'Tommy' was to retain Big Hal's confidence.

Mrs. Welland always made a fuss of 'Tommy'.

"At least you keep your room tidy," she said one day. "You're a rough'un to look at, but your heart's in the right place. I'll do your washing wi' mine if you like. You haven't got that that much as far as I can see."

Laura appreciated living with Mrs. Welland. She was a stout woman, short in stature but always clean and neat. Laura left her small stock of male clothing and personal belongings in her room, taking care to hide her necessary feminine items, and made do with the rough soap and one towel per week. She was surprised to find that bed linen would be changed only once a month and that the indoor latrine was not available to lodgers. She made do with the malodorous shack at the bottom of Mrs. Welland's yard.

"Call me Mrs. W.," Mrs. Welland had said one evening. "My other lodgers did that, though sometimes they call me other things, and they were not very flatterin' I must say."

From time to time Mrs. W. invited 'Tommy' to spend an evening with her in the small living area following the evening meal. The tiny kitchen on the left of the room was stocked with a small number of utensils, drinking mugs, plates, knives, forks and spoons.

"Just enough for no more than three visitors," she had said. "I don't like too many things in my house. It's only there to be cleaned and why waste the time when there's only me and a lodger?"

One asset of living with Mrs. Welland was her cooking. There was no skimping on the breakfast of eggs, ham and new baked bread provided each morning, nor the evening meal of a hot meat dish and vegetables, followed by a wonderful brew of hot coffee. After the first week 'Tommy' was invited to eat in the small living room with Mrs. W., who appreciated her lodger doing the clearing away and washing up afterward.

The other asset was Mrs. W.'s pony.

"I bought it for my son," she said one day, "he's gone off west to fight them red-faced folk across there, but he'll come back even if it's just to see old Flankie again. I take care of 'im, but not so good as my son did."

209

Laura soon learned that Mrs. W. did not approve of Big Hal's gang.

"You're too good fer the likes of 'im and his pals," she would say, "You're a rough 'un but yer manners are an improvement on 'im."

'Tommy' was well liked as he took part in their raids on Union buildings, kicking down fences and stealing from stores. On one occasion Laura joined in with one of the boys as they stole clothes from a washing line from an army captain's small garden. She was not, however, invited to all the planned meetings and raids, but by careful listening and common sense she managed to ascertain when and where these would be held.

As soon as she heard of a meeting and venue, she would seek out the location in advance to look for a suitable hiding place, where she could hear what was said. By now, she had got into the habit of exercising Mrs. W's pony. When traveling to the venue, she was careful to pad the pony's hooves to avoid the clatter as he trotted along, and always hung a sack of hay around its neck on arrival, in an effort to prevent the animal becoming restless during a long wait. It was from these planned, well-hidden vantage points that Laura derived her best intelligence. She made her contact aware of the information gleaned, knowing the agent would decide whether or not to disrupt the plans. She knew it was expedient not to sabotage all the planned disruptions, in an effort to prevent suspicion of subversions among the perpetrators.

During the first weeks, Laura had become aware that Big Hal was more than just a nuisance to the Union forces. He was a spy. As she listened to their future plans from her hideout, hardly daring to breathe, she would watch how the gang folded notes lengthwise before stuffing them into the craw of dead poultry, apparently ready for the next day's market, and how documents were shoved into sacks of flour which were then shaken. Sometimes, small notes were hidden in the handles of knives, or inserted within the false soles of boots. She picked out the same men on each occasion and so fathomed out who the real traitors were and who, from their absence, were no more than 'back-up' tormenters like 'Tommy'. She was able to locate the message 'drop-off'' points.

Laura was excited with her new role and felt that at last she had found her niche, so she was disappointed when, after a few weeks, the agent instructed her to extricate herself from Big Hal's guerrilla force. She was advised to start the process immediately by suggesting to Mrs. W. of a fancy to move west where 'he' had heard there were jobs available on the farms. Laura was also told that Big Hal and his whole gang would be rounded up within the next two or three weeks, based on the information she had provided.

"All the information you've provided has helped us to discover valuable documentation and disrupt their plans. You've done a damn good service," the agent, an elderly man devoid of any obvious characteristics, told her.

"A Captain Sullivan will contact you soon, probably three or four days prior to the proposed coup of Big Hal and his gang. Meanwhile, you're to carry on as if nothing's happened. Good luck."

Laura was delighted with the results. She loved this exciting subterfuge and the buzz it gave her as well as the satisfaction she gained from being useful to her country. Her former existence as a quiet, staid, school-teacher was almost illusory nowadays, and she even found it difficult to relate to her more recent life as a fighting soldier.

Captain George Sullivan had contacted her a few days later, and had taken her to a small house where she was allowed to revert to her own persona, as she began learning the process of code-breaking and writing new codes. It was a relief in some ways to spend most of her time in a relaxed atmosphere and she appreciated the bonhomie of a few young men and women on the same learning program. She did miss, however, the excitement of being out and about, finding and analyzing useful information for the Union cause. However, as she waited for her next outside job, Laura made the most of the cleanliness, calm and ability to live as a woman. She was sorry there had been no contact with Beth, whom she longed to see again.

After a while she was contacted by Captain Sullivan, who informed her she was to act as his ward for the next job. He provided suitable clothing, and two days later took her to the home of a Doctor Brendan Lockwood, a distinguished physician and his wife, Esme. Mrs. Lockwood, a poised, elegant and attractive woman, was the hostess to an evening function in the absence of her husband, who had been called away. He would not return for two or three days, Esme informed her guests, but he had particularly wanted her to carry on with the planned evening.

Laura had been given little information about her role, except she would be required to undertake what could be a dangerous task for the Union. For the function, she dressed in the modest though fashionable clothing provided. She was duly introduced to Mrs.

Lockwood as Sullivan's ward, but was surprised to be welcomed as the woman's new house house-guest for the next few weeks.

"Laura is very shy, as you can see," Captain Sullivan said to Mrs. Lockwood, "a pure, unsophisticated girl from Kentucky."

"Yes, I can see that," responded Mrs. Lockwood, "but I'll take care of her until you return from your war duties."

"I am so grateful to you for agreeing to look after her for what we hope will be a short time," he said.

Laura bristled and glared at him, taken aback at the surprise. This was not part of the script she had anticipated.

"My dear Laura," Sullivan said, with a lift of the eyebrow that suggested she should say nothing, "I haven't had the opportunity to tell you of my new plans. I'm so sorry I couldn't meet you at the railroad station this afternoon, but I hope my arrangements for the journey ensured your comfort."

Laura agreed she had been comfortable and listened while Captain Sullivan explained to Mrs. Lockwood how difficult the life of a Union captain was nowadays from a time point of view. He simpered a little more at the elegant woman, who mewed back.

"Although Laura is delightful, the care of her is not what I need right now," he concluded, patting his temporary ward on the shoulder quite firmly, as though warning her. Laura felt sick at the obvious flirting between the two of them and the situation she suddenly found herself in. She turned her head away and glowered at her feet.

"I don't have my night things, sir," she said, looking at him in hope that she would not, after all, be expected to stay. She liked living in the small lodging house and was indignant that she found herself dumped upon Mrs. Lockwood without any warning. She felt Captain Sullivan should have let her know she would be staying as an intimate guest of this unknown woman.

"Oh, that's alright," Sullivan said, "I got the housekeeper to pack your things. I left them with your butler, ma'am," he said, turning to Mrs. Lockwood with an ingratiating smile.

"I'll see they're taken up to your room, Laura," Mrs. Lockwood said.

Laura noticed that while Mrs. Lockwood's well-rouged mouth smiled, her eyes did not as she drew her further into the room where the party was now in full swing.

Mrs. Lockwood beckoned a maid over with instructions to look after the 'young lady's' luggage.

"I'm sorry, there aren't any other young people here this evening," she said. "How old are you, Laura? Eighteen?"

Laura did not know how old she was supposed to be. She knew nothing of this woman except that she was to reside at her home for a while. Laura had not been informed at that stage that the less she knew of her role, the more gauche and immature she would appear when introduced to Mrs. Lockwood and her guests.

"I was always told that it was rude to ask a lady her age," she retorted, in an effort to cover up her confusion.

"Oh dear," said Mrs. Lockwood, "a gal with spirit! " She took hold of Laura's arm, nipping it in the process. "Come," the woman said, "I'll introduce you to my guests."

Laura was relieved, realizing that in so doing, Mrs. Lockwood would tell her who she was supposed to be.

Really, she thought, *Sullivan's a bit complaisant in his duties. Or is he supposed to act like that?*

She knew only that he was part of Alan Pinkerton's Secret Service organization.

As Mrs. Lockwood and Laura walked through a crowd of women dressed in their opulent best and well-heeled, haughty men, Laura had the sense to realize she was looked upon as Mrs. Lockwood's protégée. She was quick to compare the friendly Compton parties with this false, stiff merriment. Her initial bewilderment at her sudden role ensured apathetic responses to their attempts at conversation with her.

The younger men admitted to each other that in time she would be a charmer, with her creamy skin devoid of any paint or powder, large eyes and shiny light-brown hair, a girl worth nurturing now for the harvest that could follow. Laura did not know this and maintained a little-girl image throughout the evening. Captain Sullivan did not reappear and though both craned their necks from time to time, he was not spotted.

Mrs. Lockwood glanced around the room again.

"Oh," she said, "I see Doctor Spurrell is here. Let me introduce you to him,"

He was from Kentucky and Mrs. Lockwood hoped he might take her awkward guest off her hands for a while. She took Laura's arm firmly as they zigzagged through the crowd. As they moved forward, Laura noticed a handsome young man, who appeared to be looking for someone, suddenly move toward them, a broad smile settled on his face. She felt a sudden tightening of Mrs. Lockwood's grip on her arm, which became firmer, so much so that she gasped in pain. As she did so, she glanced at Mrs. Lockwood. To her surprise she noticed a faint look of panic in the woman's eyes as she acknowledged the man with a side-way glance and a small negative shake of the head that seemed to suggest 'go away'.

The man passed by, not even glancing at them, and Laura wondered if she had imagined the incident, as they continued to push through the guests toward the Kentucky doctor

Mrs. Lockwood released her hold on Laura's arm and was astonished to notice the red marks, which Laura felt would turn to bruises.

"Oh, my dear, I am so sorry," she said in genuine concern, realizing that only she could have inflicted the marks.

"I do hate crowds so, don't you?" she went on. "I was afraid I would lose you among all these full skirts and all. You're quite a little thing, really and we must feed you up. Sullivan tells me you've not been well."

She tried to smile, but it was obvious to the astute Laura that Mrs. Lockwood was stressed. She was about to say she would like to go to her bedroom, when a youth tapped Mrs. Lockwood on the shoulder.

"Madam," he said, his accent pure Richmond, "I saw this drop from your reticule as you pushed through the crowd down there."

He pointed vaguely toward the left. Laura was puzzled as they had not come from that direction. That fact did not deter Mrs. Lockwood. She took a small roll of paper from his hand and popped it into her purse with measured nonchalance.

He left her with an elegant bow, and turning to Laura, proffered the same courtesy. Laura was impressed. She had not experienced such good manners toward her since her arrival in this house, and rather enjoyed it. For once in her life she preened. She could hardly believe it of herself.

She never did get to meet Doctor Spurrell, as Captain Sullivan appeared out of the crowd with startling suddenness.

"My dear Esme," he said. He looked relieved, which seemed to gratify Mrs. Lockwood. "I've been looking everywhere for you. I wanted to get you both some refreshment. Come over here, there are some seats. I've asked two of my men to safeguard them."

He brought them refreshments which Laura ate with enthusiasm, and when the music began, the captain asked Mrs. Lockwood to dance a quadrille with him. She accepted with eagerness. She passed her reticule to Laura for safe-keeping.

It did not take long for Laura to understand Sullivan's discreet nod at the bag as he took Mrs. Lockwood into his arms and whisked her onto the floor. She thought at first she had misunderstood the instruction, but after a second nod from him, as they passed again, Mrs. Lockwood's face suffused with the sheer pleasure of it all, she opened the bag slowly and pulled out the roll of paper.

She recognized the spy code immediately. Much of her training and work in Richmond had been deciphering both Union and Confederate codes, a task that she had found easy. This code was new, though she was familiar with the principles. The message was short; a date, a time, and a place together with a code name of the recipient of a package. It did not indicate who the recipient was, but here was proof of some sort of illegal delivery. She quickly rolled the paper and returned it to the reticule.

Five minutes later a breathless but happy Mrs. Lockwood plumped herself down next to Laura.

Sullivan asked Laura if she would care to dance the polka with him.

"Aren't you too tired?" asked a petulant Mrs. Lockwood, who needed to recover prior to assuming her position in his arms once again.

"My dear Esme, I can't be too tired to dance with my ward. She deserves one short polka, don't you think?"

The wonderful smile he bestowed upon Esme reassured her of the captain's continued interest.

"I was thinking that one so young should be in her bed by now, so perhaps I will take Laura to her room after your dance," she said, stroking Laura's left cheek with gentle care. The gesture made Beth feel a bit like a package that had become cumbersome and had to be got rid of.

On the dance floor Sullivan told Laura how he had kept a surreptitious eye on them during the past hour.

"I saw that incident with the first fellow when he realized he should not acknowledge Mrs. Lockwood," Sullivan told her, "and watched him speak with another other man and give him something. You know the rest. This guile, more or less, confirms suspicions that she's involved in a serious breach within the Louisville medical storekeepers head-quarters. Large stock losses have occurred, though no discrepancies have been proved in their records. We have to be careful though as Mrs. Lockwood's husband is one of our most respected medical purveyors. There could be serious consequences if we accuse her unjustly, or if we implicate her husband without cause. She's a Southerner, he's not, so he may be innocent of any wrong-doing. I personally believe in *his* innocence, but it's a bit like walking a tight-rope until we know for sure."

"You mean she's stealing from –"

Before Laura could finish her question, Sullivan put a finger to his lips.

"We'll discuss it later," he said.

As they danced, Laura whispered the contents of the coded message to him.

"Good job, well done," he whispered back.

As they returned to Mrs. Lockwood, taking their time, with Laura looking exhausted just as he had instructed, he outlined their plan to catch Mrs. Lockwood.

"It could be dangerous for you, but you have proved your worth during your recent career."

He grinned down at her.

Laura's excitement grew, though she did not know whether this was due to the captain's nearness or the new task she had been set.

"I think you're right, Esme," Sullivan said on their return, "we should get this little maid to her bed. I'll cancel my carriage if you can see your way to providing me with a room for the night."

Esme Lockwood could not look more delighted and quite forgot to commiserate with her young guest as she took the captain's arm.

"Perhaps you will escort us, Captain Sullivan, so that you can reassure yourself of Laura's comfort while you are away. I will also arrange for your own room to be prepared."

Laura could not help but feel sorry for poor Doctor Lockwood, until she remembered that he may be involved in the black-hearted plan to steal vital medicine from the Union Army. She knew from Clarrie the devastation that was inflicted when there was insufficient medication to treat the battle-wounded.

The next day, Sullivan left the Lockwood home. Laura had already seen him early that morning when further plans were outlined. *At long last*, she thought, she knew what her role was. She must at all costs, Sullivan had said, continue to retain the 'little lost girl' image. Breakfast had been served to her in her room, and at a time already agreed, she ran down to catch Sullivan as he climbed into his carriage brought round half an hour earlier by his driver. Mrs. Lockwood was already there, her hair tousled, face pale without the heavy rouge and powder.

Laura stood back.

"When will I see you again?" Mrs. Lockwood pouted, putting up her face for a kiss, which was planted on a cheek. She was disappointed, made worse because she was sure she had seen the driver grin.

"A soldier's life," Sullivan explained, with a shrug of his shoulders. "I'll be in touch as soon as I can, you can be sure of that."

He saluted her, waved to Laura and off he went.

Laura went forward to greet Mrs. Lockwood.

"Thank you so much for my lovely room and my breakfast," she said with genuine thanks, looking up at the tall woman in front of her.

Seeing the young girl dressed in a somewhat childish smock, her hair untidy, large eyes looking up at her with such trust, Esme's heart lurched. She was not surprised at her reaction. She had always longed for children, and was ungrateful to God that he had not blessed her marriage with them. She had said this to her local church minister many times.

"God will have other plans for you. Be patient." The minister had responded on each occasion

Esme Lockwood now looked down at Laura and wondered if the minister was right after all, and it was to be this shy creature that was to be her destiny – a young girl whom she could adopt as her own daughter, nurture her as such, just as she had always dreamed. Yes, she would have liked Sullivan to have stayed for a few more hours, she thought, but if this girl was to be her destiny, there was no time like the present to begin.

She took Laura's right arm.

"I'm so sorry to have caused those bruises on your lovely skin last night," she said.

She was pleased to see that the marks had almost gone. She kissed Laura's arm, and putting her own arm around her new project, escorted her back to her room, talking all the time of the new gowns she would buy for her.

Laura could hardly believe it all, especially when Mrs. Lockwood asked her if she would like a permanent role in the household as her personal companion.

This is uncanny, she thought, for the possibility of a definitive role in the Lockwood household was something she and Sullivan had already discussed.

She had demurred, stating that her guardian would need to give permission, but was glad to accept the invitation to stay for as long as she wished.

Mrs. Lockwood felt her own future looked bright. She would take care of this innocent young person, utilizing her under-used maternal instincts in making Laura someone to be proud of. She knew she could do it.

"Perhaps you would like to go to Richmond with me next month," she now suggested.

During their early morning discussion, Sullivan had confessed flirting with Esme Lockwood the night before in an effort to learn more about her.

So besotted was Esme, just as Sullivan had planned, that her heart had ruled her head for a time as she confessed to her Confederate allegiance, believing her lover was also a Confederate. She had spoken of her unsatisfactory, lonely marriage and an urgent need to feel useful to her country and the Southern cause. He had sympathized with her divided loyalty between her husband's proclivity and that of her own.

During their early morning talk, Sullivan informed Laura that he and his peers had been aware of Esme's strong desire for children for some time.

"Esme Lockwood has always been so discreet and careful it seemed we would never crack her shell. When we became aware of her unhappiness about being childless, we wondered if there was a way to use that knowledge. And then you came along into our spy world and we knew what to do," he said.

He stopped, trying to weigh up what Laura was thinking, as she remained inscrutable.

"That is why we chose you to act the part you did last evening," he continued. "We were forced to leave you in the dark about your role, in order to achieve that simplicity of spirit you demonstrated. We had counted on her strong maternal instincts to protect your youthfulness and innocence. That's why we played it the way we did, though I hadn't bargained for her initial jealousy of my relationship with you. I know you found it difficult, but the end result is good, I think. The unexpected benefit was your ability to decode that message."

The next weeks were hectic. Esme, as she now liked Laura to call her, announced she wanted to complete a large colored quilt to take with her to Richmond. Laura offered to help, and was soon at work stitching in the larger than usual patches, though puzzled when Esme asked her to leave one side of each square open.

"You mean like a pocket?" asked Laura.

Esme laughed. "I'll tell you why later on," was her enigmatic response.

Beth had already guessed that this was how medication would be taken out of Kentucky into Virginia, if indeed Esme was proved to be a thief.

She went along with the work without further comment, and within two days the task was completed. Esme was amazed at her skills.

"I have always been good at needlework," said Laura, with no hint of modesty.

Esme decided they could make a smaller quilt before they had to leave for Richmond.

"My friend would welcome an extra one, I'm sure," she had said.

The day came when Esme and Laura had to report to the Union headquarters of Brigadier General Jeremiah Boyle, to obtain passes to cross the line into Virginia. As the Lockwoods moved in the highest of the Louisville aristocratic circles, Esme knew there would be no difficulty in obtaining one for herself as her own husband would act as her guarantor. Captain Sullivan had assured her, through an emissary, he would guarantee a pass for Laura.

Although they had these guarantees, the two still had to wait in line to obtain their passes. During the long wait Laura noticed a quietly spoken man watching Esme. She took careful note of his bearing and stance, though his facial features were part-hidden within a thick, black beard and moustache. He wore a Stetson-style hat that covered his hair, though strands had crept through, indicating it was as black as his facial covering. She thought he looked familiar and stared at him for a while. She decided the familiarity was created by the Stetson, the kind worn by Timothy Compton whenever he returned to his Lexington home.

It was late afternoon and the room was dark when Esme and Laura left the office. As they prepared to exit, they were approached by the black-bearded man.

"Mrs. Lockwood?" he queried. He asked to speak with her, making it plain that he wanted a private conversation.

Laura made the most of the opportunity to locate a much needed latrine. On return, she placed herself behind a large column separating the seating area from the waiting area, watching the reflections of Esme and the man through the darkening glass window at the opposite end of the room. Their faces became animated as they talked together. Laura couldn't hear the conversation, but quickly drew out a stub of a pencil and her ever-ready notebook, and made a sketch of his appearance. She noted the lack of polish on his boots and the side button detail. His feet were small, as were his hands, but she did notice the increased height of the soles and heels and realized he was a small man with a need to look taller. She would get the drawing to Sullivan as soon as she could. She learned later that Esme had invited him for dinner the following day.

Later that evening, Esme told Laura the main reason for her visit to Richmond was not just to visit but to transfer contraband goods to the Southern forces. The small pockets in the quilts would be used to insert various packages.

"Once inserted, we'll have to complete the seaming and sew up the pockets," Esme had told Laura.

At this stage in their relationship, the two were close enough to have discussed in full the political situation between the North and the South. Laura had been careful to lean toward the South, and so Esme was able to confide in her that the items were medication packs intended for the Southern soldiers.

"They'll weigh heavy," commented Laura, showing no concern at the content of the packages. "How will you get such heavy goods into Richmond without anyone noticing?"

"I'm worried about that, I admit, but when we're over the line, it won't matter," said Esme, "and that's why I'm glad we were able to make two quilts, with your help."

She touched Laura's face as she looked at her with real affection.

"Two individual packages will not be noticed as much as just one very heavy package, and this way, we can now take more items across the border. However, the real problem is not getting them up to the border line, but getting them across it. That's where our Mr. Black Beard comes in. With his help we can take two quilts, whereas without his help we could only take the one. By the way, his name is Wilkie. Actually, he's Captain Wilkie, a medic in one of the Southern regiments."

Laura asked how Captain Wilkie knew about Esme's role.

"We have spies everywhere," Esme replied. "He was able to give me a good account of himself. I questioned him about his antecedents and other matters known only to our particular spy-ring. The South is in great need of medication and surgical supplies but he's been unable to get anything through because he was almost captured on his last trip, and had to alter his appearance. He asked if we could join up for this effort, and proposed I make an earlier journey than planned. So, here we are."

She laughed at the surprise on Laura's face.

"Just think," she said, "this time next week all those poor injured soldiers will be benefitting from what we are doing today."

"Does an earlier start affect our passes?" Laura asked.

"No, they're valid as from today's date for three months," Esme answered, "so if you would like to, we could stay for a few weeks in Richmond. Would you like that?"

Laura said she would, though she worried about the effect of extra clothing in their luggage.

"We needn't take anything extra. I'll buy some new gowns for us in Richmond."

"Are there still clothes and shoes to purchase there?" Laura asked.

"Of course there will be. Don't worry about that," Esme said, with supreme confidence.

Later that day, Captain Wilkie visited, carrying further news.

"I came across a former colleague, Doctor White," he said. "He needs to get to Vicksburg, where he can meet Southern friends who'll get him South. He has a Federal Order to travel to Illinois, where he has to report for transportation to the South via Vicksburg. He's a paroled prisoner, you see, though that's not known to the border officials."

Captain Wilkie explained he had been concerned that Esme and Laura's luggage could be challenged, even with their official passes simply because it was heavier than that of normal travelers.

He had been keeping his ear to the ground and when he had first heard of Doctor White and the Federal Order, he realized he may have found a possible solution to Mrs. Lockwood's dilemma.

"I am aware that anyone travelling with someone holding an official Federal Order would be regarded as legitimate, particularly if they had their own passes," Wilkie told Esme.

All three realized the benefits of travelling to Illinois and then onto Vicksburg with Doctor White in the circumstances. When they met with White the following day, he demurred at first, knowing that in his situation as a Union prisoner, he could be found guilty of a more heinous crime if they were apprehended. However, Wilkie's quick talking and Esme Lockwood's comments as she stroked his arm and looked earnestly into his eyes, convinced him he was playing a vital part in the Confederate war against the Unionists.

The snag was the speed at which they would now need to start their journey within the time scale of the Federal Order. The four of them worked on filling the quilt pockets and sewing up the contents. The normal routine of meals and bed times were kept in an effort to maintain normality and prevent stress as they worked for three long days. Eventually they were ready, their personal bags packed, and the heavy parcels placed on a trailer marked for the benefit of local 'do-gooders' in Richmond. Laura made a mental note of those names with a view to passing them to northern spy agents in Richmond.

The Federal Order proved to be their safeguard as the long journey began without a hitch. They arrived by railroad in Illinois on schedule and made their way to the train that would take them onto Vicksburg. There they were greeted by four guards, who took control of their baggage and parcels, and escorted them through a number of doors. The travelers were grateful, assuming the priority treatment was provided because of the Federal Order.

When they arrived at a large empty waiting room they were asked to wait. Someone brought in a tray of hot coffee and refreshments. Their baggage was left in a corner of the room as they waited. Esme and Doctor White began to look anxious after a half-hour had passed. Wilkie offered to locate the guards and ascertain what the hold-up was.

"We've been lucky so far with the timetable, but there are disruptions on these routes these days, and it's probably that. We're better here, I suppose, rather than waiting on the platform, so I'll find out exactly where our train is. Don't worry."

He returned five minutes later.

"I was right. There's been a hold up further down the line. We'll be on the move soon."

Four railway operatives arrived 10 minutes later. They were not the original ones and more brisk in their attitude as they entered.

Without speaking, they took hold of Mr. Wilkie and Doctor White and ordered them to strip down completely.

They both looked in horror at each other and then at the two women.

Esme looked as if she was about to faint.

Laura was aghast. Something had gone very wrong. Is this what Sullivan had meant when he had told her it could be a dangerous assignment?

One of the guards said, "Not in front of the women."

Some whispering took place among the guards, and Wilkie and White were hustled out of the room. As they struggled they were dealt cuffs around their head, and Esme and Beth could hear their protests and further struggles as they were, by the sound of it, dragged down a corridor. The soft voice of Wilkie rose as his outrage increased while Doctor White wailed that he had feared this was going to happen and should have known better. The other two guards moved toward the two women, and pushed them through the door.

"Don't hurt the girl," shouted Mrs. Lockwood. "She's innocent. She's only a young girl. She's only 18."

"Old enough to be involved in this racket," said one of the guards, his voice harsh.

Laura, appalled at the suddenness of all this action, was relieved when the other guard pulled her back as Esme was taken out of the room. He relaxed his hold on her.

"Well done, ma'am. Your timetable was perfect. Everything was just as you'd said." He winked at her.

"Sorry to have treated you so roughly. You didn't deserve all that, but it was the only way to catch Mrs. Lockwood in the act, so to speak. She can't get out of this one."

The guard was a member of the police force and their red-handed capture of Mrs. Lockwood was a coup for his team and the Union cause.

The small room in which she remained was quiet once the heavy cell doors had clanged shut and the noisy voices of the men receded. The remaining guard slashed the two parcels open and the quilts spilled out in a heap.

He waited for the return of the other guards and the quilts were ripped open, revealing large quantities of quinine, morphine, ether and other medical items, as well as surgical equipment required in the battlefield hospitals. Letters and documents containing vital Union information that would be valuable to the Confederates were also discovered.

Laura was asked to supervise the counting of all the items, as the guards listed them. The two men who had led the men away returned with a white-faced, distraught Mrs. Lockwood.

"Right, who's first?" one of guards growled.

A pointed finger indicated that Laura was to be the first. Esme almost fainted when Laura was pulled to her feet and her hands tied behind her back. Laura resisted as they tried to lead her away, looking at Esme in desperation. It was then that Esme called out that the girl had nothing to do with it.

"I'll tell you everything if you'll only let the girl go. She's innocent, only a child. Her only mistake is to be in my company. She knows nothing, nothing…"

One of the men leading Laura away turned to Esme.

"Tell me everything," he said, "and I'll do my best to see that the girl comes to no harm. I promise."

Esme told him everything, how she made use of her knowledge of the official directions concerning the duties of medical purveyors and storekeepers. She had stolen requisition orders on a visit to her husband's office, and had forged his signature prior to visiting the storekeeper's office for 'urgent supplies' apparently requisitioned by her husband. She had bribed the clerk with a promise of her body and more to come the next time her husband was away. The clerk, a small 50-something widower, was unable to resist the beautiful woman, and it had been easy to obtain the medical supplies, with promises of future co-operation.

Laura was surprised when she learned that Doctor White was a valued Union agent, and Captain Wilkie was no less a person than her friend, Beth Willoughby.

"Why didn't you let me know what was going on? Didn't you trust me?" Laura asked Captain Sullivan, during a casual but lovely dinner with him and Beth later that week.

"We had to ensure Mrs. Lockwood's confession, even though we had the proof in front of us. When she heard, through the walls of the cell we had put her in, how badly we appeared to beat up the two men, and knew the same fate awaited you, we gambled she would rebel at that thought. In her mental state she had latched onto you as a simple, open girl who needed her like a child needed a mother and she'd begun to look upon you as her own. You had not expected any of the action in the rail road waiting room, and your genuine distress and frightened face brought her maternal instincts to the fore. She would not let her chick come to harm."

"But how did you know Laura would react that way? Beth asked. "You said you had *gambled* on Mrs. Lockwood's reaction when the plan unraveled. Surely you could have arrested Mrs. Lockwood on the evidence in front of you when the quilts were ripped open."

"We had to surprise Laura as well as Lockwood with our tactics, to ensure the reaction we got from her. She may have tried to implicate Laura," Captain Sullivan said. "We had to be very certain of our case within a law court and given who she is, we knew it would be expedient to have a confession rather than a long trial. All I can say is that you and Laura were part of a psychological plan to catch out Esme Lockwood. With her arrest and imprisonment, one part of the canker in a wider based coterie has been cut out. We now have further information from her and we can make further plans to take other guilty persons out of their system."

"Can Beth and I be part of those plans? Please, please…" Laura pleaded.

"No, you can't. Don't ask again." With that he got up, paid the bill and went out to arrange for a carriage to take Beth and Laura to their new lodgings.

When he returned he said, "I've been asked to inform you that your work has been praised at the highest level, and will be recorded, but for the time being your efforts must be directed to other war services. This kind of work can have detrimental effects in the long term, and we would not wish to put further pressure on young women such as you two."

He grinned at Laura who grinned back. He kissed the two girls. Then he left. Beth and Laura returned to Kentucky together as Beth wished to spend time with Sarah Willoughby.

After a few days with Clarrie, Laura returned to Longfield, where each night she would think of Captain Sullivan, who had almost broken her heart when he had grinned at her the last time she had seen him.

She thought of his soft blue eyes with the hint of amusement within them, the strand of blond hair that forever fell over his brow, his long legs, wide shoulders and his face. It was a wonderful face, she thought, kind and wise, and oh, so desirable. She remembered the love she had felt for Rory all those years ago, and knew that it was nothing in comparison to this adult sensation. A thrill surged through her body at every thought of the captain, and a desire so strong she was both excited and ashamed. She had, she knew, fallen in love.

Laura knew it was an impossible situation and that he could never have feelings for her, and vowed he would never know how much she loved him. Captain Sullivan suspected she might, for he had seen the look in her eyes as he had kissed her as he left. Beth had also guessed his feelings when he made a special plea to her to keep Laura safe until he could travel to Kentucky again. Beth suggested he should write to Laura and he promised to do so.

Chapter 18
Gettysburg Aftermath – 1863

As the army of Northern Virginia approached the small village of Gettysburg on July 1, 1863, General Robert E. Lee had no doubt he could win a decisive battle on this strip of Union territory. He knew the Army of the Potomac, under the command of Major General George Meade, was low in morale following recent Confederate victories. In the first three days of fighting 11,000 Confederate and Union soldiers had lost their lives and a further 20,000 were seriously wounded. All were left to lie on the blood-soaked Pennsylvania land.

Following the intensive battle a third of Lee's army had been killed or wounded. He had retreated toward Virginia in an attempt to prevent further slaughter of his men, pursued by the remains of Meade's army, leaving the 25-miles-square battlefield in turmoil, with thousands of dead and wounded littered throughout.

Realizing the potential battle ahead, and in spite of the wounded left behind, Meade had ordered the medical corps and ambulances to travel with him, leaving only a bare minimum of medical support.

Doctor Rory Compton was one of the first of over six hundred doctors and surgeons to arrive at the battlefield. It was early morning. The scene before him of trampled fields where the dead and wounded soldiers lay was horrific. As the six doctors and a few nurses moved onward to the village a few miles away, the only sounds were the hooves and neighing of the frightened horses, as well as the sharp intakes of breath as riders witnessed the horrors inflicted on the men. The few soldiers who had escorted them throughout their journey fell silent as the blood of their dead colleagues soaked into the fields in the strange, odd stillness. From time to time a long moan, a high-pitched scream of agony or the ranting of a crazed, injured soldier penetrated their dazed brains. This escalated as they picked their way through the jungle of mangled bodies. The sight of these poor souls was a nightmare, beyond anything Rory or his fellow medics had expected.

One of them muttered under his breath. "Fredericksburg, Fair Oaks, Yorktown battles, they were harrowing, but this one…this one…"

He was unable to finish his sentence. Another completed it.

"This one is hideous, gut-churning, and odious!" he yelled.

His voice echoed across the line of horse riders into the stillness. They all heard the whimper from the youngest of the riders, but rode on without further comment, though Rory cantered over to the youngster, and patted his hand. The boy looked up and tried to wipe the tears from his face as he acknowledged the gesture with a weak, toothy smile.

Arrival at the village was hectic. They were met by Doctor Henry Janes, a young Vermont physician renowned for his organizational skills in the hospital. He had been appointed by Doctor Letterman to establish and be responsible for the required field hospitals.

Janes knew the main areas of battle well; Wheatfield, Peach Orchard, Cemetery Ridge, Little Round Top, Devil's Den and Culp's Hill, and had allocated an area to each of the six new physicians.

Rory was allocated to Culp's Hill. Janes had already established temporary hospital tents in all the battle areas. His initial intention was that the doctors should provide immediate medical and surgical care to the wounded and to bring the more serious down to the main medical center within the village for transportation to the city hospitals. Only then could attention be given to the burial of the dead, he told the distraught medics.

He reassured them that colleagues were already working around the clock and that other medics and nurses were on their way. He spoke of the difficulty of feeding over 22,000 people, consisting of the wounded from both armies, together with 1800 Confederate prisoners and the care teams, though the lack of medical resources was Doctor Janes' paramount concern.

The following day, after a cold, rainy night under make-shift tents, their only sustenance being crackers and hot coffee, the new medical teams began a tour of their individual areas. As they assessed the problems before them, Rory's team came across an unexpected and surprising legion of well-dressed men, women and a few children, some picking pies or sweetmeats from a large picnic basket as they gaped open-mouthed at the blue and grey clad injured soldiers moaning on the ground. These folks discussed the ghastly sights and obvious suffering. While most expressed sympathy, they did not offer help.

Rory and his companions were outraged and forgot about manners as they pushed the people away in their efforts to get to the wounded. One crowd took umbrage as Rory and his colleagues pushed through the throng of onlookers.

"Who the hell are you?" shouted a large, red-faced man, annoyed when his well-dressed lady in lilac silk had been brushed to one side as medics, nurses and ambulance-men tried to push through.

"We're here to save the lives of brave men," roared one stretcher bearer.

"Get back to your home before I make you one of the victims," yelled another

His ferocious expression ensured the back-tracking of the crowd, who muttered their own threats as they turned their heads away in shame.

"At least we're not looting from the dead men," shouted one, with a wave of his hand at a group of relic hunters, many now armed with bullets, bayonets, belts, blue and grey jackets. Some carried personal mementos of the dead.

Rory was sickened, but knew his energy and efforts must be toward the living wounded. As he progressed, taking notes, calling for stretcher-bearers or a nurse from time to time, he tripped over the small frame of a soldier, a boy of about 17 lying on his back. Perhaps the boy sensed Rory looking down at his smashed body as he called out to him.

"I can't see. Are you one of us?"

His voice was feeble. He was wearing a filthy, grey jacket.

"Yes, I'm for you," Rory said, "I'm here to help you."

He tried to keep his voice calm as he looked down on a sightless face.

The boy's eyes had been blown out of their sockets, and lay splattered across his face in a clotted mess.

"I can't see," the boy said again. "Can you help me?"

He tried to raise himself up, without success.

Rory was unable to lift him and called for help. As they lifted him onto a makeshift stretcher, the boy, who now knew Rory was a doctor, asked if he would need an operation for his eyes.

"I can't see nothin'. Nothin' at all."

His stressed voice cracked, though tears could not fall from those eyeless sockets.

Rory's calm voice appeared to reassure and soothe him, but by the time they had reached a makeshift hospital tent, he had heard the final rattle of the young soldier's breath. The orderly who had helped to carry him remarked that the death was a merciful one, as they left the boy with a horrified nurse.

"He told me his name. It's Peter Wilberson, from Ohio. Will you write down his name and rank and pin it to his tunic, so that we'll know it when we bury him," Rory said to her. He told himself that when this was all over he would try and ascertain who his parents were and write to them, or even visit them.

Rory continued his search for others who may be alive but had been left for dead. An hour or so later, he heard a scream so tortuous that he felt the nerve ends prickle throughout his body. He had already seen a group of townspeople wandering round one of the fields on his patch. They were weeping as they looked for relatives and friends known to be serving with the Union Eleventh Corp. One had found her son. It was her scream that rang out over the remaining bodies, encapsulating the desolation of the scene. Rory saw an orderly run toward her. He himself could do nothing, he realized, as he grieved for her and the hundreds of dead waiting to be found.

Trained as he was to be realistic about death, he found it hard to remain so, as he helped to lift soldiers with serious wounds onto quickly assembled stretchers. For two hours he was a stretcher bearer. This time he did not hide his tears.

Two days later, the army barricaded all approaches to the battlefield and no one was admitted without a pass.

Rory knew the deterioration of the weather, which now had long spells of torrential rain, and the lack of blankets and tents, had exacerbated the suffering of the wounded.

Inadequate nutrition was another continuing problem.

Rory also realized the situation was beginning to threaten the health and well-being of the medical staff, which could have disastrous effects. He knew his own good physical health had deteriorated.

"What happened to the Letterman Plan?" Rory yelled into the air, in exasperation. "Many of the dead could have been saved if they had received early treatment. These men should be moved into the city hospitals without any more delay."

He had seen the Letterman Plan work well on other battlefields, so he and a few colleagues tackled Doctor Janes about the problems and asked how they had been allowed to escalate. Janes informed them of a series of administrative errors at commander level and that prior to leaving his post as the army's commander, Major General Hooker had ordered a reduction of medical wagons from six per division to two. There was also a reduction in ambulances.

"On whose authority did Hooker make such an insane order?" Rory roared, as others crowded around Janes as if it had been he who was responsible.

"He said that speed of movement was vital to his army, and believed that the medical and ambulance entourage slowed it down. Apparently Doctor Letterman disagreed with the order but had no power to rescind it and Hooker's successor, Meade, tended to agree with his predecessor."

"Yes, and he's compounded Hooker's miscalculation by taking most of the medical supplies and surgeons, as well as the remaining ambulances in his pursuit of Lee," Rory said.

His voice cracked in disbelief, as his colleagues growled in agreement at the apparent blunder.

With so many wounded soldiers and prisoners to feed, food stocks remained inadequate. Janes and the medical staff were adamant that the Confederate wounded and prisoners should receive the same rations as their own men. He sent an urgent message to Letterman in Washington, who had no authority over store allocations. However, he manipulated a few strings in Washington and directed a long wagon train to Gettysburg filled with medication and surgical appliances, tents, blankets, and beef stock.

This revealed more of Meade's flawed tactics. As soon as fighting had begun, Meade had ordered his corps commanders to send all the long wagon trains to the rear as they arrived, except those carrying ammunition and ambulance vehicles. This was sensible from a military point of view, as it allowed expeditious unloading of ammunition. However, the longer trains carrying food and general stores ended up parked in Westminster, 20 miles away. The problem then was organizing an already depleted workforce to unload and obtain transport to take the goods from Westminster to Gettysburg. Chaos ensued, leading to inevitable long delays in transportation of vital supplies. Letterman was unaware of these delays, and had assumed that Janes had received the much needed extra medication and apparatus he had been able to negotiate. Goods from the trains arrived slowly, Janes told his colleagues, though not on a planned and timely basis.

On top of all this, the telegraph system had been vandalized, so the country was initially unaware of Gettysburg's plight. Once the lines had been restored and the country became aware of the predicament, hundreds of parcels containing food and clothing arrived from concerned citizens. Some of the food was found to be rotten as it was unloaded, resulting from inadequate packing and the delays in unloading and transportation. However, sufficient food remained to implement improved nutrition, though there was difficulty in keeping account of stocks and storage.

The citizens of Gettysburg also continued to support the battlefield problems. Larger houses were requisitioned for use as hospital and army headquarters, while smaller homes volunteered spare rooms for recovering wounded soldiers. Other households prepared meals on a daily basis for up to 10 soldiers, while others offered garden produce. Some baked bread and pies while soups and stews were offered by the local hostelry. Donations of clothing and blankets were so high that a small store hut was erected for them, donated by a local carpenter.

Through all this, the medical teams continued their onerous task of caring for the wounded without sufficient or appropriate treatment aids. Success stories were abundant, but there were a large number of the wounded who died due to a lack of timely medical or surgical care. It was a heart-breaking job, and many medics and nurses were traumatized by the frustration and distress of what they had to deal with.

By now 650 doctors had arrived on the scene. Doctor Janes had dismissed three from service in response to Rory's petition they were no longer fit to treat their patients. Rory's knowledge of psychotic illness was noted in his records, so Janes knew he had no option but to accept his recommendation that the young doctors be removed.

"They are not suitable for working in this environment and could do more harm than good to our wounded and dying patients," Rory had told him. "My colleagues and I have all noticed their lack of judgement. I'm sure you'll agree that cannot be tolerated. They are young in years and experience, but now present as shivering, lachrymose old men and if allowed to continue, could well take their own lives. For the sake of my patients, I will not allow them to work in my patch. They just can't cope though it's not their fault, and we can't hold this against them."

"If I dismiss them, it could well affect their future career," Janes had said.

"Rather that than have an adverse effect on the lives of the men in our care," Rory retorted, "and if you retain them, I fear they may not live long enough to have a future and a career."

"I will need to speak with Doctor Letterman about this," Janes said, "but in the meantime I will refer them back to base on the grounds of poor health. I may need you to provide a report on your findings based on your experience in these matters, Compton, but I'll let you know in due course. In the meantime, I have sufficient confidence in your knowledge and integrity to take notice of what you have told me."

There was a groundswell of sympathy for these young doctors, as well as others whom Rory suspected would be dismissed, and when asked to provide a report as a team leader who had knowledge of the perceived mental trauma, his peers added their signatures to the document.

The stench of dead horses and mules added to the chaos and distress, as did the sight of the surviving wounded animals as they staggered about. It was a luckless group of soldiers that was assigned to put those poor animals out of their misery. They were unable to bury the animals, as the interment of the dead soldiers was the priority. Farmers on whose land the animals had died were eager to help. Under the direction of military officers they assisted with ropes, and sometimes chains, to pull the animals into pyres for cremation. Folks soon got used to the smoke and smell of the burning mounds, and did not complain. They understood the necessity of the task.

Throughout the medical and burial dramas, anxious relatives rushed from far away homes to bring food and equipment or care for their loved ones. Residents opened up their homes to these folks.

Clarrie was among the nurses who arrived in Gettysburg. She was accompanied by Beth and Laura, who had thought to become ambulance orderlies, or whatever useful task, however menial, was required. Like most medics, Rory found himself in charge of over a thousand wounded men with little other professional help. When he heard of Clarrie's arrival, he asked Janes if she could be allocated to him. To have Clarrie at his side was, he knew, a stroke of luck for him and his patients.

Even with this extra help, Rory remained devastated at the number who died due to inadequate care, even though conditions had improved as more soldiers were dispatched to city hospitals or to their homes. The medical teams also remained vulnerable, exposed as they were to the continued suffering of their patients.

Rory kept a careful eye on Clarrie, who appeared to have recovered from her near breakdown in Fredericksburg, but she remained serene as she tended the grateful men. She had known what to expect thanks to her previous experience.

It was always a relief to Rory when he and his Kentuckian 'best friends' were able to squeeze an hour together. For a while they forgot their immediate tasks as they talked of home. Rory didn't mention his wife and son much, but when new pictures of his son arrived one day via a large, well-filled mailbag, he was thrilled to show them around. The pictures had, he said, been taken by his cousin Oliver, now living in Paris and a photographer of some considerable fame in Europe.

"He keeps an eye on my family," he said, and appeared to be delighted with the arrangement. "I gather Antoin is beginning to talk and Oliver got him to say 'Papa'."

He laughed, pride in his voice as he stared with longing eyes at his little son's image.

"He looks just like Mary, one of my twin sisters," he confided, a wistful, emotional note in his voice.

Clarrie remembered the other picture of his wife, Marie Louise, he had shown her at Chatham Manor, and how she resembled a younger Beth. She did not refer to it today but wondered why he had not shown them his wife's pictures she knew remained in the envelope.

Working so close to each other, she was Rory's confidante, a necessary comfort for him as he worked through the trauma of misery each day. She knew he was anxious his wife would become weary of waiting for him.

"Parisian women are more impatient, more volatile than Kentuckians," he had said to Clarrie one day. "I'm scared that she'll become restless and decide I'm not worth waiting for."

"She'll wait," Clarrie had said. "You're the father of her child, she'll not forget you."

Rory smiled.

"You always seem to say the right thing and put me back on track," he said to her during one of their chats about family life, "and you're so resourceful, with a lot of common sense in these awful conditions. You'll make somebody a wonderful wife when all this is over."

On that occasion he had bent over and kissed her cheek. Clarrie smiled now at the memory. *At least*, she thought to herself, *I can never say that I've never been kissed by a man.* She remembered how pleased she had been with the gesture but felt no regret at her unmarried status. She had overcome the bodily desires that Rory and Doctor Wallace had, without realizing, inflicted upon her during her adolescent years. She was at peace with herself, though both she and Laura did worry about Beth, who seemed once more to be consumed with thoughts of the deaths of her sister and parents.

When the photographs had been put away, the four spoke of Oliver and Timothy, wondering how their war was faring.

"Timothy's still out west," said Laura, who had heard recently from her mother, "and Oliver distinguished himself as an army photographer before he left for Paris to work with a national newspaper. I understand he risked his life more than once in that role. He ended up with a disabled left leg and wasn't able to continue as an army photographer."

"Dear old cousin Oliver," said Rory, "oh, before I forget, Beth, the last time I saw Oliver he gave me a book that had belonged to Maya. He asked me to let you have it the next time I saw you. I think Fred Hetherington gave it to her when he was helping me teach her how to read. It's Hawthorne's *The Scarlet Letter*. I'll let you have it some time. Actually, I think it's in my pack somewhere. I thought I'd read it myself if and when I have any spare time."

"If he'd still been an army photographer, I wouldn't have been at all surprised if he'd ended up here with us," Laura said.

Clarrie and Rory agreed, as they marveled yet again that they were all together on this bitter battlefield. Beth remained silent, remembering her last sight of Oliver's former friend, Hetherington, in Richmond. She wondered what they would say if she told them that story, though she knew she was never likely to do so. Clarrie noticed her reticence as they spoke of the old days and worried about her.

Later that day, Clarrie sought Rory's opinion as to whether Beth was suffering from some form of psychological stress.

"She must have worked under stressful conditions as a spy, but I don't suppose she ever saw such dreadful scenes as these," she commented.

"She might be depressed," he agreed, "though I don't see her enough to make a proper assessment. I do wonder, though, whether the work she's doing now is disappointing her, after all the excitement of her previous exploits. If it is, she may start brooding again about Maya and what happened to her. This environment is not exactly a place where joyous memories come to the fore, is it?"

Clarrie had to agree. "Fortunately, the depressive periods don't last too long, as there's so much for Beth and Laura to do. I do think she feels useful here and always puts her heart and soul into whatever task she's doing."

Beth and Laura were not as involved in the day to day medical care as more nurses and trained orderlies arrived. They were called upon more and more as stretcher-bearers to help with the removal of the dead still strewn around the large battlefield.

On one occasion, Laura was requested to take two recovering soldiers to an evacuation point for rail transport from where they would be taken to a city hospital. She was aware help would be available at the railroad, but her immediate problem was finding transport to the evacuation center. There were no ambulance men or stretcher-bearers available to help her, and she had to resort to pleading with a local farmer to lend her his horse and wagon and to help her lift the patients onto his cart.

"I'm sure pleased to help such a pretty lady, but can you afford the price?" he asked.

The sum demanded was exorbitant, but somehow she, Beth and Clarrie raised enough to meet the man's charges. When that same man came to them for help a few days later for treatment of a badly sprained ankle, he was kept waiting all day. Everyone knew it was a mean thing to do, but a lesson was learned and most local farmers became more realistic in their transport charges.

The actions of those greedy farmers were far removed from the kindness of a local mulatto woman known as Linda Smith, a citizen of Gettysburg, who canvassed the surrounding area for food and clothing for the soldiers, whether Union or Confederate. Her donations were among the first of thousands that had begun to arrive from across the country. She did this almost every day, with no thought for her own welfare.

Laura wrote to her mother about her.

"I think we should all try and tell Linda's story to our newspapers, so that everyone in our land can be aware of her, and people like her. She doesn't have to do what she does, but she can't bear the thought of all that pain and hunger that she's seen so much of. What a woman."

The Sanitary Commission remained a welcome presence. Their initial contact brought essential food supplies, which was further enhanced by the generosity of food parcels from the general public.

Beth and Laura were popular, and it was not long before they were asked to help the Sanitary Commission officers in their work of recording their stores. Laura worked with a team identifying and issuing clothing and boots, while Beth organized the food stores.

It didn't take long for Laura and Beth to work out a recording system, which was stacked in a large tent in appropriate sections, ensuring ease of access when required. The task of beginning their stock-keeping ledgers under the watchful eye of Clarrie was onerous but necessary.

"You'll need to ensure weekly stock-taking," advised Clarrie, who was impressed with the rapid collation of the stock, "and you'll also need a weather-proof store-shed as soon as possible."

Laura used her diplomatic skills to requisition the same local carpenter who had built the clothing shed, to build a shack large enough to contain most of the food. Dr. Janes agreed to pay for the required wood and labor.

Beth took control of allocating the food stores, ensuring adequate supplies of the main food-stuffs for the wounded, as well as rations for the medical and voluntary teams. She did not eat much herself, and her already slender body began to look scrawny as she went about her new work. It was during one short meal-break in the room allocated to the Sanitary Commission for meals that Laura discussed her friend's lack of appetite with her. She learned that one of the main reasons Beth rejected food was the stench of smoke created from the cremation of horses and mules.

"Thank goodness the cremations are now finished," she said to Laura. "But the stench seems to remain in my nostrils. I'm sure it's going to be there forever."

She stopped to sip her water.

"I think that's been the worst thing for me in this filthy, befouled, damned hell-hole."

Her rising voice drew the attention of women nearby who stopped eating, disbelief written all over their faces.

"Your cuss words are quite charming," Laura joked, "you really ought to hear mine when I'm at my best. Do you want to hear some?"

She swore with gusto, using excessive profanities learned during her army days. They sounded incongruous coming from Laura.

Beth and those near them laughed out loud. Their giggles rang out around the room and their companions, around 30 women, became infected. Before they knew it, the whole room was in uproar as vivid expletives rattled around.

They had forgotten that one of the clergymen was in the room, ready to take a prayer service at the end of their break, until he left the room on tiptoes. Laura was certain he went out with a smile. Indeed, he had caught her eye and winked. Would he repeat the fiasco to his colleagues that night, they all wondered.

The laughter began again. It was in this way that Laura and Beth became responsible, together with the Reverend John Appleton for setting up a concert party.

Reverend Appleton had reported to his colleagues the levity that had been generated in the Sanitary Commission's rest-room that day. He described how the women had responded to those brief 10 minutes with a joyous spirit and more energy for the rest of the day. He did not divulge the reason for the laughter, but insisted communal relaxation was needed more than ever now the dead had been interred, and many of the wounded were either in other hospitals or recovering well.

"It's clear to me that what everyone needs now is some joy in their lives," Appleton said. "Not just that of receiving letters and parcels from home but a shared link as the men grow stronger and helpers see the rewards of their labor."

Appleton recommended a concert and got his way so long as he took responsibility for its organization. He recruited Beth, who was delighted to organize music and song where possible, though how she would provide the music was beyond her at that time.

Another clergyman suggested communal book-reading sessions for the non-ambulant patients, while others suggested knitting and sewing sessions for off-duty nurses and even soldiers if they wanted to learn. Ideas for activities to ease the horror of those earlier days or relieve the boredom of recovering soldiers awaiting transport to a hospital or home were welcomed.

The medical teams, who knew the men better than anyone else, were delighted to sift out those who could sing, play an instrument, or 'do a music hall' turn. They even offered their own services. Beth was surprised to learn that Rory had a good alto voice. It was his cousin, Laura, who had inveigled him to participate, and he welcomed the event as a great emotional and intellectual boost for everybody, including himself.

The loan of banjos, fiddles, and a flute from the villagers made it possible. The audience consisted of injured soldiers from the field hospitals, and those located in the village who awaited transport to a city hospital, together with any staff that could be spared. All villagers were invited.

"I suppose army generals harden themselves to the fact that it's the plight of soldiers to suffer, but it's apparent there's no heart among our men to accept this hypothesis," one of the doctors said to the gathered audience. "And from what I see, neither do the men and women of the voluntary organizations and the wonderful villagers, whose lives we seem to have taken over. Thank you, villagers and volunteers, from the medical teams and most of all from the brave wounded."

He sat down blushing as his voice faltered. He never had been much of a public speaker, he thought to himself, as he brushed a small tear from his left eye.

But what he said appeared to have been just right as his comments were met with tremendous applause. One of the villagers stood up and thanked Doctor Janes for allowing his staff to organize the event. The applause for him was tumultuous.

The playing of various instruments made everyone who could perform arm dances or tap their feet as they listened to the happy sounds of home. The highlight of the evening was the singing in which the entire audience joined in. The evening was completed by storytelling, read in the deep, cultured voice of the Reverend Appleton.

Clarrie in particular found herself enraptured with the rendering, and felt she could listen to that voice forever.

The evening ended with hymn singing, led by Reverend Johnson, and prayers by Doctor Janes, who joined Rory and 'the girls' afterward. He was, he said, most grateful to Beth and Laura for what they had achieved.

He and Reverend John Appleton were intrigued to learn that Rory, Clarrie, Beth and Laura, had been friends for many years in Kentucky.

"We've gone through a lot together, when you think about it," said Laura, the vivacity of her early teenage years making an appearance.

"I hope that you'll have many more years together," said Appleton, "It's good to see such close friends. What a remarkable coincidence that you're all together in this place. I do hope, Doctor Janes, that you will allow us to organize another concert soon," he said.

Janes countered that hope with one of his.

"I hope, sir, that we'll all be leaving this place soon. But we'll see about another concert. It was uplifting for us as well as the villagers, I do agree."

Appleton glanced at Clarrie and strolled over to her.

"I hope your patients will feel better for this evening," he said, "though I have heard that you cheer up your patients every day just by being you."

Clarrie smiled, her face flushed.

"I'm so pleased that you were able to get time off to come this evening," he went on, "I know of your work, and your friends have told me so much about what you and Doctor Compton achieve as a team."

Beth and Laura raised eyebrows as they glanced at each other, surprised to see Clarrie blush. Rory raised his too, as he had already noted a sudden shyness in the reverend as he spoke of Clarrie earlier that day.

"Reverend, it would take me a week to tell you all about Clarrie's achievements," Rory butted in. "Not just in this battlefield, but also in Kentucky. For instance, she once organized a plan that prevented a measles epidemic and that's just one of her achievements."

"Really," said Appleton, "you appear to be an interesting young lady, Clarrie. I look forward to hearing your life story."

He continued to look at her.

Clarrie pressed her palms to her cheeks in embarrassment, as she looked at him with eyes that shone bright and glossy.

"Thank you, Reverend, but I'm not so interesting. I'm lucky to be able to do what I love doing," she added in a soft voice that cracked a little with emotion.

"It's John," said the Reverend. "Please, everyone, I would prefer you to address me as John."

Rory noticed Clarrie's embarrassment and confusion.

"Well, nurse, will you come with me to check on Private Barnes' leg, please. I want another quick check before we finish for the night."

He didn't feel guilty at whisking her away so abruptly. If John Appleton was interested in Clarrie, he would make sure he talked with her again.

Two weeks later Laura was ordered to Doctor Janes' office. She assumed it was something to do with the book-reading session she was arranging, but was surprised to be greeted by Major George Sullivan. She had heard of his promotion and of his transfer to

Lincoln's Bureau of Military Information. She congratulated him as she tried to recover from the shock.

Major Sullivan greeted her in what she felt was diffidence. He did not beat about the bush

"I want you to take over a project that I'm setting up in Washington," he said, "and with your background in teaching and espionage work, I know you're the right one for the job. I have asked leave of Dr. Janes to ask you to return with me to Washington to undertake the position. I need to fill it as soon as I can."

Sullivan's slick demeanor unnerved her. This was not the same, smiling Sullivan she remembered so well.

"What's the job?" she managed to ask, as she lowered her head, swallowing hard as she did so.

He told her about a plan for training teenage orphans in the art of code breaking and writing.

"These particular orphans have high academic skills and are quick learners. They're young enough not to be suspected of being involved in this type of work, which is a boon to us, and the fact that they are orphans ensures they would not break confidences to family members. However, for the sake of their future social relationships as they become older, we need an experienced teacher who could encourage them in their work as well as being a 'parent' figure. I can think of no one better than you."

He looked at her and she saw a glimpse of that former mischief in his eyes. She felt she would agree to anything he said. Her mind had been filled with this man for so long now, and she could hardly believe what he was saying. She knew she was an ideal candidate for the job, and was thrilled that Sullivan had remembered her.

In her heart of hearts, though, she knew she would not be able to work alongside Sullivan in such an important task. She was too proud to show her emotion, and the strain of working for him, unable to express her feelings, would, she knew, worry her. She felt he could not be interested in her as a woman and even if he was attracted to her, his short dalliance with Esme Lockwood suggested he was not the faithful type and for all she knew he was already married.

She thought of his understated greeting today, with no exceptional expression of pleasure at seeing her again. She felt suffocated as these thoughts permeated through her mind, until a sudden idea struck her. Her response was impulsive.

"I'm sorry, Major, but I cannot accept," she said, "but you know, Beth has far more experience than I have in code work. Indeed, I know only the basics. So, I'm not ideal, you see."

He looked puzzled and stared at her before closing his eyes for a few seconds. He opened them and studied his notebook, flipping over a few pages.

"You're a very clever woman, Laura. You have a similar intellect to your cousin Rory Compton, and would soon crack the art of coding. The other important factor is your teaching skill and your general demeanor that makes you an ideal candidate. I don't believe Beth has those particular skills. Hers are, as you say, the writing and deciphering of codes. Alongside that she has an ability to draw plans and even provide an immediate facial drawing, which I know has proved useful in the past."

He stopped as he studied his notebook again.

"We are aware of her skills and her usefulness, but in this regard, I deem you to be the more suitable person to carry out this work. You're the one I want for the job."

Laura frowned at him. By now she had convinced herself that this job would be right for Beth.

She shook her head.

"You don't know Beth well enough if you think she would be incapable of parenting those young people. She'd be ideal and could provide testimonials confirming that. She should be given a chance in life. I've had mine, and became head of my step-father's school, which is what I wanted. I could return to it, if necessary. How's that for an opportunity. Beth has none of that."

"I thought you would be safer in Washington…"

"So would Beth. That job you've just offered me is the ideal solution for her. You'd find soon enough how right I am, if you offer it to her. And I'll be safe enough in Cynthiana when I get back there, I'm sure."

She stood up, as he did.

They stared at each other.

"Yes, but I'm not in love with Beth," he blurted out.

She stared at him.

"What does that mean?" was all she could think to say.

He spoke softly. "I love you Laura. I can't get you out of my mind…"

"Well," she said, her mind whirling. "That settles that, doesn't it? I couldn't possibly come to work with you in Washington now."

"Have you any feelings for me? Somehow I thought you might have."

He looked anxious, as he bit hard on his bottom lip.

Laura felt the same fluttering in her stomach she experienced whenever she thought of him. She looked around the room, for a second wondering where she was as her mind blanked and her heart hammered against her chest.

She looked for a chair and sat down.

Sullivan remained standing, looking down at her.

"Yes," said Laura, "I do have feelings for you. Strong ones. I thought I was in love with someone once, but I never felt like this about him. But it's just too soon to talk about this. I must let it all sink in. Neither of us must commit ourselves."

By now Sullivan had recovered his composure. He appeared to have made a sudden decision.

"Well, as I was saying, I've kept up with Beth as well as you. I have a vacancy in my office in Washington that would be ideal for either of you until the end of this war. Her experience with codes would be invaluable. If she accepts it, I'll at least hear how you are."

He grinned at her, that wonderful grin she so loved.

"The war will soon be over and we can think about things then," she promised.

He strode over and lifted her into a standing position. He placed his hands on her shoulders and kissed her mouth. She responded, knowing full well the kiss sealed her fate. She was sure of it.

He took her to the door.

"I'll ask Janes to send Beth to me," he said, lightly kissing her forehead before brushing her lips with his.

Beth's general demeanor changed overnight to the relief of her friends. She left two days later, promising to be in touch as soon as possible.

Before she left, Rory gave her *The Scarlet Letter* book that Oliver had asked him to pass to her. She was pleased and said she would probably read it during her lonelier nights in Washington. She wondered if she could remember the story. It had been years since she had listened to Fred Hetherington reading it to her and Maya.

Chapter 19
Beth in a Crisis – Winter 1865

Beth had been writing for about an hour. All she had heard during that time was the scratch of her pen and the fluttering flames in the small fire grate. She put down her pen, stretched, crossed the room and lit her lamp.

At the large window overlooking the street buildings, she noticed the whiteness everywhere. Every crevice and corner of the buildings appeared to hold a burden of snow as it continued to fall. Before drawing the heavy blue drapes, she watched a family of four walk along the otherwise empty street, all unsteady on their feet. The man slipped onto his backside, creating hoots of laughter from the children, while his wife fussed and tried her best to help him back onto his feet. They both shouted at the boys to help, as he failed to gain a steady foothold, though their efforts made the situation worse. Beth laughed out loud at the comedy unfolding, thankful that the family could neither see nor hear her.

She looked around the small room that served as her writing/sitting room.

It's curious, she thought, *how a room can seem so quiet following a snow-storm.*

It had been furnished when she arrived in Washington two and a half years ago and had stayed the same ever since. She glanced at the ancient oak writing desk and chair and an old though cozy two-seat davenport of the same hue as the drapes. Next to that stood a more modern bookcase, the shelves of which housed various work schedules and records that received her constant attention. On the opposite wall stood two high back chairs with a serving table between them where the maid placed her tea and cake each afternoon. A soft, cushioned chair was placed in the corner, overlooking the whole room. It was comfortable and warm, and Beth loved it. It was her domain, personalized by the many photographs of her Kentucky friends.

She picked them up one by one, smiling back at those who smiled at her through the lens of a camera, usually one of Oliver's. She wondered how Clarrie and John Appleton were following their first 18 months of marriage as she remembered again their wonderful happy wedding reception in Lexington. She also pondered how John was faring in his new role as schoolmaster in the new Lexington school for boys.

She studied the picture of Laura, so beautiful in her wedding gown, as she gazed up at her husband, Major George Sullivan, resplendent in his army uniform, as he looked down on her with so much love radiating his handsome face.

She looked forward to the next family event when Rory returned home from Paris at last, bringing his wife and two children, together with his mother-in-law. It had been a sad business, she thought, when his father-in-law had passed away so suddenly last year, around the time they had planned to return to Kentucky.

"Antoin will be four years old now," she mused, "and baby Brigitte will be over a year old by the time I meet her."

She spent the longest time looking at the picture of Sarah Willoughby, who had died just a few months ago from an unexpected heart attack. Laura had returned to Kentucky for the funeral, and as she stared now at Sarah's image, she recalled how her late employer had never returned to Richmond once she had settled with her sister in Lexington. She'd had no wish to after hearing how badly damaged her house was following the final skirmishes in Richmond. She had left it to her brother-in-law to finalize all legal affairs.

Sarah had remembered her sister Beulah in her will, as well as her nephews Timothy and Oliver, and her former companion, Annie Parker. Beth had been astonished to find that she also had been remembered. At first she said she would not accept it, and remonstrated with the family. Beulah had said it was not up to her to refuse the gesture, and she must accept it with the love that prompted the significant cash gift.

"How good it is to be part of a huge family," Beth mused. "The next thing I'll hear will be Laura asking me to be godmother to her little one."

She smiled at the prospect having enjoyed the privilege of being godmother to Clarrie's first born.

She added a little more fuel to her fire, before settling back at her desk, and sighed out loud as she remembered the short conversation with George Sullivan yesterday. The news of the termination of her job within a few months was sudden and devastating.

She had argued for the continuance of the project until all 20 students had achieved their university degrees and been offered suitable work, as promised. There had been five late-comers into the scheme, and she was worried what the effect on those particular participants would be.

"I know what you're saying, Beth," George had said, "but it's a government decision to close the scheme down. Don't forget the main purpose of it was not philanthropic, but aimed at training high quality and trusted code-writers and breakers. Getting those young people through university was a bonus not essential to the scheme. At the time we saw it as a kind of reward for what they were doing for us."

"I think I can obtain agreement for the remaining five students to take up their university places and honor the commitment to pay their fees. We can't, however, guarantee accommodation for them as we need these existing premises for other projects. You'll not be left without a job, though you'd have to find accommodation. I'd help with that, if necessary, and there are two or three jobs which my team thinks you might wish to consider, unless you decide to return to Kentucky."

Beth had felt that the decision was unfair to those remaining five, and told him so.

"I realize you are committed to paying their university fees, but where will those five young people live? Who will be their carer, their mentor? It is not their fault that they were late entrants into the scheme, and it would be dishonorable if they were denied the same reward as the other boys. They can't undertake the university course without accommodation and moral support."

"I know they've already benefitted from their tenure here, but they've not earned anything, and without cash finding accommodation is out of the question. Without a legitimate address they'll find it impossible to find a decent job to earn cash in the future. Your department is just tossing them out as surplus to requirement. They are young, brilliant, vulnerable human beings, not parcels or baskets of groceries."

She sighed again, as she remembered how she'd stopped her indignant tirade as tears threatened. She hadn't wanted Major Sullivan to see her distress and she had bowed her shoulders. Her head had also drooped as she had put her hands over her eyes as if to shield Sullivan from her sight. Her breath exhaled in a short whimper as she choked back the tears.

She had found her voice again as she raised her body to its normal posture.

"They will be bereft if they're thrown into the open, with none of the prospects they had expected and to make things worse, no means of subsistence. Don't forget, please, that they have no family, they are orphans," she had said.

Her eyes had remained averted as she gazed at the fire grate, thereby missing Sullivan's concerned expression as he stared at the lovely face now distorted with concern and anger. He nodded.

"Yes, Beth, I know what you're saying, but even though the war is over from a military point, many political and financial problems remain. You'll be aware that President Johnson is already clashing with the Republicans about priorities. I'm not conversant with all of the politics, but have been informed, as other department heads have, that we must find ways of saving resources where we can, as every cent saved is essential for the country's future progress."

He had stopped for a moment in an effort to assess Beth's reaction, but she remained aloof, eyes still averted, her anger still apparent.

"This isn't the only project I've had to chop," he had said, his tone wretched, eyes desolate.

"Do the others projects involve vulnerable orphans who have relied upon us to ensure their future? Though they're not yet fully trained, I know for certain that those five youths have already provided a substantial service to the country. Have other casualties made such a worthy contribution?" Beth had retorted.

"I'm unable to comment on whether one project is any more important than another, but I do understand your concern about their plight," he had responded.

Beth chuckled to herself as she remembered how she had stared at him with the hardest expression she could muster, before asking him if he had any influence on retaining the project.

"Think of the waste of time and money if we don't retain and utilize those highly intelligent folks in the future. They've been defined as exceptional intellectuals, and the country needs that genius, I would say."

Major Sullivan's response had surprised Beth.

"I may have a little authority," he said, "but I have to say I will shortly be leaving the army, and returning to civilian life. As a married man I want to provide for my wife's future security as well as that of my children whenever they come along, so I'm planning to return to Louisville to settle into my father's business. I'm not sure how long I'll be around here to use any influence I might have."

Beth had looked at him for a while with beseeching eyes, until he spoke again.

"You argue just like my Laura," he had said at last, smiling and waving a hand in front of her eyes, "and not only with your rhetoric."

"I'll do my best to see if we can gain a bit more time in this place, though squeezing the funding out of my board for pastoral care and subsistence will be gnarly," he had said, just before he left. "I'll try and get an answer by tomorrow."

A sharp knock at her door brought Beth out of her reverie. It was the maid, Matilda, with her afternoon tea.

"Mattie," Beth said, "I think you'd better get off home now. It's still snowing and I don't want you to get caught out. Don't rush back in the morning, either. I can take care of my own breakfast for once. Leave me a bit of bread and ham, in case I want something later, but I don't want a cooked dinner this evening. So long as you leave out plenty for the students, I'll tell them to look after themselves."

Matilda, who had been with Beth ever since she arrived in Washington, looked relieved. "Thank you, ma'am," she said, "I was beginning to get a bit worried."

"Off you go then, Mattie. And remember, if it is still snowing, or there are big snow drifts, do not attempt to come in tomorrow. We'll manage ourselves for once."

Her eyes twinkled and Matilda knew she meant it.

"I'll leave things out for the boys and set your tray, just in case," she said as she went out.

"I'm not going to worry about the future until tomorrow," Beth said to herself, "I'm going to stir outside for five minutes, just to say I've ventured out in the snow, and then come back and go to bed and read. Thank goodness for books."

The book she chose to read that evening was Hawthorne's *The Scarlet Letter*, the one she had been promising herself to read ever since Rory had given it to her when she left Gettysburg to come to Washington.

The very one my dear Maya had owned, she thought. *I wonder how it came to be in Oliver Compton's possession. The next time I see him I'll ask him.*

As she settled down with a warm glass of milk and her book, she glanced at the small pendant clock that had been a gift from Beulah when she had left for Richmond, and realized it was later than she had thought.

She yawned. "I think I'll be able to sleep tonight after all," she said to herself. "That walk in the snow did me good."

She opened the book and leafed through the pages, dipping into two or three chapters to see if she could remember the story line. As she did so, a small sheet of white paper fell out and fluttered onto the floor. Not wishing to clamber out of her warm bed, she reached down to the floor and her groping fingers soon fastened onto the paper.

As she lifted it she noticed it was a drawing of a face. She rescued the eye-wear she had tucked under her pillow earlier and confirmed what she had already thought. It was a picture of Fred Hetherington's youthful face from the Lexington days. Even if Maya's name had not been penned in the bottom right hand corner of the paper, she would have recognized her sister's unique style. Maya's artistic abilities had been high, and for a few moments she was shaken to see her sister's handiwork. She turned the paper over.

Three words, 'The other angel', were written on the back in Maya's untidy scrawl, the same words she had said to Beth as she lay dying all those years ago. Beth was glad to have her pillows to lean back on as dizziness overwhelmed her.

She did not begin to read the book that night, nor did she sleep. She worried and puzzled over the closure of the project, interspersed with the shock of finding her sister's artwork by such pure chance. It was not until six o'clock that morning her tired mind concluded that finding the drawing was destiny rather than a fluke, though she could not define that inkling. She slept for a couple of hours once the thought entered her mind. She was thankful when Mattie arrived within a half hour of her rousing.

"The snow's stopped, and the sun's bright enough to thaw it. The boys are up, taking charge of their own breakfast downstairs. I think they're enjoying themselves," she prattled on, stopping only when she noticed Beth's strained face.

"Why, ma'am," she cried, "you're not well. Here, let me help you."

She fussed and worried over Beth, and spoke of calling for a doctor.

"No, don't worry, Mattie," Laura said, "I'm expecting Major Sullivan this morning and want to be up when he comes."

"At least have something to eat before you get up," she said, "and there'll be plenty of time to bathe and dress before he arrives. It's usually in the afternoon when he comes, isn't it?"

She looked at Beth's drawn, solemn face.

"Oh dear, it's my fault, I knew I should've stayed to make you a proper dinner yesterday," Mattie wailed, as she dashed off to get hot beef tea and toasted bread for her.

Beth felt better when she had bathed, dressed and eaten. While she waited for Major Sullivan, she looked at her scribblings from yesterday afternoon. She realized, as she had done yesterday, that her legacy from Sarah together with her own small savings would not stretch to pay the rental for accommodation and subsistence for five youths for the next three years, though she might be able to manage two years. City accommodation was already expensive, and she realized that it could be even more so in the future. She knew she may be able to raise some cash from philanthropists, though did not know at this time how to go about doing that.

She decided to ask Laura's mother, Delphia, how to set about it. She did realize, however, that today's philanthropists would be inundated with requests for many years to come, and she was uncertain she could persuade them of the importance of this particular cause.

When Sullivan arrived later that morning, she was informed she must accompany him that afternoon to his office suite, as the chairman of the officiating committee, John Forder, wished to interview her.

He told her of how he had been able to persuade Forder's committee they must try to retain these potentially powerful young brains in their grasp for future projects. Forder was considering a reprieve for a further 12 months only. Furthermore, all remaining university fees and subsistence would be paid by the government, though the five remaining students would be required to fund their own accommodation for the remaining two years. He confirmed that the committee members were adamant in their unwillingness to offer a loan or a grant for accommodation.

After Sullivan left, Beth worked hard on her personal presentation as she acknowledged the shadows of sleeplessness evident under her eyes. By the time he had returned to accompany her to the interview, she felt more settled. She had more or less accepted the situation and had made tentative plans in her mind to utilize her own funds for the boys. She now knew she would have 12 months in which to finalize her intentions.

She entered the chairman's office without trepidation. She would make one final plea, and if it did not succeed, then she knew the way forward. John Forder greeted her with a firm handshake

He was a small, balding, plump man, though Beth noticed his kind, dark eyes above all else. Although short in stature, he was inches above Beth. He tried not to look surprised as she walked in, her petite figure and excellent features a complete opposite to the intimidating, middle-aged woman he had expected. He had been ready for verbal combat, but instead looked down with pleasure at the smart woman standing in front of him. His respect and liking for her was instant.

"I have heard of your good work, ma'am," he said, "and I thank you for what you have achieved with those young people. From what they have told me, it's been your encouragement that's helped them become so valuable to our cause during the war. As you know, those who have completed their education have now been infiltrated into various management teams."

"Thank you, sir," she responded.

He pointed to a chair, and asked her to sit.

He did not sit at his desk as she expected him to, but chose the chair opposite hers. Major Sullivan remained standing in the background. Beth succeeded in suppressing a giggle, as she pictured Forder sitting behind the huge desk, knowing she would have been unable to see his short frame behind it. She was, however, unable to keep her amusement from her eyes and the sparkle within them appeared to enrapture Forder. Sullivan, recognizing a hint of humor in that sparkle, shifted his feet, hoping this would alert her to his unease.

Forder coughed a little, before he spoke and Beth was surprised at his apparent anxiety. "Let's get straight to the point," he said, "I know that Major Sullivan has advised you of the need to cut our costs within all our departments, not just this one. We can't make concessions as this could create even more unrest among the different divisions if it became known and experience tells us that it would eventually. That would lead to even further disruptions and eventual chaos so any savings made from current plans would be swallowed up in trying to put order back into the disarray. You can see that, can't you?"

Beth nodded and Forder looked relieved.

"Major Sullivan has told me of your plea for the five young men who will remain within this project until they have completed their university course," he said, "but my committee has decided the project cannot continue. However, we do have some sympathy. As you are aware, we will not require the premises for 12 months, so their accommodation will remain for that period. This will allow those boys currently studying at the university to complete their course and the other five will have it for their first year at the university. Your own position will, of course, remain for that period also."

Major Sullivan shifted his position, and the chairman turned from Beth in some irritation. "Sorry, Major, do bring that side chair over here and sit with us. Sorry for the discourtesy. Unintended, I assure you."

He waited until Sullivan was seated. Beth smiled at him, appreciating his gesture toward his subordinate.

"It has now been agreed we will pay the full fees for the whole university course for all students, as a patriotic gesture," he said. "It is a 'one-off' gesture, of course, and we will not be disseminating this information to anyone but you. You will not discuss this with anyone, not even the boys involved, at any time. I want your confirmation that you agree to this."

"Of course, sir, and thank you on behalf of the boys for the privilege," she said.

"Now we come to the pastoral welfare of those five boys," he said. "My committee has thought it over and cannot agree to the continuance of the current accommodation or their subsistence after the next 12 months, for the reasons you've just accepted. I've asked you here this afternoon to listen to any other comments you may have others than those already put forward by Major Sullivan on your behalf. If you have further suggestions or criticisms, please talk to me now."

"I understand your position, sir, and that of your committee," Beth said. "I have to assume your committee has taken into consideration these boys are orphans, thrust into that position because of the war, and have no means of financial support. Is that correct, sir?"

Forder appeared nonplussed.

"My committee and I are well aware these young people are orphaned," he said, "though it didn't engender a particular discussion, as I recall."

"During their deliberations, sir," Beth said, her voice thick with emotion, "did your committee of well-fed men, probably with plump children loving every minute of their family lives, anticipate these boys would jump up with thankfulness from their make-shift bed under the shelter of a tree each morning, eager to get to their free university studies?"

"Did they feel that the boys would enjoy foraging for scraps of food and water wherever they could, before attending their classes, in their eagerness to learn? Did they anticipate that the boys would look forward to the end of the day to begin rummaging for their supper in the kitchen bins of large houses and hotels, before collecting their hidden rolls of blankets ready to make another make-shift sleeping area?"

"Did they think for one minute how hard it would be for these five young men, blessed with extraordinary intellect, to study with only the moon to light their books? Perhaps the committee could imagine these penniless, hungry boys, with no home or any hope of having one, being joyful enough to have a snow-ball match with each other in their free time during the freezing winter months?"

"Well, let them think again, sir. Their university places would be useless, because those boys would suffer severe malnutrition and ill-health within a month of that sort of life and wouldn't be able to complete even one term."

She stopped for a moment. Her agitation was obvious to Forder and Sullivan, as her voice wavered.

In the sudden heat following her harangue, she began to undo the top button of her dress, before realizing what she was doing. She refastened the button and began to brush the skirt, as if removing tiny bits of fluff.

For a moment she avoided looking at the two men. Neither had moved, or even cleared their throats as some men did in difficult situations. She felt light-headed and closed her eyes, waiting for the dizziness to subside before she spoke again.

"Like so many orphans nowadays, that's what their life would be like. It would not be long before they fell into crime to help them exist. Sir, they would not be living, but existing. What a waste of those exquisite brains. Did your committee think about any of those things?"

Still there was no response, and Beth could see that Forder was as anxious as he was displeased. Beth's anger increased, more at this reaction than anything else.

"Shame on you, sir, and shame on your committee, if those thoughts did not occur to you, especially after the support all those boys provided for your espionage teams day after day, sometimes night after night, whenever needed. You used their extraordinary brains, not realizing that they are human beings without a family to support or love them. Well, I'll support them. They'll go to the university and benefit from it. I'll not let them down."

By now her voice was a whisper

The chairman gulped before he asked in a restrained voice.

"How will you do that, ma'am?"

She stood up.

"I shall arrange for accommodation and subsistence from my own purse," she said, "and will seek a post as a lady's companion to provide myself with a roof over my own head. I will not renege on my promise to these young men as you and your thoughtless committee have done."

She moved toward the door. Both men leapt up to assist her, but she declined with a disdainful hand as she turned the door knob.

"You'd better see her home, Sullivan, then return to me immediately," she heard Forder say, his voice subdued, as she stepped through the door. She thought she detected a slight shake in his voice, and then realized she'd imagined it as no man of that strength of character would be shaken by the rantings of an irate woman.

The following day she was surprised by an early morning visit from Major Sullivan and John Forder.

Forder spoke first.

"You gave me much to think about yesterday, ma'am," he said, as he accepted a cup of hot tea served by Mattie.

Sullivan handed a cup to Beth and took his own from Mattie, before he sat alongside Forder on the davenport. Beth preferred to sit behind her desk.

"I even spoke to my wife about what you said yesterday," he said. "She was appalled."

"Appalled? Why? Would she like your children to be in the position of my boys here in 12 months' time?"

Sullivan stepped in. "Listen to what the chairman has to say, Beth, please," he said, glaring at her.

She lowered her head in acknowledgement of his disapproval.

"Ma'am, what I am saying is that you painted a brilliant picture of life as a wartime orphan I must say, and the reason my wife was appalled is that my committee had not fully appreciated the outcome of our action. I had not myself realized the enormous problem, but my wife is involved with a charitable organization that supports families with no income because of the deaths of so many soldiers.

"To my own shame I admit I have concentrated on the security of our country without fully understanding the nature of her patronage, nor the quandary the orphans suffer. There are always political issues that take precedence in our discussions, and lack of time is our ever present challenge, though I accept it's not a valid excuse. I ask your forgiveness for not understanding your plea."

Beth was astonished and it was her turn to remain silent as he looked at her.

"The outcome is that my wife and I will take in your five boys at the end of their stay here in a year's time. We have ourselves lost two of our sons in the war, and the younger one now lives in Maine, so their rooms are available. My wife would be glad to have them and be a mother figure to them, just as you have been. There will be no cost to your purse or any others but mine when they came into our care. The fulfilment of our country's initial promise to them when they came into the project will be reward enough."

This time Beth allowed her tears to fall, and she snuggled her head into Forder's shoulder as he rushed to comfort her.

"My dear girl," he said, "you're such a courageous little thing. We always longed for a daughter like you. I would like you to befriend my wife, Lucy. She would love you to come and see her. Will you?"

Beth, together with Sullivan and Laura, journeyed to the Forder's home the following weekend.

Lucy was a cheerful, plump, middle-aged matron, who stood no nonsense from anyone, especially her husband, which is not say she was unkind in any way. She made a fuss of Beth and Laura, as the men toured the Forder's large estate prior to a sumptuous dinner with other guests. During the men's 'whisky time' as Lucy called it, the women discussed the musical evening laid on for later that night.

Beth had never been to such an event. She knew the words of some songs, learned in her childhood, and had heard the beating of drums and clashing of cymbals, as well as the soulful sound of old Jeremiah's flute down in the po'white village near her childhood home. She had occasionally heard the lamentations of a piano set upon by Oliver or visiting children, as they made efforts to entertain their elders at John Compton's home in Lexington. She had danced as a child when a friend had visited her parents long ago, bringing with him a banjo with five strings and a long fretted neck. From this he had produced jolly tunes that set their toes tapping for hours.

But none of these previous experiences prepared her for what she listened to that night.

Lucy had arranged the concert in her small though adequate ballroom. A welcoming fire burned in the grate, and the flames of two candelabras cast shadows around the corner in which an open piano was situated. Oil lamps provided light in the remaining corners, suffusing a shade of gold around the rest of the room, in which comfortable davenports and chairs had been placed facing the piano. The music began at eight o'clock. Lucy and a baritone sang a couple of duets together, and other guests performed piano solos. Everyone enjoyed the tranquility and when John Forder announced that a special guest, Monsieur Jacques Bouchier, was coming at nine, Beth felt the sense of expectancy.

She had no idea who this Frenchman was, but gathered from the guests he was an amateur violinist, who had not been allowed by his family to enter the professional music world. She realized he must be a musician of note, as the room became quiet as the hour approached. The guests were all seated when a white-haired man, dressed in black from his shirt to his shoes, entered, carrying a violin. The guests rose and applauded him.

Without a word he tucked the instrument under his chin as his right arm hung at his side, his hand clutching a bow. Lucy was at the piano, her hands awaiting his signal to move, as she looked up in awe at the maestro in front of her. He took his time, but at last raised his bow and gave a slight nod to Lucy

Beth had never heard a true violinist. She realized later that it was her good fortune to first hear it played by this great amateur. He played a Brahms valse; a small, tender, warm item. Beth could not move, nor take her eyes away from Monsieur Bouchier as the sweetness of the sounds entered her bones, creating a creeping quiver down the whole of her spine. As the charming reiterating melody played on, she felt tears gathering. As it swept over her, tears brought on by a rapture she had never before felt, began to streak down the sides of her nose. She was unable to stop them, but didn't care.

Suddenly it was over.

The Frenchman did not move. It was as if he remained in his own rapt world of music and didn't want to leave it. At first there was no applause from the audience, as there had been for the baritone and piano solos. Beth watched in awe as each awakened from their own reverie with a sigh of wonder and contentment, just as she had done.

When the applause did come, it was thunderous and tearful, as men and women clasped each other in symbols of peace and love. No one, not even Lucy, approached the violinist, for at least five minutes. It was well known that it took him that long to descend from his own nirvana after playing with such perfection. Beth never forgot that night and her introduction to 'real music', and the euphoria never left her memory.

The evening led to further meetings with Lucy. Older by a number of years than Beth, Lucy was a vivacious woman, who in spite of losing sons in the war, remained conscious of what she felt was her duty to the country. She focused her attention on a number of projects, the main one being the plight of orphans, whether due to the war or other reasons. She admired Beth's sentiments as they were so similar to her own, as well as the stance she had taken over the plight of those five remaining young people still in her care. Together they established a group of women who were prepared to work toward the future care and education of homeless orphans. Beth now knew in her heart that her future lay in this charity work.

Her existing work did not leave too much time for the charity at this stage, and she knew also that she must, for the sake of her own psyche, solve the question mark surrounding Maya's drawing of Hetherington. Whenever she thought of the cryptic words on the back of the drawing, she wondered again what they meant just as she had when she heard Maya whisper them. She realized that Hetherington must know something.

Obsessed as she was by this question, Beth had asked one of her senior students to check into Hetherington's current situation. He was one of the best espionage agents from the project, and with the information Beth had been able to give him, it had been an easy task. He reported that Fred continued to work with his father near Nashua, New Hampshire. The family had moved from their large mansion into a smaller home within a more convenient neighborhood, allowing Hetherington's now aging father to be nearer his office. It seemed that Fred had not yet been appointed as his father's successor, indeed his working position within the firm remained a humble one.

The mansion, still owned by the Hetheringtons, remained empty, though her student's report indicated internal deterioration. Beth wondered if it had been requisitioned by the army during the war, though there was nothing in the records to say it had been. There were, however, many records within that vicinity that had been destroyed during a war-time fire in the legislature buildings.

"What a shame it isn't nearer Washington," she had said to Lucy Forder. "We might have been able to utilize it for a home for orphans."

"No chance," said Lucy, "it would have been snapped up by the government if it had been."

They had both laughed, knowing it to be a true enough conjecture, but did concede New Hampshire might find it useful for such a purpose.

Laura and George Sullivan had divided their time between Washington and Cynthiana since their wedding, and it was not long before Laura became part of the meetings that Beth and Lucy now enjoyed. Now that her worries over her students had rescinded, Beth enjoyed these new openings, though often felt restless as she thought of the future. She felt a need for a change, and decided to accept the Sullivan's offer of a lift to Cynthiana on their next visit. She wanted to talk everything over with Clarrie as well as Beulah and Delphia, just to get her head around the potential changes in her life.

As it happened, they had little time for personal chats when they arrived, as they were greeted by the unexpected return of Rory and his family. Laura, Beth and Clarrie spent much of their time together, not wishing to impose themselves on the Compton family at that important time. George and John joined them occasionally when they found time from 'messing about on the river'.

When she was alone with Clarrie one day, Beth discussed the finding of Maya's drawing and the subsequent report she had requisitioned. She also told her of the empty Hetherington mansion.

They chatted a while about the old days, though Clarrie had to admit that she had met Fred on only two, maybe three, occasions.

"I seem to remember some chat about how he had left Lexington when it was obvious Oliver wasn't coming back," she said, "though I can't remember just when, can you?"

Beth confessed that she couldn't remember either.

"I think it was before Maya died," she said.

She chose that moment of brief quiet to inform Clarrie of her future plans.

"You know, Clarrie," she said, "since that awful time when I thought my last five boys would lose the same chances the others had, I've thought a lot about the hundreds of orphans there must be in our country nowadays. It was my tirade to John Forder that made me think of it all in depth. It has crossed my mind that the empty Hetherington mansion could be an amazing place to establish an orphanage. It could at least house some of the New Hampshire orphans.

"I'm thinking of going to New Hampshire in the near future to talk to the Hetheringtons about its possible use. I also want to see Fred. He must know something about that drawing and what Maya meant by 'The Other Angel', and even why that piece of paper was in her book."

"There could be some substance to your idea for the mansion," said Clarrie, wearing her metaphoric business hat, "but it would be expensive to set up, as would the running costs of caring and educating the children. It would cost thousands and that's not including the maintenance costs of the building. Hetherington would have to include that in the annual rental charges. A lot would depend on how much Fred's father would charge for the rental, assuming the local legislature approved funding for an orphanage."

Beth had no option but to agree, but Clarrie wondered what her friend was planning. She had hoped her dismal analysis of potential costs would remove any idea of taking up such a challenge from her friend's mind.

"Well, let's change the subject. I'll tell you my bit of news, shall I?" She twinkled at Beth.

"Oh, no, don't tell me. You're going to have another baby?"

"Yes, yes," beamed Clarrie. "Who'd have thought it? And you are to be godmother and honorary special aunt. He, she, whoever, will love you, I know."

"I was only thinking the other day which one of you will be the first to come and ask me to be a godmother again," she said. "I am so very thrilled for you, Clarrie."

She hugged her friend hard, hoping for a goddaughter to love and cherish. She was just about getting used to Clarrie's son, born within a year of the wedding.

The next day there was little time for further discussion. Beth, together with Clarrie and her family, had accepted the invitation of Rory and Marie-Louise to their home-coming party at Longfield with their children Antoin and Brigitte. Beth could hardly take her eyes off Brigitte, a most beautiful child. She wished that Oliver could have been there with his camera, as she wondered what the child's future would be. She was glad both of the children had escaped the horrors of the Civil War. Antoin, a lovable little boy who understood French instructions much better than he did English, resembled his French grandfather, according to the petite, elegant Madame Alazet, though he did have Rory's fair coloring.

The following day Beth returned to Washington with George Sullivan, as Laura had decided to spend a few more days with Rory and the children.

Neither mentioned their work as they discussed in full detail the wonderful few days and the arrival of Rory and his family. George enthused about Marie-Louise and mentioned that she had a look of her. Beth had heard the suggestion once or twice during the past few days and suggested it was their similar hair color and style that gave the vague indication of them being look-alikes. She had noticed, as the family saw Beth and George off, that Marie-Louise wore her long hair in a wonderful Parisian chignon that morning. Everybody, including Beth, had said how breathtaking and very French she looked.

Chapter 20
A Turning Point

On her return from Kentucky, Beth wasted no time in organizing a trip to New Hampshire via rail to Boston, where she stayed overnight. She travelled on to Concord by passenger coach the next day. John Forder had organized an overnight stay in Concord, and she completed her journey to Nashua the following day. The coachman dropped her at the small hotel, also recommended by Forder.

The manager was impressed with her good looks and demeanor and allocated her a quiet, well-furnished room that he reserved for his 'special' guests. She just had to ask and the world would be hers, he had said.

He was curious about Washington, and asked numerous questions about the city and President Johnson. What was he like? How did he compare with that great man, Lincoln? She smiled at his enthusiasm and told him that the president was a good man who had yet to prove himself, and no, she had not had tea with the First Lady but lived in hope of doing so. He was fascinated when she told him how she saw the president and his wife taking the air in their horse driven carriage from time to time.

The law office of Samuel Hetherington was easy to find the next morning and Beth left a note for Fred asking him to meet her at the town's only coffee house at noon. Beth saw him before he noticed her. He appeared taller and slimmer than when she had seen him in Richmond. *He must be in his mid-twenties now*, she thought to herself, and noted a few grey swathes at the sides and brow of his hairline. This was a common phenomenon nowadays amongst young men who had returned from war-time exploits and dreadful experiences.

She watched Fred as he stepped into the coffee shop and looked around. At first he didn't recognize her, dressed as she was in a long green gown and matching brimmed hat, with a large maroon feather adjusted to cover her face as she looked downward. This adjustment served its purpose and gave time for Beth to study Fred before claiming his attention. When she raised her head and rearranged the feather with a blasé flick of a delicate manicured hand, he saw her. He stared for a long moment, unsure as to whether it was she, as he took in her well-cut clothes bought specially for the occasion and the discreet rouge and powder adorning her face. He told her later it was her expressive eyes that confirmed to him who she was.

"Well, Bethesda, how are you? What a surprise and how kind of you to look me up. I never ever expected to see you again," he gushed.

She allowed him to kiss her cheek as curious onlookers wondered who this smart, pretty woman was greeting the rather dull Mr. Hetherington junior with obvious affection.

"He's a dark horse," said a swarthy builder, who had already noticed Beth and had planned to set up a chat with her. A few of the men stared at the couple, until the barkeeper told them to "watch it", before he walked over to them.

"Afternoon, Mr. 'etherington. Can I git yerself and this pretty little thing somethin' to eat or do yer just wanna coffee?"

Fred consulted with Beth and ordered two milk coffees.

"We'll be taking our food elsewhere, and mind your manners in the meantime," he said. He had not liked the casual attitude shown to his guest.

Their first half-hour together engendered earnest conversation about how everybody he had known in Lexington had fared. He was interested to hear about Rory and his family, the marriages of Laura and Clarrie, and that of Rory's Aunt Delphia, as well as the 'doings' of Oliver's parents.

"What did Oliver's father do with his beautiful horses during the war?" he asked. Beth knew he had sent them to a 'safe farm' near New York, though knew little about how they had fared. She promised to find out more and let Fred know. He asked few questions about Oliver's welfare, though appeared to have been aware he had been in Europe for part of the war.

Beth asked him about *The Scarlet Letter* and how it had come into Oliver's possession.

"I do remember giving that book to Maya once," he said. "I don't know how it came back into my possession, but I can recall I asked Oliver to get it back to you when he could. It was after your sister died. I thought you should have it."

"Maya used to love you reading it to her," she said, "and maybe you hung on to it by accident one day after reading to us."

Fred shrugged and repeated that he couldn't remember. They spent a little time after that chatting about their days by the river as young teenagers, and how he had helped Beth and her sister to learn to read and write and speak a little French.

"That was the beginning of my French prowess, and you'll be pleased to know I'm now fluent," Beth said, as they finished off their coffees and ordered fresh ones. "How lovely those days were: no thoughts of war, or limbless men, or blind ones walking with white painted sticks, or those injuries seen and somehow coped with on the Gettysburg battlefield."

She looked at Fred with the wonder of the earlier tranquil days. Perhaps one or two of the jealous male customers in the café thought they were looks of love as Fred returned her gaze. He had looked surprised when she mentioned Gettysburg.

"What do you know about that battlefield?" he asked. "Surely you weren't there."

He was surprised to hear her story of how she and her three friends had all ended up there after the battle, arriving within days of each other. He shook his head in amazement.

The barkeeper carried the drinks across to them. As Fred paid for the drinks, she noticed how flustered he had become as she withdrew Maya's drawing of his face from her reticule. She handed it to him.

"Why did she write 'The Other Angel' on the back of her drawing of you?" she asked.

He shrugged, his face flushed.

"I don't know," he said.

Beth noticed an odd, almost furtive expression that she could not interpret spring into Fred's eyes for a few seconds.

"Were you still in Lexington when Beth died?" she asked.

His left eye twitched as he answered. "It's a long time ago now, and I really can't remember. Why?"

"I just wondered if you could remember all the commotion there was. The police and even the local army were involved in tracking down clues."

"Did they find any?" Fred asked.

"None, except her bloomers were flung onto a nearby bush. And there were hoof marks around where I found her. She was still alive, though she died soon after I got to her. We never did find out what had happened."

"What did she die from?" asked Fred. "Was it a fall from a horse?"

For a moment Beth was silent as she wondered why Fred thought Maya had fallen from a horse.

"It's not certain that she fell from a horse, Fred. We never had a horse of our own as you know, and neither of us ever rode one, of that I'm sure. We all surmised that she had gone to that spot to meet someone who had ridden there. We never found out who it was, though."

She told him then how her parents had died. She could see from his dazed expression how that news had upset him. He took hold of her hand.

"Oh, Beth, I hadn't heard about that. You have suffered so much," he choked. "I didn't know."

She could see the shock in his ashen face, as he swigged down the remainder of his coffee.

"I'll have to get back soon," he said.

"What? Surely the boss' son can take a longer midday break. I've come a long way to see you. Can you stay a bit longer?"

Fred stared at her for a long moment. "Why have you come, Beth? It's a long way from Washington, I agree, and I'm beginning to wonder just why you're here."

"First of all, I wanted to find out about this drawing and why she wrote 'the other angel' on the back. It was obvious to me I must meet up with you again as I thought maybe you'd know."

"I s'pose it was the natural thing for you to do," he said, though his eyes and voice had lost their original luster at seeing her.

"She called me an angel just once," he said.

"Why, Fred, why did she call you that?"

"I don't know why Beth, I can't remember."

"She hadn't died when I reached her. I asked her who had hurt her, and she spoke the very words written here just before she died in my arms."

Beth tapped the back of the drawing with two fingers.

"I'll never forget her very last words to me," she said.

Fred looked confused and troubled. "Let's go for a walk," he said, as he noticed some of the patrons were now staring at them as Beth's voice began to rise. He took her elbow as they walked toward the door.

"Young Fred's got 'imself a right 'un there. What does she charge, Fred?" someone bellowed.

Fred's face was livid. He turned back and walked up to the youth who had called out. Without preliminary he shot out his right fist. The youth fell off his stool, blood spurting from his nose.

"The lady is an old friend from Kentucky. She's a true lady, but as you've never seen one, how would you recognize that plain fact," he shouted, before pushing another thug away.

"Do you want to keep your job?" he snarled at that thug, who backed off.

Fred returned to Beth. "Let's go down to the hotel where we can talk in peace. They know me and I'll introduce you to the manager if you haven't already met him. He'll stop any rumors if anybody starts something up."

They walked a short distance in silence. After a few minutes Fred said, "You want to know when she called me an angel. Well, it was right after we'd been together."

"Been where together? What are you talking about, Fred?"

"You know what I mean. Together, in a…um…" He stopped and sighed and then in a great rush said, "In a…ahem…carnal way."

Beth stopped in her tracks. "What?" she screamed.

"Some of the local boys dared me to. Most of 'em knew Maya was known for being…'um…easy. They told me I didn't know what I was missing…"

Before he could finish, Beth struck him hard across his face.

"What are you implying, Hetherington?" she asked, her face furious. "My sister was pure, untouched. She wanted to remain so for her future husband. My parents were very strict and Maya wouldn't have gone against our mother's rules."

She stopped in her tracks and stamped her feet in her anger, as she raised her hand to him again. Fred caught her arm before it could strike.

"Let me finish, Beth," he said, as he continued to rub his face with his free hand. "Your sister was *not* pure."

He told her how he and some of the other young men were smitten with Beth. She was beautiful, vivacious, intelligent, and quite willing to bestow her favors on those she liked. They were usually the richer boys. Oliver was never interested in the local girls, but he did encourage me when he realized I was attracted to her. Up to then, neither of us had interest in girls – but Maya, well, she was a rather special girl. At least I thought so. Oliver knew how I felt about her and frankly encouraged me to take up the challenge from the other boy. He said I hadn't the guts to take her. In fact, he followed me on the first meeting I arranged to make sure I didn't run off. At my second meeting with her, down by the river, I let her strip me naked, and she made a good job of that seduction. I became besotted with her…"

He stopped as Beth sobbed. "I don't believe you, not my Maya, my little Maya…"

He dodged out of reach of Beth's hand once again. In doing so spied a log on the side of the track leading to the hotel, and led her to it, where they sat well apart.

"Yes, Beth, it's true. She made me feel so good that I returned for more when she sent me a note a couple of weeks later asking me to meet her. That time it was even more amazing. Then she sent me another invitation a few weeks later. It was a new venue and I had to ride there."

"When I arrived, she had already stripped off her underwear. I saw them laid across a hedge. She lifted her skirt and allowed me to see her beautiful body. Oh, she was so very lovely. She laughed at me, but she wouldn't let me touch her. She told me that she was bearing a child, our child. She said that we must marry quickly, so that our child would have a start in life without the stigma of a forced marriage. Or words to that effect, I can't remember just how she said it."

He stopped to look at Beth, his face contorted with sorrow.

"Forgive me, Beth, but I told her that I couldn't marry her. Oliver had told me of your family's curse, you see."

"Curse?" Beth shouted.

"Well, yes, Beth. He told me once that any child born to you or your sister could be either light or dark-skinned because of your family heritage and that even if you birthed light-skinned children, their descendants might still produce darker ones. Though I was besotted with your sister, Beth, I was unable to accept that. The time may come when it will be acceptable, but it isn't now and I knew my parents would disown me. As well as that, I had no means to support a wife let alone a child."

"So you killed her?"

Fred was ashen-faced.

"No, I didn't. I told her I couldn't marry her because of the curse. She flew at me, hit me, bit me, pushed me onto the ground and kicked my head. It was all so sudden, but I didn't defend myself because I didn't want to hurt her. I must have been dazed for a while, because when I came to my senses, she was astride my horse. She was laughing at me and said she wanted to marry me so she could be mistress of a mansion one day. I'd never told her I had an older brother who would inherit it. There'd been no need to do so, even when Oliver had once shown her photographs of my father's mansion. He'd taken them during his one and only visit to my home."

"She said on that awful day that this was an opportunity for her dreams to come true, and that if I refused to marry her she'd start the rumor I had raped her. She said her baby would be proof I'd done so. I can tell you Beth, I was scared. Then my horse reared, I don't know why, but whatever the reason, she couldn't keep her balance and slipped off the saddle. She did land with a bang, I must say."

"You left her there to die," Beth whispered.

"Well, no, she was breathing, called me a scum bag, and she even sat up. I tried to help her to stand, but she wouldn't let me. She seemed alright, though her head was bleeding a little, but I must admit I did ride off. I looked round once and by then she was standing up, screaming after me, calling me terrible names, telling me she would tell everybody I'd seduced her. I was glad to get away, Beth."

"You must have heard about the commotion after we found her."

"I didn't, no. I returned to Nashua the next day 'cos I wanted to be as far away from her as possible. I'd told Oliver about it, and he also felt I should move on. I never returned to Lexington. There was no point as he and I were no longer close."

Beth sat on the log, staring in front of her, too shocked to move.

"What I've told you, Beth, is the truth. You can always discuss this with Oliver. He knows the whole story. I know him very well, and he's not a liar and wouldn't lie about something like this. Neither would I. He did write and tell me a while later that Maya had died, though he never told me how or when. That's the last time I ever heard from him."

Beth would not allow her tears to flow, though Fred saw her distress.

"My dear Beth, I am so, so sorry to disillusion you about your sister," he said. "I never would have, but I can't allow myself to be accused of killing her."

Beth nodded. In her own grief over the years, she had forgotten her own suspicions of Maya's behavior before her death, and they now slotted back into her mind.

"It's a lot to take in right now, Fred, but I can tell you she wasn't pregnant. When her bloomers were found, everyone thought she'd been attacked for sex, but there was no evidence that she had been. The doctor who examined her would have known if she had and I know he would have told me. He may have told my father that she'd been sexually active well before that day, but if he did, Papa never told me. Perhaps that's what created his deep depression. Poor Papa."

She wept then, and asked Fred to go back to his office as she wished to recover on her own.

Chapter 21
It All Comes Together

Beth was surprised to receive a visit from Fred's mother later that evening.

"Call me Mary," she said, as she introduced herself. "Fred told me you're connected with the Lexington Comptons and I did meet Oliver years ago. His parents were very good to him when he was a student in Kentucky."

Mary Hetherington, a slim, grey-haired woman, of average height, sported the new shorter hairdo that a few fashionable women were daring to wear nowadays. Her clothes were impeccable, of the latest Washington style, her complexion unadorned, though clear and rosy. She could have been described as plain were it not for the ready smile that reached her eyes and which never seemed to leave her face.

"Can you come for dinner tomorrow evening, or the evening after? When are you returning to Lexington?" she asked, almost in one breath.

Beth explained she had not yet made arrangements for her return, though it would be within the next few days.

"I'm going to rest this evening, but would love to meet your family. As soon as my plans are made, I'll send a note so you can find a convenient time for my visit."

Mary asked about her work with orphans and spoke of her own concern at the plight of war orphans across the States. She told Beth of those in Nashua who could be seen trawling the streets each evening as they scavenged for food thrown out by cafes. Vandalism and theft was rife. A number of housewives and mothers took it in turns to provide soup and bread for the 40 or so who roamed around, and kept a careful eye out for those who were badly clothed or shod, or ill. These were reported to the local authority and taken into care where necessary for a short spell, before they were put out again to fend for themselves, in order to provide a placement for a needier child.

"I chair a local charity that tries to help them, but the extent of the problem is overwhelming," she said. "We've placed babies and toddlers in suitable homes, but it's difficult to find places for the older ones."

Beth told her of Lucy Forder's research in other cities, all of which were experiencing similar problems.

"Lucy's research indicates the problem must be solved soon, otherwise we may have a generation of thieves and rascals who've never had a chance at all to overcome their fate," Beth said. She watched as Mary's face screwed up in dismay and worry at the thought.

While she was unable to discuss the nature of her own work, Beth spoke of her association with Lucy and her husband with whom she had developed a strong friendship.

She described Lucy's work with the orphans in Washington, and her fantasy of establishing orphanages throughout the country, each working to a national defined scheme.

"Lucy wants to include not only essential care, but also education and life opportunities." Beth said and explained how Lucy's committee had sighed many times over the possibility of achieving this dream even though they never expected to.

"Lucy won't give up her ambition without a fight, though. She wants to establish a 'center of excellence' as a showcase, and dreams of local authorities sending their representatives to it in the hope they'll emulate the plan in their own areas."

"You mean a kind of 'tool' to highlight and solve the problems of war orphans throughout the country?" asked Mary, her voice thrilled with excitement.

"Exactly," said Beth, "and we all agree with Lucy that it's better to understand a scheme with the evidence of one's own eyes, rather than sitting around a table reading a report."

She was gratified when Mary nodded her agreement at the vision.

"The trouble is there's no suitable accommodation within the Washington area to set up such an establishment, so Lucy's now looking country-wide to find somewhere, in order to make a start on a national project. There is some interest at government level, but this could wane unless she can get a move on. Without a suitable building, of course, she's unable to do so. That's one of the reasons I'm here."

"One of the reasons?" Mary queried.

"Yes. You see, my coming to New Hampshire was by chance, really. I needed a short break from my work. I could have gone to Kentucky, but I had a notion to go somewhere different. Someone told me about the beautiful countryside of New Hampshire, and they suggested the Concord area. When I studied a map, I realized it wasn't too far from Nashua, where I knew Fred's family lived. I then developed a sentimental longing to link up with him again, as well as wallowing in the countryside."

They laughed at Beth's sentiment, both understanding the yearning. Beth hoped she would be forgiven by her Maker for lying about her reason for visiting her son. It would have been impossible to tell Fred's mother the real reason had been to discuss Maya's drawing.

"I realized Fred may have moved on, given all the changes that the war brought, so I asked one of my students to ascertain whether Fred was still in the area. He soon confirmed that he was, but that the family had moved home. His report described how he had found your mansion empty and though it showed signs of deterioration, it wasn't beyond repair. He showed us a photograph your local newspaper office had telegraphed to him."

She stopped and looked at Mary, whose face was a picture of enthusiasm.

"You realized you'd found your large building?" Mary asked

"Well, we thought there was a possibility, though we didn't dare allow the idea to take hold. We decided that I should take a look at it when I was in the area."

Beth told Mary that John Forder had already been in touch with the local authority and preliminary legal negotiations had progressed. Forder had done this in order to save time, knowing the government department overseeing the proposal was threatening to withdraw the financial support within days.

"No one's been in touch with my husband," Mary said. "I would have been made aware if they had."

"Negotiations haven't got that far yet," Beth said. "They've been looking at the legalities, but I have an appointment to meet with your husband tomorrow, along with Gordon Barrington, one of the legal executives."

Beth then realized her lack of discretion and a stab of apprehension coursed through her body.

"Oh, Mary, do you mind keeping this to yourself until after I've seen your husband, please? I'm afraid I got carried away with your enthusiasm."

"Of course I will," Mary said, "the last thing I want to do is jeopardize this marvelous concept."

Mary left soon after that, having made arrangements for Beth to have dinner with them the day after the appointment with her husband.

By the time Beth had prepared for bed that night, she had accepted Fred's revelations about Maya's indiscretions and his description of the accident that had taken her life. Having vowed so many years ago she would ascertain what had happened, she was consoled at the thought that, at last, this had been achieved. Fred's explanation did ring true, she thought, though she did wonder if it would have been better not to know about her sister's indiscreet behavior. There was no doubt in her mind now that Fred was in fact 'the other angel' Maya had referred to. However, the mystery of whom or what was the 'first angel' remained. She decided to write to Rory about the outcome of her talk with Fred, as he had been around most of that long ago summer and may have heard Maya say something about another 'angel'.

"Maya's death has been pivotal to all the changes in my life," she mused, as she climbed from her bath tub in the tiny space next to the bedroom. "I don't suppose I would have been here right now if she'd survived. Dear Mama and Papa could still be alive and I'd never have left Kentucky and gone to Richmond or to Washington."

She smiled as she thought of her Kentucky friends, and how the past few hours had brought them into her thoughts. She longed to be with them again in the way they had been before the war. If only they could have been together for this short respite to New Hampshire, which was as beautiful as folks had told her it would be.

She imagined the four of them exploring, walking through the woods and valleys, stopping to eat their food along the way, or calling at a hostelry to imbibe the local 'brew' alongside a delicious concoction of provincial produce. Perhaps Rory would have borrowed one of Oliver's cameras to record it all.

As she fantasized, her imagination failed to take into account her sister Maya's tragic death or the subsequent deaths of her parents. Nor did she think of Clarrie's happy new life with a loving husband and her son, with another baby on the way, or of Laura's current happiness with her handsome husband. But at least by now she was able to think of Rory without the intensity of emotion that had imprisoned her for a long time. She sighed as she remembered those perfect days of early youth and friendship in the lovely Blue Grass area of Kentucky she knew so well, before she fell asleep.

The next morning the fantasy was still with her, though it faded as thoughts of the meeting with Fred's father later that morning overtook her. The twist of fate that had brought the Nashua mansion to the notice of Lucy and herself was in the forefront of her mind.

It was a stroke of luck, she felt, that Mary Hetherington was involved in the welfare of orphans here in Nashua. She was unsure how much influence Mary might have over her husband's decision whether or not to release the building. It was certain, however, that if the project went ahead, there would be Mary's steady hand to help guide the project. She couldn't believe how everything appeared to be falling into place.

As she prepared herself for the meeting, Beth remembered how John Forder had vetoed Lucy's suggestion that the negotiations should stay between Hetherington and the Nashua local authority negotiators.

"It would be more diplomatic for the suggestion to come from your organization, Lucy," he had said, ever the diplomat. "I've already researched Hetherington, and he's a wily old lawyer who knows how to put on the pressure to get the best deal. We can't afford more than we will offer, and if you are keen enough to send along your own representative, he'll be more likely to accept the negotiator's offer. It's so lucky that Beth decided to visit his son, and I believe she'll be a tremendous asset. After all, if she hadn't made enquiries about her friend's current whereabouts, we wouldn't even have heard of Hetherington Mansion."

Another member of the committee, usually a placid, unexcitable individual, piped up. "I'm a great believer in fate, Divine Intervention, coincidence, call it what you will, so let's not upset this," she said, with uncharacteristic fervor.

So it had been agreed that Beth would try to sell the idea to Hetherington.

After breakfast she asked the hotel manager for the timetable of passenger coaches to Boston within the next few days. She was directed to the local funeral director, Bob Lea, who also served as the community's travel expert. His office was just around the corner. Bob was a cheery soul, small, elegant and full of chat. He agreed to take her to Concord in three days' time when the next Boston coach was due. He also provided her with the necessary rail timetable for her onward journey to Washington.

She ascertained from him the route to the Hetherington Mansion. Bob told her that Fred's brother, Robert Samuel Hetherington, had enlisted in the Second New Hampshire Voluntary

272

Infantry Regiment, and been killed in the Williamsburg battle. Robert, five years older than Fred, would have inherited the mansion. Bob could not understand why Hetherington was allowing the mansion and grounds to wither away. The rumor was, he told Beth in a quiet whisper, that Hetherington didn't wish his younger son to inherit, though nobody knew why.

She returned to the hotel, reserved her room for the required extra nights and went up to change into the comfortable old boots she had remembered to bring with her, anticipating one or two long walks during her stay. She also sent a note to Mary, confirming the arrangement for dinner the following evening. After those chores, she commenced her mile long trek to the mansion.

Caught as it was in the sunshine of late morning, the large old house was attractive, though the gardens were unkempt. There had been no attempt to retain any semblance of tidiness, just as Bob Lea had said.

She was unable to open the gate leading to the gatekeeper's lodge, a large building at the bottom of a long, straight drive. She remembered Fred telling her his father's two gardeners and their families had lived there. The lodge was now closed up, with no sign of existing habitation, but she knew she couldn't scamper over the high gate as she might have done a few years ago. In any case, her long gown prevented this, but walking around the perimeter of the grounds, she found a hole in a hedge large enough to clamber through. She did notice a few inches of thread scrunched up at the hem of the gown, where it had been caught and pulled by the brambles. It reminded her of the black garments she had worn as she waited in the brambles during her assignment in Richmond, when she first saw Confederate secret agent Hetherington.

As Beth peered through the ground-level windows, she realized the large number of rooms.

"If the upper floors are as large, there should be plenty of room for a dormitory or even a few single rooms for older orphans," she thought.

She noted a good sized kitchen with worktops and a large cooker. Pots, pans and a selection of cooking utensils were slotted into compartments here and there, and a large wooden table surrounded by at least a dozen chairs, was visible down one side. There was plenty of room for a kitchen dresser. She noticed there had been one there though now removed, according to the visible marks she could just make out on the floor. She noticed some dilapidation within, though it was not as extensive as she had

273

expected. She wished she could get inside as she tried the locked doors and long windows.

The gardens were in a worse state than at first glance. Those around the back of the house, used for growing vegetables she supposed, were devoid of any existing growing patches. The front and side areas were overgrown, though a pattern remained which Beth felt could be reinstated once it had been cleared of dead vegetation. She thought it would be a wonderful place to teach homeless orphans about the real beauty of nature and a natural environment to teach orphans the skills of building and maintaining a garden.

Having now seen the property from the outside, Beth could envisage its effectiveness as a 'center of excellence' that could motivate a meaningful national project.

She returned to the hotel, and following a light meal served in her room, she tried to rest until the time for meeting Mr. Hetherington. Gordon Barrington from the local authority arrived 45 minutes before the meeting, with a view to discussing their tactics.

She had already dressed in a skirt and jacket of cerise velvet, the shape-enhancing jacket cut in last years' Washington fashion. She had chosen light grey shoes with a fashionable medium heel, adding height to her petite figure. She didn't wear a hat, but had styled her light brown hair into a French-style, similar to that created by Marie-Louise, which enhanced her elegance. She wore no make-up or jewelry, and looked a lady in every respect. She was aware of her impressive appearance, though wondered how she would be received by Fred's father. She picked up a small grey purse as she left her room to meet Mr. Barrington.

Beth was impressed by Barrington's appearance. A man of medium height and build, he looked smart in a pair of tailored pants, a dark blue tailcoat jacket and a matching waistcoat. His white shirt was enhanced by a pale blue cravat and he carried a top hat and a leather document case. As she walked toward him he pushed a book with a Greek title into his case.

She thought he looked Hellenic and felt it would not have been inappropriate had he been reading from a Greek parchment as she took in his blue, somewhat sad eyes and chiseled features. She wondered how Rory's cousin, Oliver, would have used the light to allow his camera to enhance the cheekbones of this man, as well as capture his handsome profile. She liked his warm smile and tried

around now and you know yourself, as a lawyer, the government's reconstruction program is already in difficulty. We are lucky to have this offer of finance. I've already informed you it will be withdrawn within three days."

Barrington stopped and raised his left eyebrow to an almost triangular arch, with a nod of confidence. He remained standing, his glowering stance commanding as he looked down at the desktop rather than at Hetherington's face. Hetherington understood the insult.

Beth admired Barrington's approach. Had she been aware that the stance was taken because of Hetherington's previous lewd scrutiny of the charming young woman who accompanied him, she would have been surprised.

"There are other calls on the available finance, you see, and there are no bargaining options around nowadays, nor likely to be," Barrington concluded, as he resumed his seat opposite Beth.

Samuel knew when he was beaten, but started on another line of attack.

"I assume the administrator will be a local person, someone with a sense of financial acumen and staying power, someone with administrative and leadership skills. If the wrong person is appointed, then it could well flop."

"There has been some discussion on this matter, sir, but we do have a description of what the job will entail. If our proposal is acceptable to all parties, likely candidates will be interviewed," Barrington said.

"I assume, I will have a say in whom you appoint," Hetherington said.

"No sir, you are the lessor, and we will pay you for the privilege of using your premises. You will have no further say in how the scheme is run. None at all."

"Will you advertise the position locally?" Samuel asked.

"We may do, sir, if our own recommendations do not prove suitable."

"Will I be in a position to recommend someone?"

"Yes, sir, of course, but you will not be involved in any decision making as to whom the interview panel recommend."

"I shall need to discuss this proposal with my wife," Hetherington said. "I shall let you have my decision within two days."

"I need to remind you, sir," Barrington said, "that once you sign a contract, it will be binding. I am sorry, sir, but that's the way of things today."

Samuel stood up, unsteadily, his face red with suppressed antagonism toward Barrington as he walked them to the door. He had not liked the way the man had spoken to him. Surely the owner of the property had a say in who should be in charge during the 10-year lease. He would see about that.

As Hetherington opened the door for them, he turned to Beth.

"I hope you will be nominated to run the center," he said, "I hope you put yourself forward for the job."

"I already have a worthwhile job in Washington, sir, but thank you for the compliment," she said as she walked out.

She and Barrington assumed the final comment indicated he would be accepting the proposal. Beth was delighted with the outcome and thanked Mr. Barrington.

"You were so professional in the way you handled him. I'm so delighted with the result," she said as she gave him a light kiss on his cheek.

As Barrington stroked his cheek where her lips had touched, it was evident he was too.

"There's just one thing, though, Mr. Barrington. I do share Mr. Hetherington's unease as to who will be responsible for the overall running of the center. Do you have people in mind willing and capable of doing the job?"

"Not yet. Are you interested, ma'am?"

"No, not at all," she said, "but I know of a likely candidate, one whom the community knows, and who I know will do a fantastic job for the orphans and for the overall project."

"Who?" asked a surprised Barrington.

"Frederick Hetherington. He knows the building and the community and he already helps his mother with her work with orphans. He dislikes his current job and wants a way out without creating problems within his family. I know he would like to work somewhere like Washington or move further west when he marries Estelle, but he doesn't want to leave his mother. She still grieves for his brother, you see."

He rubbed his chin for a while, before saying that he would put the suggestion to the appointment board.

"We don't really want a fight with Hetherington over this and it could well be a solution that'll ensure a move forward. It's a pity you're not interested, Beth."

He raised his hat to her and left.

Beth was quite taken aback that he had used her first name, though was in one way delighted, as she smiled at his receding figure.

The rest of the afternoon was hers and she decided to do what she had come for in the first place, plenty of healthy country walking. She had already planned a long walk through some of the countryside around Nashua, and donning her old boots and an elderly skirt and jacket packed specially for the purpose, she prepared to set off with a pack of food provided by the hotel. She wished she had one of Oliver's cameras with her, so she could show off the lovely landscapes of the New Hampshire countryside when she returned to Washington.

The long, peaceful walk provided time to think, and by the time Beth returned to the hotel, she had resolved to speak again with Samuel Hetherington. His office was closed by then, but she pushed a prepared note through the door, marked for his personal attention, stating she would be at his office at 8.30 a.m. the next morning. She knew he would be there, because Mary had already told her of his dedication to his business and the hours he worked.

She slept well that night and was awakened at seven o'clock by a maid bringing her pre-ordered boiled egg, toast and coffee. She dressed in her cerise velvet skirt and a toning high-necked blouse, and styled her hair in a flowing mane, fastened at the sides with hairclips decorated with small cerise stones. She wore her stouter black heeled shoes and carried a small reticule. The weather was warm and she decided she did not did not need the jacket. As she stepped out of the hotel, watched in admiration by early risers, she appeared serene and impressive as she set out on the short journey to the Hetherington law offices. She hoped she would not meet Fred, but didn't really expect to, as Mary had told her his hours were shorter than his father's.

She rang the bell and was surprised when Hetherington himself opened the door.

"What a delightful surprise your note was," he gushed. "To what do I owe this very great pleasure?"

He walked her to his office, and nodded on the way to a hovering woman, dressed in a black long skirt and high-necked white blouse, her grey hair drawn back into a neat though unflattering chignon. She appeared to have a perpetual frown on her face, suggested by the deep, horizontal lines between her eyes.

"Tea please, Amy," Hetherington barked at her.

"Yes, sir," she said, and curtsied before she hurried off.

Beth could not believe it.

"Christopher Columbus," she exclaimed to herself, "she curtsied. She actually curtsied to him."

She was dumbfounded but also amused. She worked hard at settling the line of her lips from one of derisive mirth to that of a serious woman keeping an appointment with her lawyer.

The incident cooled her manner toward him and she ignored his compliments about her appearance. She sat down abruptly, without invitation, on the same davenport she had used the day before. This time he sat opposite her. Her voice was more aloof than she intended, as she spoke of the reason for her visit.

"I listened to you carefully when you suggested you'd like to be involved in the appointment of the leader of the new orphanage, assuming it will go ahead."

She stopped, waiting for his acknowledgement of her statement, which he did not offer, though he continued to beam at her.

"I agree with you that you or your wife should be approached as to your recommendations, as you both know the community, the strength of individuals and your own property. Naturally you want the best for that, as well as for the community, and the orphans."

"Of course," he said, "I'm glad you understand that. After all, I'm a person of stature in this community, though I say it myself, and if we do go ahead, it is my property that will be utilized."

"Yes, sir," Beth agreed, "and I would go further and suggest you should even be on the appointing panel."

Amy came in with the tea, poured it and left with the same efficiency she had displayed earlier. Beth noticed she served Hetherington first, fussing with the amount of sugar and milk that was poured into the larger of the cups. She dealt with Beth's request for tea with no milk, and turning to her boss, offered her curtsy. He grunted at her to leave.

Beth had expected, so was not surprised at, the venomous look Amy gave her as she left.

Poor little Amy, Beth thought, *she's eating her heart out for someone who really isn't worth the bother of it all.*

"Now," Hetherington began, "I take it that you took my comment seriously yesterday," he said.

"What comment?" Beth asked.

"My comment that you should be the one offered the job. I assume you're here seeking my recommendation to Barrington. And by the way, please call me Samuel."

"No, Samuel, that is not why I'm here," Beth said

She decided to change her attitude from indignation to a more solicitous tone.

"You were wise to bring up this matter and to point out your own worthiness in suggesting a possible candidate, but I'm not interested. I did say that I had my own job in Washington."

"Yes, you did. I hoped my comments may have changed your mind, but obviously not. You think I know the best person for the job, do you? Are you referring to my wife, and do you think I should put her forward?"

"I don't think that at all, Samuel. Your wife's main preoccupation is caring for you and your home, and she does her work for the orphans around that, not instead of it."

"You've got someone in mind, then, haven't you? Someone from Washington, is it?"

"No, Samuel, someone more obvious than that. Your own son, Fred, would be ideal. He's legally trained but we both know his heart isn't in the profession. Nevertheless that training is essential to the post and I know from my own days in Lexington that he's a good teacher and a good organizer. He also knows your mansion inside out.

"He's a fair minded man, who really has more potential than he may have shown you. That's my professional judgement of him and I have an idea your recommendation for his appointment would be well accepted by the local officials."

"You know his background well, do you? Did you know he's experimented in another way of life…a bit of a deviant? He had young Oliver Compton over one summer, and it was obvious to me…"

He didn't want to go any further, fearing to distress this delectable young woman.

"No, I'm not aware of that. I've known him for a long time and his problem is one of shyness. I don't think his fiancée, Estelle, would agree with you either," Beth said, in her matter-of-fact tone, with a slight shrug of nonchalant shoulders.

Samuel was astounded when she neither blushed nor appeared surprised.

"But if you're referring to his friendship with Oliver Compton, from what I gather, it was nothing more than a close attachment of two lonely boys. It's not unusual, especially among shy youngsters who can feel isolated and lonely when they're away from home. I am aware they had witnessed a bad episode concerning an older college student and a wayward village girl which ended in the student's death and it had a bad psychological effect on them for years. Their joint experience in witnessing the tragedy made them close and they sustained each other all through college and beyond. They were two boys who had been deeply shocked, who needed guidance at a vulnerable stage of their lives. Did Fred get it from you?" Beth was angry and it showed.

"I vaguely remember hearing about it from the headmaster of the college. I'm not a fool, and of course I spoke to the boy. Told him not to be so nebbish about it – after all, it wasn't the end of the world, was it? Not for him, anyway. He shouldn't use that as an excuse for his weak-kneed posturing with that milksop he called a buddy. I couldn't stand the sight of them together. How dare you speak to me like that?"

"You brought it up. Samuel. What I know is that you should have felt concern for him. You should have felt understanding, compassion and a great deal of love for what must have been a misery for him."

"What a lot of rubbish, and I thought you were a bright girl," Samuel spat out.

"Fred's a fine man, and is looking forward to marriage and producing fit, healthy children," Beth said, "but he's hampered right now because he's in the wrong job with you. He needs to spread his own wings and be allowed to be himself. He should be given a chance."

"Does he know you're here? Did he send you to plead the case for him? That's just like him. He's feeble, weak, insipid, a man who didn't even fight for his country. Look at how he wears his hair, no style, too long, a foppish wash-mop on top of his head.

"He hopped off down south, without consulting me, to work in some wishy-washy law firm, and returned pleading sickness so that he wouldn't have to fight for his country like his brother. How can I respect or love a so-called man like that? Get out of here, woman."

He reached for a bell that lay on a nearby table.

Beth stood up and snatched it from his hand.

"How dare you?" he shouted. "This is my room, not yours. Now, get out."

Beth popped the bell in her reticule before pouring out another cup for Samuel from the teapot Amy had left behind. As she handed it to him, she smoothed his brow with her other cool hand.

"I'm sorry to upset you. I didn't mean to do so," she said, her soothing, soft voice full of the real concern she felt. "Please drink this, and then I'm going to tell you something about Fred that you don't know."

He looked startled, gaping at her with his fleshy lips wide open. His eyes bulged as he took the tea and gulped it down.

As he placed the cup and saucer on the table, she took out the bell from her reticule and placed it before him.

"If you really want me to go now, ring for Amy," she said.

He pushed the bell back to her. "Tell me," he snapped.

She looked straight into his eyes.

"First of all, I must tell you that I am committing the sin of breaking my oath to my country and my God. An oath I undertook when I became an agent for the secret services. I will cope with that in my own way, but I want to tell you that your son, Frederick, also undertook a similar oath when he became a secret agent."

Samuel's head jerked forward as he gave a short bark of laughter before it slumped toward his chest. The silence that followed for almost 30 seconds was surreal.

"Go on," he said in a shaky, disbelieving voice, as he raised his head. He laid his hands on his breastbone, the slender, smooth fingers fanned out as his ashen face looked at her.

"Part of the oath is that we should never, ever reveal what we have done and seen, both during the war and in peace-time. I am aware of your son's involvement only because he and I participated in a particular espionage project in Virginia. When that was completed, I didn't see him again, though I often wondered what had happened to him."

"What flag were you under?" he said.

"The Union flag," she said, looking into his eyes.

She had not liked breaking her oath, or that her words had implied Fred's flag had been the same as hers.

It is done now she thought, *I can't retract it.*

Samuel's face was distraught.

"He never told us. When he returned safely from the south, and made no attempt to join his dead brother's regiment, I resented it," Samuel said, squeezing his eyes shut. "I've given him hell ever since. I didn't know."

"I'm so sorry that Robert died," she said, "but so did Fred in a way. He saw terrible tragedies, dreadful injuries, probably more than he would have seen as a serving soldier. He has lived to carry those thoughts in his head forever, to grieve over them, to worry that he may have been the cause of some as a result of his espionage work. He received a serious injury to his head on one occasion, but

283

fortunately they got him to a medic in time to help him survive. He covers that large scar with his long hair, the very hair you despise."

Samuel's groan was long and deep. She sat beside of him and held him in her arms.

He released himself and looked at her with a downcast expression as he tugged at his bottom lip, his forehead wrinkled.

"Tell me more of the other things he did. I need to know. Please," he begged.

"I have broken my oath," she said, "and I'm not prepared to say any more. Fred will not, I know, break his oath. He has refused to talk about those days even with me. I trust you, Samuel, not to divulge to him what I have told you. I value his friendship and good opinion, but he will loath me if he knows what I've done in these past few minutes."

Samuel pushed fallen hair out of his face as he bit hard on the inside of his left cheek.

A knock at the door interrupted the tableau. Samuel raised a hand as if to ward off anyone from approaching or speaking to him, and shuffled to the door.

"I'm not finished here." He said to Amy, "I'll let you know when I'm free."

"It's Mrs. Talbot, sir. She's been waiting a while, sir, and is quite angry."

Samuel's stare at her was incredulous. He uttered an expletive and Beth could hear poor Amy's gasp.

She saw Samuel lean toward the wall for support and she rushed to him. Amy gasped again, though this time with concern.

"Are you alright, sir," she asked, as she strove to help Beth.

They led him to his seat.

"He's had some sort of turn," Beth said to Amy. "His wife says he's been overdoing it. Do you think you can get someone to prepare another cup of tea? You bring it in, though, if you don't mind because I don't think Mr. Hetherington would like anyone else to see, or hear, that he's unwell. What do you think, Amy?"

Amy understood the veiled instructions but was pleased to have been trusted above anyone else to help with Mr. Hetherington's 'turn'.

"This is the first time in 15 years," she said, "that I've seen Mr. Hetherington sick."

She looked at Beth in disapproval. "I hope that you didn't bring on this attack."

"No, she didn't, Amy." Samuel's voice remained shaky, but he was anxious that Amy did not blame Beth.

"Beth's a friend of my son, and called in to see me this morning because I wasn't so well last evening. She's just making sure I'm alright. Between the two of you I'm sure I shall be, but another of your cups of tea would be ideal. Can you send my son to me, as soon as he gets in, because I might decide to go home for the day. Give my apologies to Mrs. Talbot. I trust you of all people to be able to placate her."

Amy beamed at this acknowledgement of her worth and dashed off to fulfil her master's wishes. This time she did not curtsey.

Before Beth left for Washington, she acted as a witness to Samuel's agreement to lease his mansion to the local authority. He had accepted without question the full terms and conditions put to him.

Before doing this, he'd had a long talk with Mary, as well as his son, who wondered at his father's sudden change of attitude. Fred was, of course, staggered when his father suggested he would like to nominate him for the post of officer-in-charge of the orphanage scheme, assuming it got off the ground, and assuming Fred would like him to do so.

"Should you be appointed," he said to Fred, "I hope you will include your mother in the project, one way or another. She's works so hard for these orphans, and I'm sure she would love it."

Fred nodded. "Of course I will," he said.

It was clear to Beth when she attended their home for dinner that Samuel had not mentioned her input into this unexpected transformation of attitude.

Fred and Estelle called on her at the hotel the following morning, and Fred mentioned it. It was Estelle who had offered a reason.

"It could be that the sudden collapse in his office has scared him a bit," she said. "People of his age begin to worry about their own demise when something like that happens without warning."

Beth thought that was a good point and said so, glad there was something on which to hang the sudden change of attitude. She liked Estelle. Almost as tall as Fred in her heeled shoes, her large brown eyes were her redeeming feature, though her long, thick brunette hair was another asset. She was a shy, slender, presentable girl, who just missed being pretty. Her personality had not yet begun to emerge, though Beth had caught a glimpse of a future woman of depth and astuteness, someone who read and thought a lot, who would be an asset to Fred and his new career, assuming he was appointed. Beth wished she had more time to get to know her better, but she knew at some time in their lives they would be together again.

During that day Beth received a surprise visit from Mr. Barrington.

"Hetherington's put in a nomination for his son to take on the job of managing the project on our behalf," he told her, "and there's every reason to think that he'll be appointed. He's got the legal background and carries his father's reputation as a skilled businessman, lawyer and negotiator. Hetherington Junior will have a hard job proving that he's inherited all those skills, and he still has to get through the interview. However, an advantage in his favor is that his mother is already involved in improvements for the orphans here, and that's a good incentive for any son to work to. I think it's fairly safe to say he's probably the most suitable person under consideration right now."

"Is that what you've come to see me for, to tell me that?" asked Beth.

"Yes. I thought you'd like to return to Washington knowing what you've managed to achieve," he said, smiling.

When Beth left Nashua with Bob Lea the following day, she was disappointed that Mr. Barrington had not been there to see her off, together with the Hetheringtons, Amy and the hotel staff. She had thought, indeed hoped, he would have been.

There was a waiting-room at one of the cross-roads near Concord, where the coach would pick her up, and with a pack of food and a bottle of cool water, she prepared for a lonely wait, as she waved her final goodbyes to Bob Lea. She was not to be so lonely after all. Gordon Barrington was already there. She didn't see him at first, sitting as he was in an inconspicuous corner. He stood up and coughed

"A friend brought me over, and I stayed with him over night," he explained, when she had got over the surprise. "I just couldn't bear the thought of you travelling all that way to Washington on your own, so I've taken a few of days off and will escort you there."

They looked at each other for a long time without saying a word, but by the time they got to Boston they had talked for so long their throats were parched and sore.

Gordon spoke of his experience in the war. Like Hetherington's elder son, he had enrolled in the Second New Hampshire Voluntary Infantry Regiment and had also fought in the Williamsburg battle.

"I didn't know Hetherington," he said, "but I do know it was a hard-fought, horrific battle, where many soldiers on both sides were killed. I was one of the lucky ones because I was found quite soon after the battle and my life was saved as a result. Another day left on that field and I would have died. I had bullet injuries to my pelvis and left leg and lost a lot of blood, but thank goodness I was cared for by a brilliant surgeon. I was unable to walk for a long while, but I still had my brain power so I was retained and pushed into work in the local legislature offices afterwards, where I've been ever since."

He stopped for a while, remembering. "I lost a number of friends in that battle, and more since then in other battles. I can't yet see the worth of that war, with all those young men gone, but perhaps future generations will have the benefit of any good that it brought."

He was again lost in his memories before he added, "I met my wife during the first month of starting my job here," he said

Beth smiled at him, encouraging him to continue.

"She was named Kathleen, after her Irish grandmother, and a sweet girl, full of fun. She was a bit flighty, which was perhaps to be expected, or so my mother said as she was four years younger than me. Kathleen was very tiny, so when she gave birth to our son, a huge fella weighing in at over nine pounds, her body couldn't stand up to the shock. She died within two days of his birth."

"I blamed myself, of course," he said, his face now white with emotion, "but the midwife and the doctor said her pelvis had not matured enough for the delivery of a large baby. This was put down to her poor nutrition as an infant; not because of parental neglect but some sort of debilitating illness she'd had. I never knew what that was. I was so heartbroken at the time I didn't think to ask. Now I wonder if it was a hereditary illness, but according to my mother, who lives in Ohio, George is as fit as a fiddle and he's grown larger than life itself since I last saw him."

He grinned with pride.

"How often do you see him?" asked Beth.

"I don't see him often enough, just a couple of times a year. I go over to Ohio in April for two weeks and my mother brings George to Nashua in early September. We write every week."

"Why doesn't your mother move to Nashua? You could bring him up together then."

"Her roots are in Ohio, as is her second husband, three dogs, her three brothers and a sister who has six teenage children. I also have a sister who lives out west with her brood, hoping to strike gold, I think."

They both laughed at the description of his large scattered family.

"Do Kathleen's parents have any input into George's welfare?"

"No, they have enough to do, as their elderly parents live with them in the farm cottage. They don't show much interest in their grandson at all, and seem happy with the arrangement we have. They see him two or three times when he comes to Nashua, but that's all."

Beth told him her own story, even her life as a secret service agent, though she left out the actual experiences. When she explained her heritage, he was surprised.

"It must be difficult to live with that," he said, "How does it affect your psyche, living as a white woman in such a time?"

The question startled her in its unexpectedness.

"I am aware of my heritage," she said, "and as for living as a white woman, I *am* a white woman. My skin and hair color is a part of my inheritance from white grandfathers and great-grandfathers. I am the same as any white woman except that I happen to have some black ancestors. I'm luckier than many women of my age in Kentucky because I've received an education and know my capacity for learning and achieving is equal to any full-blooded white. Race should not come into it. My psyche, as you put it, is not affected, though sometimes I feel my life is a charade, perhaps because people like you wonder at how black people's minds function. Well, let me tell you, I have the same brain capacity every other human being has, irrespective of nationality."

She was silent for a while.

"My only difficulty is that I am reluctant to bear children. That's why I'll never marry. Even though there are two consecutive generations of white blood in my lineage, and assuming my husband was white, I could still produce a black child. It would be detrimental to the child's well-being and I would not wish for that."

Gordon realized he had been insensitive with his question. She was right. He also realized she was a wonderful woman, attractive, educated, thoughtful, brave, and a deep thinker to whom he could relate with ease. He knew he could marry her like a shot, given the opportunity, despite her wish not to bear children.

"Tell me more about yourself," he said. He listened hard and when she explained why she lived and worked in Washington, and how she came to be here in Nashua, he was aware how much she had achieved.

His eyes looked directly into hers, and Beth felt her insides somersault.

"What a brave woman you are, Beth," he whispered, reaching for her hand.

A strange emotion suddenly swirled around her. It was if he had drawn her into himself with his sad eyes, gentle voice and handsome face. She felt as if her whole body had undergone a molecular renewal which she knew would change her forever. She had fallen in love with a man from Nashua who worked as a lawyer for the legislature, a man who had a son called George in Ohio, a man whom she had known for only a few days.

Chapter 22
A New Generation

Clarrie wakened abruptly and sat up in bed. She was anxious about something, but couldn't remember what it was. Her heart was beating faster than usual. After a few confused seconds she realized. There was no sound of the running or chatter of her toddler son, or the mew of her few months old daughter seeking sustenance. She rushed out of bed, agitated, and then she remembered.

The children had spent the night with her mother and step-father. This was the day of the reception she had been planning together with Laura as a welcome home surprise for Beth and her husband, Gordon.

She breathed a sigh of relief and rested for a brief moment on the edge of the bed. John must have got up earlier as she noticed a cup of tea at her side of the bed, now cold. She picked it up and drank it anyway. It tasted good. She dashed across to her window from where she could see her mother's house, though trees planted around it when it was first built had now grown, providing the privacy they were there for. She opened the window in the hope of hearing her children, and yes, there it was: the joyful sound of Robin's chatter and laughter. She tried hard but couldn't hear the gurgles of baby Martha, named after her maternal grandmother, though everyone tended to call her Marty.

Probably still sleeping or having her feed, Clarrie thought, as she smoothed the yellow satin bedspread with her hand. She had forgotten to lift and fold it the previous night, but was not surprised, given that she and Frances had been baking and setting the tables in the large tent her husband and a few of his older students had set up at the back of their house.

She put on her working clothes. There was a smell and frizzle of cooking bacon and sausages as she hurried into the kitchen. She glanced at the old clock on top of the kitchen dresser that Timothy Compton had made for them on his last visit home. Thank goodness it was not as late as she had thought.

She caressed the dresser as she passed it. She loved it. Timothy had a flair for carpentry and had offered to make this, and a similar one for Laura, to celebrate their weddings. He was due to arrive today for the reception, and she looked forward to seeing him. Beulah, his mother, had told Clarrie only yesterday that he was considering leaving the army and establishing a carpentry business. They all hoped he would, for John missed the presence of his sons, with Oliver away in the big cities with his photography and Tim serving his country as an army captain. They were not sure whether Oliver would be here for today's reception, given that Fred Hetherington and his wife Estelle would be there. Indeed those two had already been established in John and Beulah's home for the past two nights. Clarrie really liked them and was pleased to have been the first to be told of their forthcoming baby.

Goodness, thought Clarrie, as she accepted a plate of fried food from Frances, *soon there'll be so many children of the next generation that we'll need to build a new town for them*. She chuckled at the thought.

She thanked her bustling, happy bakery manager, now a plain little dumpling of a woman, but wholly lovable.

"Have you had a breakfast, Frances?" she asked, "it's going to be one heck of a long day for all of us."

"I have indeed," Frances said. "I'm really looking forward to seeing Beth's face when she sees all this," she said, spreading her arms toward the door, and the large garden tent. "It all reminds me of your mother's wedding day. Wasn't that a wonderful event?"

Clarrie agreed it was.

"So much has happened since then, Frances, and I was just musing about how things are changing all the time. I've just done a mental count of the new generation members and within a few years our own generation will have become secondary in the scheme of things."

"Not really," said Frances. "There's still a lot to do to bring up these lovely children to be the kind people their parents, grandparents, aunts and uncles are."

Frances smiled as she said this, knowing her own place in Clarrie's family was precious to both of them. She sighed as she remembered her brothers who had given their lives for their country. She had never forgotten how her beloved Clarrie had brought the two boys together on that shocking battlefield.

Clarrie finished her meal, and then searched for a clean pinafore. As she donned it Laura dashed in, her newborn in one arm and a toddler holding on to the hand of the other.

"Will your mother be able to cope with these two as well as yours?" Laura said, looking anxious. "I don't want to put too much on her, but I know my mother said she would help her out. What do you think?"

Martha came into the kitchen at that moment.

"Your mother and Walter came over from Cynthiana last evening," she said, "and they're staying with us for two or three days. Delphia's already delved in with the chores. Of course we can take your little ones, Laura. Come along with me, Charles," she said to Laura's first-born, as she took the new baby into her arms. "Just let me have their clothes for the reception when you've got a minute, and we'll see everything is fine. Forget about us and them until then. We'll be along in time for receiving Beth and Gordon."

"That's a good idea," Frances said to Clarrie. "I'll go up and get Robin's and Marty's things."

"You haven't met Gordon yet, have you?" Laura asked Martha. "I've only met him that once when we went up to Washington for their wedding. He's such a nice guy and you'll fall for him. He looks like a Greek prince, though he's just an ordinary lawyer from Ohio, who had the luck of meeting our darling Beth."

"No, I haven't," Martha said, "but your mother has. If you remember she went to Washington with Beulah and John for the wedding. Delphia's told me all about him, so I feel as if I know him already."

"Why didn't they get married here?" asked Frances, as she returned with the neatly folded clothes for the children. "They could have had their reception on the actual wedding day instead of ten months later. I can't understand it, I really can't."

"Well, they couldn't find the time to come all this way to Kentucky to get married," Clarrie explained, "as neither of them could leave their jobs straight away. Beth still had to complete her tenure with her government job and there was plenty to do as she wound it all down. It was a similar situation with Gordon, as they required his expertise in establishing the New Hampshire orphanage and he was anxious to be involved in that. So, they decided to be married in Washington, and take it in turns to spend their free weekends in either Nashua or Washington. Gordon also wanted his son to get used to the idea of moving from his gran's, where he's lived most of his life. They weren't sure how the boy would take to such a huge change so it was a gradual arrangement. As you can imagine, George soon fell under Beth's spell and now he's looking forward to being a family with his father and new mother."

"George and his grandmother went to the wedding ceremony, but I remember he was very subdued then," Laura said. "He's a very nice looking boy, nearest to Antoin's age, though a little older, but he'll soon make friends. Walter has found a place for him at a local school."

"Remind me," said Martha, wrinkling her nose, "whose child is Antoin?"

"He's the first one of the new generation – he's Rory's son. He was born in France, if you remember," Clarrie said with a laugh, understanding her mother's dilemma in remembering which child belonged to which parents.

Frances walked across to Martha's house holding onto Laura's son and their clothes. She said she wanted to see Robin and Marty before beginning the next stage of the day's festivities.

"What's this I hear about Beth and Gordon adopting twins? A boy and a girl? Laura asked Clarrie.

"Not sure, really," Laura said, "except there had been plenty of publicity about the proposed Nashua orphanage, and the children appear to have been dumped near a church, in hope the orphanage would take them in, I suppose They're about three years old, and were suffering from malnutrition and dreadful neglect. Gordon learned about them from a colleague, and when he saw them in that state his heart went out to them. The children went into medical care and responded well, and the physician explained that they were young enough to overcome their physical and mental trauma, according to Beth's letter."

"Apparently, Beth went to Nashua that weekend and saw the pathetic state they were in. You know what's she like – so kind and tender. We may never know why they decided to adopt, but I'm guessing that's why they got married when they did. I'm not sure, but maybe children can only be adopted by married couples."

"It's a handful to take on," said Laura, "especially when their roots are unknown. What happens when she becomes pregnant with her own children? How will she cope with a step-son, those twins and her own?"

"She did write and tell me bits about it all," said Clarrie, "and I remember my mother being in tears when she read her letter. Beth said she'd been inspired by what our family had done for Frances and Jack all those years ago. Anyway, they'd already decided they wouldn't reproduce themselves because of Beth's heritage. They felt it could complicate George's life, and the baby's, if there was a color problem."

"Christopher Columbus! I'd forgotten that possibility," Laura said.

She wondered aloud how Gordon's son felt about the adoption.

"Apparently George takes after his father in nature as well as looks. His grandmother told me at the wedding he's a caring little soul. Beth wrote that when George heard about the twins and their story, it was he who piped up with the idea. Maybe he realizes he'll miss the bustle of life in Ohio," Clarrie said, "but whatever the reason, I admire their decision, don't you?"

Laura nodded and grinned. "Another three souls to add to our 'next generation' list," she said.

The next hour was spent preparing the beef, lamb and poultry for cooking. The vegetables and baked items had been assembled the evening before. Small serving rehearsals were carried out under Frances' eagle eye, until she announced the girls brought in to help were proficient. The girls thought the hard work was worthwhile as they were allowed to eat what they wished in the second kitchen, where food was available for staff to eat prior to the event.

Martha had asked her cook to look after the meats while she and the family set about preparing themselves for the event, which by now was only an hour away.

Neither Beth nor Gordon were aware of what was to come, as guests had been asked to arrive at the Alexander bakery premises, where wine and sweetmeats were available in a smaller tent pending the arrival of the main guests. There were to be 80, including Lucy and John Forder from Washington; Samuel and Mary Hetherington, together with Fred and Estelle from Nashua; and a couple of Gordon's friends from his office. Gordon's Ohio family had also arrived en bloc and a local hostelry was delighted to receive such a large, happy contingent for three days.

A number of Beth's former Washington 'students' and two of her staff had accepted the invitation, as had the Jolliffe family from Richmond. Of course the whole Compton family were included, as well as those staff with whom Beth had worked during her times as Beulah's personal maid and a couple from Sarah's Richmond household.

Vinnie and Annie Parker from West Virginia were attending with their brood of three children, along with Delphia and Walter Twigge. Rory and Marie-Louise Compton with their children were among the first to arrive from Cynthiana, accompanied by William, Longfield's farm manager and his wife of just over a year, Melanie. There were other Lexington locals who had known Beth all her life.

As guests arrived at the Alexander Bakery, there was excited chatter between Rory, Laura and Clarrie.

"Who would have thought that so much would have happened to each of us," Clarrie said. "When the four of us met, we were only teenagers, and what we have all done since then is remarkable."

"It certainly is," agreed Laura. "Teenagers do tend to mix with diverse people in their early years as they experiment with life, but the fact we are still good friends after all those shattering war years and the experiences we lived through is exceptional."

Laura asked Rory how he thought the meeting between Oliver Compton and Fred Hetherington would be.

"They were youths learning about life in those days," Rory said. "They've both had experiences of different life styles and will now meet as adults, knowing who and what they are and how they wish to live. Wait and see, you'll find they get along."

There was much excitement when news arrived from the Compton farm that Beth and Gordon and their new family, were on their way, together with John, Beulah, Timothy, and Oliver with his camera slung over his shoulder.

Beth could not believe the welcome and burst into tears as Gordon comforted her, close to tears himself.

The next few hours were spent laughing, eating and drinking. There was so much wonderful food. Plates wallowed in steaming beef, chicken legs and lamb chops while other dishes were piled high with potatoes, peas, cabbage, onions and carrots. There were Alexander home-baked bread rolls and delicious gravies to help the food go down. To follow there were ample fruit pies filled with apple or berries, supported by jugs of fresh cream. Dishes of cheese accompanied all this, with pieces cut into delightful shapes of animals or flowers, for the children. When this was cleared, the tables were filled with tiny colorful cakes, and jars of redcurrant jelly, more jugs of cream, together with dishes of red apples and russet pears. Jugs of hot tea and cool elderberry wine appeared. It was all topped off by a large wedding cake baked and decorated by a proud Frances.

As the party ate, they also talked, reminiscing about the past and sharing hopes for the future. The children played together, with an occasional scrap ending with streams of tears down one or two little faces. George and the adopted children, Basil and Cecily, looked healthy and smart in their new blue-checked clothes. They were reticent at first, but in time couldn't help but join in with the jolly crowd of youngsters. George was particularly popular with his broad, attractive Ohio accent and comical chatter about his family life there.

At last the four long-term friends were able to get together. Beth was still tearful as she thanked them. She described the large though dilapidated house she and Gordon had purchased twixt Lexington and Cynthiana and how they looked forward to restoring it. She told them of the upgraded post Gordon had been offered within a prestigious Lexington law company, following a reference from John Forder. Beth said she would be busy taking care of her new family but could, in due course, become interested in local charitable work. Laura said she would hold her to that, as although she was a stay-at-home mother nowadays, she was still a shaker and mover whenever she got the time.

Beth also spoke of their joint decision not to have children of their own and as everyone was aware of the reason, they praised the couple for providing a home for the abandoned waifs, who were already showing signs of personality and promise.

"Who would have thought," said Rory as he raised a glass to toast the four of them, " that within a decade the whole of our four lives would have turned out as they have and that we'd still be together?"

Their talk evolved into discussion about the future of the country's current reconstruction program and all hoped their children would not have to cope with the kind of war that had taken away much of their own youth.

"We must do all we can, as friends and good citizens, to protect our children and grandchildren from such atrocities," Rory said. "We're sensible, educated people, and we must impress on the children and the whole nation, if we can, that such a war should never ever happen again."

"Do you ever think of standing for public office, perhaps as a congressman or a senator, or even president?" Laura asked Rory.

"Well, funny you should say that but within a year or two I could be asking one of you to be my campaign manager," Rory said, noting Clarrie's interested glance.

One never knows, we've achieved a lot, and we could achieve more, he thought, as he considered the possibilities that lay ahead.

As more wails emanated from the playing group, they began to think of getting the children to their beds.

Before he left, Rory took Beth to one side.

"I got your letter a few months ago about your visit to Nashua. I'm pleased you found out just what did happen to Maya," he said. "Thanks for sharing the whole story with me, and yes, of course I'll keep it confidential. There's just one thing. We now know who the 'other angel' was, and I think Maya may have been referring to me as the 'first angel'."

"You?" Beth was astonished.

"Not in the same context as Fred's involvement," he assured her.

He told her then of the morning he had first seen her and Maya at the riverside, appearing 'like goddesses' out of the water just as he had undressed behind a bush, ready to dive in.

"I'd never seen either of you before and was scared stiff of letting you know I was there in case you thought I was stalking you. I kept very still but must admit I didn't close my eyes."

Beth blushed.

"The sun came out from behind a cloud just then and caught the bush. I think the sun made it translucent for a short time and Maya may have been able to see me. By the time she brought your attention to the bush, a cloud had covered the sun again. I heard Maya say that she had seen an angel. Maybe she thought she had. My blond hair could have looked like a halo in the sunlight. She could well have carried that experience in her mind ever since, really believing she had seen a heavenly messenger from God.

"I've thought since I received your letter that her lust for Fred may have reminded her of the incident, because the seduction was in a river setting. Maybe that's why she wrote 'the other angel' on the back of her drawing. That's my theory Beth, though we'll never know for sure," he said.

Beth looked stunned for a few seconds.

"Well, it's a possible explanation. There is no other. I shall think about it. I'm glad you told me about seeing us that day, Rory, and that I shared the whole story with you," she said. "I know now Maya's death was an accident and though Fred was involved indirectly, it wasn't his fault. I do feel, though, that he should have helped her more."

Rory felt the same but did not want to stir things up again by agreeing with her.

She felt him looking at her and smiled up at him.

"I have a feeling you'll be seeking public office in the near future," she said, grinning. "Are you happy with your life, Rory?"

"I'm content yes, but sometimes feel restless, wanting to do just that bit more, you know."

He glanced at her again. "Are you happy, Beth?"

"Yes, I've found my soul mate," she said, smiling, "and I have my own family now, just as my three dearest friends have. I'm a complete person again. We can all look to the future now, to the next generation of hope."

"It hasn't been an easy journey for any of us," Rory said, taking her hand, "but the four of us have been fortunate in that we haven't had to march through life on our own. We still have each other, as well as our partners to help the next phase along."

As he said this, Clarrie, Laura and their respective husbands caught up with them. They saw Marie-Louise making her way toward them, with Gordon in the rear, walking as quickly as his stiff leg would allow. The eight linked arms and in one long line walked down the hill toward the children's playground area, where most of the guests had also wandered. The waning sun shone at the back of them, creating a picturesque profile. One of the children looked up, shouted, and began to run, causing those who could to do the same.

The gathering of guests applauded the sight of the silhouetted second generation parents, who in turn watched with love as the third generation ran into their waiting arms, whooping with laughter.

"To the future," the eight friends shouted in their mutual joy.